DESCENT
— OF —
SHADOWS

Book 1

DESCENT
of
SHADOWS

◆

Book 2

RUINS
of
LIGHT

◆

Book 3

BREAK
of
DARKNESS

DESCENT
─ OF ─
SHADOWS

RYANNE GLENN

Detroit, Michigan

DESCENT OF SHADOWS

Editorial Services by:
Keith Osmun, Quill Pen Editorial
E.D.E. Bell

Line Edited by:
Camille Gooderham Campbell

Cover design copyright ©2018 by:
Jennifer Zemanek, Seedlings Design Studio

Interior Design by:
G.C. Bell

Published by Atthis Arts, LLC
Detroit, Michigan
atthisarts.com

ISBN 978-1-945009-30-3

Library of Congress Control Number: 2018964164

This book is dedicated to those who struggle.

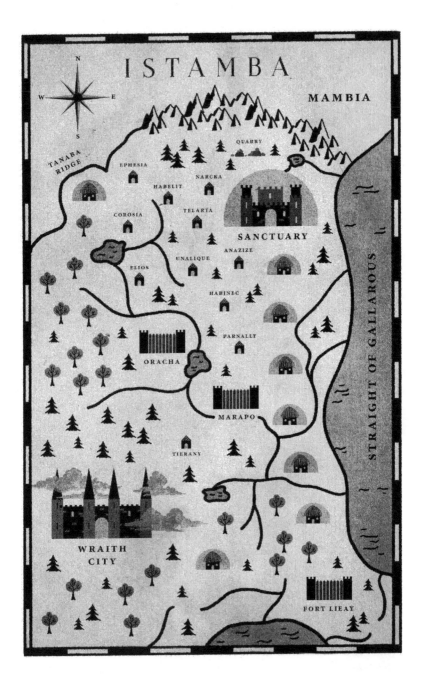

1

Anna peered over her shoulder at the ground below, then back up at the window she was inching toward. She was barely halfway there, and her shoulders were already burning from the effort. Her fingers ached; needle-like pricks assaulted her fingertips, weakened from clutching the old stone. She tried alternating her grip to shake out her arms, but the discomfort continued. Wind whipped past the tower and Anna frantically latched back onto the crumbling stone. A few pebbles came loose above her head; she shielded her eyes as they tumbled to the ground far below.

"Great," she mumbled. It hadn't been so windy when she'd started climbing.

She shifted her foot and found another hold closer to the small window of the tower. She carefully moved her hands up, hoisting herself even with the opening, and peeked around the corner. The small room was well-lit, and she could see her father speaking to the Captain of the Guard. They were poring over a large piece of parchment laid out on one of the rickety tables in the small tower.

"Our last troop of scouts just returned," the Captain said. "Only four have reported in."

"Out of how many, Captain?" her father responded, his eyes still focused on the map.

"Six, my Lord."

"Eight gone," her father continued, "but returning scouts report no activity near the city. Roland must be moving his wraiths, but where? I'll go out after the feast and look for myself. In the mean-time, post a few extra sentries at the northern and western gates and double the guards around the main hall. Be as discreet as you can. I don't want to cause any panic, especially during the festival. Morale is already wavering from the low crop yield, and I don't want to make it worse."

Anna's eyes narrowed. She figured her father had forbidden her from venturing into the woods because of something the wraiths had done, but they'd kept to their city for hundreds of years. Why would they start venturing out into human territory now?

The door to the tower opened and a woman strode through it. Anna ducked back behind the wall to keep from being seen, almost losing her grip on the stone as she moved. Her heart fluttered as she realized how close she'd been to falling.

"Evvard," her mother said, "the people are waiting for us below."

Anna peeked back into the room. It didn't seem like her mother had seen her.

"Ah, my beautiful wife," her father said. "I must make my appearance at the feast, Captain. I'll leave you to do what you think is right, but I will caution against sending out more scouts. I don't want to lose any more men. If you can, please join the celebration— perhaps a small break will bring some clarity to the situation."

"Of course, my Lord. My Lady," said the Captain with a bow.

"Have you seen Anna today?" her father asked, after the Captain had passed through the door.

Anna ducked back behind the wall, though she thought she saw her mother's eyes flick in her direction.

"Not since this morning," her mother replied, "but I'm sure she's in her chambers preparing for the feast."

Anna groaned quietly. She was supposed to be getting dressed. She heard her parents' footsteps leaving the tower and she glanced back at the ground below. If she hurried, she could still get back to her room before her parents got there.

She began making her way back down the side of the tower, trying to use the same holds she'd found on the way up. She tried to move quickly but going down was proving to be much harder than going up, since she couldn't see the holds below her. Finally, she dropped onto the roof of the guard house and ran across it before lowering herself to the ground. Ignoring the startled looks from the guards and villagers, she ran inside and up a back staircase, not stopping until she reached her chambers and shut the door firmly behind her.

Anna walked over to her wardrobe and threw open the doors. Various dresses hung inside, and she ran her hand over the silky fabric, frowning. Dresses were so cumbersome, and her leggings were much more comfortable. She examined what she was currently wearing.

The white tunic she'd put on that morning had embroidery along the edges; it would be fine for the feast. She brushed off some bits of dust and debris from the tower and buckled a decorative belt around her waist. Her leggings weren't torn, so there was no need to change those. Her boots weren't in the greatest shape. She had mud on them from walking around the Fort that morning, and she hadn't had time to clean them. Not that she would've bothered on any other day, but according to her mother, she had to look "presentable" for the feast. She shrugged and figured they'd do well enough.

Anna shut the wardrobe and walked over to her window, as her father's conversation in the tower came back to her mind. The bright green of the forest contrasted sharply with her mood. How she longed to be out there, exploring the familiar paths. Being out in the trees was her only respite from the Fort. The only kids close to her age were either a couple of years older or a couple of years younger, and she didn't get along well with either group. But when she was out there, climbing and listening to the animals, she didn't feel so alone.

Even though she now knew the reason her father wouldn't let her out of the Fort, it didn't make her feel any better. Besides, her boots held hidden sheaths. She could borrow a dagger from the weapons master when she went out. Or better yet, her parents could give her a set of her own. She begged for a set constantly, but her parents had yet to relent. They still believed she was too young, but she could use the recent disappearances to her advantage.

Anna grabbed a brush and began yanking it through her dark hair. With each pass of the brush, her scowl deepened. She wouldn't have had to bother if it hadn't been so windy.

"Would you like me to help?" a voice asked from the doorway, startling Anna.

She glanced over her shoulder and saw her mother, Lady Eileen Lieay, stepping into her room. Anna sighed in relief, glad to have help.

"Could you braid it?"

Her mother nodded and took the brush from Anna's hand. She worked through the tangles easily, ignoring Anna's winces, and gathered her hair into a simple braid before pinning it into an elegant knot at the back of her head.

"I don't know what you do to your hair every day," her mother said. "It gets more tangled every time I see it."

Anna shrugged in response and turned around to allow her mother to examine the front of her hair. She didn't want her mother to know what she'd been up to.

Lady Lieay pinned a few hairs back before she was satisfied, then glanced down once more, finally noticing her daughter's worn leggings and boots. "Perhaps you would consider a gown instead of those leggings you insist on wearing every day?"

"The dresses are itchy," Anna replied.

Lady Lieay raised a brow. "Mmhmm. And you can't climb towers in a dress."

Anna's face reddened, and her mother stepped forward to brush some grit from Anna's shoulder.

"I just wanted to know what was happening," Anna mumbled.

"I know," her mother said. "Your father and I were trying to keep you safe. But make sure you don't tell anyone else. We don't want to cause a panic."

"So, what's Father going to do?" Anna asked.

"We'll talk about it later." Her mother winked and left the room. "Be in the banquet hall soon," she said on her way out.

Anna smiled at her mother's retreating figure. Of course, her mother had seen her in the tower; she never missed anything. Spotting her amulet lying on her desk, she grabbed the leather cord and slipped it around her neck. She ran a finger around the edge, feeling warm tingles from the contact. The opalescent figure gave her some comfort, and though she couldn't make out the design anymore, just having it on helped her breathe a little easier.

She left her chambers and made her way to the banquet hall, weaving through the crowd of people until she finally reached the main building. Villagers and soldiers alike were milling about inside, enjoying food and drink from the most recent harvest. Goblets and mugs clanked together, ale and cider splashing out onto the floor as friends embraced one another. Roasted potatoes and charred husks of corn were piled high next to each other, filling the air with their aroma. Anna's mother glanced at her and she made her way over to where her parents were receiving the guests.

"Anna," Lord Lieay called, embracing his daughter, "I see you still refuse to wear a dress." Anna eagerly returned the hug. Just being in her father's arms made her feel like the wraiths didn't even exist.

"You sound just like mother," Anna said, pulling free. "But if I had my own daggers—"

"Anna," he said, "we've talked about this."

"Yes, but that was before the scouts went missing." Anna snapped her mouth shut when she realized what she'd said.

Her father sighed but smiled. "I thought I heard something in the tower. Were you hiding inside, or did you climb up?"

Anna felt her face burn once again. "I climbed up. But what if something happens and I need a weapon?"

"Anna, you don't know what it's like out there. I'm trying to keep you safe."

"But—"

"No," he said firmly. "Now go on. Your mother and I need to receive the guests."

Anna stalked away from her parents and began making her way around the hall. Platters with baskets of fruit and freshly baked bread and pastries dotted the room. Candles lined the hall and ribbons were strung across the ceiling, covering the uneven beams. The old tables had been polished and repaired and were set up along the edges of the hall, leaving a large open space in the middle for dancing. The villagers conversed with one another as they steadily trickled in from the side and back entrances. They paid their respects to their Lord and Lady, excited to join the festivities.

A servant offered her a tray piled high with pastries. Anna grabbed a sweet cake and nibbled the spongy texture while walking through the crowd. She talked with a few people she knew, but mostly kept an eye on her parents. Her father wore his finest vest of deep red fabric with silver buttons. Her mother's dark hair had been braided and coiled up on her head, and she had woven red flowers through the braid. Though they looked like they were just observing the festivities, Anna knew better. Her father's smile looked strained, and her mother's gaze constantly shifted around the hall. Occasionally, her father's hand would drift down to the sword hilt on his hip. They were nervous, more nervous than they were letting on.

The musicians started an upbeat song and music floated through the large hall. One by one, the villagers paired off to dance, and the woes of everyday life seemed to be forgotten. For a while, Anna didn't see worried eyes shifting back and forth between shadows and sun, and the drawn expressions brought on by a shortage of crops were nowhere to be found.

Quickly becoming bored among the adults, Anna began making her way through the crowd back to the dais where her parents were standing. The hall doors burst open behind her and she snapped her head around to see what had happened. A guard stumbled through, clutching his stomach with a bloodied hand. Anna's attention was so fixed on the blood that she nearly missed his words.

"They—they're here!"

The guard gasped as a gold sword point was thrust through

his chest. He crumpled to the ground, revealing dozens of wraiths behind him. Their limbs were smoky and blended with the shadows, so that Anna couldn't discern their shape. She froze as more wraiths forced their way into the hall. The doors were shoved roughly open and shadows poured in. Anna could hear screams from all over, but in her daze, they were muted, as if heard through a heavy door. Anna's heartbeat echoed in her ears as she was jostled by the villagers trying to find an escape from the horde of wraiths funneling into the hall. Her mother's voice distracted Anna from the commotion.

"Guards," commanded Lady Lieay, "let loose the hatches!"

The few soldiers remaining ran to the walls and pulled on the old ropes. Dust plumed from the hatches in the roof as they fell open, allowing sunlight to flood the hall. The wraiths grimaced as the sun hit them. Their shadowy forms became solid, and they looked almost human, save for their red eyes glowing like embers picked from a dying flame. Still, they continued forward, appearing unconcerned that they were now vulnerable to the humans' blades. Anna's parents pulled their swords from the sheaths at their hips and charged the horde.

Anna, trapped in the mass of escaping villagers, pushed her way to the edge of the hall, where she knew of a hidden staircase that led to the second-level balcony. The steps creaked and groaned under her weight. Pulling herself over the last broken step, she inched out onto the balcony, carefully side-stepping the holes and rotten places that pitted the dusty walkway.

Anna heard a cry from one of the soldiers, which drew her gaze down over what remained of the railing. Her parents fought together like a couple in a deadly dance, putting themselves between the wraiths and their people, flanked by guards who fought to keep their Lord and Lady safe. But the guards couldn't keep up with the battle, and Anna had to look away as soldiers she'd known her whole life fell to the ground, motionless.

The sound of metal striking metal reverberated through the hall, and Anna glanced back down at her parents. She saw her father thrust his sword through a wraith's chest. The wraith turned to dust before him, joining the small ring that surrounded her parents. Now, with only the two of them together, they were having trouble staving off the enemy. A wraith lunged at her father and drew a large gash across his chest. Anna stifled a scream. Her mother tackled the wraith, but her dress caught on the rough wood of the dais and the wraith pushed her back into the wall. Anna could hear a crack as her mother's head hit a hard beam behind her.

"No!" Anna breathed out, her voice cracking in terror.

"Reserve forces, go out and round up what's left of the villagers. No one escapes," rasped one of the wraiths. His gravelly voice raked over Anna's ears, like metal scraping metal, entrancing her with a harsh melody. He pointed to a few of his soldiers. "You stay with me to finish off these two."

Anna remained frozen as she watched the remaining wraiths close in on her parents.

I can't leave them, she thought.

She forced the ice from her veins and rushed back down the creaking stairs. When she reached the bottom, she grabbed a sword from one of the fallen soldiers. The wide blade was much heavier than the daggers she usually practiced with. For a moment, she wondered if she could lift it. Taking a deep breath, she gripped her amulet tightly. She couldn't leave her parents. She wouldn't. She forced her arms to lift the sword, and rushed to her parents' side.

"Anna, no!" her father yelled.

"I won't leave you," Anna called.

She hefted the sword, aiming the point at the advancing wraiths. She'd never seen a wraith before, and tried to ignore her shaking as they approached her and her family. They became flesh while they stood in the bright light of the sun streaming in from the hatches above, yet not quite flesh: their skin was like porcelain glass, and shadows shifted and moved just below the surface of it. One took a short step forward into the shadows and almost melted into them. If it weren't for his glowing red eyes, she never would have seen him in the darkness.

"How pathetic," one of the wraiths sneered, "but all humans are weak."

Her father charged forward and slashed the closest wraith to dust, but his blade was knocked from his hand with a blow that jarred his whole body; he sank to the ground, weak from his wound. A pool of blood gathered underneath him, and Anna's breath hitched in her throat. Her heart raced and her chin quivered as she sucked in breath after breath, trying to calm herself. She fumbled for her amulet and held it out toward the wraiths. She pressed the center of it, and sunlight poured from the figure, briefly illuminating the few shadows in the hall. When the light faded, the three wraiths were still there, and Anna's heart dropped to her stomach.

"Was that supposed to kill me, girl?" one of them taunted her.

Left standing alone, she trembled before the wraiths, the sword visibly shaking in her hands. One of them lazily hit her blade, sending it flying away. Her legs went numb and she struggled to remain upright. Feeling a nudge against her calf, she flicked her eyes down to see her mother holding out her dagger with a faltering grip.

Anna ducked to the ground and seized the dagger. As she grasped the handle, her frantic breathing calmed and a strange warmth spread through her. She let the feeling fill her, and time seemed to slow. She sank the blade into the first wraith's chest and he disintegrated, transforming into dust that drifted to the ground. A golden haze blurred the edges of her vision, sharpening the oncoming attacks.

The two remaining wraiths lunged at her simultaneously. She managed to twist away from the first sword, but the other caught her shoulder. She cried out in pain, grabbing the offending sword and yanking it from the wraith's hands. She plunged it into his chest, and then spun to the side, narrowly avoiding her final attacker as he swung his weapon at her head. Diving through his legs, she emerged behind him and thrust the dagger into the back of his neck.

As the last wraith disintegrated, Anna dropped the weapons. Breathing heavily, she stared at the piles of dust on the ground.

How . . . she thought. She heard a groan from behind her, and her eyes flicked toward the sound. She turned, and dropped to the ground beside her parents.

"Mother?" she choked out. "Father?"

Her father let out a soft moan. His shirt was soaked with blood and his face was ashen and drawn in pain. His breathing became more and more shallow before stopping altogether. Tears blurred her vision as she stared at her father's chest, willing it to rise and fall again, when her mother's slight movement caught her attention. She turned back to her mother, whose hand was clenched over a wound in her stomach.

"Anna," whispered her mother, "I'm so proud of you, but you have to leave before more of them come. Go to the Sanctuary."

"I can't leave you. I won't."

"I love you, Anna, but we won't make it."

"What if they come after me?"

"Use the safe houses, and remember: *Humanity is Strength.*"

Her eyes found Anna's one last time before fluttering shut.

"Mother!" sobbed Anna. "You . . . you can't leave me!"

Anna threw herself over her mother's body, willing her to wake. As she lay there, she could hear distant shouting coming from outside the hall. She wiped her tears on her sleeve and worked to lift her head. Her father rested, still, beside her. The stench of blood filled her nose, mingling with the dust from the wraiths her people had managed to kill.

Standing up on shaky legs, she teetered over to the wraiths' weapons that had dropped next to their dusty corpses. The gold glinted harshly in the sun streaming through the hatches, highlighting the finely made weapons, better than anything the humans had. The wraiths' weapons were forged with their own blood; the process turned all metal to gold, yet somehow made them nearly indestructible. Soldiers usually kept a killed wraith's weapons, but Anna couldn't take the swords. These were the weapons that had killed her family, and she couldn't bring herself to touch them.

Anna reached down and grasped her mother's last gift: the dagger. The gold was dull with the dust from the recent battle, but she could still see the familiar pattern on the six-inch blade that depicted the cycle of the sun over the ocean. Seeing the motif filled her with energy and hope. With this dagger, she'd carry her family with her, always. She tucked it into the hidden sheath in her boot and walked out of the hall without looking back.

I will not forget this day, Anna thought. *King Roland will pay for what he's done.*

2

Anna surveyed the quad outside the hall. She could still hear faint shouting coming from the Fort's center where she assumed the wraiths were rounding up the rest of her people. Not seeing any wraiths in the area, she ran to the tree line, feeling safer once she'd reached the cover of the forest. Putting the sun on her left, she ran north for a while until she began to hear birds and other wildlife again.

Anna slowed her pace to a walk. She'd never explored this far north before. Every step she took sent waves of pain through her wounded shoulder. Her sleeve was soaked with blood and she was afraid to look, not knowing what to expect. In a way, the pain helped. She managed to focus on its sting, instead of the horrors she'd seen. Though the start of the festival had only been that morning, it seemed like days ago.

As the sun began to set, the shadows around her grew longer, making the forest more ominous. Anna began seeing nonexistent assailants in every shadow. A bird called out and, startled, Anna broke into a brisk jog.

She pulled her amulet out and held it level with the ground. The amulets were supposed to help humans find safe houses while out in the forest, but she'd never had to use it before. Whenever she was traveling, she'd always had her parents to show her the way. Sorrow filled her at the thought of them, and she swallowed a hard lump in her throat. She couldn't afford to be distracted now.

She glanced back down at the amulet; a gold dot was pulsing near one edge. She altered her course accordingly and followed the amulet's pull. After a few more minutes of walking, she could make out the faint shimmer of the barrier. She ran the last few hundred yards, only relaxing when she was safe inside the shield.

Anna had never stopped to appreciate the safe houses before. During one of the first major clashes between humanity and the wraiths, the humans had set up secure shelters along the more treacherous paths in the forest. The small huts had the same wraith-proof barrier that surrounded the Sanctuary.

Since magic had disappeared nearly a thousand years ago, no one had been able to replicate the ancient spell that created the barriers, so no other settlements aside from the Sanctuary were protected. Unfortunately for her, that meant at least five days of travel without protection, except for these small refuges.

Anna shoved open the door, nearly causing it to come off its rusted hinges, and stepped inside the small room. The roof creaked overhead as a breeze shook the structure. Bugs scurried from the barren shelves that had been their home. Crates were stacked in the corners, taking up nearly half the small room. They were all rotting, and the bottom corners had given out on a few, unable to withstand the weight from inside. Anna wrinkled her nose at the staleness of the air.

Scouts from the Sanctuary were supposed to restock the huts with food every few months, but it looked like that chore had been neglected in the past few years of tentative peace. Anna also suspected people from the Sanctuary didn't like traveling this far south. She knew from her lessons that the northern and southern territories generally didn't get along. She blamed the Council. They called themselves the 'ruling body of Istamba,' but people in the south had chosen to follow Anna's parents instead, which only made the Council tighten their grip on the land. The Council didn't have much power in the south, but her parents had commanded respect wherever they went. No matter where Lord and Lady Lieay were, people knew how good they were in battle . . . or . . . how good they used to be—

Anna stopped her train of thought. She wouldn't think about what had happened; she couldn't. She distracted herself by sifting through the crates. There was a bag of nuts that she could try to eat, but any other food had spoiled long ago. She was glad to find there were supplies she could use. Having left her home with nothing but her mother's dagger and the clothes she wore, she was in no condition to be picky. Thankfully, there were a few shirts and other bits of clothing still mostly intact. Spying an old blanket, she tore it into thin strips before slowly peeling away her ruined sleeve, revealing her wound.

Anna winced as she gingerly blotted up some of the blood. Without water, there wasn't much she could do to clean it, but thankfully, it didn't look too deep. She wrapped some of the blanket strips around her arm to keep pressure on the wound, before pulling on an old hunting jacket from one of the shelves. She set up a makeshift bed using the remaining clothes she'd found, and shut the door tightly, trying to make it look from the outside like the hut hadn't been disturbed. She went back to the pile of rags and curled up, falling into a restless sleep.

Anna woke to sunlight filtering through the cracks in the walls of the hut. Groaning, she pushed herself up and stretched her aching muscles. Her shoulder throbbed, but her improvised bandage had stayed in place and she wasn't as worried about her wound starting to bleed again. She was still weak, and any movement sent pangs through her entire arm. She wished she'd paid more attention when her mother was trying to instruct her in the ways of healing.

I never thought sleeping on the ground would be so painful, Anna thought.

Grabbing an old bag from one of the crates, she stuffed the rest of the nuts into it, along with a few of the empty waterskins in hope that she might find a stream or lake soon. She adjusted the jacket to rest more gently on her wound and walked over to the door. Grasping the handle, she stopped. What if there were wraiths out there? If there were, she couldn't last long here. There wasn't enough food, and it was far too cold with only old rags to keep her warm at night. She needed to get to the Sanctuary, as her mother had said. Her hands started to shake, and her breath came in short bursts.

This is ridiculous, she thought, locking down on her fear. *They probably think they got everyone in the Fort. I doubt they'd be looking for me if they thought I was already captured.*

Anna squared her shoulders and cracked open the door. The darkness of the hut caused her to squint against the brightness of the new day. Glancing around, all she saw were trees and the occasional bird flying overhead. Still, terror gripped her, and she forced herself to circle the hut, listening and looking for any signs that something could be near. Hearing nothing but wildlife, she sighed.

"I can't stay here forever," she said to the forest around her.

Taking one last look around, she stepped out through the golden barrier and continued on her way north. Lost in her thoughts, Anna continued on her path, letting the forest pass her by. She consulted her amulet occasionally, but according to the small glow from the edge of the figure, the next safe house was directly ahead of her, somewhere. Coming to a small clearing, she stopped to rest and eat a handful of nuts. She filled both waterskins from the stream that cut through the clearing. She was just starting to walk again when she heard a twig snap to her left. Pulling out the dagger, she turned to where the sound had come from.

"Stay back," she called. "I'm armed!"

"Whoa, whoa, whoa," a voice responded from the trees. "I'm human!"

A boy emerged from behind a large tree. He wasn't much taller than Anna and only looked a little older. His chestnut hair was ruffled and covered with leaves and dirt. His clothes were tattered and frayed, and Anna could see small scars and scratches through the holes in his sleeves. His face was drawn, and his hazel eyes shone with apprehension as he examined Anna, her dagger glinting in the sunlight.

"Who are you?" she demanded.

"I'm Alex Marduk, from one of the western villages near the

old wraith city. We were attacked, and I ran. There were so many wraiths, I didn't know what else to do," he muttered.

Anna's eyes narrowed before she relaxed slightly. "Sorry. We were attacked as well. I guess I haven't really let my guard down since."

"You were attacked too? Where are you from?"

"I'm Anna Lieay from Fort Lieay. They came, just yesterday, during our annual harvest festival. We didn't have much time to prepare before they took over the banquet hall."

"Did anyone else manage to get away?"

"No. Just me," Anna said, hanging her head. "My parents—" She swallowed hard and looked back up at him.

Silence stretched between them as they stared at each other for a while, contemplating what each had just revealed. Reluctantly, Anna lowered the dagger and placed it back in her boot. Though she was glad to see another human, she was still on edge, and if other places had been attacked, there were more wraiths roaming the land than she'd thought.

"Is that a wraith's dagger?" Alex asked, staring at her boot.

"Yes. It was my mother's. From the first one she ever killed. She gave it to me before . . . before she . . ."

"Oh. I'm sorry, you don't have to say it."

Anna let out a shaky breath. "It seems so foolish now. I was arguing with her and my father about getting my own dagger set before we were attacked. I never wanted one like this." She trailed off, thinking back to the argument. She'd trade a hundred daggers if it meant she could have her parents back.

Alex nodded. "I just thought it was one you kept from a wraith you killed. That would have been amazing. Only one person from my village has ever killed a wraith, and he has a gold sword. I've always wanted the chance to get a gold weapon for myself, but it's pretty hard to believe you could actually kill one."

Anna's eyes narrowed. Just because she was young didn't mean she couldn't take care of herself. "You think I'm not good enough to kill a wraith? Because I'll have you know, I killed three. That's how

I was able to escape. And if you still think I'm too weak to take care of myself, then I can get my dagger back out and show you just how strong I am."

Alex held out his hands in front of him, his eyes wide. "Whoa, calm down! I didn't mean to offend you. It's just that I've only known one other person who's ever fought a wraith and lived, and he trains constantly with a sword. Did you really kill three of them? Why wouldn't you keep their weapons? They're only the finest ever made."

"You're right. I should have kept the weapons that killed my parents." Anna crossed her arms and glared at Alex. Sure, being attacked was overwhelming, but it wasn't any reason to stop thinking.

"Oh. I didn't think about that."

Clearly. Another silence settled between them.

"Where are you headed?" Anna finally asked.

"I'm not sure. I was just trying to get away from any wraiths that might have been following me. What about you?"

"The Sanctuary," she responded. She nodded her head toward her path north. "With its barrier, it's the only safe place right now. If more villages were attacked, there have to be more survivors than just us. I can only hope that they're headed there as well. There are little safe houses about a day's travel apart from here until the Sanctuary, in case a person traveling needs to hide from a wraith."

Alex kicked at the ground. "I don't suppose I could tag along."

Anna chewed on her bottom lip. She didn't really know him, but he was human and running from the wraiths like she was.

"It would be nice to have some company," she finally said.

"Thanks! It'll be nice traveling with such a great warrior," he responded with a smirk.

Anna's lips turned up slightly, revealing a hint of a smile.

"Let's get going, then. The next safe house is still a few miles away."

The two continued on past the clearing, back into the dense forest. Alex tried to ask her questions, but everything they talked about drifted back to the wraiths. Eventually, they decided to walk in silence. Soon, the sun began to sink behind the trees and the pair began to hear the sounds of nocturnal animals from the woods. Soft hoots came from one direction and were answered by sharp screeches from another.

"Are we almost there?" Alex asked, nervously glancing around. "I'd like to be in a safe house before it gets dark. The wraiths are supposed to be stronger at night."

Anna looked back at her amulet. The small dot hadn't changed positions. "We're still headed the right way."

Alex looked over. "How do you know?"

"My amulet," she said, gesturing to the figure in her hand. "The glowing spot shows you which direction to go to get to a safe house."

"This?" he asked, touching the center before Anna could stop him.

As his finger brushed the center of the amulet, sunlight poured from the figure, forcing Anna to look away. When the light cleared, Anna scowled at Alex. He'd just wasted their protection for the night.

"What did you do that for?!" she demanded.

His eyes widened and he backed away from her slightly. "Sorry! I didn't know that would happen."

She groaned. "Well, now we can't use it again until I charge it with the sun tomorrow. What if we need the protection tonight?"

"Yeah, but isn't that a safe house?" Alex said, pointing ahead of them. "We won't need it."

The trees rustled behind them, echoing through the empty night. The two shared a look and took off as fast as they could toward the now-visible hut. They burst through the doorway, bending over to catch their breath.

"I'm sorry about the amulet," Alex said, once his breathing had returned to normal.

"No," Anna responded, "I shouldn't have yelled at you. You didn't know."

"I'm just glad we made it in here. Who knows what that noise was?"

"Honestly, it was probably just a bird. Wraiths can't find the safe houses since they don't have amulets, so I doubt one would be this close."

"That's a relief."

Anna smiled. Perhaps Alex wasn't so bad. He looked just as scared and nervous as she felt. She scanned the hut and found it similar to the first, though the walls looked to be a bit stronger. At least they wouldn't have to worry about it caving in on them in the night.

"I'll look through the crates, but the last house didn't have much of anything. Just a bag of nuts and some old clothes."

"Good plan. I'll, um, lock up, I guess."

Anna nodded and started rummaging through some of the old crates. Like the last hut, almost everything was ruined, but there was another small bag of nuts and some jerky that seemed okay.

"Well, there's a bag of nuts. Hooray," she announced sarcastically. "There's also some old jerky that looks like it should be fine to eat."

"It's no banquet, but I'm starving."

Anna nodded, and felt the pains in her stomach returning at the reminder. She had barely eaten anything at the festival, and the last bag of nuts didn't do much to sustain her. Grabbing one of the old shirts, she tore it into strips before taking off her jacket. She carefully unwrapped her shoulder, trying not to break open the wound. Alex gasped when he saw it.

"What happened?" he asked.

"A sword caught me when I was fighting. It doesn't seem too deep, but it really hurts."

She pulled out one of the waterskins and poured a little on one of the rags before dabbing at her wound. Her face contorted in pain, but she remained quiet. When most of the blood had been cleared away, she turned to Alex.

"Could you help me rewrap it?" she asked. "It's tough on my own."

He nodded and gingerly wound the scraps of cloth around her arm. She winced at each turn of the fabric.

"How's that?" he asked.

Anna examined her arm. "Works for me. Thanks."

"Any time." Alex glanced around the room. "It looks like there's only a few jackets and an old blanket, so sleeping's going to be tough."

"If we're going to be part of an army, we need to get used to sleeping on the ground."

"Army? I never thought about that."

"What, were you planning to forget about everything that happened in your village? Sit idly by while others go to war for you, when you have the ability to fight?" Anna glared at Alex, feeling her face going red.

"Calm down! I just hadn't thought much past making it to the Sanctuary alive, but if it comes to it, of course I'll fight. I want the chance to avenge my family as much as you do."

Anna shook her head and rubbed her eyes. "Sorry. I haven't slept much the past few days and haven't thought of much else but revenge since I left the Fort."

"What was it like? To kill one of them?"

"Honestly, it all happened so quickly. But I remember being utterly terrified, like in a nightmare. While it was happening, it was like it wasn't even real. Our Captain had taught me a few things about using a sword, but it was never more than the basics. Then all at once, I was standing alone against three of them with absolutely no idea what to do. They were so strong and so much faster than me. I honestly don't know how I ended up getting out of there alive."

"Impressive."

"I'd rather not talk about it, if you don't mind. I've relived it enough times already."

"Fine by me. I'm exhausted."

Alex took one of the old jackets and handed the blanket and the other jacket to Anna. She started to protest—after all, she already had an extra jacket and she didn't need the blanket as badly—but he'd already turned over on his side. Deciding not to wake him and argue about it, she rechecked the door to be sure it was securely shut before rolling herself up in her own jacket. She pulled the blanket over herself and fell into a light sleep.

The pair woke at dawn, both too nervous to try falling back to sleep. Anna shook the frost off the blanket before rolling it up and stuffing it into her bag, not knowing what the next safe house might hold. Maybe there'd be another, so they could both have one. If not, she'd let Alex use it that night; it was only fair. Anna yanked her hair free of her unraveling braid and pulled it up and away from her face before turning to Alex.

"I guess we should get going," she said. "We have a long way to go today."

"Ugh, how far?"

"About twenty miles, if I remember correctly. The safe houses are supposed to be about a day's walk apart. They're designed that way."

"Well, at least we'll be safe at night. Do you know how many days until we get to the Sanctuary?"

"Four, I think. I just hope there's some better food in the next few houses."

"No use waiting around here," Alex said as he opened the door.

The two left the safe house and continued on their way north. They managed to make it to each of the next safe houses before sunset. The nights were tense. Even with the barriers guarding the houses, every noise startled her, a potential attack from the dark.

The situation wasn't ideal by any means, but Anna was glad for the company. Someone else relying on her to get to the Sanctuary gave her something to focus on and helped her keep relatively calm throughout the journey.

Four days later, a break in the trees revealed stone towers outlined in gold through the branches. She had seen the Sanctuary before, but the barrier always took her breath away. Though the safe houses had small barriers surrounding them, the one around the Sanctuary was massive. Granted, the Sanctuary itself was nearly twice as large as Fort Lieay, but it was still a shock to see the gold shimmering brightly in the afternoon sun.

While the Sanctuary was safe from the wraiths, the barrier did nothing to protect the Sanctuary from the elements. Thousands of years' worth of wind, rain, and sun had ravaged the outer walls. The tallest spires were crumbling, and many of the watchtowers were nothing more than piles of rubble. The lower buildings, including the barracks, stood mostly intact. The shorter structures escaped the worst of the wind storms, but even they could not escape time. Still, the Sanctuary still stood. It was almost as stubborn as Istamba's people.

The crumbling towers of the Sanctuary were becoming clearer with every step. Anna felt like her chest was no longer constricted and the knot in her stomach slowly faded away. They would be safe once they were through the barrier.

Alex looked over and gave her a wide grin, his thoughts likely mirroring her own.

A loud crack resounded through the trees just to their left, and her eyes widened. They'd come too far to be attacked in the last few hundred feet. She and Alex began sprinting toward the barrier, pumping their arms and legs with all their might.

"Are those soldiers in there?" Alex panted. "They don't look happy to see us."

Passing through the shimmering barrier, the pair came to a halt in front of an officer, both breathing heavily.

"What do you two think you're doing? Running at the Sanctuary with everything that's happened? It's a good way to get yourselves killed!" yelled the officer.

"We thought we heard a noise behind us, and after the past few days, running seemed like the best option," Anna replied. "We're sorry, um, Sir," she added as an afterthought.

"How far south did you come from?" he barked out.

"Fort Lieay," she answered.

The officer nodded. "There's food inside, but stay in the main hall. Soldiers will be coming around to collect reports from different villages."

"Is there somewhere I can get my shoulder bandaged?" Anna asked, pulling down the jacket to reveal her wound.

"Nasty," he said. "Infirmary's just down the hall from the food. You'd best get that looked at before it gets worse."

Anna nodded, and Alex pulled her toward the main building. The pair found their way through the worn halls, dodging soldiers and refugees who paid them no mind. Locating the infirmary was easy—injured people were flooding the large room to have even their small scratches and bruises looked at. Most with mild injuries were being sent away with a quick wash and some balm, but others were directed to the beds lining the room. About half of the beds were already populated with wounded refugees. Healers walked up and down the rows, trying to help the patients as best they could.

Anna walked over to a healer who had just finished with another patient. As Anna approached, she heard the patient arguing about a small scrape on his elbow. Anna scoffed when she saw it. She'd gotten worse scrapes from falling in the forest. Finally, the man stalked off, leaving the healer free.

Anna took off her jacket. "Could you re-bandage this?" she asked.

The healer nodded and led Anna over to an open cot, where she pulled out fresh linen and cut away the rags.

"This doesn't look too deep," the healer remarked as she cleaned and treated the wound. "How long ago did it happen?"

"About six days."

"Hmm. You heal fast. Just keep it clean." The healer finished tying off the new bandage and sent Anna on her way. After thanking the woman, Anna left the infirmary and went back down the hall with Alex.

They had to dodge a few people to get to the main hall, but the smell of roasting potatoes drove them on. Joining the long line of people, the pair made their way up to the serving table. Anna's eyes shifted around the room while they waited. Though they were safe within the barrier, the events of the last few days still had her on edge. Large cracks had spread across the vaulted ceiling of the hall they were in, but nothing had fallen yet. Old, rickety tables were set haphazardly throughout the large space, almost all populated by refugees. Most of the diners were talking in hushed murmurs, as if their enemy could hear them.

"Beans and potatoes are better than old jerky and nuts," joked Alex, pulling Anna out of her thoughts. "Where should we sit?"

"How about there?"

Anna marched up to a table where two people were already sitting. The first was a boy paler than anyone else she'd seen, with longer sandy hair. Most was pulled back and secured at the base of his neck, but some pieces had pulled free and flopped in front of his eyes. Though his clothes were in good condition, they were covered in dust. He was making large gestures with his arms, causing the girl across from him to laugh. Her clothes, by contrast, were spotless, but they did have quite a few patches decorating her arms and elbows. Her bright red curls bounced with every giggle.

"Are these seats taken?" Anna asked the boy.

"Be my guest," he replied. "I'm Oliver, by the way, Oliver Talon, and this is Ele Rivers."

"Anna."

"Alex. What's so funny?"

"Oh, Oliver was just telling me a story," Ele replied, choking down her laughter.

"Anything interesting?" Alex asked.

"Just something a soldier did earlier. He was yelling at some refugee about watching where they were going. Then he ran straight into a page. Ink and scrolls went flying everywhere, and the soldier was so embarrassed." Oliver switched topics. "Are you two from the same village?"

"No," said Anna, "I'm from Fort Lieay, and Alex is from one of the western villages."

"Ooh, north or south?" Ele asked.

"South; you?" Alex said.

"Oh, I'm from the north. I ran into Oliver on my way here. He lives really close."

"Really, where?" asked Anna.

"Narcka," Oliver continued. "We weren't attacked like the out-lying villages, but when people started coming through our village headed for the Sanctuary, we followed. My parents have always been kind of paranoid when it comes to the wraiths. Then again, who isn't? Although I've never seen one personally—wouldn't that be terrifying? The stories are bad enough. I just think—"

Ele rolled her eyes. "Oliver, stop talking. You're going to scare them off."

Oliver shrugged. "Sorry. Sometimes I get going and I can't stop. Did anyone else from Fort Lieay make it?"

"Not that I've seen," Anna responded. Her shoulders drooped and she crossed her arms, as images of bodies lining the banquet hall flooded her mind. She gave a quick shudder and said, "It was so scary. A huge group of them came all at once, overwhelming our men. We were completely unprepared and not even my parents could hold them off."

"Well, unless your parents were legends, I don't know who could have," Oliver said. "So few people have even come close to killing a wraith. Although that could be because there haven't been that many around. Or maybe they just attack in packs and they over-whelm a person. Or they attack at night. Or—"

"Oliver," Ele interrupted.

Oliver snapped his mouth shut, his face going red.

"So, who were your parents?" Ele asked.

"Lord and Lady Lieay."

"Whoa!" Oliver exclaimed. Ele elbowed him in the ribs and he looked back at Anna. "I mean, I'm sorry for your loss."

Alex looked around anxiously. "As much fun as this conversa-tion is, can we talk about something a little less morbid?"

Anna wasn't upset by the conversation. This was their life now; why should they avoid it? "Are you two planning on joining the army?" Anna asked, looking pointedly at the couple across from her.

"Oh, that's much less morbid," Alex added sarcastically.

Anna rolled her eyes and turned her attention to Ele.

"Well," began Ele, "it didn't seem like much of an option. The only new recruits I saw were much older than we are. I think we're too young."

"Yeah," said Oliver. "You have to be older to join the army. Otherwise, I'd do it."

"I'm not worried about our age, but Alex said he'd fight too," Anna said, gesturing to Alex.

"Er, yeah, about that . . ." Alex said, looking away.

Anna's mouth fell open. "You don't want to fight?"

Alex coughed. "It's not the fighting I mind. It's the dying part I'm not too keen on."

"I'm pretty sure that's what the training's for," Oliver said.

"Excuse the interruption," interjected a soldier, "but I'm collecting accounts of the various attacks. Have any of you been interviewed yet?"

"He and I have," Ele said, gesturing to Oliver and herself, "but these two just arrived."

"Follow me, if you would."

Anna and Alex stood and followed the soldier into a hallway and through a few doors to a small room.

"Please have a seat." The soldier gestured to a couple of the chairs in the room. He sat across from them at the desk and pulled out a piece of parchment. "Who would like to go first?"

"Uh, I'll start," Alex said, glancing at Anna.

"If you would, begin with your name and village."

"Um, okay, well, I'm Alex Marduk, and, uh, I'm from Tierany. They didn't come until the late afternoon, so most everyone was in their homes. I was out in the forest when I heard voices. I climbed the nearest tree, trying to surprise whoever it was, when I saw the gold weapons. I wasn't hidden very well, but they didn't look up."

"Did you see what happened in your village?" the soldier prompted.

"Yes. I climbed down after they passed and followed them. As soon as I got there, a wraith grabbed me and hauled me toward one of our corrals. They had emptied it and put people inside, I guess to be taken back as slaves." Alex fell silent and eyed Anna. She knew it couldn't be easy talking about this. She gave him a small smile of encouragement before the soldier got his attention again.

"Then what happened?" he asked.

"Uh, well, we worked together to overwhelm the guards and everyone started running in opposite directions. I ran until it was dark and I didn't look back. I climbed a tree to try and sleep, but mostly I just sat up and listened for anyone coming. When the sun came up, I started walking again. About midday, I ran into Anna, and we continued on here together, staying in those little safe houses on the way."

"Did you see if anyone else from your village was able to get away?" asked the soldier as he finished jotting down the story.

"No. When I had the chance, I just left. I haven't seen anyone here I know."

"Thank you." The soldier took out a new page and turned to Anna. "Now for your account. Anna, was it?"

"Yes." Anna swallowed hard. "Anna Lieay, from Fort Lieay. We were having our annual harvest festival when they attacked. My father had sent out numerous scouts that day and a few days before, but the ones that returned didn't see anything odd. He had even increased the guards around the Fort, but he was concerned about causing a panic, so he kept alerts to a minimum. The day of the festival, he had extra sentries posted, but even that wasn't enough." Anna stopped and looked at her lap. Images of her father in the watchtower flashed through her mind. Memories of his strong figure standing tall were overwhelmed by his broken body lying in the destroyed hall.

"The attack?" The soldier prodded. "Did you see it?"

"Yes. When they attacked, the majority of people were in the main banquet hall so they were trapped." Anna squeezed her eyes shut, remembering the wraiths cornering her people. "I don't know for sure, but I assume they surrounded the hall to eliminate most of the guards. One did get away and came into the hall to warn us just before the wraiths swarmed in. I tried to escape using some back stairs that led to the upper balcony, so I was able to see most of the attack. My parents managed to kill a few and were able to put up enough of a fight that most of the people found a way out of the hall. After backing my parents into a corner, one of the wraiths—he acted like the leader—stepped up and ordered most of them outside to gather the villagers that had escaped. The rest stayed to fight my parents."

Anna's last words came out as nothing more than a whisper. She could feel her chest tightening, and as hard as she tried, she couldn't banish her memories of the fight. She saw her mother and father falling to the ground over and over again. Alex laid a hand on her arm, and she flinched. She took a deep breath before continuing.

"I ran back to the main floor, grabbed a sword from the ground, and went to help defend my parents. After he killed one more, my father fell, and I was left alone against three of them. I don't know how, but I managed to kill them. I grabbed my mother's dagger and ran away. I didn't want to, but I could hear voices outside talking about checking the hall for survivors. After leaving the territory, I headed north, looking for the safe houses my parents had told me about. I stayed in the first one on my own, but I met Alex the next day, and we traveled here together."

"And your parents? Any chance they could be alive?"

"No," Anna choked out.

"That's too bad. We're going to need every soldier in this war."

"Well, I'm sorry their deaths are such an inconvenience! I suppose they should have thought about that before giving their lives to save their people!" Anna yelled, leaping up. She stormed to the door and gave the soldier one last glare before exiting and slamming the door behind her.

4

Anna rushed through the halls of the Sanctuary, tears streaming from her eyes. Climbing some stairs, she found an empty balcony and collapsed onto the hard stone. Once there, she hugged her knees to her chest and sobbed. Since the attack, she'd been so focused on getting to the Sanctuary, she hadn't given herself time to grieve. Telling the story to the soldier brought all her emotions back.

"Anna," came a faint call.

Anna wiped the tears from her face and lifted her head to see Alex walking out onto the balcony. Why couldn't he just leave her alone?

"What do you want?" she snapped.

"To see if you're okay. Do you have a problem with that?"

"Why do you care?"

"I know these past few days have mostly been spent running from the wraiths, but I think we can call each other friends. And as your friend, I'm here for you."

Anna took a deep, shaky breath. After a long pause, she said, "With everything that's happened, I guess I just haven't had time to process. And that soldier . . . ugh! It's like no one even cares that my parents are gone."

"It's okay to be sad. I didn't talk to anyone for weeks after my parents passed away."

"Your parents? I didn't know."

"It happened a long time ago. It's hard at first, but it gets a little easier each day. You just have to find something to fight for."

Anna took another deep breath. For some reason, Alex didn't seem as upset about the attacks as she was. If he could be so strong, then she could too. As she stood, Alex caught her in a tight hug. She pulled away from his touch and stared at him.

"What are you doing?" she demanded.

His face reddened. "I'm sorry, I just thought—"

"Well, you thought wrong." She turned away and looked out over the Sanctuary grounds. "I'm sorry I was a little harsh," she said after a few moments. "There wasn't anyone close to my age at the Fort. I'm not really used to having someone around like this."

"I understand, but we should go back downstairs. They're going over rules and assigning refugees to sleeping halls."

The two went back downstairs and into the main hall, where soldiers had lined up on a platform at the back of the room and the refugees had assembled in front. They noticed Ele and Oliver, and sat next to them as one of the soldiers gave a safety briefing.

"Can I have your attention, please?" called the soldier. "I am Captain Terra. I know you all have had a rough few days, but hopefully you can find some peace while you're here." She paused and paced to the other side of the platform. "I won't lie to you all. We are entering a war with some very dangerous enemies, but if you follow a few guidelines, you'll all be safe within the barrier. You'll be assigned to a living hall within the main structure. This is where you will sleep, and it will act as your common area.

"Unless you are summoned, you are to stay out of the westernmost corridor of the Sanctuary. Those rooms are dedicated to officers and battle planning. As the war progresses, the army will need your help. Of course, we will need volunteers to fight, but we'll also need healing aides, supply organizers, and refugee directors. I'm sure as time goes on and more people arrive, we'll come up with more jobs. Everyone who's able is expected to contribute.

"We do have some expectations of you while you're on rest breaks. Under no circumstances are civilians—that's you—allowed to be near the barrier without a soldier escort. If you want to be outside, there are plenty of courtyards within the complex. Unless you are accepted into the fighting force, stay away from the training grounds. Our soldiers will be training with dangerous weapons, and we can't guarantee your safety if you go near the quads.

"Additionally, we have a few calls and signals that can be heard throughout the Sanctuary, and you'll need to know what they are so you won't be alarmed when you hear them. The main ones are sharp horn blasts, either one, two, three, or four. These are signals for soldiers to report to different quadrants of the barrier. If you hear those, all non-military personnel are to remain inside the main structure. Three bells will call you to meals. Soldiers will be served first so they can return to training. Occasionally, you'll hear a bugle blast, welcoming a regiment returning from a mission.

"The signal you'll all need to be familiar with, though, is a constant bell ringing. This means an attack on the Sanctuary is imminent. If you hear this, healers are expected to report to the infirmary, weapons managers are to report to the armory, and most everyone else will report to the inner rooms for safety. Although wraiths cannot get through the barrier, our soldiers will still be engaging the enemy and any nonessential personnel will need to stay clear of the quads. I don't intend to frighten you all, and it is highly unlikely you will hear this signal, but you all need to be aware of it.

"I know I've given you all a lot of information at once, but everything we do is to keep you safe. Tomorrow at midday, there will be a training session for new recruits. Any who don't volunteer will have their skills evaluated and will be assigned where they will be of most use. For now, these soldiers will show you to your living halls." She gestured to a few soldiers who were lined up beside her. "Divide yourselves up into groups of men and women, and we'll get you settled in. If you came here with your family, we have separate rooms on the second floor for family groups so you can stay together."

With a nod, the Captain left the room. Everyone in the hall

stood with varying levels of urgency and separated into groups as the Captain had ordered.

Anna glanced at Alex and Oliver. "I guess we'll see you two at dinner." She and Ele linked arms and headed over to where the women were gathering.

"That Captain was pretty intense," Ele said as they walked.

"I think everyone is on edge. It's been years since the wraiths have openly attacked us like this. Besides, the leaders here have to get us used to army life pretty quickly."

The two joined a group of women and followed them to a large interior room. Various cots and mats were set up in four lines that took up the whole length of the room. Some had already been claimed by earlier arrivals. Anna and Ele found two make-shift beds next to each other and sat down. Anna dropped the bag she had taken from the first safe house to mark the bed as hers. Pulling off her hunting jacket, she stretched gingerly, testing her shoulder. It twinged slightly, but she could barely feel it. The healer was right; she was healing quickly. Well, that was something to be grateful for. Maybe the wound hadn't been as bad as she'd thought it was.

"What happened?" Ele asked.

"I was fighting a wraith while trying to escape, but I wasn't quick enough."

"You were lucky. Most people who face a wraith don't escape. Did you actually kill one?"

"Three."

Ele's jaw dropped. "Really? How? My parents wouldn't even consider teaching me how to use a weapon until I was older."

Anna shrugged. "It was either them or me. I'm pretty sure they took a look at me and weren't expecting much of a fight. I guess I caught them off guard."

"Can I have everyone's attention?" called out one of the soldiers. "We have limited resources, but we should be able to supply everyone with a change of clothes. To get to the supply rooms, go down this hall, take the first left and a right in the final corridor. You can go there before or after dinner, but keep in mind, we may not have the right sizes for everyone."

"Why don't we head to the supply rooms before we meet with Oliver and Alex for dinner?" Ele suggested.

"Sounds good to me." Anna pulled what few clothes she'd managed to salvage from the safe houses out of her bag. "Maybe I can trade these in for something that fits."

"Lead the way."

Two hours later, Ele and Anna met Oliver and Alex outside the main hall for dinner. The aroma of roasted potatoes and fresh bread filled the air. Anna clamped a hand over her stomach as it growled loudly enough to be heard over the various conversations echoing throughout the hall. The small group joined the line for food, and then claimed the same table they'd had at lunch.

"What do you think of the Sanctuary so far?" Alex asked between bites.

"It's a little chaotic, especially as more and more people arrive," Ele began. "I'm sure when a war isn't going on, it's nice, but right now I feel like I'm in everyone's way."

"I've already gotten lost," Oliver said. "I don't think I'll ever find my way around."

"I see you have no problem finding the food," Ele replied.

"Well, the smell helps."

The group shared a laugh before falling silent, each focusing on their meal. Oliver finished first and began sneaking small pieces of bread off Ele's plate. Ele noticed and brandished her fork like a sword. Oliver grabbed his own fork, and they fought each other for a few moments before Ele broke down in giggles and handed Oliver the rest of her bread.

"So," Anna said slowly, "there's a basic training session for new recruits tomorrow at midday. Are any of you going to join me?"

Alex opened his mouth to answer, but was cut off by a boy at the next table. "You're volunteering?"

"Yes," Anna said, turning. "What's it to you?"

"Oh, I was going to volunteer too, but I wasn't sure if they'd let me. But if you're able to volunteer, I'll definitely be okay."

Anna's eyes narrowed. "Are you saying I'm not good enough to fight?"

"Oh, no, no, that's not what I meant at all. You just look really young and . . . small."

Anna inhaled sharply, face warming.

The boy gave a nervous chuckle. "Heh, hold on. That came out wrong. Uh, I'm Liam, and I'm, uh . . . I'm just going to leave." He stood and backed away from their table and out of the room.

"Well, that was awkward," Alex finally said.

"I'm sure he's nice once you get to know him," Ele said.

"It doesn't matter." Anna turned back to Alex. "And you never answered. Are you going to volunteer with me?"

"I guess. I'm not going to let you have all the glory."

"I'll be there," said Oliver.

"Me too," added Ele, "but it looks like they're cleaning up dinner. I think we have to get back to our common area. Let's go, Anna."

Anna and Ele rose from the table and said goodbye to their companions before returning to their sleeping quarters.

5

nna woke to three sharp horn blasts and soldiers in motion around her. They were surrounding their sleeping area. Other women were waking up as well, confusion spreading throughout the hall.

"What's going on?" a worried mother asked.

"Nothing to be concerned about, Ma'am. Just a routine drill so our newest recruits have a chance to practice."

Anna scowled. A drill so early in the morning, around people who'd lost their families only a few days before? That didn't seem like the smartest move.

"I'm going to find out what's really going on," she whispered to Ele.

"But they aren't letting anyone leave."

"Who said I was going to ask for permission?" Anna replied with a grin.

She made her way to the edge of the room. It was slow going, but she managed to weave through the waking forms around the hall. She finally reached a small alcove near the door where two soldiers were arguing.

"Why are we here?" one of them asked. "Aren't we causing more panic?"

"I don't know. They didn't tell me any more than they told you."

"Excuse me, Sir," one of the women asked, "is there any possibility that I could go outside for a moment? I need a little air."

"I'm sorry, Ma'am," one of them said, turning. "No one is to leave this room for the moment."

As they argued with the woman, Anna snuck past the soldiers' backs and walked through the halls. As she stepped outside, she took a deep breath of the crisp morning air. The sun was just beginning to peek over the trees. A light mist hovered above the grass, blurring the trees beyond the barrier. Soldiers marched across the quad, cutting through the haze with purposeful strides.

I knew something must be going on, she thought. *This many people couldn't be doing the same drill at the same time.*

She climbed up to the roof of one of the barracks to get a better look. She could almost see the whole southern quad. Unfortunately, she could also see the group of wraiths approaching the barrier. She felt her chest constrict. Memories from the attack on her home came flooding over her and she couldn't fight off her fear. She gritted her teeth and forced the memories back. She couldn't—wouldn't—allow herself to be intimidated by the wraiths' presence.

General Collins finally appeared from within the Sanctuary and began organizing the frightened new soldiers. They had just gotten a line into place a few feet inside the barrier when the wraiths came to a halt. Anna could count all thirty of them from her elevated position. In the morning light, their red eyes glinted, taking in the shambled appearance of the humans. Their golden armor shimmered and gleamed while the humans' leather armor looked shabby and unkempt. The two groups stared at each other for a while, waiting to see who would speak first. Then, the wraiths parted to allow a single one to step forward; they seemed to cower as he passed.

Anna was forced to squint as the sun reflected harshly off his full armor. Like the rest of the wraiths' armor, it was completely gold, as were the two swords hanging from his waist. A gold crown adorned with black jewels rested upon his head. His form shimmered in and out of focus as clouds passed in front of the sun. His skin was almost translucent, and shadows shifted just beneath the surface like flames writhing against a drizzling rain. Darkness clung to him, as though he couldn't quite pull himself from the shadows to become pure flesh. Anna shuddered as he got closer, his eyes a gleaming red.

This must be King Roland, she thought.

"General Collins, I presume," King Roland said.

Anna was entranced by his hypnotic words. He spoke softly, but his voice carried across the quad up to where she sat. His very demeanor dripped with power and authority, and Anna felt herself wondering why they were fighting him in the first place. She wanted to invite him in and surrender. Looking at the soldiers, they seemed to share her thoughts. Some of them were leaning toward the barrier and a few had even taken a step forward.

"Get back, men," Collins snarled.

Anna, along with the human soldiers, snapped out of the strange trance. Only then did she remember another of the stories her father used to tell her about wraiths. Many of them could enforce their will on humans. Usually they had to make direct eye contact, but the older, more powerful wraiths could exert their influence by being in close proximity to a human. The King was the strongest of all. Her father had also said that beating this effect was possible—you just had to have a strong mind and a strong will. Anna let the faces of her parents fill her mind, and feeding on her anger, she was able to block the King's manipulation.

"You must not be a good general if you cannot control your men," Roland remarked.

"And yet we must be a threat for you to come all the way here."

Roland's eyes narrowed in anger and he let out a sharp hiss. "Well, I was dealing with a few problem spots." He gestured behind him and Anna looked out over the forest. Pillars of smoke were rising over the trees, evidence of more villages the wraiths had destroyed. Anna felt her breath catch. All those people, just gone.

"You'll never get through the barrier," Collins snapped.

Roland's mouth curled into a nasty smile. "I figured I'd give you a chance to surrender before I kill what's left of your people."

"We surrender, and we're forced into slavery."

"Exactly."

"We'd rather die."

"That can be arranged, and with what little I see here, I don't anticipate having much trouble with your . . . 'army.'"

Anna had heard enough. She climbed down from the barracks roof and crept closer to the line, ready to give this so-called King a piece of her mind. As she reached the ground, she saw Collins turn to give a signal, and each of his soldiers pulled out a bow, aiming at the wraiths. Roland gave the General a sneer before nodding to one of his soldiers and turning away from the Sanctuary.

Anna saw one of Roland's soldiers move his hand to his belt and withdraw a small dagger which he threw at the General's turned back. The dagger passed easily through the barrier. Anna ran at the General and tackled his legs, causing the two of them to tumble to the ground. The dagger soared harmlessly over their heads. In the confusion, Roland and the wraiths disappeared into the forest. Anna untangled her arms from the General's legs and watched the wraiths vanish into the trees. Collins stood quickly and dragged her up by the arm.

"Careful!" she exclaimed. "My shoulder."

The General loosened his grip on her arm. "What do you think you're doing out here, young lady?"

"How about a thank you? I did just save your life," Anna replied.

She walked over to where the dagger had stuck in the side of a nearby barrack and pulled it free.

"Can I have this?" she asked, holding it out.

The General stared at Anna. "Do you have any idea how fast that dagger was moving?"

"Fast enough to kill you, I'd guess," she said, "and you never answered me."

"I suppose you've earned it," he said slowly. "Who are you?"

"Anna. Anna Lieay."

The General nodded, and Anna could see that he recognized her name.

"What are you doing out here?" he asked.

"Your soldiers started waking everyone up in the sleeping quarters, telling everyone they were running a drill. Given the circumstances, that didn't seem very smart to me. I snuck out here and climbed the barracks so I could see what was happening." She paused. "You know, if you would've just stationed the soldiers outside the doors, no one would have been the wiser. It wasn't really necessary to have them enter the sleeping quarters."

The General sighed. "I'll take that into consideration next time. I suppose I can overlook your presence if you can promise to tell no one of what transpired. There are a lot of scared people here, and it wouldn't do to spread panic."

"I understand." Anna turned and walked back inside, pausing to call over her shoulder, "Oh, and thanks for the dagger."

She tucked it into her boot, then made her way back to the common area where Ele was waiting for her.

"What happened?"

"Not much. There were some wraiths at the barrier asking us to surrender." Anna snapped her mouth shut as she realized what she'd said. She had told the General she wouldn't say anything, but it just slipped out.

"That sounds like something to me."

"General Collins just rejected the invitation to surrender and they left," Anna said, trying not to make it sound like a big deal. "Breakfast?"

Ele sighed and shook her head. "Does nothing shock you?"

"Not really."

Anna led Ele past the mess of mats and cots to meet up with Oliver and Alex for breakfast. They each grabbed a plate of food and sat at a small table to wait for the boys. Ele looked up from her food to see Oliver striding toward them with Alex close behind.

"Good morning," Oliver announced brightly.

"Did soldiers come into your room this morning?" Alex asked. "They wouldn't let us leave ours."

Ele nodded. "Apparently there were some wraiths at the barrier asking us to surrender."

"Shh," Anna said, still regretting that the words had slipped out, "the General asked me not to tell anyone about it."

"You saw them?" Oliver asked.

"Mmhmm. And I saved the General from a dagger, which he let me keep." Anna pulled the dagger from her boot and laid it on the table, the gold blade gleaming.

"I guess you're ready for training, then," Alex said.

"Definitely."

"We should probably hurry up," Ele interjected. "I doubt they appreciate tardiness."

The four of them quickly finished off the rest of their food and rushed out to the eastern quad, where a large group of people were already assembled. Most of the recruits were older, but Anna saw a few around her age.

"Fall in, recruits," announced an officer. "Assemble in lines. Soldiers will be coming around to collect your names."

The younger recruits assembled near the back of the lines and waited for the soldiers to come around. One of them finally got to Anna and gave her a questioning look. He glared at the rest of the line before speaking.

"Young lady, we are trying to assemble an army that will protect humanity from the wraiths. You and your friends need to go inside to be assessed and assigned to an aid station."

"We want to volunteer, Sir."

He glared at Anna before signaling to the ranking officer.

"What's the problem, Soldier?" asked the officer.

"These children say they want to volunteer."

The officer chuckled and turned to Anna. "Get back inside, girl. This is an army, not a nursery."

Anna glanced at Alex before answering. "We know. We want to do our part."

"I will not have children endangering themselves. I already have enough to worry about. Get back inside and report to an aid station. That is your part in this war."

"No!" Anna yelled. "We want to fight. We've lost our homes and our families, and we want the chance to fight for our people just as much as you do."

"All of you, back to your common areas now," shouted the officer, "or I'll have you detained. That's an order."

Anna opened her mouth once more, but Alex pulled her away before she could retort.

"Anna, they're pretty angry. Don't make it worse."

Anna yanked her arm from Alex's grip, feeling her face go warm. "First off, quit grabbing me. I can walk on my own. And secondly, why can't they let us join training? I want to fight for my land just as much as anyone else."

"I'm sorry for grabbing you, but they won't let us do anything if you keep yelling at them. We'll get our chance. Let's just go back to the dining hall and wait for lunch. Then we can find someone to talk to."

"Fine," Anna said with a huff.

Alex led her to a small table and sat down, with Ele and Oliver joining them moments later. They sat and talked for a few minutes before Anna noticed the soldier from the recruitment assembly. He was speaking to a few others who looked like they could be officers. The soldier gestured angrily in Anna's direction before leaving the hall.

"I think they were just pointing at you," Oliver said, "and they didn't seem too happy. Maybe we shouldn't have tried to volunteer. Or maybe you shouldn't have yelled at an officer. They tend not to like that."

Anna shrugged and tuned Oliver out. Everyone needed to stop telling her what to do. She wasn't some helpless child wandering through the Sanctuary. She'd figure out how to fight one way or another. If only the officers would give her a chance to prove herself. She glanced at Ele, and saw over her shoulder that someone was approaching their table. He came to a stop behind Ele, and Oliver fell silent.

"Miss Lieay?"

Anna stared at him. "Yes?"

"Follow me, please."

The man turned and left without waiting for an answer.

"I guess I'll see you later," Anna said, rising from her seat.

She smiled and left the main hall, leaving her friends staring after her in confusion. She caught up to the man and fell into step beside him.

"What's this about?"

"You have been summoned by the Council. Take your next right and their chambers are on the right."

Anna nodded and rounded the corner, coming face to face with a pair of soldiers blocking the entrance to the Council chambers.

"State your business," one of them said.

"I was summoned by the Council," Anna replied.

"Name?"

"Anna Lieay."

"Go on in."

~ 6 ~

Anna stepped through the door and found herself in a large room with a domed ceiling. This room seemed to be in better shape than most that she'd seen. The ceiling was free from the cracks that populated nearly every room in the Sanctuary. A great mosaic of the Sanctuary's crest covered the stone floor, matching the tapestry that hung behind a raised table. Anna grimaced when she saw the seal. She'd always hated it. A fist rose from decorative scrollwork and extended before two crossed swords. It was supposed to represent humanity's battle prowess and strength, but to her, it had always reflected the Council's ego.

Seven people sat behind the table, conversing softly with one another. The few glances she was spared were cold and distant. Never had Anna felt so small. She could see the General sitting off to the side, but his hard face didn't give her any comfort. There were a few other people next to the General, but she didn't recognize any of them. She assumed they were other officers. After a few moments, the general chatter died down and the entire council turned their attention toward Anna. Their combined gaze nearly made her shrink back, but she held her ground.

"Andromeda Lieay," the woman in the center stated. Her dark hair was streaked with grey, and her eyes were sharp, piercing straight through Anna's core. Anna remembered her father saying once that the head of the Council was a woman named Althea. This must be her.

"I like to be called Anna, please."

Ignoring her, Althea continued, "It has come to our attention that you have been encouraging your peers to join the Sanctuary's fighting force, as well as joining yourself, without permission. In addition, you talked back to a commanding officer, deliberately disobeying a direct order."

"I'll apologize for yelling at the officer, but not for trying to join basic training. I don't see what the problem is. Soldiers are going around asking for volunteers. We're just doing what they said."

"We cannot have children on the battlefield."

"I'm thirteen. I don't think that makes me a child."

"This is not a discussion. You and your friends will report to the aid stations and your attendance at basic training will cease immediately. Is that clear?"

"You're going to deny us our right to fight in the army? Look at all the soldiers you have now. Very few survivors from the initial attacks are joining up as new recruits. You may get a few dozen more as refugees continue to come in, but it's nothing compared to the wraiths' forces. If you look at the remaining pool of refugees, you really only have me and my peers left."

Anna took a few steps forward before continuing. "Not only are we able to fight, we want to. Besides, there's a reason there are so many of us. During the initial attacks, the wraiths went for people they knew could fight back. They passed us by, thinking they'd round us up later. But we were the ones who were able to escape. They didn't see us as a threat, and I believe they will continue to ignore us, which will give us an advantage in a battle. I know none of us have fought in an army before, and most of us have never handled weapons, but that's what training is for. All we need is a chance and I know we can be the difference between winning and losing this war."

"A pretty speech, young lady, but you still don't understand the moral issue involved. How can we, in good conscience, send children out in the field?"

"I do understand. But most of us have lost our families. Taking away our chance to avenge them is the worst thing you can do."

"I'd say getting you killed is the worst thing I could do," Althea said with a glare.

"But that's why we want to train," Anna retorted. "Besides, no one would volunteer unless they absolutely wanted to fight. We just—"

"That is enough."

Anna scowled and glanced over at General Collins. He was staring at her with an odd look on his face. She didn't know if he'd told anyone else what she'd done that morning, but surely it was proof that she could handle herself against the wraiths. She turned her head back to the Council and waited for them to continue speaking.

"Andromeda, will you wait in the side room?" the General asked loudly.

Anna glanced back at the General and sighed. "Yes, Sir." Her heart sank as she walked toward the door. They'd never let her fight. They didn't understand anything.

As she exited the main chamber, someone shut the door behind her. The thick door latched into place, but if she stayed quiet, she could still hear the Council bickering inside.

"I can't believe we're actually entertaining this idea!" a man's voice called out.

"They're too young," said a woman.

"What else can we do?"

"The wraiths will look at our army and laugh. How can we intimidate them with a group of children?"

Anna's scowl deepened. Sure, she and her friends were young, but it's not like they were completely useless.

"Enough, please," a man's strong voice called out.

"General Collins. You don't normally voice your opinions. These are Council meetings, after all."

Anna heard a long pause before the General spoke. "I am within my rights."

"Very well. What do you have to say?"

"I think we should let the younger volunteers into basic training," he announced.

Various conversations broke out among the Council members.

The General spoke up over the crowd, "Please, hear me out. Andromeda made many good points about our current situation. The younger recruits could add nearly three hundred soldiers to the force, and that's a low estimate. They may be untrained and untested, but I was watching a few of them earlier, and I believe most, if not all of them, have some raw talent.

"I'm not saying we should send them out to the forest right away, but we should at least let them train. If they are trained, perhaps they could take over the barrier patrol duties and free up older soldiers to venture out into the field. Furthermore, we don't have to let any of them see combat until we're sure they can handle themselves. This way, they feel like they are still a part of the war effort, but we aren't actively sending them to their deaths."

Anna's heart soared. She'd figured the General was going to be as bad as the Council, but from what she was hearing, perhaps he would give them a fair chance after all.

"It's too dangerous," another voice said.

"They're probably going to try and fight anyway, with or without our permission. If we let them train, at least they'll know how to defend themselves," Collins said.

"You make an interesting argument, General, but how can we be sure they can handle the training?" Althea asked.

"This morning, when Roland came to the barrier, Andromeda was out on the southern quad. She said she watched our exchange. When Roland turned to leave, one of his soldiers threw a dagger at me while my back was turned. Anna was able to knock me out of the way. Without her, I doubt I would be here now. If she could resist Roland's pull and save me from a fast-moving dagger with no experience, think what she could do with some training. I believe her peers will flourish as well. They should at least be given a chance."

"This is ridiculous," another man said.

"I fail to see how, Councilman Sage," Anna heard the General say. "As it stands, we do not have the numbers to face Roland and his army directly. If we want to protect the future of humanity, they may be our only option."

"They're just children."

"Would you rather they try to fight behind our backs?"

Silence fell over the room and Anna longed to be inside to witness the reactions.

"You're the one responsible for running the army," Althea finally said. "Do you think you can handle the addition of these younger recruits?"

"I do."

"Very well, General. But you will take full responsibility for whatever happens. If they fail, it's on you. Understood?"

Anna gritted her teeth. They wouldn't say such things about the older soldiers, and many of those would probably drop out of training. Why couldn't the recruits all be treated equally?

"Yes," Collins said.

"All in favor?" Althea asked the rest of the Council

Anna waited, barely breathing as she listened to hear what the verdict was.

"Motion carries," Althea said. "Send Andromeda back in."

Anna jumped back from the door. When it opened, she wearily stepped through and moved to stand back in front of the Council. Looking up, she forced herself to hide a smile and plastered a frown on her face.

"Andromeda," began Althea.

"Anna, please," Anna interrupted.

Glaring, Althea continued, "Andromeda, this Council has decided to grant your request."

Anna finally let the smile appear on her face.

"But before you get too excited, we have some provisions."

"Of course. Anything."

"We will open up basic training to anyone thirteen years of age or older. A new recruit will have to complete all of basic training plus all of the intermediate level of training to prove to higher-ranking officers that they can handle themselves in battle. If they cannot, they will return to help with the refugees or wherever else this Council sees fit to place them, without question. Are these terms understood?"

"Yes. Completely. Thank you all so much for this opportunity!"

"A special training session for younger recruits will begin tomorrow on the northern quad, one hour after sunrise. Any recruit not present will forfeit their right to join the army. Dismissed."

Anna bowed her head in thanks before exiting the Council chambers. Going over the encounter in her head, she was pleased with how she'd handled herself. The Council was intimidating, but she'd held her ground and even gotten what she wanted. She hardly noticed she had reached the dining hall until she was shaken out of her thoughts by a distant voice.

"Anna," Ele called from one of the tables, "over here!"

Anna weaved through the crowd to reach Ele and her friends.

"You alright?" Alex asked. "Not long after you left, a bunch of soldiers rounded up everyone under seventeen and led us in here. They won't let us leave."

"I'm fine. I was summoned by the Council."

"The Council? What happened?"

"They found out I was encouraging people they considered too young to fight to join basic training."

"That doesn't explain why they've rounded us up."

"Well, do you all still want to fight?"

"Anna," Ele said, "do you not remember what just happened on the quad?"

"Yes, but when I was talking to the Council—"

"Attention," called a soldier from the front of the hall. "Attention! The Council has a special announcement concerning new army recruits. After careful consideration, the Council has decided to open basic training to anyone thirteen years of age or older. There will be a special training session tomorrow morning at eight, sharp. Report to the northern quad. Any not present will forfeit their right to join. Thank you." The soldier gave a curt nod and left the dining hall.

Anna took in the shocked faces of her friends and smiled. "As I was saying, when I was talking to the Council, I convinced them to let us fight."

"How did you manage that?"

"I just told them why I thought we should be allowed to fight and how it would benefit the army. Aside from that, I think General Collins helped a lot. He had me wait in a side room for a bit, and I guess whatever he said was enough to change the Council's mind."

"So . . . tomorrow morning?" Alex said with a grin.

7

King Roland stood in the center of the smoking remains of the small village. He held his sword loosely in his hand, blood dripping from the point and soaking into the ash and dirt below.

"There's nobody left, my Lord," one of his soldiers said. "Shall we move on?"

Roland closed his eyes and took a deep breath. He tried to focus on the sound of the crackling fires around him, but nothing soothed his mind. He hadn't really expected the General to surrender, but a part of him had hoped they would take any option but a war.

He opened his eyes and paced around the perimeter of the village, ignoring the looks from his soldiers. They could wait. He stepped briefly into the shadow of a large building, shuddering as the darkness penetrated him, prickling him with the touch of a thousand knives. He stifled a hiss. His followers didn't need to know how difficult his transition was becoming. With each passing year, it became more and more painful to shift from flesh to shadow, and every time he shifted back, he felt as if part of him was left behind in the darkness.

A daka swooped down and landed before one of his soldiers. The bird held out its leg, offering the small scroll attached. The soldier took it and scanned the page.

"Word from your advisors, my Lord."

"Give it here," Roland said, hissing as the sun hit his outstretched hand.

His soldier offered him the scroll, and Roland snatched the paper. He quickly scanned the words on the page before crumpling it and tossing it into the burning remains of a nearby building.

Whispers from the south were growing. The unseen threat of another group of wraiths weighed heavily on his mind. He had to gain control of Istamba as soon as possible, lest the rumors of these other wraiths held any truth. The sooner he could secure his place as ruler, the easier it would be to defend his territory from any other invaders that might have their eyes on the land.

Fury welled within him. It was ridiculous that he had to wage war for a land that should rightfully belong to him. He'd given more to Istamba than anyone else. He'd lost his family for the Sanctuary and they'd given him nothing in return. Now he would take what he deserved.

"We will return to the city as quickly as possible," Roland commanded.

"What about the other villages in our path?" one of his soldiers asked.

Roland fixed the soldier with a cold glare. "Leave them. They will surely starve before the humans manage to get to them."

He sheathed his sword and marched away from the village, leaving his wraiths to catch up.

8

Ele and Anna both woke early the next morning. They met Alex and Oliver in the dining hall before heading outside to the northern quad where their training session was to be held. A large group of recruits was already assembled, and more were joining the group from all directions. A soldier was going through the crowd, taking names for the General's record.

At an hour after sunrise, exactly, a soldier came up and stood before them. She stood completely straight and her mouth was set in a tight line, but Anna could see kindness behind her cool, grey eyes. Her hair, pulled sharply back away from her face, was so blonde it was nearly white. She showed no emotion as she surveyed Anna and her peers.

"Listen up, recruits," she bellowed. "I am Captain Xandra Price. I'll be one of the officers overseeing your basic training. Before we begin, the Council has a few expectations of this group. As you might expect, many people are apprehensive about letting you train, considering your age. Prove them wrong, or leave.

"If you stay, you will all be expected to pass both basic and intermediate training. In order to assimilate you into regiments, you'll need to reach the skill level of the older soldiers. If you can't, you will be assigned to one of the aid stations, and you'll go without complaint. Is that understood?"

A mumbling of agreement spread through the group.

"I said, is that understood?"

"Yes, Ma'am," they echoed.

"That's better. There are a few things concerning protocol you all have to learn if you are going to be a part of this army. When a superior officer asks you a question, you answer quickly and respectfully. Understood?"

"Yes, Ma'am," came the reply.

"As far as ranking officers go, we don't have many now, but expect that to change as we progress further and organize more recruits into regiments. Each officer wears a command pin that you'll learn to recognize. Our three Generals have different pins than the other officers, so you should be able to recognize them easily. Unless they speak to you first, there isn't any reason you should be talking to the Generals. When an officer enters the room or immediate area, you are to salute and remain that way until they say so."

Captain Price made a gesture with her arm. "To salute, form a fist with your right hand and place it over your heart. Your elbow should point straight out and your arm should be parallel to the ground. Demonstrate."

Anna held her arm out, mimicking the Captain; soldiers strode up and down the lines, correcting the new recruits' form.

The Captain resumed her place in front of them once she was satisfied with everyone's salute. "Our forces are small compared to our enemy's, so we will be progressing through training as fast as we can. The more villages we can save, the less the wraiths can take. Your days will be full, but if you want to continue training, you'll learn how to keep up. Each day, you'll begin with conditioning, then move through a variety of weapons. The conditioning is necessary if you're to be able to go against wraiths with their enhanced strength and speed.

"Before moving onto intermediate training, you will all become proficient in basic weaponry. Once we deem your skills good enough to move on, your training will become more specialized. For now, let's get started on some conditioning. Organize yourselves into four even lines."

Everyone shuffled to get into position. The Captain and another soldier stood at the front while two more brought up the rear. They jogged around the inside of the barrier, once around the Sanctuary for a run of just over six miles. The Captain kept them at a steady jog, and any who dipped below the pace were yelled at by the two soldiers at the back.

About halfway through the run, Anna could feel her pace slipping. Alex panted beside her. His face was red and sweat dripped off his chin. Her legs felt like jelly and her head pounded with each step. A boy on the other side of her ducked out of line and threw up near a tree before collapsing. Anna's stomach lurched, but she wouldn't let herself give in.

As their run continued, Anna saw more and more people dropping out from the run. A girl just ahead of her collapsed on the ground, chest heaving, while another boy leaned heavily against a tree, tears streaming down his face. A few took a short break before rejoining the line at the end, though Anna saw they were yelled at more than some of the others. Anna forced herself to keep going, using the people who dropped out as motivation. She wouldn't allow the Council to have the satisfaction of her quitting.

After what seemed like an eternity, they finally returned to the training area. She saw gaps in the lines where she assumed recruits had dropped from exhaustion. The Captain didn't give them a break, though. She pushed them through strength exercises before running through some final stretches.

"Alright, that's enough for now," the Captain said. "Before training begins every day, you'll run through the same workout we just did. A soldier will lead you for the next two days, but after that, you'll be expected to do these on your own. When your time decreases for your lap, we'll have you run two. Let's move on to some sword drills."

Anna sucked in another deep breath. All she wanted to do was collapse on the ground, but she was determined to push through and continue the training. She pushed away the thought of having to run again tomorrow, and told herself to focus on what was next.

The Captain motioned behind the group. Anna turned and saw

a few more soldiers carrying a bunch of practice weapons. The new recruits jumped up and rushed to grab swords, their exhaustion from the morning's training turning to excitement. They were all eager to begin what they considered real training.

Once everyone had a sword, they were arranged in lines and the Captain showed them a routine of basic maneuvers. They went through the routine over and over again with soldiers walking up and down the lines to help perfect their form. A few more recruits threw their swords down and left the quad, not ready to fully commit to the training. They practiced for two hours without a break before the Captain called for a halt. Nearly everyone collapsed from exhaustion.

"I never said you could sit!" shouted Captain Price. "Everyone up! On your feet!"

The group groaned, but managed to pull themselves up. Anna, who had remained standing, could feel her legs wobbling, and her arm hurt from the effort of holding a sword for so long. That, combined with the workout they had gone through, was enough to make her sleep for days. But, she figured, it was all part of their conditioning. She knew they wouldn't have a chance to rest in battle.

Captain Price stared at them, yelling to hurry, until they had lined up again. "Now that you've got some basic sword instruction, we'll move on to throwing. When you're in the middle of a fight, anything can be thrown, including your sword, but for now, we'll focus on spears, axes, and daggers. Follow me."

They followed the Captain to a separate training area where they saw racks of spears and axes lined up next to a few chests. A soldier opened the chests to reveal various sizes of daggers, bows, and quivers of arrows. Across from the weapons on the opposite end of the field, twenty targets sat in a line.

"We'll get to archery later," the Captain said. "For now, everyone grab some kind of dagger. If there aren't enough, you'll have to share."

Anna grabbed a training dagger that looked to be about the same size as her mother's. She'd never actually thrown a dagger before, and she was a little apprehensive. The workout and sword drills had left her weak, and she wasn't sure how she would muster the strength to throw it.

"I don't know how you're still standing," Alex whispered. "I'm about ready to collapse."

Anna grimaced. "Me too. Just think, lunch has to be soon."

A soldier stepped up in front of the group, silencing the chatter, to demonstrate the various ways they could hold and throw a dagger. After the demonstration, the recruits divided up in front of the targets and attempted to mimic the soldier. They rotated through a few times, taking up the rest of the morning.

"That's enough for now," Captain Price shouted. "We'll pick up with spears and more long-range weaponry after lunch. Get something to eat and meet back here in half an hour."

Everyone breathed a sigh of relief before trudging into the main structure. Ele and Oliver managed to catch up with Anna and Alex; together, they found a table at which to eat and rest. Anna grabbed a large jug of water and took a long drink before passing it around to her friends.

"Drink as much as you can," she said. "The Captain of the Guard at the Fort always said to drink extra water when working hard."

Ele grabbed the jug gratefully. "Anything that helps, I guess."

"This is intense," gasped Oliver through mouthfuls of food. "I thought they'd never let us rest."

"I know," replied Alex. "Are they trying to kill us?"

"I don't think so," Anna said. "I think they're trying to get us to quit. I have a feeling a lot of people are still against us fighting because of our age. If we quit, they get their way. We just have to keep up with the training."

"Is that all?" Alex grimaced.

Anna smiled but said nothing, instead focusing on her food. When their rest break was nearly up, the four of them walked back out to the training area. Anna glanced around, but couldn't see Captain Price anywhere. Instead, a woman about her mother's age was talking to a few soldiers. Her black hair was streaked with grey, and she leaned on a gold broadsword. The point dug into the dirt near her feet as she twisted the handle back and forth. Anna's eyes traveled upward and located the officer's pin glinting on her chest.

"Listen up, recruits," announced the new officer. "The General has allowed you to begin basic training. Now, I may not agree with his decision, but as I have no choice, it falls to me to make sure you don't get yourselves killed. I am Major Ravenall, and I will be in charge of providing valuable knowledge that will keep you alive."

Anna glanced at Alex, unsure of what to think of the Major.

"First rule of war," the Major continued. "Know your enemy. We'll start off easy. Who are we fighting?"

A boy sitting next to Ele raised his hand.

"You," said the Major.

"Michael, Ma'am. We are fighting King Roland and his army, Ma'am."

"Did I ask for your name?"

"Well—"

"No. But you are correct. King Roland has been hiding behind the walls of the wraith city for years, and now, for some reason, he's decided to attack. With some training, we will beat the wraiths. But if we are to defeat them, we must learn everything we can about them. What we do know is small compared to what we'd like to know. However, some of the Sanctuary's records have provided invaluable knowledge. What do we know about the wraiths' abilities?"

Ele raised her hand.

"Yes, Recruit?"

"Aren't they a lot faster and stronger than we are?"

"Yes, but not so much that you can't hold your own. A sol-dier must train every day so that he remains fit enough to fight. Attacking in daylight gives us an advantage. In direct sunlight, they are almost human. They are still strong, but they can be hurt like any of us. The more shadows they have to hide in, the harder they are to kill. After sunset is when they are at their best. If you ever come up against a wraith after dark, your best bet is to run the other way as fast as possible."

"Are you saying that it's impossible to defeat a wraith after dark?" someone else called out. "Isn't that what the amulets are for?"

"Speak out of turn again, and I'll have you run laps all day. To answer your question, that's exactly what I'm saying. The amulets aren't strong enough to help you kill one after dark. They'll help create a distraction so you can get away. Speaking of the amulets, how many of you have your own?"

About thirty recruits raised their hands.

"That's more than I was expecting," the Major said. "From what I've seen, only the oldest families have their own. The Sanctuary does have a few in reserve that we loan out to people leaving the barrier. Since we're on the subject, what can you tell me about the amulets?"

Anna raised her hand. "They were created hundreds of years ago by the magicians of the Sanctuary. When we still had magic, families would travel here to have one made when a baby was born. They have to soak up the sun's energy during the day so you can use them at night. They also point the way to the safe houses in the forest."

The Major raised her eyebrows. "Impressive, recruit. Since magic has been gone from the land for some time, we are unable to make new amulets, so they have been passed down through families. Does anyone know how they work?"

"Umm, magic?" Oliver murmured, earning a laugh from the group.

The Major scowled. "Thank you for your assessment. Obviously, since they were created with magic, that's how they function, but that's not what happens when they are activated. As your fellow recruit pointed out, the amulet should be placed in the sunlight during the day so it can soak up its energy. At night, should the wearer come across a wraith, the amulet will release a blast of light. The light causes the wraith to solidify and weakens them, allowing the human to escape. Unfortunately, each amulet can only store enough energy for a single use each night, and must be charged every day. Like your comrade said, they also point the way to the safe houses. We'll talk about those later.

"We've gotten a little off what I wanted to cover today, so let's go back to the wraiths themselves. We've touched a little on strength and speed, but these attributes vary from wraith to wraith, much like some humans are stronger or faster than others. Now, there is one other important ability that we haven't discussed yet. Anyone?"

The Major looked around expectantly. The new recruits avoided eye contact, hoping someone else would answer.

Persuasion, Anna thought to herself, *unless there's something else I'm forgetting about.*

"Persuasion," the Major finally said. "Wraiths have a knack for getting you to do whatever they want. The older the wraith, the stronger their ability. However, a strong resolve can help you overcome the urge to obey them. Let one idea fill your mind so completely that the wraith cannot put any new ones in. Some soldiers use an emotion or a memory. This becomes much more difficult in battle, so when you're training, I want you all to practice thinking of one thing. That's all I've got time for today. Captain Price is going to take you back to continue your long-distance combat training."

Captain Price came to stand next to her and addressed the recruits. "I hope you all took advantage of your break. I'm going to divide you up into groups. Unless told otherwise, you will remain with the same group for the remainder of your training. Group One will move to the far side of the field with me and learn to use a spear. Group Two will stay here and continue to practice with daggers. Group Three will move back to the training field to work with swords again."

The Captain then read off names, splitting the group in three. Anna and Alex ended up in the first group along with Ele, Oliver, Liam, and a few other trainees that Anna noticed had gotten the hang of throwing the daggers rather quickly. She figured Group One was probably the best place to be, and based on the expressions she saw, a few who weren't selected realized this also. The Captain led them to the end of the field and began their instruction on spears.

"While daggers are easy to conceal, spears are versatile. You can use them as a melee weapon in combat, and they can also be thrown. If you make it through the next stage of training, you'll be taught how to fight hand-to-hand with a spear, but for now, we'll focus on throwing. Take the spear in your dominant hand and make sure it's balanced. Aim at your target, step, and throw in one smooth motion. Divide up and start."

The group shuffled a bit to form lines, anxious to begin practicing. When it was Anna's turn, she grasped the spear and bounced it a few times in her hand. She had thought the lunch break had helped ease her soreness, but just the weight of the spear strained her aching muscles. Hefting it above her shoulder, she took aim and threw it with as much strength as she could muster. It struck the far left of the target and stayed there, its point embedded in the wood.

"Well done, recruit," called the Captain.

Anna examined the other targets. She noticed she was one of the few to hit one and make it stick, even if it wasn't near the center. However, as she stepped back from the line, one of the older boys stepped up and hurled a spear at the target. It hit dead center and sank in past the spear point.

Alex looked at Anna. "Who is *that*?"

"I have no idea," she whispered back.

The Captain walked over to the boy and pulled him aside. Anna tried to hear what they were saying, but they were speaking too quietly.

When the Captain was satisfied with the recruits' progress, she had Group Two work with spears and Group Three work with daggers, but she moved Group One back to an open field to work with swords again before dinner. After dinner, they were reunited into one large group for another grueling workout before the Captain finally released them to enjoy an hour of free time before the Sanctuary-wide curfew at an hour past sunset.

Alex collapsed on the well-trodden grass of the quad once they were dismissed, and Anna sat down beside him. The workout that morning had been by far the most difficult part of the day, and she knew she'd be sore tomorrow. Really sore. But learning how to use the weapons had turned out to be a lot of fun.

"I could fall asleep right here," Alex groaned.

"Me too, but I think I'm going to stay out until curfew and run through those sword forms they taught us," Anna replied.

"Really? You haven't had enough for today?"

"If they're really trying to get us to quit, I don't want to give them the satisfaction. Besides, I joined the army to fight and protect my land. I'm not about to give up now."

"Okay, I'll join you." Alex dragged himself into a sitting position and rolled his shoulders.

"Join her for what?" Ele asked, walking up to the pair with Oliver trailing behind.

"We're going to do some extra training during our free time so they don't have an excuse to kick us out of the army."

"Do you ever quit?" Oliver exclaimed. "We only have an hour before curfew!"

"You might be better resting," Ele warned. "You'll do no good exhausting yourself."

Anna pictured Roland's cold gaze. She couldn't just sit around and wait to be attacked. "Then we don't have much time to waste," Anna replied. "Besides, what else is there to do?"

"Might as well," Oliver agreed. "Could we fight each other, do you think? Learning maneuvers is great and all, but what good are they if we don't get to use them?" He stopped, as if unsure of the idea.

"As long as we take it easy," Ele cautioned, her drawn face projecting her concern. "I'd like to be able to move tomorrow."

"Sure. There should be some practice weapons on the eastern quad," Anna said.

"What's on the eastern quad?" called a voice.

Anna turned and saw Liam striding toward the group.

"Not that it's any of your business, but we were going to do some extra training," Anna said.

A grin spread across Liam's face. "Sounds fun. Count me in."

"Who said you were invited?"

"Um, me? Come on," he pleaded, "there's nothing else to do around here. And if this is about what I said yesterday, I didn't mean it. I just wasn't sure who they were going to let train."

Anna looked at her friends. Alex and Ele both shrugged. "I guess it couldn't hurt," Anna finally said.

"This'll be great!" Liam exclaimed. "We'll be better than everyone else in no time."

He linked arms with Anna and Alex and tried to pull them to the eastern quad. Anna and Alex shared a look before they both pulled free from his grasp.

"I'm sure," Anna said.

She brushed past Liam and led the way to the eastern quad. The group arrived to find the quad empty, save for a large collection of practice weapons. They each grabbed a sword and paired off, trying to apply what they had learned in an actual fight.

Each night, between dismissal and curfew, they'd meet and put what they'd learned to practical use. Eventually, word spread through their basic training group about their unscheduled sessions, and their group grew to about fifty. Most of the participants had their own small groups that they interacted with, but a few joined Anna and her friends.

Occasionally, Anna would see some of the training officers watching, but they never said anything. Colonel Grimshaw, General Collins' second-in-command, watched most often. Though Anna had never actually spoken to the Colonel, her presence was intimidating enough. She hardly spoke to anyone and her mouth was always set in a tight line. She had cut her hair short so people could see the long scar running from above her ear to her shoulder where a wraith had attacked her as a child.

General Collins came and watched one night with the Colonel, and the next day, the training officers split their regular training group up again. Those that put in extra practice were pushed harder than before, but Anna didn't mind. It felt like the officers were treating them more like real soldiers.

She could feel herself growing stronger and faster with each new day of training, and her skills quickly began to outmatch those of many of her peers. She and her small training group were even gaining attention from some of the other soldiers. Even Major Ravenall began to warm up to them a bit. Their sessions with her turned to strategy lessons with a little of Istamba's history sprinkled in. They learned different methods of group attacks, as well as basic survival skills they would need if they ever went into the forest.

Week after week, the recruits trained. They were introduced to all types of weapons, from broadswords to spears, from bows to axes. As the days passed, Anna noticed that their training group continuously grew smaller as trainees either dropped out of their own accord or were asked to leave based on their performance. What had started as a group of two hundred and fifty now had a little less than one hundred.

A few months after they had begun basic training, Captain Price assembled what was left of their original group for an announcement.

"Quiet down, recruits! You've reached the end of basic training. Tomorrow, you will all be tested to determine whether or not you can continue to intermediate training. You will be put through conditioning exercises to determine your physical fitness as well as weapons testing to determine your proficiency. Those who do not pass the testing will be reassigned to the aid stations. Get a good night's sleep and meet Major Ravenall on the quad tomorrow morning for a quick session before the tests. Dismissed."

Anna and Alex left the quad and went back inside to the dining hall. Sitting at their usual table, they waited for Ele and Oliver to join them before they began eating.

"You two ready for the test tomorrow?" asked Ele as she sat down across from Anna.

"I think so," Anna replied. "I hope those extra training sessions will give us an advantage."

"I just hope they don't go harder on us because of them. I've seen a few officers watching us before and right afterward, our daily training got harder."

"I don't think it will be too bad," Alex replied. "Are we still meeting tonight? I haven't really had the chance to look around the Sanctuary and I thought we could rest up for tomorrow."

"Sounds alright to me," Anna said.

"Have you seen the gardens?" Ele asked.

Anna shook her head.

Ele motioned for the group to follow her. "They grow all the vegetables in these courtyards within the main structure. There isn't a whole lot of room within the barrier, so they grow the plants up and on the walls."

The friends dodged soldiers and refugees as Ele led them further into the main structure. They passed through the kitchens and she waved to her aunt, who was stirring a large pot of soup. Anna felt a twinge of loneliness as she longed for her own family. Ele pressed on through the kitchens to a long hallway, empty save for a cook wandering in and out of the rooms.

"All the rooms here have been converted to gardens," Ele said.

Anna walked over to the first one and stepped through the open archway. The scent of fresh herbs mingling together tickled her nose. Small plants were lined up in rows throughout the entire room. Wooden boxes filled with more plants had been nailed to the wall, extending up nearly fifteen feet.

"How is it so bright in here?" Oliver asked.

Anna's gaze traveled up to the roof of the tall room. A mirror was angled to reflect the sun from a tall window down onto the plants below.

"There," Anna said, pointing, "that mirror is directing the light to help the plants."

"Couldn't they just plant some gardens in the forest?" Alex asked. "Why go to all this trouble?"

"Because the forest isn't protected by the barrier," Anna said. "If wraiths could destroy our food, we'd die before we could win. This way, the food is safe and the cooks can easily access it."

Oliver shook his head. "It just seems so strange. It looks like those plants have been growing from the walls for years. How would our ancestors have known to think of that?"

Anna smiled. She had asked her father the same question when he'd taken her to visit the Sanctuary when she was younger. "According to my father, the Sanctuary was designed thousands of years ago to house all of humanity in times of crisis. Like Ele said, this entire hall is filled with rooms just like this, but I doubt more than a few of them are even being used right now."

"I guess if it works, there's no sense in wasting space," Alex said.

"Right." Ele yawned. "Why don't we get to sleep? I'd rather not be tired for our test tomorrow."

"Ugh, I almost forgot," Oliver said.

"We'll see you two tomorrow," Anna said, and she and Ele went back to their sleeping room for some much-needed rest.

9

"W elcome back, recruits," called the Major the next morning. "As you all know, you will be tested for weapons proficiency this afternoon. For now, we have another lesson in our history: the barrier. What do we know about it?"

"The first humans of the Sanctuary made it to keep the wraiths out," a girl said.

"Correct. The barrier was erected by the first humans to settle this land when the wraiths began attacking them. So, it's ancient. As such, it can fail sometimes, and a single wraith occasionally makes it through unscathed. *That* is why we run barrier patrols at all times, day and night. You, as the newest recruits, will be on barrier duty once you complete basic training, but don't worry—it's rare that a wraith can slip through the barrier on its own. However, the barrier does have another flaw, a more dangerous one: a wraith can get in *if invited*."

"But why would a human willingly invite a wraith in?" someone asked.

"Remember what I said about persuasion? A wraith can coerce a weak-minded soldier into offering that invitation. All it takes is a *yes* when the wraith asks to come in. For this reason, refugees and civilians are not permitted to be near the barrier without an escort; soldiers are more aware of the wraiths' psychic abilities and should be able to fend off any such attempted influence. And this isn't only true for the main barrier here. Our safe houses throughout the forest are also protected by small barriers, which have the same properties and flaws as the big one. As I've mentioned before, the amulets can lead you to their locations, so keep that in mind when you're out in the forest. One of those safe houses may save your life one day, but only if you don't invite a wraith in."

"If the first people were able to create barriers outside the Sanctuary, why can't we do the same? We could protect villages across the land," one of the girls suggested.

"Genius! You must be the smartest person to have ever passed through the Sanctuary. No one, in our entire history, has ever thought about creating new barriers until now!" The Major's voice was heavy with sarcasm.

"Well, I—"

"Of course we've thought about it! The means to erect a barrier were lost centuries ago; there haven't been magicians in Istamba for nearly a thousand years." The Major paused and glanced around at the recruits. "That's all I have for you this morning. Your tests will take place after lunch. The rest of the morning is yours to spend as you choose."

After lunch, Anna lined up with the rest of the trainees hoping to transition into the intermediate level. Alex stood by her side, tapping his foot. She could feel the nervous energy rolling off him in waves. Captain Price stepped up in front of the group.

"We'll start off with two laps around the Sanctuary. Those who cannot make it in an hour and ten minutes will be cut from the second round of testing. Those who pass will have their abilities tested with a sword and one ranged weapon of their choice. Is that clear?"

"Yes, Captain," came the unanimous cry.

"Good. Begin your laps."

After an initial burst of speed, most of the runners fell into a steady jog. Anna, Alex, and a few others who had been doing extra conditioning work on their own led the group at a more aggressive pace. Anna lost track of her surroundings as she slipped into her running rhythm. She wasn't worried about this part of the testing at all. She and her friends were in better shape than most of the recruits, as were the other people who had joined their small group sessions. She had begun a tentative friendship with a few of them. Liam and Rebecca were among the more open people. Though Anna and Liam had gotten off to a rocky start, he'd since apologized and seemed nice enough. Rebecca, Anna had learned, was extremely kind and absolutely deadly with a bow. She'd even offered to help Anna with that part of her training. Anna had readily accepted, but after only a few lessons, she'd quickly realized she would never be great with a bow—which didn't trouble her much, as she preferred to throw daggers when range was needed and hoped never to have to rely on archery.

Noticing that she'd come to the end of her first lap, Anna shook herself out of her thoughts and focused once again on giving the run her best effort.

As she passed the Captain, she heard her say, "Thirty minutes gone."

Anna nodded and increased her pace. She had yet to make two laps in under an hour, but she was determined to do it this time. She could hear Alex's heavy breaths just behind her, but they were fading. She was pulling ahead of the group. The next few miles passed by, and she could feel the weariness setting in. Rounding the final corner, she could barely make out the Captain ahead when she saw Liam gaining on her out of the corner of her eye. She knew he'd always loved running, and he had yet to lose one of their races, but Anna yearned to beat him, just this once. She pushed through her aches and drew deep breaths, trying to give oxygen to the screaming muscles in her legs.

Liam wasn't about to give in easily, though. He used his long stride to his advantage, taking one step for every two of hers. Faster and faster they went, until the two were racing in a frenzied sprint toward the Captain. Digging deep, Anna gave one final push, increasing her slight lead to an arm's length before stumbling to a halt in front of the Captain, with Liam only seconds behind her.

"Nicely done, recruits," said the Captain. "Fifty-eight minutes.

That's a new record. Cool down and get some water while we wait for the rest of your comrades."

Anna gasped out a 'thank you' and headed for the water station. Liam followed her, breathing just as heavily.

"Wow, Lieay, didn't know you had it in you."

"I had to beat you sometime," she replied with a grin.

Their cooldown finished, they sat down in silence to watch the remainder of the recruits stream across the finish line in waves, showing various emotions as they reached the end of their laps. The Captain handed the last group of runners plain white armbands.

Once everyone was present, Captain Price spoke up, "Those of you with a white armband, report to the aid stations tomorrow. You can try basic training again in a few months. Everyone else, you will move on to the second round of testing. Follow me."

Anna dragged herself to her feet. Weariness was beginning to set in, her legs felt like jelly, and she longed for a short break, but that didn't seem to be an option.

They followed the Captain to the sparring field. Arranging themselves in lines as they had been taught, they waited for her to speak.

"You all have managed to run twelve miles in under an hour and forty minutes, therefore . . ."

"Um, Captain?" asked one of the recruits.

"Yes, Recruit?"

"Didn't you say we had to make it in under an hour and ten minutes?"

The Captain smirked. "Yes. We tell you that so you'll push yourselves, but in truth, very few can actually make that time. Our best soldiers can on a good day, but certainly not trainees. Two of you even made the run in less than an hour; an impressive feat. Now, let's see if you can handle your weapons." She gestured for the group to divide down the middle. "Those of you on the right, grab a practice sword; those on the left, go to the throwing targets and choose a ranged weapon."

Anna grabbed a practice sword and got back in line to await her turn.

"I will call two of you forward at a time, and you will each enter into a short duel with one of these six soldiers," the Captain said, gesturing at the half-dozen experienced troops standing behind her. "The duels will continue until one person wins or I call a draw. You two, come forward."

The two recruits the Captain motioned to stepped forward and began their duel. Anna had positioned herself near the middle of the group so she could watch the first few fights before having to face one of the soldiers herself. Each fight only lasted a few minutes before the recruit was defeated. Though no one won their duel, the Captain nodded in approval and told most of them to resume their place in the ranks for the next round of training. However, a few recruits were beaten almost immediately, and were dismissed with white armbands.

Alex and Ele, who were standing beside Anna, were called up next. Alex squared up to his opponent and charged him with ferocity. Ele advanced toward her opponent on light feet, circling, darting forward and retreating in a dangerous dance. After five or so minutes, neither person in either pair had won. The Captain called for a halt.

"Good work, recruits. Get back in line. Next two, come forward."

Anna stepped forward with a girl she didn't recognize, and two fresh soldiers strode to meet them.

"Begin."

Anna held out her sword, but didn't attack. Smirking, the experienced guard swung at her right shoulder. Anna raised her arm, blocking the blow easily with her sword. Twisting the point away from her body, she struck the underside of her opponent's sword and leapt forward. She attacked with a flurry of strikes, alternating sides so that the soldier was forced to block right and left in quick succession. When he fell behind, she slapped the flat of his blade with the edge of her own, knocking it from his grip. She flicked her sword up to his throat and waited for the Captain to speak.

"Impressive, recruit. We may just make a soldier of you yet. Get back in line."

Anna nodded and returned to her spot next to Alex to await the final test. The Captain finished up with the rest of the recruits in the sword group and sent them off to the throwing range. When they got there, a soldier directed them to line up and proceeded to explain the final test.

"You will all choose one weapon to demonstrate your competence with ranged attacks. You will have five chances to hit the target. I and my fellow soldiers will assess your ability and determine whether or not you will move on to the next level of training. The first five in line, step up to a target."

The first five stepped up, and Anna saw Rebecca among them. She chuckled to herself, knowing how good Rebecca was. Glancing back at the training officer, Rebecca let lose all five arrows in quick succession. The first struck hard in the center of the target and each one after that split the previous arrow in two. Rebecca turned away from the target and set the bow down, head held high. The training officer nodded approvingly and motioned for her to stand off to the side. The other four had hit the target with adequate accuracy, and they joined Rebecca.

Anna watched the remainder of the recruits show off their ranged abilities without much excitement. A few people caught her eye, though. The first was Ian, the boy she'd noticed on her first day of training who was exceptionally good at throwing spears. He often trained at their night sessions, but wouldn't speak to anyone except his sister, Mariana. The second was another boy—Michael, she thought—who tripped over every other step. Despite his clumsiness, only Rebecca's skill with a bow outmatched his.

When Anna's turn came, she chose five daggers of about the same size. She was better at close combat, but did her best to practice throwing daggers whenever she could. The small weapons were easily concealed, and she was determined to develop her skill with them as best she could. She stepped up to the line and hurled them at the target. All of them stuck in the center ring but one, which landed just outside. Earning a nod of approval, she joined the rest of the passing group to wait for the rest to finish.

The soldier overseeing their test congratulated those that had passed, and led them back to the sparring field.

Seeing everyone assembled, Captain Price stepped up in front of them. "Congratulations, all. You have officially earned the title of Soldier. There will be some changes now that you've passed basic training; you will all be put in the roster for patrols and guard duty. You will also be moved to the northern barracks. Additionally, you will all be required to wear a grey armband so that other soldiers and officers may identify you as a soldier. As far as your actual training, you'll be broken up into smaller groups according to your strengths. You'll still practice with all weapons, but you'll focus on one or two and be placed in regiments accordingly. Report to the eastern training quad tomorrow morning. The rest of the night is yours. Dismissed."

"I never thought basic would end," Ele said as they walked back to the dining hall.

"I'm actually excited to be moved to the barracks," Oliver said as he bounced from foot to foot. "It feels like we're actually part of the army."

Anna smiled. "We are! Speaking of, we should probably head over there. We don't want to have last pick of the available bunks."

Alex nodded and stood to follow Anna.

"I'm going to head to the kitchens," Ele said, a huge grin on her face. "My aunt will want to know how the tests went. Grab a bunk for me, Anna?"

"I'll go with you," Oliver said. "I'm sure my parents are keen to hear what happened as well."

Anna nodded and headed in the direction of the northern barracks with Alex. "We'll see you two tomorrow," she called over her shoulder, though her heart had fallen at the mention of family. What wouldn't she give to be able to talk to her parents again? Her friends were great to talk to and she loved having them around, but it still felt like there was a hole in her life. The two people she had counted on for everything no longer existed anywhere but in her memory.

"You want to walk around a bit?" Anna asked Alex after they had chosen their bunks.

"Sure."

They wandered around the eastern quad before circling up to the north.

"I didn't know there were trees inside the barrier," Alex said. "I thought it was all just grass and dirt like the quads."

"I guess they left these ones alone," Anna paused for a moment. "Don't they use these trees for training games?"

"Oh, yeah, I remember they told us to stay away from here," Alex said, smiling.

Anna pulled Alex away from the trees and they wandered up toward the northern edge of the barrier. There was a small lake just outside the barrier, and a series of wooden troughs led from the bank to a gate at the back of the Sanctuary's main structure.

"I thought it was dangerous to have our necessities outside the barrier," Alex said.

"I don't think wraiths come this far north. They'd have to go all the way to the coast to get here from the east and they'd have to go through mountains from the west, so I think the water's safe where it is."

"Huh."

Anna glanced at Alex. "Is something wrong?"

He stared at the water system for a moment before answering. "No, I just thought everything here was built with magic, but this seems so . . . normal."

Anna smiled. "Well, magic did disappear a long time ago. Humans have had to adapt to survive. Actually, aside from the barrier, I don't think anything here was built using magic."

"That's too bad."

Horns sounded around the Sanctuary, signaling curfew.

"I guess we'd better get back to the barracks," Anna said.

Alex chuckled. "Yeah. Wouldn't want to get kicked out right after we've officially become soldiers."

Anna laughed, and the two returned to the barracks.

— 10 —

The next morning, the newest soldiers assembled on the eastern training field as ordered.

"Line up, soldiers," came a harsh command.

The soldiers straightened up their already neat lines, trying to appease the officer moving to stand in front of them. He wore gold bracers on his arms and an old steel sword hung at his waist, though the handle was wrapped in gold thread. His leather chest piece displayed an officer's pin, along with several other medals and trinkets. His hair was combed back sharply, and Anna doubted that she'd find even the smallest speck of dirt on his uniform if she looked. As he surveyed their lines, Anna could see his scowl deepening and his eyes narrowed to slits.

"I am Colonel Griffen Wells. I'll be leading your strength workouts and overseeing most of your training. Let's begin."

The Colonel proceeded to direct the group through grueling strength exercises before having them run three laps around the Sanctuary without even the slightest break. He yelled at them for even the slightest imperfection in form and demanded they work ever harder, while he stood idle in front of them. The soldiers assisting him barely said a word, and several times Anna caught them shooting dirty looks at their commander. After their laps, he had them go through the same exercises again, berating them again for not being good enough. Anna's arms and legs ached, but she continued to push through, silently telling herself to stop complaining. By the time they'd finished the brutal workout, it was time for lunch.

"Alright, soldiers, you'll have an hour for lunch, then assemble back here for your next training session. Dismissed." Colonel Wells stomped away from their training group, muttering underneath his breath.

A collective groan came from the group as they dragged themselves to the dining hall, desperate to rest for a moment. Though Anna and her friends were in better shape than most of the group, the morning's workout had taken its toll. She snagged a plate of food and collapsed at the nearest table. Alex, Oliver, and Ele were right behind her.

"Is it just me, or does it seem like that Colonel hates us?" asked Alex between bites of food.

"I know the other officers were hard on us," responded Oliver, "but he actually seemed to be trying to kill us."

"Maybe we should train harder on our own so we can keep up," Ele said.

"I'm alright with that," Anna replied, "though I don't know if the rest of our little group will go along with it."

"I think they will. They must have noticed how much tougher these conditioning routines are. Maybe they'll like the idea as well."

Anna shrugged. Noticing some of the soldiers in their training group heading back outside, she motioned to her friends, and they stood and followed everyone back out to the training ground. They lined up and waited for Colonel Wells to direct their next session; however, they were glad to see Major Ravenall instead. Though the Major had been brusque at first, Anna had come to like and respect her for being level-headed and truly caring about the army and the Sanctuary. She was still tough on their group, but Anna had come to understand that the Major was like that with everyone.

"First off, I suppose congratulations are in order, but just because you've passed basic doesn't mean you get to slack off. Now that you're considered soldiers, we need to correct the information you've been given about the warning signals that can be heard across the

Sanctuary. You were told that the horn blasts are signals for soldiers to report to a certain quad, correct? We tell refugees that so they don't worry, but it's only a partial truth. If you hear horn blasts, it means we have wraiths approaching the barrier.

"If this signal sounds, soldiers in regiments are expected to report to the designated quad. One blast is for the north, two for the east, three for the south, and four for the west. Soldiers not in a regiment—you—are to report to your stations. You'll get those assignments at your barracks. We'll have drills to help you get more comfortable with your responsibilities. Understood?"

"Yes, Ma'am!"

The Major nodded her approval. "Good. Now we can speak about information a little more relevant to combat. Wraiths. How can they be killed?"

Oliver raised his hand. "They turn to dust, Ma'am."

"Correct, but I asked how they can be killed, not what happens when you do. Anyone else?"

"Stabbed through the heart?" someone else guessed.

"That's one way. Wraiths heal very quickly, so you'll have to give them a substantial injury to kill them. You could also cut their head off." The Major paused and a slight smile crossed her face. Anna's eyes went to her feet and the Major gave a dark chuckle, as if remembering something, before looking back at the training group as she continued, "Any serious injury to the neck will also turn them to dust. Any other injury is unlikely to kill them, but it might slow them down enough for you to deal a killing blow. Keep in mind that if a wraith can return to its insubstantial or shadow form, it can heal almost anything. That's why it's impossible to kill one at night. In direct sunlight, they'll be wounded like humans."

"How do they heal themselves?" a boy in the back asked.

"We don't really know."

"Well, how do they create more wraiths?" another girl asked.

"We don't know that either," the Major responded.

"Do they know anything?" Alex whispered, and Anna stifled a dark laugh.

"We think it has something to do with shadows, but if you meet a wraith who's willing to explain it to you, we'd love to know," the Major said. "However, if someone in your group suddenly has body parts that look like shadows, it's safe to say they're probably becoming a wraith. The best option at that point is to kill the human before they fully turn.

"Major?" asked one of the soldiers.

"Yes?"

"Is that why the wraiths take people? To change them into more wraiths and make a bigger army?"

"They may do that to a few people, but we doubt it. Though many of them were once human, they look down on us. The people they take, they put to work. Since they hate direct sunlight, they force humans to build up their city. They also produce smoke to cover it and block the sun. If you are ever unfortunate enough to go near the dark city, you'll first see its large cloud.

"Now, the forest may seem like the worst place for us to be, given how much shadow the trees create, but we do have an advantage over the wraiths. When wraiths are near, animals will either leave or go into hiding. It doesn't matter what form the wraiths are in. So, if the forest goes quiet, be ready for a fight. There is one exception, however. Wraiths use dakas to send messages between their forces. For those of you who don't know, dakas are black birds about a foot tall. If you see a daka, try to shoot it down and take anything it's carrying; in particular, you want to look for small scrolls attached to the birds' legs. If there are no questions, I need to get to my patrol. Colonel Wells will take it from here."

The Colonel stepped up in the Major's place to address the group. "Listen up, soldiers. Patrol and guard schedules will be posted outside your barracks every night, so unless you are scheduled for either, you will report here for individualized training. Divide yourselves up into groups based on your strengths. Archers, swordfighters, and throwers."

The group moved to follow his demands. Anna stood with the swordfighters along with Alex, Oliver, and Ele. The Colonel directed

each group to separate training areas with a few experienced soldiers to supervise. After they were divided up, the Colonel left the
training ground and went inside the main structure. Anna could see
some of the other soldiers visibly relaxing as he left, and although
she'd tried not to let him affect her, she couldn't help the feeling of
relief that came over her.

They ran through some advanced drills before pairing off and
sparring with each other. They practiced with standard swords for
a few hours before moving on to specialized swords. Anna chose to
learn how to fight with dual swords. Oliver and a few others chose
broadswords. Some tried their hands at other weapons, such as axes
or double-bladed spears. With the Colonel gone, the training officers
seemed more comfortable. While they still pushed the trainees, they
made their directions easy to follow and gave praise where it was
due. Anna began to feel like a real soldier instead of a nuisance the
Colonel had to endure.

Anna left her friends on the training field earlier than usual that
night and wandered around the Sanctuary for a bit until she found a
secluded balcony on one of the upper levels. She sat on the edge and
admired the way the barrier shimmered in the moonlight. After six
months of living at the Sanctuary, she'd found some semblance of a
normal life, or as normal as she could expect with a war going on.

She remembered a group of refugees coming through the barrier
a few weeks before. Officers had dismissed training early that day
to manage the extra people. It was a horrible sight. People clung
to one another, tears making tracks in the dirt and grime on their
faces. Children latched onto their mothers, or in some cases to each
other. Their eyes were red and none of them would look at any of
the soldiers. The sight of these people, driven from their homes and
sobbing for those they had lost, haunted Anna's dreams for the next
few days. She'd thrown herself into training after that, working hard

and then harder still so that she might be the one standing between the wraiths and the next village they chose to attack.

Anna forced the memory from her mind and reflected on the past few months. The conditioning and strength workouts each morning were difficult, but her body soon became accustomed to the exercise. After lunch every other day, she would be scheduled to guard either the armory or food stores with senior soldiers, along with Alex or Ele. Though no one ever tried to take weapons or food without authorization, the Council still wanted soldiers posted. Anna didn't mind; it allowed her to get to know more of the soldiers and pick up small pieces of information regarding the war's progress.

On the days she wasn't on guard duty, she would train with the swordfighters until dinner, before joining the other soldiers in intermediate training for hand-to-hand combat. They hadn't done any form of direct combat in basic, and Anna quickly amassed a collection of bruises. Being one of the smaller soldiers, she was targeted quite a bit. Most of the other soldiers saw her as an easy win, at first, but she learned to use her speed to her advantage.

After they were dismissed from formal training, Anna would stay out and continue training with her small group. Through those sessions, Anna got to know some of her peers much better. A few still kept to themselves, only joining in for group combat drills, but she talked with Liam and Rebecca quite a bit. Anna knew she'd never be great at archery, but Rebecca and Michael were perfectly fine giving the whole group lessons. They had insights that the training officers couldn't give. Anna found that she could apply many of their tips to throwing daggers, like judging wind and angles for throwing longer distances.

As Anna reflected on the past few months, she realized how much contentment she'd found in her new life. Of course, each day was difficult, physically; it made her proud of how far she had come. She missed her parents desperately. Every morning when she woke up, she had to remind herself that they were gone, but as time passed, it became easier to exist on her own. Her new friends helped distract her from memories of her past, and she was grateful to have met them.

She let her fourteenth name day pass without recognition, though her friends tried to call attention to it. She missed her home and her family, but she'd reached a sort of peace at the Sanctuary. She was surrounded by good friends, and though she couldn't forget the death of her people, training was a good distraction. Even if she never got to leave the barrier, it made her feel like she was working toward something. Perhaps if she worked hard enough, the General might put her, and her friends, in a regiment.

11

General Collins ran a hand through his hair as he examined a list of the youngest recruits. Captain Price and Major Ravenall had given him their rankings of the recruits in terms of overall skill. He was supposed to have a list from Colonel Wells, but Wells had 'conveniently' forgotten. He had asked the Colonel again, but all Wells had to say was that all of them should be expelled from the fighting force. At least he had the two lists to compare. While most of the recruits were fairly evenly matched, there were about twenty who stood out from everyone else.

"What do you think of these lists?" he asked Colonel Grimshaw.

She glanced down at the parchment. "Names on a page don't matter much to me. What's important is how they work together."

Collins chuckled. "I have to pick *someone*, Iyla."

"These soldiers stand out to me the most," she said, pointing to a handful of names. "Their skills are solid, and they know how to work with others. I think that's what's important in a new regiment."

Collins nodded, reflecting back on the few training sessions he'd watched. They only served to reinforce his original decision to allow the young recruits into training in the first place. He knew the Council wanted to remove him from command, which was why they'd let the young soldiers attempt training. They'd anticipated that the recruits would wash out quickly, and he felt certain they'd planned to use that failure to replace him with someone more loyal to the Council's interests. With the Lieays gone, the southern lands were ripe for the taking in the confusion of the war, and he suspected the Council would try to trick Anna out of her birthright.

He glanced over the two lists again. Anna Lieay topped both of them, and the assistant training officers had nothing but praise for the young soldier. He owed her a lot, though she didn't know it. Her determination had spread throughout her training group, and he firmly believed that her presence was what made their group so successful, and thus, why he was no longer in danger of being removed from command.

"What about Anna Lieay?" he asked.

Colonel Grimshaw smiled widely. "I like that girl. If anyone deserves a command, she does."

"She's quickly learned different weapons and she's a great fighter. I think she shows potential."

"It's more than that, and you know it," Iyla said. "She runs those training sessions herself. And the others respect her. Don't you remember that fight?"

Collins nodded. Two recruits had started arguing one night, and yelling had escalated to throwing punches. Anna had stepped between them and separated them. He didn't hear what she'd said to them, but after that, they shook hands and walked away. She'd sported a split lip the next day in training, but no one had said a word about the incident. The recruits in her training group obviously looked up to her, even though she was one of the youngest among them at fourteen. She was a natural leader and seemed to inspire the others around her to work harder.

"I'd almost forgotten about that," Collins finally said. "I know she's only fourteen, but we need new blood in our officer positions. The problem now is convincing the Council of it."

"Ha! It's your army. Just do it," Iyla said.

Collins snorted. "You're a terrible influence."

"General Collins." A woman's voice interrupted. "Colonel Grimshaw."

Collins looked up to see the head Councilwoman standing only a few paces away. Her flowing blue robes brushed the floor. She adjusted the gold crest hanging from her neck and cocked her head slightly, waiting for an answer.

Nodding to the older woman, he said, "Althea, I thought you'd be in the Council chambers already."

"I'll go check on the regiment," Iyla said, before turning to the Councilwoman. "Althea."

Althea nodded coldly and looked back at Collins. "I'm just on my way to the meeting, as you should also be. How goes training?"

"Quite well." The General adjusted his pace to hers, as she seemed intent on walking with him. "Everyone seems to be adapting to army life without too much trouble. I am especially impressed with the younger recruits."

"Oh?"

"Yes. I'll be addressing them in my report."

"Then we should go in."

She strode into the Council chambers, the General close behind her. Taking her place in the center of the curved table, Althea addressed the room.

"I call this Council session to order."

Everyone stood, saluting the crest hanging over Althea's head as they recited the Sanctuary's creed in unison. "May we, the people of Istamba, pledge our loyalty to this great land. We pledge to protect humanity and all it stands for. Through our strengths and through our weaknesses, may we prevail, and may the strength of humanity govern this land, now and forever."

Once everyone was seated, Althea spoke. "We will begin with the Council members' reports. Councilman Phillips, supply report?"

Collins stifled a yawn. Each of the seven Council members was in charge of one thing at the Sanctuary and Althea insisted on them reporting every time they had a formal meeting. At first, he had made sure to take in everything that was said, but he soon realized how little of it actually pertained to the war.

Most of the reports, Collins tuned out. They always said the same thing, anyway. Scouting and reconnaissance missions needed to be sent to a few different villages. Troops needed to be on the lookout for any extra supplies, whether it be food, clothes, or medical supplies. The refugees weren't as happy as they could be, but at least were alive.

"Councilman Freeman, how is the armory?" Collins heard Althea say. The armory was a major concern for the General. The steel weapons weren't nearly as durable as the wraiths' gold ones, and their stock of spare weapons was running dangerously low.

The balding man cleared his throat. "Every regiment has been outfitted with one weapon per soldier. Patrol and guard loans are stretching the supply a bit, but some regiments are already returning with wraith weapons. If missions continue to go well, we shouldn't have an issue. The volunteers for the armory have been very helpful. They have completely catalogued the armory and know exactly where our weapons are going."

"I'm glad to hear that," Althea said. "Councilman Sage, how is the examination of the barrier coming along?"

Collins cracked his neck and looked through his proposal once more before examining each of the Council members. Althea and Byron Sage were the most vocal. The others rarely offered anything of value unless they were giving their reports, and even then, he used the word 'value' loosely. If anyone was going to argue against his idea, it would be those two.

"Not good," Councilman Sage said. "The barrier itself is holding steady, but I've made no progress on its creation nor its history. I've been combing through the library and there is almost no mention of it. None of the journals date back that far. There may have been some at Fort Lieay, but that's much too far south to venture with the wraiths."

"Keep looking. If we can manage to replicate the barrier, we may be able to end this war with minimal losses. Councilwoman Altman, have you received responses from the other lands?"

"I've received word from our northern allies. They will not pledge any soldiers to our cause. They believe the risk is too large, given the wraiths' numbers. They will, however, continue trading with us. As

I understand it, they're in need of timber and will gladly exchange food and supplies for sturdy trees. I have not been able to send word to the lands across the sea. The only port we had was located in Fort Lieay. I doubt the wraiths left any ships that could sail."

"It is unfortunate that Mambia will not come to our aid, but at least they are keeping trade lines open. If there are no other reports from council members, we'll move on to officer reports. Are there any pressing matters that need to be addressed?"

"Yes," one of the men said, standing.

"Major Welleck, what is your issue?"

"My regiment has been on barrier patrol all day, every day. I know as the newest regiment, the job falls to us, but there is no time to train. If we could have another regiment take some of the patrol time, it would give my troops an opportunity to train and keep in fighting condition, should the need arise."

"I think that can be arranged," Althea said. "General Collins?"

Collins took a moment before he realized he was being addressed. He nodded quickly. "I'll find a regiment to transfer."

"Thank you," Major Welleck said.

"If there are no other officer issues, General Collins, please give your report on the new recruits."

"Their training is going well. Some of the more advanced soldiers have already been assimilated into existing regiments, but most have been placed together in new regiments. We are nearly at officer capacity and I've established a clear chain of command. As the war progresses and the new officers get used to their responsibilities, I expect communication and relations between regiments to strengthen. I am especially impressed with the youngest recruits."

Byron Sage, Althea's second in command, spoke up. "The youngest recruits . . . Do you mean the children?"

"Yes. They may not be as strong as some of the older soldiers, but they are surprisingly adept when it comes to handling weapons. I'm not sure if they're all just naturally gifted or if teaching them so young allows them to process and retain what they've learned more rapidly. Most are moving through the training at record speeds."

"Are they really that good?" Althea asked. "They're only children, after all."

"They're performing beyond their years. Some have even been able to best a few of my experienced soldiers in sparring matches. I know we had originally decided to keep the youngest soldiers out of the fighting, but I think we should place a few of them in their own regiment."

"What?" Councilman Sage exclaimed. "You can't be serious."

"I am serious. They are a highly skilled group of individuals."

"The results would be disastrous," Althea said.

"That's what you said about allowing them to join training," Collins reminded her. "I've already selected the top recruits and am prepared to alert them of their new assignment immediately."

"I'm afraid I can't allow that, General."

"With all due respect, Althea, I'm in charge of running the army."

"You go too far, General," Althea warned him.

"I've not gone far enough. You were convinced that allowing the younger volunteers to join basic was going to destroy the army, but because of them, my soldiers are working harder than ever. They deserve to be given the same chance as anyone else."

Althea's eyes narrowed. She glared at Collins for a few moments. The silence in the chamber was almost tangible.

"What is your proposal, General?" Althea finally said.

"I think we need to create a new regiment made up of only younger recruits. It would be a small regiment specializing in scouting missions. Sending our more experienced regiments to scout is a waste of resources, since those missions hardly yield results. This way, we keep up the younger recruits' morale by giving them something to do, but we aren't intentionally putting them in harm's way, and we free up other regiments for battle assignments. For now, the young ones could take over the barrier patrol from Major Welleck."

Althea sighed. "Very well, General, but you will take full responsibility for whatever happens. I trust you'll be placing a seasoned warrior in command?"

"With all due respect, I disagree," Collins said, courteously but firmly. "I think one of their own needs to lead them."

"A regiment of completely untested recruits is a recipe for disaster."

"On the contrary, we have three regiments comprised of only new recruits. The only reason you have a problem with this regiment is because of their age. I want a younger soldier to gain command experience. But if you're concerned, we could have a few experienced soldiers in the regiment to keep it on track. I know of a few soldiers who may be willing to volunteer."

"And who would you recommend be given command?" Byron asked.

"Anna Lieay. She is strong and intelligent. Captain Price reports her to be one of the best soldiers in the group and Major Ravenall has said she has a good head for strategy."

"But what makes you so sure she can handle command?" Althea demanded.

"She and a few of her peers have taken it upon themselves to run their own extra training program after the formal sessions. Anna has taken charge of the group and directs them through drills, work-outs, and mock fights. She's already performing many of the duties of a commander, and I am confident she can handle more."

Althea glanced at the rest of the Council. They were nodding in agreement.

"I object! I object most strongly!" Colonel Wells shot up. His face was red and his hands were clenched at his sides.

"You don't have any right to object," Collins shot back.

"He has a right to voice his opinion," Althea interjected, "as do you." Althea turned her face back to the Colonel. "Colonel Wells, why do you object to the General's proposal?"

"We cannot have children in their own regiment and we certainly cannot have a child in command! I was against allowing them to train in the first place, and now I understand they're to be given assignments? We're fighting a war, or have you all forgotten that?"

"I understand your concern, Colonel," said the General, "but you've seen them train. Most, if not all of them, are exceptionally skilled. They deserve to be given the same chances as our other soldiers."

"They aren't that good. I've found them arrogant and lazy—that Lieay girl most of all. You don't have my support, and I'm sure many of the ranking officers would be against this as well."

"And yet, none of them are protesting my proposal," General Collins said, motioning to the other officers in the room.

"Are you sure you aren't just against Andromeda because her parents refused to make you head of their guard?" Byron interjected.

"That's completely beside the point," the Colonel said, crossing his arms.

"This is not your decision," Althea said. "Whatever animosity there is between you and the younger soldiers, you need to resolve it."

"Then I insist that she be tested. I want to see for myself that she's able to handle herself."

Collins gave the Colonel a hard look. "You just want me to place one of your friends in command."

Althea waved the General to silence. "What do you propose, Colonel?"

"Single combat. I can test her myself."

"Single combat?" Althea asked. "Andromeda is only a child."

Collins waved Althea down. "No. Colonel Wells, we will grant you the test. However, if Anna wins, you will stand down and allow her to take command of a regiment."

Colonel Wells glowered at him. "Fine," he spat through his teeth.

"Very well," Althea said. "You will face Andromeda in single combat before their training session tomorrow morning. In the event that Andromeda is successful, she will be granted command of her own regiment. Councilman Sage, will you supervise?"

"Yes."

"Then it is decided. If there are no more reports—nothing? Good, then this Council is adjourned."

❧ 12 ❧

The next morning, Anna and her training group were assembled out on the eastern quad, warming up after breakfast.

"Who's that?" Alex asked, nodding to a pair advancing toward the group.

Anna looked up and saw Colonel Wells walking with another man. He wore long flowing robes of deep blue; the general wardrobe of a Council member.

"He must be a Council member," Anna said. "They're the only ones who wear that color. But the Colonel being here is odd. He usually leaves us alone."

"Right," Ele agreed. "Why would he want to be around us for more than is absolutely necessary?"

Anna and Oliver chuckled and Alex kept staring at the duo. Colonel Wells yelled for everyone to assemble in lines and everyone nervously shuffled to get into position.

"Soldiers," said the Councilman, "there will be a small change to your training regimen this morning. Those of you scheduled for patrols and guard duty today, proceed with your regular routine. Those of you who aren't, stay here."

The soldiers moved to follow his orders, and a small group was left to see what the pair wanted.

Colonel Wells stepped forward. "I'd like everyone to pair off and run one-on-one combat drills with standard swords. Lieay, you're with me."

He drew his sword from the sheath at his hip, the steel grating harshly against the scabbard. Confusion filled Anna as she examined the Colonel's sword. Why would he want to partner with her? Anna raised her eyebrows at Alex. He shrugged in response before pulling Liam aside to duel.

Anna grabbed a practice sword and squared up to the Colonel. They stared at each other for a few seconds before the Colonel made the first move, a ferocious attack. Anna met his sword with hers at every blow. The Colonel may have had more experience, but she was younger and faster. Instead of merely defending herself from his attacks, she went on the offensive, striking hard, and then harder. Feigning a jab to his left side, she twisted her sword at the last second and caught the guard of his blade. She yanked the weapon from his grip and brought the tip of her blade up to hover at his collar. He nodded grudgingly, conceding the match.

Anna slowly lowered her sword and saw that the Colonel was breathing just as heavily as she was. After only facing her fellow new recruits for the past few months, she wasn't sure how she was actually progressing. Beating an officer had given her a huge boost of confidence.

The Colonel, however, was glaring at her. His face was slowly turning red and Anna could see that the muscles in his jaw were tightly clenched.

"Congratulations, Andromeda," the Councilman said.

"Um, thanks," Anna replied. She had almost forgotten the Councilman was watching, though why he cared about this training exercise, she had no idea. Maybe he just wanted a progress check on their training group.

Anna turned her back on the Colonel, and Alex gave her a triumphant thumbs up before he brought his hands to his mouth, eyes wide. Hearing a rustle of movement behind her, she turned in time to see the Colonel thrusting his sword at what would have been her back and was now her chest. She smacked the palms of both hands against the flat of his blade, pushing it away as she lunged to the side and grabbed for the hilt, simultaneously sweeping a leg out to knock the Colonel further off balance.

She wrenched the sword from his grasp and brought the point to his throat, shouting, "What is your problem?"

The Colonel glared at her, but the shock at his failure was evident on his face. Councilman Sage walked up and took the sword from Anna's hands.

"Colonel, that was highly unprofessional. You are suspended from your command, pending a formal hearing with the Council. Andromeda, get to the infirmary and have your hands attended to." He turned to address the rest of the group. "The rest of you, go back to your regular training schedule."

Anna threw one last scathing glare at the Colonel before marching off toward the infirmary, mumbling under her breath. What was his problem? The Colonel didn't exactly get along with their training group, but he should be directing his anger at the wraiths, not his own people. Alex and Ele rushed after her, trying to catch up.

"Why would the Colonel do that?" Ele demanded.

"I'm not sure. I know he never liked me, and I know he hated my parents, but I never thought he'd attack me with my back turned like that."

Alex nodded furiously. "He could have killed you! I know he doesn't like us, but I never thought he'd actually try to hurt us."

"At least he's suspended," Ele said.

"For now," Anna replied, "but I don't see him staying out of command for long. The army needs every soldier it can get. Besides, he's a Colonel and he's been here for a while. They'll probably let him off with a warning."

Anna glanced down at her hands, which had begun to throb. Oozing cuts bisected both her palms. She'd tried to push off the flat of the weapon, as they'd been taught, but remembered being told that anyone who had to go barehanded against a blade would almost certainly sustain some slashes, and the goal was to prevent them from being vital ones.

"How am I supposed to hold a weapon with my hands like this?"

"I'm sure the healers can fix your hands," Alex replied. "Remember how quickly your shoulder healed?"

"I suppose." She tried to blot some of the blood off on her pants, but quickly brought her palms together as pain shot through the wounds and up through her arms. She shook her head. "I just don't understand what the purpose of the whole thing was. And the Councilman . . . Why would he care what we've been doing?"

Alex shrugged. "You're the only one of us who's even spoken to the Council."

"Speaking of which, I didn't know your name was Andromeda," said Ele.

"Ugh, I hate it. It's too long and formal," Anna said. "You know, you two didn't have to come with me. I know where the infirmary is."

"What else do I have to do?" Alex replied.

"I'm actually going to meet Oliver in a few minutes," Ele explained. "He said he wanted to try out a few sword moves before we meet up for hand-to-hand combat tonight."

They reached a junction in the hall and Ele broke off from the pair.

"I'll see you two later," she said, waving.

Alex and Anna continued on to the infirmary. Anna walked over to a healer and held out her hands. The healer examined the wound and grabbed some supplies.

"These don't look too deep," the healer remarked. "They should heal quickly. Change the bandages daily and use this salve each time. Try not to hold anything too tightly for the next few days so the wounds can close."

"I suppose that includes a sword," Anna mumbled.

The healer pursed her lips. "You could, but I would caution against it. If you leave the wounds alone, they'll heal faster. If you absolutely have to fight, wrap some rags around your hands for extra padding."

Anna nodded her thanks and took the salve. She and Alex dropped the small bottle off at their barracks and wandered through the Sanctuary for a few minutes before coming to a stop at one of the southern doors. They could see Ele and Oliver sparring with practice swords on the quad.

"Andromeda?" asked a voice from behind them. "Andromeda Lieay?"

"Yes?" Anna turned to see a page saluting her.

"A message for you."

The page held out a small scroll, and left as soon as she took it. Anna scanned the message and rolled her eyes.

"What is it?"

"The Council wants to see me again."

"What, no escort? You had one last time."

"Well, that corridor is reserved for the army. Only soldiers are allowed there without an escort. Now that we've passed basic, we can go there on our own."

"Good luck."

Anna smiled and headed back inside toward the Council chambers. She racked her brain for a possible explanation as to why they would want to see her again. Maybe she shouldn't have defended herself against the Colonel—he wouldn't actually have stabbed her, would he? Generally, you weren't supposed to yell at an officer, and disarming one was likely frowned upon as well. Then again, the Council was probably looking for any excuse to take the younger soldiers out of training. Entering the huge room, Anna stared at the Council and waited for them to speak.

"Andromeda," Althea began.

"It's Anna," she replied.

Althea glared at Anna, "Are you going to insist on correcting me every time you come before us?"

"I've asked you to—"

"Anna . . ." The General's warning tone prompted Anna to fall silent.

Althea nodded to the General and continued, "This Council has decided to create a new regiment, comprised of recruits from the youngest training group. The regiment will be a small force of only eleven soldiers, specializing in small reconnaissance missions that should go unnoticed by our enemy. We believe the youthful appearance of the regiment will allow them to pass unnoticed where our more experienced forces cannot go."

Anna nodded slowly, hope blossoming within her. If they were explaining all of this to her, did that mean she was going to be placed in the regiment?

"Additionally," Althea continued, "General Collins has expressed his wish that a younger soldier gain command experience; therefore, we have elected to place you in command of this new regiment."

Anna stared at the Council in shock, thinking she misheard.

"You want to what?"

"We would like to grant you command over your own regiment," Althea repeated.

Anna took a few deep breaths to collect her thoughts. "Why me? I mean, I'm flattered, but it always seemed like the training officers hated me. And Colonel Wells just attacked me for no reason."

"The training officers are instructed to be hard on everyone," Althea said. "As to Colonel Wells . . . placing such a young soldier in a command position has never been done before. Colonel Wells insisted on testing you himself."

"You do know he came at me with a sword while my back was turned. A real one. Not a practice sword."

"An unfortunate incident, but—"

"I could have died!" Anna exclaimed.

"And yet, here you are. You seem to be completely against what we have offered; you don't want the command position, we can—"

"No, I accept," Anna said quickly.

Althea's eyes narrowed a fraction. "Good. Here is your command pin," Althea said, handing Anna a small pin in the shape of a dagger. "You will be expected to attend the large group training sessions when they are held, as the other regiments do, but from now on, you will set your own training schedule. The Council has already chosen the members of your regiment, and we have appointed an experienced soldier to aid you. They have been notified and are waiting near the westernmost barracks, where you will be housed."

"Thank you," she said, still in disbelief.

"Lieutenant Lieay," said the General, "you may begin command of the 77th regiment."

Anna saluted the General and left the room.

My own regiment, she thought. *I can hardly believe it!*

She passed through the main hall and out a side door, heading toward the west barracks where her troops were supposed to be waiting. As she walked, her excitement was slowly replaced with apprehension. What if the soldiers the Council selected didn't want to follow her? She knew they'd all be from her training group, so she was confident in their fighting abilities, but what if they didn't get along? The older recruits at least knew how to work together. Granted, they were all farmers and craftsmen who were attempting to learn to use a sword, but they seemed to get along fairly easily. Her peer group was much better trained and far more disciplined, but aside from her small group of friends, she noticed that they rarely even tried to get along with each other.

Another worry crept into her mind. *The Council.* They were giving her a chance to prove herself, or rather, the General was. Anna smirked. As much as the Council tried to pretend they were in charge, General Collins was the true leader of the army. The villagers-turned-soldiers followed him, not the Council. Her confidence grew with the thought that Collins believed enough in her to give her this chance, and she knew she had to make the most of it. Any mistake, no matter how small, and she and her regiment would be back in basic training—or worse, expelled from the fighting force permanently.

Anna shook her head to clear her mind. It wouldn't do to dwell on all her worries the first time she met her regiment. Instead, she turned her attention to the command pin. Aside from the Generals' pin, they all looked fairly similar. It was made of the same steel as the old swords, shaped like a dagger, about two inches long. Because it was a Lieutenant's pin, it didn't have any embellishments, but she knew that with each additional rank she earned, a small steel bar would be added lengthwise across the blade.

⚡ 13 ⚡

Anna scanned the members of her regiment as she approached. She saw some people she'd already become friends with, including Rebecca and Liam. Most of the others had joined in their nightly training sessions, but like so many of the younger soldiers, they'd kept to themselves. There were a couple of people she hadn't met yet, but they looked nice enough. One person stood a little way off from the group. He stood tall, back straight and head level. His left hand rested casually on the hilt of his sword. Though his clothes were worn, they were clean and neat. He turned around so she could see his face.

"Jonathan?"

The man smiled widely. "Anna, good, you're finally here."

"You're part of the 77th? How'd you get stuck with this assignment?"

"I volunteered. I'm sure you know the Council was unsure about putting such a young soldier in charge of a regiment. General Collins approached me and asked if I would supervise. I think he knew I was friends with your parents and thought a familiar face would make it easier for you."

"Weren't you risking a lot by accepting?"

"I don't see it like that. You may be young, but you've progressed amazingly in your training. Besides, if your parents are any indication, I'd say you're a safe bet for a great leader."

"Thank you. I . . . I wish they were still here."

"You can't change the past, Anna. But hopefully we can make a better future."

"Anna," Alex called, coming to meet her, "you're part of the 77th too?"

She turned toward him, apprehensive. She hadn't considered how her friends would react to her being their superior officer now. She took a few steps forward, and his eyes found the pin on her chest.

"You're a Lieutenant?" he asked.

Anna nodded slowly, wondering at his tone.

A smile broke out on his face. "That's great! Is that what the Council wanted to talk to you about?"

Anna felt a weight lift from her chest and she smiled. "Yeah. It came as a complete shock. I thought they were going to expel me from the fighting force, and instead, they promoted me."

"If anyone deserves it, you do."

Anna gave a small smile. "I'd like to think I earned it."

Alex held his hands out apologetically. "That's what I meant."

"Thanks. I think everyone is here, so I guess I should say something."

Anna left Alex and walked around to stand in front of the barracks.

"Line up," she called loudly.

Jonathan moved to stand in a line next to Alex, Ele, and Oliver, but everyone else looked around, confused.

"Are you serious?" one of the girls asked. She was the shortest of the group by a good three or four inches. Her round face was sweet and surrounded by a halo of golden waves. Anna thought she looked like she belonged in a castle surrounded by fine things and needlepoint instead of a battlefield, but the girl's icy blue eyes held a dangerous glint, as if daring someone to challenge her.

"As your commanding officer, I expect my orders to be followed," she replied calmly. The blonde girl's eyes thawed slightly, and she moved to stand next to Oliver. The rest of the group slowly followed suit.

"You're the commander?" another girl asked after they had lined up. Her dark curls complemented her dark skin, and her amber eyes shone with kindness and warmth. She and the boy standing next to her looked remarkably similar, probably a sibling, but his eyes were hard and unforgiving. As Anna looked more closely at him, she recognized him as the boy who had impressed their training officers with his spear-throwing ability. He stood taller than everyone else, including Jonathan. Liam was closest in height, but while Liam was gangly and thin, this boy was burly.

Anna realized she hadn't answered the girl, and nodded. "Yes. I'm Lieutenant Anna Lieay. If you would, I'd like everyone to call out their name one by one so we all know who's here."

"Michael Telin," a boy on the end said. He had dark brown hair, cut short and severe, but his green eyes held life and hope.

"Kyree Akeman," the blonde girl said.

"Mariana Young, and this is my brother Ian," Mariana said, pointing to herself and the boy next to her. His jaw remained set.

"Liam Carver."

"Rebecca Aldrich."

"Jonathan Greggory."

Ele, Oliver, and Alex followed. Anna glanced out past the barrier. The sun was slowly sinking behind the trees.

"There isn't a whole lot of daylight left, so we'll jump into training tomorrow," Anna said. "Tonight, I'd just like to go over a few logistics."

Turning, Anna went into the barracks with the rest of the regiment following her. Their new living space was fairly nice compared to some of the other barracks she'd seen. It was definitely better than the barracks they'd been staying in up till now. The soldiers still in training were assigned to live in the worst accommodations, nothing more than long halls filled with bunks divided by a single walkway, barely wide enough for one person to walk down. The bunks in the trainee barracks were carved into the stone walls, three beds high. Anna and the younger recruits had slept alright, but the older soldiers barely fit into the small beds. It was good motivation to perform well enough to be transferred to a regiment.

The regiments had the best barracks. Most of them had actual beds and furniture. They also had a lot more room for weapon storage and personal belongings; not that they had many to begin with. Anna surveyed her new barracks and was pleased with what she saw.

The entryway was wide, with small alcoves at regular intervals. Each alcove had a few racks and shelves, likely for weapons and armor storage. Directly after the entryway was the main sleeping area. The walls were bare, but the stone was strong and smooth, a sharp contrast from the cracks that ran throughout the walls of the main building. Eight beds lined each side and a small chest sat at the foot of each one. Toward the back of the long room, she could see another set of doors. Walking over, she opened them to see a large weapons closet. There were a few dusty weapons already hanging up that looked as if they would shatter with a single hit. If she and her regiment ever saw battle, this would be a great place to keep extra weapons that they couldn't use every day. Turning back around, she saw that her regiment had filed into the sleeping area.

"Everyone, take a bed," she said, "but try to stay in the ones toward the front in case the Council decides to assign anyone else to our regiment."

They all moved toward the beds, then paused to let Anna choose first, as commander. Anna sat down on one of the two nearest the door, and motioned for Jonathan to take the other, across from her. Alex took the one right next to her, and that seemed to act as a signal for all the others to find their places, shuffling and negotiating.

Once every soldier in the new regiment had claimed a bed, Anna addressed the group. "The rest of the night is yours to move your things over from the other barracks and get settled. Be ready for training tomorrow."

Anna left the barracks and took a deep breath of the cool night air. A slight mist hung over the Sanctuary, and the dark clouds in the distance hinted at an evening rain. She wandered over to the western quad and watched as Major Ravenall directed a training session for her own troops. A frown crossed Anna's face. She had no idea how to command a regiment.

She left the quad and headed into the center of the Sanctuary. About a month ago, she'd found a small library down the hall from the Council chambers. There were old journals and training books that she hoped could give her some insight into command.

In the library, she pulled a few journals off a shelf and began reading. They were an old general's from a few years back. He'd had to recruit a small force to take care of some human plunderers who were going from village to village, stealing what they could and burning the rest. Anna remembered her father telling her about those attacks, years ago, and she shuddered at the memory. The thought that one human would harm another was awful. It was bad enough that the wraiths attacked them, but to have the threat come from your own people . . . it was almost unthinkable.

After skimming through five of his journals, she stood and stretched, feeling stiff from sitting in one position for so long. For all her effort, she'd learned almost nothing about command. His training methods were superficial at best and never created any sort of comradery. The General just sent messengers out asking for volunteers to fight and he only got some farmers to volunteer.

Anna scowled. Really, there wasn't much difference between that 'army' and the one Collins had now. The refugees and villagers at the Sanctuary were just farmers, traders, and craftsmen who'd been thrust into war. Aside from a few dozen career officers stationed here at the Sanctuary, her father had maintained the only formally trained army at Fort Lieay, and all of them had been killed during the wraiths' initial attacks. Sure, the villagers and refugees were put through training, but it was nothing compared to what was needed to fight the wraiths, and it was very different from what Anna and her peers went through.

She shook her head at the memory. She and Alex had finished conditioning early one day and had gone to watch the older soldiers train. Where she and her peers had been put through grueling workouts and drills designed to get them to quit, the older soldiers had just been given a sword and told to figure it out. Watching them made her furious. If they treated all the training groups the same, they might have a functional army, but the Council had chosen to focus on making her peer group's lives miserable. As a result of their harder training, Anna could see that her training group was far superior to most of the other soldiers in the Sanctuary, but because of their age, the Council refused to acknowledge it.

Anna sighed loudly. It was so frustrating. She and her friends had often talked about it, but the conversations only ended in headaches and angry nights. Of course, if they tried to talk to anyone older about it, they were dismissed as 'irate children' complaining about every little thing. Finally, they had given up trying and resigned themselves to the fact that they would never see battle.

"But now I have a chance to prove myself," Anna whispered to herself, "and I can't mess this up."

She grabbed the last journal, hoping for something interesting, and left the library. Nose buried in the book, she ran headfirst into General Collins. Anna shifted her grip on the journal and saluted.

"I'm so sorry, General. I wasn't watching where I was going."

"Obviously," he replied with a smirk. "Where are you headed?"

"Back to my barracks. I was just researching some training techniques."

"Ah, yes. I'm sure you're nervous about your first day as a Lieutenant tomorrow."

"Yes . . . um, General? Can I ask you a question?"

"Of course."

"How do help your troops make connections with each other when you're training?"

The General's brow furrowed. "I'm not sure what you mean."

"Well, how can you be sure that your troops will work together as a unit? In a fight, there's not a lot of time to be calling out orders."

"We do a great deal of practice with formations and strategies. I've found that pre-planning potential battles can help with the chaos of an actual fight. If my troops have an idea of what to do in a similar situation, we can look at the battle like one of our practices."

"But what if the battle doesn't go as planned?"

"I trust my troops to follow orders and that's the most valuable thing you can have as a commander."

"But—"

"Can I give you a bit of advice?"

"Of course."

"Establish yourself as a strong commander and appoint someone you know will be a strong second. You have the right to appoint whomever you wish, but I would recommend Jonathan Greggory. Your troops need to know that you are in command and you will not expect anything less than their obedience. I promise you, it will keep you alive in the field."

Anna nodded. "Thank you, General. I'll keep that in mind. But it's time I get back. I'd like to have an early start for tomorrow."

Anna saluted the General once more and started to leave.

"Oh, and Anna," he began.

"Yes," she said, realizing he hadn't called her by her full name.

"Congratulations."

Anna smiled and continued walking toward her barracks. She found her troops sparring out front using fallen branches instead of proper swords. Even those who weren't fighting were standing around watching and shouting advice, no matter how horrible it was. Their laughter brought a smile to her face, but it faded as she remembered what the General had said. He'd made it clear that strong commanders didn't laugh with their troops, nor would they condone such actions. He would most certainly advise her to put a stop to what was happening immediately.

She sighed quietly and watched them for a few more minutes. Everything she'd read in the journals, everything General Collins had said—those weren't ideal methods at all. She'd seen the results of their advice at work in the other regiments: mediocre at best. Why should she try to be like all the rest, when it obviously didn't work? If she was going to make a difference in this war, she was going to have to be her own person and prove that different wasn't always wrong.

Her parents were the perfect example of that. They'd been

strong and powerful, and they never did things the same way as other people. It didn't matter that they were gone; she could still follow their example.

A ghost of a smile appeared on her lips as she thought about tomorrow. She was going to be different. She was going to show that there was more than one way to lead, more than one way to train, more than one way to win a war. She could bend traditions and still be a strong commander. Maybe a wise leader examined traditions and decided when they needed to change. Besides, the Council did say that as long as her regiment attended the large group sessions, she would have full control over the rest of their schedule.

The latest fight in front of her came to a conclusion and she called for a halt.

"Lights out in twenty minutes," she called. "I want everyone to be fresh and ready for tomorrow."

"Does that mean you're going to make us run laps?" Oliver said with a groan.

"I guess you'll just have to wait and see," she responded with a sly smile.

Anna woke early the next morning, too anxious to continue sleeping. She felt confident about her plan for the day, but she was apprehensive about going to the group training session that afternoon. It would be their first act as a regiment and she wasn't sure what to expect.

Since the morning signal to rise had not yet sounded, she left her bed without waking anyone and went outside. Circling the building, she saw an old ladder near the back. She climbed up and looked around the simple stone roof. It was completely flat, with a small ledge about a foot tall all the way around. As a safety wall, it was useless, but it would stop small items from rolling off.

This would make a great sparring area, Anna thought, *it could help teach control and body awareness. The threat of falling off the building would be a fantastic motivator.*

She walked to the easternmost side and sat on the edge, her legs dangling. She stayed there for close to an hour, watching the birds flit back and forth as the sun rose above the trees. Figuring her troops had slept long enough, she went back inside to wake them up.

"Rise and shine," she called.

Jonathan was up immediately, probably used to strict commanders who wouldn't tolerate any hesitation or disobedience. Alex wasn't far behind, but he was still rubbing the sleep from his eyes as he dressed. Oliver and Ele sat up, but they were having trouble keeping their eyes open. Everyone else either glanced at her from their pillows or simply rolled over, ignoring her order. After all, basic and intermediate training had never started until after breakfast.

Anna looked at Jonathan.

"What do I do?" she whispered.

"Show them you mean what you say. A good leader needs to show confidence."

Anna nodded. Taking a deep breath, she added, "Anyone still in bed in ten seconds will run laps all day."

Her troops were up immediately, tripping over themselves to get ready. Jonathan gave Anna an encouraging nod before ducking into the entryway to buckle on his sword.

"Breakfast in ten," Anna said. "I want everyone walking over and eating together. We haven't had as much time as the other groups to form a cohesive unit, so we need to do everything we can to speed the process along."

There was a mumble of agreement among her soldiers before they all filed out of the barracks. When they walked into the dining hall, Anna noticed most of the other soldiers staring. Everyone must have heard that a new regiment had been formed, and they probably weren't expecting the youngest recruits to take on real responsibilities or see action.

"News spreads fast around here," Alex whispered.

She could feel eyes on her while she got breakfast and sat down. Alex took a seat next to her, and Ele sat on the other side. They ate in silence for a few minutes before Liam started talking with Oliver. Though it was awkward at first, conversations picked up and remained steady throughout the meal, and Anna soon forgot about the stares coming from around the room.

After a while, Anna raised her voice to cut through the chatter. "If everyone's finished, we need to get to the armory to pick out weapons."

"We're done," said Ele, gesturing to herself, Oliver, and Liam. The others nodded eagerly. So far, they'd only been able to borrow practice weapons for training and had never been able to keep them.

Together, they stood from their table and left the main dining hall. Anna led her troops down a few halls, nodding to various soldiers as they passed. Jonathan fell into step beside her and nudged her shoulder.

"You're doing great," he whispered. "Almost like you were meant to lead."

Anna smiled, but said nothing as she continued down the hall. After a few more turns, they finally came to a large door with a guard on either side. At a nearby desk, two refugees were hovering over a book, mumbling to each other. She assumed they were the weapons managers, in charge of recording every weapon in the Sanctuary and ensuring that the regiments had enough armaments to defend themselves in the forest. As Anna approached, one of them looked up and smiled.

"Welcome. You must be the newest regiment. 77th, correct?"

"Yes, Sir," Anna responded. "I was told we'd be able to pick out weapons this morning. We could also use some armor if you have it."

"Of course; however, our supplies are being stretched. We ask that each person only take one set of whatever they are best with. As far as armor, we only have leather at the moment. The larger sizes have mostly all been taken, but I believe you should be able to fit in the smaller sets. Those are all located at the very back. When you have what you need, check in with my assistant so we can record what you've taken."

"Thank you."

"Oh, and if you manage to retrieve any weapons while out on missions, please send them over. The more weapons we have in reserve, the better off we'll be."

"Of course."

The group filed into the armory and wandered through the sparsely populated racks, each trying to find something they could use. Alex managed to find a broadsword that fit his hand relatively well. Ele found a delicate rapier that complemented her quick fighting style, while Oliver picked up a longsword that he could swing around.

Ian spotted a huge axe and tested its weight. She'd seen him hurl an axe just as easily as he could throw a spear. During one of their training sessions, he'd thrown one so hard, it splintered the throwing target. Anna shuddered at the memory and was glad he was on her side.

Rebecca rushed over to the bows, running her hand over each of them until she found one she loved. Michael wasn't far behind her, but he didn't take nearly as much time choosing. Kyree scowled at every sword she came across. Finally, she settled on two medium-length daggers. Toward the back of the room, Anna found a pair of twin blades that suited her. Jonathan, already in possession of a sword, waited for them in the hall.

Anna noticed a soldier glancing repeatedly in Jonathan's direction and she positioned herself near the door to try and listen. He'd probably noticed how young they all were and was wondering what Jonathan was doing with them. Maybe she could get someone else's opinion of having her in command.

"Jonathan, right?" the soldier asked. "Jonathan Greggory? I'm Ruprect Tole."

"I'm sorry, have we met?" Jonathan asked.

"No, but I was assigned to weapons advisory before you came back here for supply."

"Ah, and now you're on guard duty?"

"I tried to volunteer, but they wouldn't take me on account of my shoulder. I fell from one of the watchtowers a few years back and now I can't lift my arm much higher than my chest. Still glad to do my part, though."

"We need people defending our home as much as we do out in the forest," Jonathan replied.

"I guess—not that the wraiths could get in. I wanted to ask you, though, did you really know the Lieay family?"

"I spent a lot of time at their Fort, so we grew to be fairly close friends. Why?"

"What were they like? I've heard some outrageous stories about them. Could they really kill a wraith in the dark? Did they actually know how to make more amulets?"

"I'm not sure where you heard any of this, but no to both. They were amazing warriors, but no one can kill a wraith on a moonless night and only the magicians of old could make more amulets. Why the curiosity?"

"Oh, just something I heard the wraiths talking about. Got me thinking a bit."

"What?"

"Oh, yeah. When they attacked my village, a few of them started arguing. One wanted to kill us all and the other wanted to take some for slaves. The second one claimed it was only the Lieays that all had to die."

"What about the Lieays?" Anna interjected with a steely glint in her eye.

Ruprect scowled at the interruption before answering, "Just that they were all supposed to be killed, on orders from King Roland."

Anna's brow furrowed. The wraiths didn't leave anyone in the hall alive, but she thought they'd taken a few for slaves.

"What else did you hear?" she demanded.

"Nothing much. While they were arguing, some of us slipped away. But it's not something you need to concern yourself with," Ruprect said, patting her shoulder.

Anna's eyes narrowed and she shook off his hand. Though she barely came to his shoulder, she lifted her chin and straightened her shoulders. "Anything you tell one of my soldiers is my business."

Ruprect looked at her in confusion before Jonathan spoke up. "Ruprect, may I present my commander, Lieutenant Lieay."

Ruprect paled. "Oh, um . . . I didn't mean . . . I . . ." he sputtered.

Anna let out a huff of annoyance and stomped down the corridor. Jonathan gave an apologetic shrug and followed. The rest of the regiment trailed behind, admiring their weapons and straightening their new armor as they went. Anna glanced back and motioned for Jonathan to walk next to her.

"Who was he?" she asked with a scowl.

"Ruprect Tole. He held my position here while I was living at Fort Lieay. I don't really know him."

"Hmm. I wonder if what he said was true."

"I think he just enjoys hearing himself talk. Besides, I don't see why it would matter."

Anna's frown deepened. *Of course it matters,* she thought. If Roland wanted all the Lieays dead, then she was next on the list. But why would the Wraith King want them dead in particular?

"It just doesn't make sense why Roland would want all of my family dead." She kept the other thoughts to herself. "What did we ever do?"

Jonathan thought for a moment. "Well, the Lieays have always been a prominent family in Istamba. Perhaps he just wanted to make a statement."

"Maybe," Anna replied.

"You have more pressing things to think about, you know. You still have to appoint a second, and you're in charge of leading our training today."

She didn't know what was more pressing than finding out King Roland wanted her personally dead, but remembering training was enough to distract her for the moment.

Anna's face fell. "I forgot about appointing a second. Collins suggested appointing you, but I think that would be a mistake."

Jonathan tried to smile politely, but it turned into more of a grimace. "Thanks, I think?"

"Oh, sorry! I didn't mean it like that. It's just that if this regiment is supposed to be one of younger recruits, I think it should be led by us. We need to show the Council that we aren't a liability and are just as capable as the older soldiers. I'll rely on your expertise either way, and I sure appreciate it."

Jonathan nodded slowly. "I can see your reasoning, but I have to disagree, especially if Collins wanted me as your second. I'm here to help you, you know."

Anna shook her head. "Collins didn't order me to appoint you; it was just a suggestion. Granted, it was a strong suggestion, but he also put me in command. I know we're better trained than nearly every other regiment. I know how good of a leader you are and what a great second you would be. But the only reason the Council wants to hold us back is because of our age, and I'm afraid if I make you my second, I'd only be reinforcing their thoughts. I think General Collins might give us a fair chance, but I need to show the Council that we're capable. Frankly, I'll need your support."

Jonathan sighed. "You're even more stubborn than your parents. I'm a little wary of going against Collins' wishes, but you have my support. Just don't doubt yourself. If any of the other officers see you act with weakness or indecision, they'll never give you the respect you want. Change your mind if it's important, but otherwise, make a decision and stick to it."

"I'll keep that in mind. Thanks for understanding."

"That's what I'm here for."

As soon as they reached the barracks, Anna directed everyone into the sleeping area.

"Before we start for the day," she began, "there's something we need to take care of. I need a second in command, but I'd like your opinion."

"Really?" Mariana asked. "Aren't you just supposed to appoint a second?"

"Normally, yes, the commanding officer appoints their own second, but we're a new kind of regiment, and I'm going to do things my way. Now, I know you didn't get to pick me as your leader, but I'd like to hear your opinions about your second, since you'll have to follow their commands when I'm not around. And I respect your advice." She paused to take in her troops' reactions. Jonathan was nodding encouragingly, so she continued. "Any thoughts?"

Anna's troops glanced around at each other. No one wanted to be the first to speak, and Anna wondered if this was such a good idea.

"Well," Jonathan finally said, "I suppose I can put my opinion out there. I think Alex would be good. You two have known each other the longest and I think you'd work together smoothly."

Anna scanned the rest of the regiment. Some were nodding, and others were looking away or examining their new weapons. Alex wasn't looking at anyone, too embarrassed to meet their eyes. At least she'd known Alex for a while and could trust him.

"Alex, you'll be my second. Now we can start training. Everyone up on the roof."

Confusion spread throughout her troops, but they followed her out of the barracks and up the ladder onto the roof. A slight breeze lifted the ends of her hair as Anna climbed up. She turned her face to the sun and took a deep breath, soaking in the warmth.

"So what are we doing today?" Liam asked.

"Honestly," Anna began, "not very much. You're going to run training today."

"We're what?" asked Michael. "Lieutenant, I don't think—"

"Firstly, it's Anna," she interrupted. "We'll be living together rather closely, so I think we can drop some of the formalities. If we're around other officers, you should use my title, but otherwise, it just takes too much time. While we're on the subject, I don't need any of you saluting me whenever I walk in. Secondly, I don't want to run any formal drills today. We had enough of that in training. I really just want everyone to get used to all of our different fighting styles."

"What? We aren't going to train?" Ian exclaimed. "If you aren't going to take your position seriously, then I don't see the point of my being here."

Ian turned to leave the roof.

"Stop," Anna commanded. "Collins entrusted me with this regiment for a reason, and you'll just have to accept that. As I said before breakfast, we don't have as much time as the other regiments to come together as a unit, and I don't believe fighting forms will help us do that. Besides, we've all passed basic training and they wouldn't have put us in a regiment if we didn't excel in intermediate training too. I have complete faith in your fighting abilities, but in order for us to build trust, we first have to know each other. Will you try it my way, please?"

Ian sighed and relaxed slightly. "I guess I could give this a chance. But if this doesn't work . . ."

"I will personally request your transfer."

Ian nodded and rubbed the back of his neck, eyeing everyone in turn. Kyree reached up and twisted a curl around her fingers. Michael scratched one of the various cuts he had on his arms.

"Where did that come from?" Rebecca asked softly.

"I fell," Michael replied, his face going red.

"What does everyone prefer to fight with?" Anna asked.

"Just a sword for me," Oliver said.

"Same here," Ele replied, nodding.

"I like daggers," Kyree said, "They're small and easy to conceal."

Liam snickered. "Like you?"

Kyree's eyes narrowed, and she launched herself at Liam. She ripped his sword from his scabbard and flipped him on his back before he even had time to blink. She flicked one of her daggers to his throat and knelt on his chest. A broad smile spread across her face, and Liam started laughing. Soon the others joined in, and Kyree stood and offered Liam a hand to pull him up.

"At least I won't blow over in the wind," Kyree said, still smirking.

Liam laughed and retrieved his sword. "Okay, lesson learned."

Anna smiled, glad to see the group connecting. Liam came off as a little abrasive sometimes, but those around him learned quickly that he was a good friend. He just spoke without thinking.

"I saw you picked up a bow, Michael," Kyree said. "I thought you used a sword."

Michael shrugged. "I can, but I prefer ranged fighting. I usually end up tripping over my feet or my opponent's if I try close combat."

"I prefer a sword," Mariana said. "I tried dual swords a little in training, but I couldn't ever get the hang of it. You use two, don't you, Anna?"

Anna nodded. "It takes a little more concentration, but I prefer two. I'd love to be a better archer, but Rebecca and I quickly learned that ranged combat is not my strength."

Oliver gasped in mock surprise. "What? Our fearless leader has a weakness? We're doomed!"

The group laughed, and Anna gave him an exaggerated scowl. "Watch yourself, Soldier."

Oliver stepped forward and motioned Anna toward him. "Come on, Lieutenant. Show me what you've got."

Anna let a small smile show, and the two wrestled for a few minutes before Anna finally pinned him. She stood and Oliver began bowing.

"I'm not worthy!" he joked, drawing laughs from the rest of the group. Anna rolled her eyes and helped him back to his feet.

"I'd love to know where Rebecca learned to shoot," interjected Jonathan.

"Really?" Rebecca asked.

"You're the best archer I've ever seen. There has to be a good story behind it."

"Archery was an important part of my village. Everyone wanted to be the best. There was a game we used to play all the time that really tested your ability. Two people would start facing away from each other about fifty paces away. They would each get an unstrung bow and a couple of arrows with padded tips. On *go*, you would have to string the bow, turn around, and hit your opponent before they managed to do the same. For festivals and celebrations, we would fill the arrow tips with color that would leave marks on your clothes. Whoever had the most marks at the end of the night had to clean up. I always hated cleaning, so I got pretty good at it."

"That sounds like a lot of fun," Anna said. "Maybe we could include that in training."

"If we ever train," Ian mumbled.

Anna fixed Ian with a glare. "Do you have a problem with my leadership?"

"Ian, apologize," Mariana snapped. She stared at him, fire burning in her eyes. They stared at each other, and Anna waved a hand.

"No apology needed, but if we're going to work as a unit, you need to talk to me if you have a problem with my orders. Clear?"

"Yes, Ma'am," Mariana answered, standing taller.

"Sorry," Ian mumbled as he came to stand next to his sister.

"We used to have strength competitions," Mariana mentioned, trying to smooth things over.

"Oh? What were those?" Anna asked.

"Exactly what she said." Ian huffed.

"I didn't mean—"

"Ian!" Mariana exclaimed.

"I was just trying to keep them off your back."

"Ian, I'm not a child anymore. I don't need to be protected."

She crossed over to the other side of the roof and sat on the edge with her legs dangling over. She crossed her arms and her face turned red and her mess of curls trembled in anger. Ian hung his head and walked over to her, trying to apologize.

"Uh, Jonathan," Alex stammered, "how did you end up living at the Sanctuary?"

"Oh," Jonathan said, nervously scratching the scar on his jaw. "Well I'm originally from Marapo, but I always wanted to move to the Sanctuary. I left home when I was sixteen. After a few years of living here and training a bit, I became a scout. I would travel to different villages to make sure things were running smoothly and keep watch on wraith activity. Roland's people may not have left their city, but occasionally a few wraiths would venture up from the far south. I actually spent a lot of time at Fort Lieay, which is how I met Anna. They moved me to supply advisory not too long ago, but after the attacks, they reassigned me to the fighting force. Now I'm here."

Their conversation was interrupted by bell tolls.

"Lunchtime, I guess," Anna said. "We have to attend the group session after lunch, so take your weapons. I want everyone eating together again."

Anna led the group back down to ground level and waited for everyone to follow.

Oliver was one of the last to descend the ladder. "Last one to the dining hall owes me their lunch."

He wagged his eyebrows and took off toward the main building. The group paused for a heartbeat before shaking off their confusion and sprinting after him. Liam easily overtook everyone, and they all came to a halt in front of the dining hall doors with Jonathan bringing up the rear.

"You owe me your lunch," Oliver said to him, panting.

"You'll have to take it from me," Jonathan challenged him, earning a laugh from the group.

They all went inside, drawing everyone's attention again, as they had at breakfast. Anna found it easier to ignore the stares this time, though, and led her regiment to the same table they'd taken before. Conversation flowed easily this time, and Anna couldn't have been happier. When everyone was finished, they stayed at their table for a while, telling stories and getting to know each other better.

"I hate to stop this," Anna interrupted them at last, "but we do need to get to the group session."

Her troops groaned but rose and followed her out to the eastern quad. All the regiments not on patrol or out on missions were already gathered. Anna noticed General Collins organizing people.

"Regiment 77, finally! Now we can begin," he said with a small smile.

Anna held her head high, but she could feel her face burning. General Collins didn't appear to be angry, but she needed to do better. After all, it was her job to make sure they got where they needed to be on time, and thus her fault they were late.

"We've only got an hour," Collins said, "so I'd like everyone using swords today for close combat. Pair off with someone not from your regiment for partnered drills. Archers, head to the range."

As soldiers looked for a partner to spar with, Anna noticed that they tried to avoid her troops. She scowled. *We may be young, but we all know how to defend ourselves,* she thought. Eventually, each one was paired off, leaving Anna, General Collins, and one other soldier without partners.

"Lieutenant, Samuel," Collins said, "you two can be with me. We'll trade off."

Anna nodded and squared up against Samuel. After a few minutes of exchanging blows, neither of them had gained the upper hand, so Collins called for a halt. He gave Anna a break and faced Samuel, beating him within a few moves. Then Anna went up against the General. She was a little apprehensive, as the last officer she'd fought was Colonel Wells, but the General had always treated her with respect. Despite her nerves, she was eager to see how her skills measured up against the General's.

She charged him, hoping to beat his attack. She'd seen him fight before and knew that he was easily one of the best swordsmen in the Sanctuary. Though the General had just faced Samuel, he was still stronger than Anna. Each blow from his sword jarred her entire arm, but she tried to hold on as long as she could. Finally, her grip loosened enough for Collins to send her sword to the ground. He nodded in approval and motioned for her to face Samuel once again.

Near the end of the hour, Anna was facing the General one last time. After fighting him a few times and watching him against Samuel, Anna figured she had a pretty good idea of his style. He was stronger, but she was faster. When he attacked, Anna simply defended herself. Instead of wearing herself out with useless attacks, she hoped to let the General tire himself out. Only as his attacks got slower did Anna go on the offensive. Finally, she saw a small opening and jabbed her sword at his side. With a great thrust, she forced his sword from his hand and sent it flying with a clang. She was even more surprised than he was. He gave her a short smile and a curt nod before retrieving his sword and motioning Samuel forward for one last fight.

When the hour was up, Anna was covered in sweat, but she was pleased with herself. She'd managed to beat Samuel quite a few times and only ended in a draw with him twice. Of course, her greatest triumph was beating Collins. She'd beaten a General! It brought her great satisfaction, especially knowing so many other soldiers had seen it happen.

"Nicely done, you two," the General said, before raising his voice to address everyone, "That's all I have for you today. You can return to your individual training."

The various regiments formed up and marched away, leaving the 77th alone on the quad.

"How did everyone do?" Anna asked.

"Not too bad," said Liam. "Mostly draws, but I managed to beat my opponent a few times."

His statement was met with a general mumble of agreement.

"Lieutenant Lieay?" said a voice.

Anna turned around to see a page holding out a small note. Anna read it and scoffed. "I've been summoned by the Council again. You all head back to the barracks. I'll be there as soon as I can."

She headed inside to the Council chambers and handed her summons to the guard at the door. He took it with a nod and motioned for her to go inside.

"You seem to be making a habit of being here," Althea stated, once Anna stood before the Council.

"I'm just responding to the summons, Ma'am," she said.

"And you continue to make a bad impression."

Anna swallowed her retort. She was a Lieutenant now and needed to remain above their taunts. "Ma'am, how can I assist you?"

"We've received word of your training methods, and this Council is less than pleased."

Anna felt her face burn, but she tried not to let her embarrassment show. "We attended the group session as was required of us, and the rest of the day was mine to plan."

"One of our aides saw you and your troops talking and laughing on the roof of your barracks. Did you run any drills at all?"

Anna raised her head a fraction of an inch. "You were spying on me?"

Althea looked down at her notes before looking back at Anna. "This Council took a huge risk by giving you command of a regiment. Now we find out that you have squandered the opportunity, and you have the audacity to stand before us now and act as if you did nothing wrong. We've considered discharging you from the army for severe misconduct. Explain yourself."

"I've squandered no opportunity. You said I was in charge of my regiment's training schedule. You said, so long as we attended the group sessions, I was to decide how our training is conducted. I am doing that to the best of my ability."

"You're supposed to be using your free time to train."

"We are." Anna took a few steps forward. "And I will continue to report at the General Assemblys, as is required of me."

The door to the Council chambers flew open behind her and General Collins stormed in. Althea turned her glare from Anna to Collins before saying, "General, we are in the middle of something. If you'll wait outside, we'll see you in a moment."

"Since you're addressing one of my officers, I'd say this concerns me."

Anna hid a smirk. Having the General at her side made her feel more confident about the whole situation, and judging by the Council's reactions, they'd called her here without the General's knowledge. In fact, that probably violated some rule. Althea sighed, and Anna glanced at the other Council members. Their faces were passive, like they didn't want to deal with this right now.

"Lieutenant, please wait outside," Collins stated.

Anna was startled out of her thoughts. With a quick nod, she turned from the Council and walked out the open door, which, as before, the guards closed firmly behind her. This time, she stood off to the side, her head held high as she waited for the General to come back out. Though the Council seemed angry, Anna wasn't too concerned about what would happen. The General obviously wanted her in command for a reason, and she didn't think it was likely that he'd remove her from command so soon after granting it to her. That would reflect on him as well.

Finally, the door opened again, and the General stepped out. He motioned for Anna to follow him, and led her down the corridor to a small room. As soon as he ushered her in, he shut the door behind them. There was a small desk in the center of the room, littered with maps, papers, and a few daggers. Collins went around it and sank heavily into the chair behind it. Anna realized that this must be the General's personal office.

"What am I going to do with you, Lieutenant?" he said slowly.

Glad to hear she hadn't been demoted—or, she hoped, removed from command—Anna flicked her eyes to his face. "You can let me know, Sir, if you have any feedback on my leadership. Otherwise, I should return to my troops."

Collins shook his head, and a small chuckle escaped his lips. "Yes, of course." He fell silent and stared at her for a few moments. Anna felt uncomfortable under his stare, but refused to break eye contact.

He sighed deeply. "Lieutenant, I'm going to speak frankly with you. I knew your parents well. I know of the relationship they had with the Council, and I'm sure you're at least partly aware of it."

"It was hard not to be," Anna said. "So many people tried to convince my father to take control and unite Istamba into one kingdom. He always protested, saying he loved Fort Lieay too much to leave. And I think he didn't want to cause an unnecessary war."

Collins nodded. "Truthfully, I was on their side, and now that they're gone, it falls to me to stand between the Council and full control. Luckily, they don't have any clue how to run an army, so for now, the army is still mine. Now, I'm not saying I want to rule Istamba myself, but I know the Council, if left unchecked, would likely run this land and its people into the ground, and I intend to stand in the way of that. But if the Council sees any sign of weakness, any deviation from the norm, they will take advantage of it. I placed you in command of Regiment 77 not just because you were one of the better soldiers, but also because I believe you truly want what is best for the people of Istamba. However, if you're going to make a difference in the lives of your people, you have to be careful. Stop angering the Council."

"So I'm just supposed to let them walk over me? How is that being a strong leader? I fully intend to reclaim my parents' land from the wraiths and prove myself to the people, but I can't do that if the Council thinks I'll do anything they say."

Collins shook his head. "I'm not saying you have to bend to their will. I'm saying you have to avoid aggravating them until you've established yourself, until you've earned a broader respect. I'm glad to hear you want to follow in your parents' footsteps, but you'd be foolish to think the people will follow a child; especially right now."

"I may be young, but—"

The General held up a hand. "You're more capable than most of them out there, even now, but that is how the Council is portraying you: as a child. You need to do your best not to act like one." She bristled, and his eyes softened. "Listen to me, Anna. Those Council members will steal every bit of power they can and if you want it back, you might have to play by their rules, at least for the time being." Collins looked down at one of the notes on his desk before speaking again. "Get back to your troops and keep your head down for a while. Remember, I won't always be there to step in."

Anna nodded and opened the door. Just before she stepped out, she turned back to Collins and said, "You know, General, different isn't always wrong."

"Maybe, Anna. But think about what I've said. Please."

She saluted and closed the door behind her. On her way back to the barracks, she contemplated the odd meeting. Since she'd arrived at the Sanctuary, she'd been focused so much on training that she'd never considered the political ramifications of her parents' death. With her parents gone, leadership of the southern half of Istamba would fall to her, by tradition. Leadership passed from generation to generation, but her parents had always said that she couldn't take it for granted, that she needed to earn the people's trust and respect. She hadn't considered how, until now.

The General had actually made a lot of sense. Why should her people follow her? She was only fourteen, and just because her name was Lieay didn't mean the people would follow without reason. She didn't just have to prove herself; she had to prove she was better suited to lead than the Council. Collins likely supported her, but he wasn't just going to give her a crown and bend the knee. She was going to have to fight for every bit of respect. If she and her regiment ever saw battle, she might be able to earn some.

Anna stopped just outside the barracks and heard laughter coming from the roof. Smiling, she climbed up and saw Oliver and Michael wrestling, blindfolded. She snorted. Of all the things to do, and on the roof of a building no less. Everyone else was shouting random information, some helpful, some nonsense. Finally, Oliver managed to grab Michael's arms and sit on his chest. He let out a triumphant cry and pulled off the blindfold.

"Anna," Kyree called, "you and I are up next!"

Anna laughed. "If you insist."

They went on, trading partners and trying different restrictions until Anna heard someone knocking on their door below. She excused herself and climbed down, surprising the page when she came around from the back.

"Yes?" she said.

"Lieutenant Lieay, prepare your regiment for training games to commence directly after breakfast tomorrow morning. Report to the northern training area to receive your assignments."

He turned and left without waiting for a reply.

"Thank you," Anna called to his retreating figure.

Anna went back up to the roof and called for a halt in their games, much to the disappointment of her troops.

"I know, I'm sorry," she began, "but we need to be fresh for tomorrow. We're to report to the northern quad for regiment training games."

"Finally! I've wanted to participate since I got here, but they were for regiments only," Liam said.

"Well, now you'll have a chance. Lights out in twenty."

⭑— 15 —⭒

The next morning, Anna and her regiment headed to the northern quad where the barrier encompassed a large area of forest. Anna had always thought it was a waste of protected space and wondered why they couldn't use it for farmland. She'd asked Major Ravenall one day. After she'd run a lap for speaking out of turn, the Major told her that soldiers needed real terrain to drill on without the threat of wraiths. The new recruits had wanted to participate since they'd first heard of the games, but only the regiments were permitted to participate.

"I'm so excited!" said Oliver. "Our very first live combat drill as a regiment!"

"Don't get too excited," Anna told him. "I just received assignments for round one. We're up first and we're facing Regiment 21."

"What?" Everyone started yelling at once.

"Whoa, whoa, whoa," shouted Jonathan over everyone. "Calm down."

"How can we calm down?" asked Ian. "That's General Collins' regiment. We've been a group for what, a day? How are we going to go up against the best regiment in the army?"

"Why would they do this?" Kyree asked.

"I'm assuming it's because the Council disapproves of my training methods," Anna said.

"Well, maybe we should have actual training instead of talking all day!" Ian snapped.

"Enough," Anna commanded. "I stand by my decision about yesterday. I know everyone thinks we're going to lose, but I know we can pull through this."

"But," Michael said, "we don't have any strategies or battle forms or—"

"We don't need any of that." Anna sighed and looked around at her troops. "Listen. Everyone I've talked to, everything I've heard about being a commander, it all has one thing in common. The troops—you—are expected to blindly follow my orders, no matter what. Instead of trusting your skills and thoughts in battle, I'm just supposed to trust that you'll follow my orders.

"But I don't think that's any way to run a regiment. Because when it comes down to it, there's no possible way to anticipate and plan for every scenario out in the field, and if something goes wrong, I don't want any of you getting hurt because you can't think for yourselves. If you've taken the time to watch the other regiments train, they become completely lost if their forms break down. That's how you lose good soldiers. We all went through the same training and I have complete faith in your abilities. Now I'm asking you to have faith in me."

"What did you have in mind?" Alex asked.

Anna raised her chin an inch, a grin tugging at her lips. "The games take place in the back part of the Sanctuary and mostly stays in the trees. Collins chose to be defensive, so we'll be on offense. Our goal is to retrieve the idol that they've placed somewhere in the field of play. There's a small clearing toward the back of the quad, just inside the barrier, that's very easy to defend. We don't have the numbers Collins has, so they can easily put up a line there that we won't be able to break through. I know you all can handle yourselves in a fight, but the General has good soldiers too. We can't break through using normal means. We don't have the numbers and we don't have the experience."

"Um," Liam said, "I'm not hearing much of a plan. All I hear is how outmatched we are."

"I'm getting to it," Anna said, glaring. "The trees in the field are strong with large, close branches and leaves that are easy to hide in. Being the strongest climbers, I propose that Alex, Michael, and I climb some of the first trees out of sight of the General's men and move toward the idol above ground. The rest of you will slowly advance toward their line and push them back as far as you can. Liam will stay toward the middle to make sure he stays in play. When one of us in the trees gets close enough, we can drop down, grab the idol, and move toward the General's soldiers from behind. When they see us with the idol, we can throw it over their line to Liam, who can run it back out to the start. On my signal, the rest of us will sprint in all different directions to distract them, then work our way back to the start. I'm hoping that all of us running at once will cause confusion, allowing most, if not all of us, to get back to the beginning safely."

"What will your signal be?" Mariana asked.

"Oh, er—How about I just yell scatter?"

"Wait," interrupted Liam, "we can't throw the idol. Isn't that against the rules?"

"Not to my knowledge. We just have to get it back to the start without the person carrying it being marked. The practice swords have chalk covering their ends."

"What happens if we get marked?" Kyree asked. "Do we have to leave the fight?"

Anna shook her head. "No. But they take points away from our ranking depending on how many people are marked and where. Whoever has the idol can't be marked at all, otherwise it doesn't count as a win—so you can't take it if you've already been marked, or get marked while you're holding it."

"Feels like whoever's on offense automatically has a huge disadvantage."

Anna shrugged. "Nothing we can do about it now. Alex, Michael, you have one of the more dangerous jobs. Are you alright jumping from tree to tree?"

The two looked at each other. "I can do it," said Michael.

"Me too."

"Alright," Anna said. "Let's head to the start."

The other regiments not out on patrols were gathered together a way off from Anna and her own. General Collins and his men had already armed themselves with the practice weapons specifically designed for the games.

"The weapons are over by the grain store," Anna said, "Alex, Michael, make sure you pick something you can carry through the trees. Liam, take something you can run with. Rebecca, bows aren't allowed in these games, so you'll need to pick up a sword. Everyone else, just choose something you're comfortable with. You'll just need to put up enough of a fight that the General and his men don't get suspicious."

Her troops sifted through the blunted practice weapons while Anna went to inform 2nd General Horne that she and her troops were ready.

"Regiment 21, Regiment 77, are you ready?"

"Aye," replied Collins.

"Ready," Anna said, putting as much confidence as she could into her voice.

"General Collins, take the idol and proceed into the forest. Lieutenant Lieay, you and your regiment will wait here until I give you the signal to start."

Collins moved his regiment into the forest. As the last of his troops disappeared into the trees, Anna turned to Alex and Michael.

"Alex, you take the center route, Michael, the left, and I'll take the right. These first few trees have some low branches that will make them easy to climb. Move quickly, but quietly. If they realize what we're doing, there's no way we can win. I know it'll be tough, but try not to rustle the leaves too much. Understood?" The two nodded and she faced the whole group. "Liam, remember, stay toward the middle of the group. We need you to stay in play long enough to get the idol to you. Be sure to keep a lookout for one of us to throw it.

If you get marked by one of them, tell Mariana. Mariana, are you willing to take Liam's place if need be?"

"Yes."

"Any concerns or questions?" She scanned each team member for a response. "Alright. Let's head to the edge of the tree line. No use putting this off any longer."

The group moved into their positions. Anna stood nearest the trees on the far right, with Alex in the middle and Michael on the far left. Liam stood near the center of a triangle formed by the rest of the troops.

General Horne signaled for the 77th regiment to start. Anna, Alex, and Michael began climbing the nearest trees, and quickly disappeared into the leafy canopy. The rest of the regiment moved forward as a unit, fanning out so as not to be caught by surprise from the sides. About a minute after the group headed into the trees, they met the General's defensive line.

Anna saw her troops meet their opponents as she passed over the two lines, high in the trees. As she climbed over branches and moved from tree to tree, she occasionally caught a glimpse of Alex as he also moved through the trees, matching her pace. Eventually, she saw the shimmer of the barrier and angled her path left to meet up with the other two near their target. Finally, she came to the edge of the trees and saw the small clearing with the idol in the center. Looking to her left, she could just make out Alex and Michael, waiting for the perfect moment to drop down.

Anna couldn't see any of Collins' men in the clearing, and she hadn't seen any in the immediate area as she passed over. She could hear the sounds of the battle and figured now was as good a time as any to take the idol. Catching the attention of her partners, she signaled, and the three dropped into the clearing. When no one came at them, Anna grabbed the idol and they began making their way toward the back of the General's defensive line.

Eventually, she could see the backs of her opponents as they sparred with her own troops. Hiding behind a large tree, she scanned the fight until she spotted Liam, unmarked by the chalk that coated the practice weapons. She stepped out from behind the tree and waved her sword in the air, trying to catch Liam's attention. When he glanced up, he nodded and backed away from the main fight. He adjusted the grip on his sword, and tapped Ian and Mariana to cover him so that he could catch the idol.

Once Mariana and Ian were in place, Anna stepped out from behind her tree and threw the idol as hard as she could into Liam's open hands. As soon as he had the idol securely in his arms, he turned and ran, leaving Ian and Mariana to cover his retreat.

General Collins turned around and saw Anna, Alex, and Michael behind them. His sword drooped slightly and he gritted his teeth.

Seeing her chance, Anna yelled, "Scatter!"

At her call, her troops ended their one-on-one fights and took off running after Liam. Their opponents stood motionless for a heartbeat before gripping their weapons and following as best they could. Anna noticed them glancing back and forth at each other, trying to figure out which battle situation they should mimic. The older soldiers didn't know which way to look. They tripped over tree roots, looking to the General for orders instead of looking where they were going.

Collins frantically scanned the field and shouted out, "Just . . . get after them."

Anna, Alex, and Michael took advantage of their opponents' momentary pause to dart ahead. The younger fighters were much nimbler and had less trouble running through the trees as they ducked under branches and jumped over roots and fallen sticks.

Michael's toe caught one of the roots and he fell hard, crying out in pain. Anna and Alex seized him under the arms and hauled him to his feet, dragging him along until he found his footing and was able to run. A few seconds later, Anna could see the quad. She stumbled through the tree line and found the rest of the regiment gathered together, their breathing returning to normal. No one seemed to be marked by the chalk that coated the practice weapons.

"Do you have it?" Anna asked as she walked over to Liam.

"Right here." Liam grinned and held up the idol, surprising the other regiments and onlookers.

By this time, General Collins and his men had finally managed to reach the quad. He looked from Anna to Liam to the idol, confusion still etched on his face.

"How did you manage to get past our defensive line?" the General asked. "We had the entire field covered from edge to edge. There's no way you could have walked past us without being seen."

Her regiment let out a few scattered chuckles and Anna grinned. "Well, you're right. We didn't walk past you," she said.

"What?"

"The trees," she explained. "Alex, Michael and I climbed the trees at the start, here, and moved across the branches until we reached the clearing where you kept the idol. The soldiers fighting your men were just a distraction so we could take the idol without you noticing. As soon as we had it, it was easy to throw to someone who was still in play."

"Very clever," Collins said. "I have to admit, I was apprehensive about facing you today, considering your lack of a formal training program, but I see your methods are proving effective."

General Horne walked over and took the idol from Liam. "Congratulations, Lieutenant. You have won your first war game. Your win against the top regiment exempts you from the rest of the games today. You're welcome to stay and watch, or you can return to your own training schedule. General Collins, unfortunately, this loss puts your regiment down quite a way on the ranking list. You'll have to stay for a few more matches."

To Anna's surprise, Collins was downright grinning at her. She grinned back and turned to her regiment.

"Lunch?"

Her troops cheered and ran off to the dining hall, leaving Collins' troops staring after them in bewilderment.

The next morning, Anna gathered her troops at the training area near the western quad.

"Rebecca, Michael, head to the archery range to shoot. The rest of you, pair off and we'll do some one-on-one sword drills. Ian, Kyree, if you like, you can head to the range as well, otherwise, I'd like you using a sword."

Ian glanced around. "I'll go throw my axe."

"I'd like some more practice throwing my daggers as well," Kyree said.

"Granted. I'll send someone to get you in an hour or so."

Anna squared up against Alex and began sparring. They spent the hour trading partners so everyone got to face each other. Though they'd all gone through the same basic and intermediate training, each person had their own fighting style and Anna enjoyed facing everyone. It stretched her ability with a sword and helped her approach each fight in a different way. She hoped that this kind of training would help her be unpredictable in a real fight and give her an advantage in the field. If she could get another regiment to join in their sparring, they could become even better. After the hour was up, she called for everyone to stop and sent Mariana to retrieve the others from the range.

"Alright," Anna said when everyone was assembled, "I have to go to General Assembly. Alex, will you lead everyone in some conditioning exercises?"

"Yes, Ma'am," he said, exaggerating a salute.

Anna rolled her eyes and left for the meeting room. Higher officers and regiment leaders were required to attend meetings once a week to receive assignments and updates on wraith movements. This was Anna's first as a Lieutenant, and she was extremely nervous. Most of the officers she'd met were cordial, but they were still a little wary of her age. Colonel Wells was no longer on suspension and he was attempting to block any progress that Anna made with the other officers. At least the Council members didn't normally come to the meetings.

She finally reached the meeting room and chose a seat toward the back without speaking to anyone. Colonel Wells glared at her from across the room, and Anna sank into her chair, trying not to attract notice. She felt thankful that General Collins walked in just then and called everyone to attention.

Anna followed suit as everyone rose and saluted. The various regiments that had been assigned to missions outside the barrier gave their reports, then Collins launched into information about the wraiths.

"Our scouts have only been able to reach as far south as Oracha," he said. "According to them, the wraiths are staying near their city, but I would expect that to change in the coming months. I anticipate that they'll start moving their attacks north to try and expand their influence. Just be on your guard around the barrier. I don't want to worry the refugees, but a few wraith scouts were spotted near the western edge."

Anna swallowed nervously. She'd been so focused on training the past few months, she'd almost forgotten that she'd have to fight wraiths for real. To have some penetrate this far north sent chills down her spine, especially since her barracks were the closest to where the wraiths had been spotted.

"Much past that," Collins continued, "I don't have a whole lot of information for you. I don't want to keep you from your training, so we'll go right into assignments."

Anna tuned out most of the missions. The General started with the Colonels and worked his way down the ranks with the assignments. Those who were assigned to missions outside the Sanctuary left as soon as they had the necessary information, eager to get started so they could return to the safety of the barrier as soon as their task was done. Finally, he got to her assignment.

"Lieutenant Lieay."

"Yes, General?"

"Your regiment will take over barrier patrol from lunch until dinner for the next week. My hope is that you taking a share of the patrol duties will release other soldiers for more training."

"Of course, General," Anna said, trying to keep her voice even.

"If there are no questions, this Assembly is dismissed."

The officers stood, and Anna quickly made her way out of the room. She didn't want to speak to them, nor did she want to deal with Colonel Wells. Disappointment filled her as she walked. When she'd been given command of the regiment, she figured she'd be given an actual assignment, not stuck on barrier patrol. The combat games had proven that her regiment could work as a unit and handle themselves in battle, but the Council obviously still saw her and her troops as untrained children. Lost in thought, Anna barely noticed she was back at her barracks until Rebecca called her name.

"Anna! How'd the Assembly go? Did we get an assignment?"

"Kind of. We're on barrier patrol from lunch until dinner. Status shouldn't change until next Assembly."

Anna's announcement was met with a groan from her troops.

"I know it's not ideal, but we just have to get through it. As the newest regiment, we're bound to get the worst assignments. If we do a good job, they'll eventually take us off patrol and give us a real mission. I want everyone on the roof in ten. You all need to know what we talked about in Assembly, and I'd like to get a few drills in before lunch."

Jonathan leaned in close and whispered, "Usually commanders only tell their seconds."

"I don't want to do things the usual way," Anna said, lowering her voice slightly. "If we're going to fight this war, everyone needs to be aware of what's going on, not just myself and a select few others."

"Very well," Jonathan relented, and they all climbed up the old ladder to hear what Anna had to say.

"Collins started out by talking about our resources and numbers," Anna said. "We've had quite a few of the older soldiers drop from the force after some of their first missions. Some of them realized army life just wasn't for them, and others apparently didn't want to put in the effort to train. However, it sounds like fewer people our age have dropped out of training, and the officers have no choice but to assimilate them into existing regiments to compensate for the losses."

"Ironic, isn't it?" Liam said. "They didn't want us to fight and now they need us."

"I don't think they're happy about it," Anna mused. "The General is the only one who will actually acknowledge our contribution."

"What about the wraiths?" Mariana asked.

Anna sighed and shook her head. "Collins didn't say much about them, and I got the feeling he didn't know much. As far as I can tell, our scouts aren't trained in combat. They really just focus on how quickly they can run, so it's hard for them to get close enough to get quality information. We do know that the wraiths are mostly staying south. They don't appear to have advanced farther north than the line created by their initial attacks."

Anna paused and looked at each of her troops. "I don't want to scare you, but Collins did say that a few wraiths were spotted near the western edge of the barrier. He wasn't going to tell the refugees, but since our barracks are so close to where the sightings were, I thought you should all know."

"Does Collins want people checking on the west barrier?" Liam asked.

"Not that he said. Most of the missions for the other regiments are to check on villages we haven't heard from recently. Until someone goes to see what happened, we don't know if the village has been destroyed, or if the people living there just can't make the trip on their own. Collins didn't have much else to say. Now, everyone up! I'd like to run a few drills."

An hour later, the regiment heard the bell signaling lunch. Tired and sweaty, they all climbed back down and splashed some water on their faces before heading off. They sat at what had become their usual table and talked throughout the meal. About halfway through, Anna sat back and listened to the others chatting. After only a few days together, her regiment was acting as though they'd been together for years. Anna smiled to herself. It was exactly what she'd wanted. As lunch ended, she led her troops back outside to present her plan for their patrol that afternoon.

"We'll be the only ones on barrier patrol. I know we don't have that many people, but we should be able to make this work. Ele, Oliver, Mariana, you start at the northern quad and go along the barrier heading east. Rebecca, Michael, and Kyree, start at the southern quad and go west. Ian, Jonathan, start at the east and go along the barrier north. Liam, Alex, and I will start at the west barrier. I know you aren't excited about this, but we have to start somewhere. Let's go."

Her troops moved to follow her orders, preparing for the long afternoon. Anna hoped that the patrols would pass without any incident. She nodded as she, Alex, and Liam passed Ele, Oliver, and Mariana on their own patrol. Though they were only responsible for afternoon patrols, it seemed to last hours longer. Anna was grateful when the dinner bell rang and the next group of soldiers came to take up their watch. She met her troops briefly to eat and led them back to their barracks for some drills. After a while, Anna stopped training so that her troops might have some free time.

"We still have an hour until curfew," Liam said. "We could keep training."

"I know, but I thought I'd give you all a break." Anna smiled. "Besides, I'm really happy with the progress we've made, and I think some free time is warranted. Just make sure you're all back at the barracks before curfew. I don't need another reason for the Council to yell at me."

Her troops nodded and broke off into smaller groups. Some

went inside the barracks while others made their way to the main building of the Sanctuary. Anna felt a twinge of loneliness as they left. Most were heading to see some sort of family.

Oliver's mother and Ele's aunt both worked in the kitchens. They were very supportive of Oliver and Ele joining the army, which was odd to Anna. All the soldiers and Council members repeatedly said how dangerous it was, yet many of the young soldiers' parents didn't have an issue with it. Anna wondered if any of her companions or their parents had ever actually seen a wraith. Her own father had been terrified for her when he saw her try to face the wraiths back at Fort Lieay.

She'd asked Ele's aunt why she wasn't concerned about her niece fighting. The older woman said that she knew Ele would try to fight anyway. At least this way, she'd have proper training and would know how to defend herself. Oliver's mother had agreed, adding that their children were going to grow up eventually. The two women reminded Anna of her mother, and made her yearn for her own family even more.

Alex waved a hand in front of her eyes, and Anna realized she had been staring at nothing for a few minutes.

"Are you okay?" Alex asked.

"I'm fine," she said. "Just thinking."

"Missing your parents?"

Anna looked at Alex and sighed. "Is it that obvious?"

Alex shrugged, and Anna's shoulders drooped.

"I miss them so much. Sometimes it just hurts." Anna looked down and scratched the new scar across her palm from the Colonel's attack.

"Come with me," Alex said. "I want to show you something."

Anna followed Alex up to the northern quad. He led her around one of the old grain stores that was no longer in use before coming to the barrier. He looked around for any sentries that might be watching before stepping through it, out into the forest.

"What are you doing?" Anna whispered. "We can't leave the barrier!"

"We're not going far," he said. "Trust me."

Anna glanced back at the main building before nodding slightly and following him out of the safety of the grounds. He led her through the forest for a little while before the trees cleared and gave way to a large rock face. He marched over to a small opening in the cliff and passed through it. Anna eyed the forest behind her nervously. Birds were softly calling to one another, so wraiths weren't near, but she couldn't help but examine every shadow, just in case.

Finally, she took a deep breath and followed Alex through the small opening. The crevice opened up to a small box canyon. The walls extended a few hundred feet into the air where the dark stone blended into the sky. The stone was smooth, but chipped away, revealing dark purple veins running through the rock.

"What is this place?" Anna asked, still gaping at her surroundings.

"It's just an old quarry," Alex said. "It doesn't have a name, as far as I know. It looks like people used to come up here and mine the purple stuff from the stones, but I'm not sure why."

Anna walked over to a large boulder and sat down.

"How'd you find this place?"

Alex shrugged and sat next to her. "I'm kind of a restless sleeper. I like to explore at night."

"Just be careful. I won't turn you in, but if another officer catches you . . ."

"I know," he said. They sat in silence for a few moments before he spoke again. "So, how do you think the war is going?"

Anna gave him a questioning look. "You know as much as I do. Collins really didn't have much to say."

"I know what Collins said; I want to know what you think."

Anna paused to think for a moment. "Well, I think they need to start teaching the scouts how to defend themselves. How are we supposed to fight Roland if we don't know anything about him or his movements? If our scouts were properly trained, they could take more risks and hopefully get us more information."

"Surely they're trained a little," Alex said.

"Nope. They go through harder conditioning, but very few of them have even touched a weapon. If they ever come across a wraith, they're supposed to run away as fast as they can."

"Hmm. Seems a little useless, then."

"That's for sure," Anna agreed. She stared at the sky for a few moments, taking in the stars before standing. "We should probably get back. If we get caught outside the barrier, I'll be in serious trouble, especially if it's after curfew."

Alex nodded. "I'm pretty tired anyway."

The pair left the canyon and carefully entered the barrier. Once they were sure no one had seen them, they went back to their barracks.

Night fell over the Sanctuary, the barrier shimmering under the full moon. Shadows covered the surrounding trees, hiding the single soldier from any who might be patrolling the grounds. The soldier slowly left the barrier, ensuring he wasn't seen, before venturing into the forest beyond. He walked for a few minutes, his footfalls barely heard over the commotion of the nocturnal animals scurrying about in the trees above. Finally, he reached a small clearing, illuminated by moonlight.

The surrounding area went silent as two shadows floated into the clearing opposite him. The shadows solidified slightly, becoming silhouettes of something resembling humans. Their red eyes narrowed as they took in the soldier.

"It took you long enough," the soldier said, trying to calm his shaking hands. "I've been waiting almost a year for contact."

"Our King decides our movements, not you," hissed one of the wraiths. The soldier shuddered. The wraith's voice raked over his ears, compelling him to listen no matter how hard he fought the influence.

The soldier swallowed hard. "It's difficult to report on human activity with no one to report to. Our deal is still on?"

"If you manage to provide us with valuable information."

The soldier drew in a short breath, but dared not reach up to wipe away the sweat that had formed across his brow.

"I take it you have some information for us," the second wraith said. She took a small step forward, eyes glinting. The soldier took a slight step back. His heel snapped a twig, and the sound echoed through the silence in the trees.

"Not exactly," he said. "The Council doesn't really share much with anyone except for General Collins. And he only talks to his officers."

"Then we came all this way for nothing," the wraith whispered, her words so quiet that the soldier barely heard her. The two moved backward, blending into the trees.

"Yes," the second wraith echoed, "perhaps you are not worthy of becoming one of us."

"Wait," the soldier cried desperately. He stepped forward, one arm outstretched as if to grasp the darkness.

"Yes?"

"I found out that you can get through the barrier if you're invited in. But I'm not sure how well it will work when you're a shadow. You may have to do it in the daylight."

One wraith stepped back into the moonlight, a ghost of a smile appearing on her lips. "And you will be the one to invite us in?"

The soldier shook his head. "I can't. I can't have anyone suspecting me of anything."

"Then this conversation is pointless."

The soldier scratched his palm nervously and his breath quickened. "Maybe if there were refugees walking near the barrier, you could persuade them to let you in."

The wraith's eyes narrowed, contemplating the soldier's words. "I suppose if that's all you can manage to give us."

"I'll have more soon, I promise. A lot of new troops have been assigned to regiments now, so I'll be able to get more information."

"How many regiments?" snapped one wraith.

The soldier glanced around at the trees before answering. "Umm, at least fifteen, but it could be more. There are still a lot of soldiers going through training."

"I suppose you aren't completely useless," the wraith rasped.

"We'll be in contact again soon. And you'd better have more information for us then."

The shadows flickered as the wraiths faded back into darkness. Sound came back into the forest, and the soldier let out a shaky breath before returning to the safety of the barrier.

— 18 —

The next afternoon, Anna divided her troops up once again for patrols. Her soldiers grudgingly obeyed her orders. Anna knew their frustration wasn't directed at her, but at the General and the Council. It was difficult for them to see the other regiments going out on missions when they knew they were better trained.

"I don't think I've ever felt so useless," Alex said after they had been circling the grounds for a little over an hour.

"I know," Anna replied. "I wish there was something I could do, but the Council probably thinks they're keeping us safe. We're still children to them."

"It just makes no sense," Alex said. "We're better disciplined than most other regiments, and I bet we're better at fighting."

"Hold on," Liam interrupted, "are those a couple of refugees near the barrier? They aren't supposed to be that close without a soldier escort."

Anna glanced over and saw two refugees staring into the trees. Shadows walked out of the trees, turning to flesh as the sun hit their forms. She saw one of the refugees nod, and the golden barrier shivered and bent to allow the wraiths into the Sanctuary grounds.

"I'm more worried about the wraiths! Come on!"

Anna drew both her swords and charged the small group of wraiths stepping through the barrier.

Liam and Alex were close behind her as she thrust her blade out, narrowly blocking a wraith's sword from harming the refugees. Placing herself between the wraiths and the refugees, Anna squared her shoulders and sized up her opponents.

There were about ten of them, a small enough force to get all the way to the Sanctuary without being noticed, but still large enough to cause some damage if invited in. Though none of them wore heavy armor, they were protected by gold weapons and thick leather padding. Anna swung her sword at one of the wraiths while Alex and Liam attacked as well, doing their best to keep the refugees safely behind them. Anna glimpsed Liam's sword coming for her head. She ducked just in time to see the blade sink into a wraith's chest over her shoulder. She swiped her sword at another wraith, and he fell to the ground. She plunged her sword through his neck, and he turned to dust before her eyes.

After killing about half the group, Anna saw a wraith jump at Liam. Startled, he dropped his sword and started wrestling with his attacker. She saw another wraith coming for Liam from behind.

"Liam!" she cried, as she tried to fight her way over to him. Liam glanced over at her, startled by her call, and one of the wraiths clubbed him on the head. He fell to the ground, limp and still.

Memories of her mother falling in much the same way consumed Anna's mind. She felt a warm rush of energy spreading from her center. Her limbs tingled with strength and power, spurring her to fight even harder. She spun to one side, barely managing to block an attack on Alex. He seemed startled by her help, but launched himself at the next opponent.

Anna could barely see her blades as she furiously jabbed and slashed at her enemies. She and Alex pushed them back toward the barrier, hoping that if they were driven out, they couldn't come back in. A couple of the wraiths fell through the golden barrier, and they didn't try to return but turned to shadow in the darkness of the trees. Anna paid them no mind, keeping her attention on the few wraiths still within the barrier. Together, she and Alex managed to defeat the remaining ones.

Anna sheathed her sword and took a few deep breaths, trying to calm her racing heart.

"Are you two okay?" she asked the refugees.

"I think so," one responded. "How did they—"

"Get in? Wraiths have a persuasive effect on humans who aren't trained to withstand the pull. They influenced you to invite them in. That's why you aren't allowed near the barrier without an escort," Anna said with a stern look.

"We're so sorry," one mumbled, "but we just wanted to walk near the forest."

Anna looked at his companion. She was staring at the small piles of dust, her face pale and her bottom lip quivering.

Her officer's pin glinted in the light. "I need your word that you won't approach the barrier unescorted again. And you'll stay with me to make a report."

"Our word, Ma'am," the man replied, reaching out to hold the woman's hand.

Anna knelt down to check on Liam.

"He seems okay, just unconscious. Alex, can you get him to the infirmary? I'm going to take these two in to make a report."

Alex nodded and hoisted Liam over his shoulder. "Good luck."

Thinking for a moment, Anna stopped Alex before he could walk away.

"Are you okay?" she asked.

Alex looked confused. "What do you mean?"

Anna glanced back at the refugees before whispering, "You hesitated, that's all. I know you haven't seen a wraith since they attacked your village, but you can't be hesitating in battle. That'll get you killed."

A strange expression crossed Alex's face, and Anna couldn't quite decipher it. Finally, he held his palms out, offering an apology. "I saw them and it took a minute for my training to kick in. I'm sure I'll be fine the next time we fight."

Anna looked closely at him for a moment, her hand on his shoulder. "Just be sure. I don't want you fighting if you're going to get hurt." Anna turned back to the couple. "You two, come with me."

The couple followed Anna inside to a small room in the western wing that the army used for strategic planning. There was always at least one officer there, usually more. Various tables were set up around the room with maps and plans spread out on them. Officers and soldiers were examining different maps or supply lists.

"Major Ravenall?" Anna asked as she walked up to a group in conversation.

The Major brushed a stray hair from her face and fixed Anna in a stare.

"Lieutenant Lieay, aren't you supposed to be on barrier patrol?"

For a brief moment, Anna felt like she was back in training. She squared her shoulders and forced herself to meet the Major's gaze. She was a Lieutenant now and she wouldn't appear weak before another officer.

"Yes, Ma'am; however, there was an incident. These two were near the barrier and allowed a small group of wraiths in."

The Major's eyes widened. "What? Wraiths got in?"

"They did, but we took care of it. They're all dead, Ma'am."

She paused and stared at Anna for a moment. "Good work, Lieutenant. Nevertheless, any breach needs to be reported directly to General Collins."

"What about these two?" Anna said, gesturing to the pair of refugees she'd brought in.

"A soldier will take their statement. Follow me."

Anna followed the Major to the Council chambers. Once there, the Major said a quick word to the guards, and they were let in immediately. As they entered the room, Althea looked up.

"Major, Lieutenant. Is there a reason you're here and not at your posts?"

"There was a breach during the Lieutenant's barrier patrol," the Major said. "We're here to make a report to the General."

"A breach! Why haven't you sent more troops to take care of it?"

"It's been taken care of," Anna said.

"Lieutenant?"

"My regiment sealed the breach. Most are still on patrol. I sent the wounded to the infirmary, and I came in to make the report."

General Collins had moved over, next to the Councilmember. "Major, you may return to your post," he said. "Lieutenant, your full report."

Anna nodded, and told the General and the Council what had happened. When she finished, she folded her hands in front of her and waited for the Council or Collins to speak.

"You and two other soldiers fought and won a battle against ten wraiths, and none of you were seriously injured?" Althea asked.

Anna paused for a moment before answering. She hadn't thought about how easily they'd defeated the wraiths until she heard Althea put it into words. After all, fighting wraiths was what they'd been training for.

She swallowed and said, "We don't know yet about one of the injuries, Ma'am. But, yes, we killed ten wraiths."

"Who were the two soldiers with you?"

"Alex Marduk and Liam Carver."

"Well, Lieutenant," said General Collins, "I believe I speak for everyone here when I say I'm impressed. Very few soldiers would be able to successfully defend the barrier with those numbers, and fewer still could do it without fatalities. Althea, I know you recommended Lieutenant Jones, but I believe Lieutenant Lieay takes precedence after this."

Althea stared at Collins for a few moments before nodding stiffly.

Anna's brow furrowed as she wondered at the exchange, then the General stood up and walked toward her.

"Lieutenant, for your bravery, I am promoting you to Captain." He walked over and unlocked a metal case of drawers, pulling an item out. He stepped forward and removed her Lieutenant's pin, replacing it with what she recognized as a Captain's pin, complete with the additional bar. He placed her old pin into her hand. "Be sure to promote your second to Lieutenant, and the three of you who fought will receive Stars of Valor. I'll have a page sent over with the Stars. Dismissed."

Anna saluted General Collins and Althea before leaving the Council chambers. Though she was still in shock from the sudden battle and then promotion, she was filled with a sudden pride. Maybe following in her parents' footsteps wasn't as daunting of a task as she'd thought.

Turning down a hall, she headed to the medical wing where Alex and Liam were supposed to be. She never got that far, however. She ran into the pair halfway down the hall.

"Are you okay, Liam?"

"I'm fine. Just a bump on the head."

"Those can be serious. Report immediately if you have any symptoms." Liam nodded. "Dinner is in about an hour and we'll be off patrol after that, but for now, here," she said, reaching forward to pin the Lieutenant's pin to Alex's chest.

"What's this for?"

"They promoted me to Captain for our victory, and told me to promote you to Lieutenant."

"You're joking."

"Nope, and they're sending over Stars of Valor for all three of us."

"Wow," Liam said, "I get one too? I did get hurt."

"Of course. You fought bravely, Liam."

She hesitated, hoping Alex didn't notice the catch in her voice. She hadn't told General Collins about the way that Alex had frozen. She knew it had been his first time seeing a wraith since the attack on his village, but freezing in a fight like that was dangerous. She didn't want to tell Collins, considering how hard she and her friends had worked to get into the army. Anna forced the thoughts from her mind. She still had a patrol to finish.

"We have to get back on patrol," she said. "We can tell the rest of the regiment what happened at dinner."

Though the barrier breach had been an interesting break from the normally dull afternoons, the remainder of their patrols that day passed without incident. When the bell rang for dinner, Anna breathed a sigh of relief and headed for the dining hall with Alex and Liam following. The rest of her regiment had apparently passed an uneventful afternoon, but they'd all heard that something had transpired at the western barrier with Anna, Alex, and Liam.

"Come on, Anna," Oliver pleaded, brushing his hair back. "Something happened with your group and we all want to hear about it. We even saw some soldiers picking up a few gold weapons from around the barrier."

Alex scowled. "Oh? Why didn't *we* get the weapons?"

Anna shrugged. "I guess the Council doesn't think we deserve them yet."

"But what happened?" Rebecca asked.

"Some refugees were near the barrier and they got influenced to invite some wraiths in. I wasn't sure how the fight would go, but we held our own," Anna said.

"There is definitely more to this story. Stop teasing."

Liam jumped in. "It was amazing and terrifying at the same time. Aside from the initial attacks, I'd never seen a wraith up close before. They were faster than I thought they'd be, but I wasn't that scared. All that training we did just . . . kicked in, and I was fighting on instinct. I went into the fight ready to kill some wraiths. It was awesome."

"Liam, you spent most of the battle unconscious," Alex reminded him.

The regiment laughed and Liam turned bright red. "That's . . . I . . . um . . ."

A page came over and saved Liam from having to respond. "Captain Lieay, the General instructed me to give these to you."

Oliver's eyes moved to Anna's pin, and the regiment fell silent. Anna nodded and took the small pouch the page offered. The page saluted and left the table. Anna opened the pouch to see three pins—the Stars of Valor. She'd never seen one before, but they were little gold stars, about an inch in diameter. She gave one each to Alex and Liam, and pinned her own next to her Captain's pin.

"They made you a Captain?" Oliver asked, noticing the pin.

"They said it was for bravery, and Alex is now a Lieutenant." She pointed at Alex's pin, which no one had noticed until that moment either.

"What are the stars?" Ele asked.

"The General said they were Stars of Valor. I guess you get them if you perform an outstanding act. He wasn't very specific."

"Maybe now they'll let us have a real assignment," Oliver joked.

"There's another General Assembly tomorrow morning, so we'll see," Anna replied. Secretly, she wasn't so sure she wanted a real assignment anymore. Seeing Liam get hurt wasn't something she ever wanted to happen again. But she did join the army and she knew what she was getting into. She would fight whenever and wherever she was assigned. *If only there were a way to fight the wraiths without putting others in danger,* she thought.

***

The next morning, Anna led her regiment to the western quad for some two-against-two sparring rounds before she had to leave for Assembly.

"I think that's good enough for now," Anna announced to her troops. "You can all continue training if you wish, or take a break. The rest of the morning is yours, and I'll see you after Assembly." She sheathed her sword and headed inside, Ian following closely behind her.

"Hi, Ian. Did you need something?" Anna asked, glancing back at him.

"No," Ian said gruffly. "My sword's off-balance. I was hoping to exchange it."

"Oh," she said.

Anna and Ian both kept their same pace, leaving Anna to walk a few steps ahead of him. She tried slowing slightly, but each time she did, Ian also slowed. She resisted the urge to sigh aloud. She'd been nothing but nice to Ian, and it still seemed like he despised her.

Mariana had said he was just stubborn in nature, but Anna wasn't so sure. Finally, they reached the main hall and broke off in separate directions.

"Good luck with your sword," Anna said before she left. Ian merely grunted in response.

Anna glanced down the western hallway and saw Colonel Wells coming out of one of the rooms. She groaned internally and ducked into an empty room to avoid him. Knowing him, if he saw her, he'd use his higher rank to make her run some sort of errand in order to make her late for the Assembly. She'd just managed to hide behind the door when she heard him call out.

"Soldier Young, may I speak with you for a moment?"

"Colonel Wells," came Ian's voice, "I don't want to keep you from Assembly."

"I sent my second as a proxy."

Anna rolled her eyes. Collins expected regiment commanders to be at Assembly if they were at the Sanctuary. She didn't think targeting her soldiers was enough of an excuse for Colonel Wells not to be there.

"Oh. Well, what can I do for you, Sir?" Ian asked.

"Nothing, nothing. I just wanted to see how things are going in the 77th."

Anna scowled. He couldn't leave them alone even for a moment.

"Things are fine, Sir. We're working well together," Ian answered.

"I heard a rumor that you weren't completely satisfied with the Captain's command. Is that true? Do you believe she is unfit for the position?"

Anna felt her breath catch in her throat. Ian often voiced his displeasure with how she ran training. If he told the Colonel . . . there would be no telling what the senior officer could do.

"Well, we had our issues in the beginning, but it was nothing we couldn't handle."

"But she led you wrong, did she not?" asked the Colonel.

"Sir? I'm not really sure what you're asking."

"You're a smart young lad, Ian, so I'll be honest with you.

I'm asking you to testify against Captain Lieay's leadership to the Council. With her removal from command, the position would be open. I'd need to find a replacement, and I always reward those who are loyal."

Anna bit her lip hard to keep herself from storming out to confront the Colonel. How dare he ask this of one of her soldiers? If he wanted her removed, as he clearly did, he should be talking with General Collins directly. Her breathing began to quicken as the silence stretched longer and longer. Finally, she heard Ian clear his throat.

"With all due respect, Sir," came Ian's voice, "Anna is a fantastic commander. She's strong and level-headed, and I couldn't think of anyone better to serve under. We may have disagreements from time to time, but who doesn't? Anna is my leader, and if you think I would ever speak against her—especially to benefit myself—then you are sorely mistaken. Now, if you'll excuse me."

Anna heard heavy footsteps stomping off in the other direction, followed shortly by another set of lighter footfalls. She peered out in the hallway and found it empty. Though she was still angry at the Colonel, Ian's words filled her with confidence. All this time, she'd thought he hated her, but maybe he wasn't so bad after all. Thinking back, she realized his challenging her all the time required her to really think through each of her decisions. Because of him, she was likely a better commander. She'd remember to tell him that.

She relaxed a bit, leaving the small room and continuing down to the General Assembly. But her mind wasn't really on the meeting. She barely heard everyone else's assignments, only paying attention to her own. Of course, she was disappointed again. They were given another barrier patrol assignment.

When General Collins ended the Assembly, Anna stayed behind. Once everyone else had left the room, she went up to Collins.

"Captain Lieay," he said. "What can I do for you?"

"Well, I was wondering if we could talk about my regiment's assignment." She contemplated talking to him about the Colonel's actions, but she didn't want him to think she was complaining too much. Besides, she wanted to handle that issue on her own.

Collins sighed. "I'm fairly busy right now, Captain. Can we speak about this some other time?"

"I urge you to let me speak now," Anna said firmly. She locked eyes with the General.

"Captain, it's not your place to question my decisions or the Council's."

"It is when I believe your decisions are wrong."

The General's eyes narrowed. "Dangerous words, Captain. I could suspend you for that."

Anna softened her tone and tried a different tactic. "Please, General. I know we're young and you don't think we're capable, but the attack yesterday proves we can handle ourselves. We went through the exact same training as everyone else and we deserve to be given the same chances."

Collins stared at Anna for a few moments, contemplating what she'd said. His face remained a blank mask, and she couldn't figure out what he was thinking. She knew they were young, but she thought she'd made some good points, and he hadn't been fair on them. They'd gone through training in record time. Besides, three of them did manage to kill the small group of wraiths on their own.

"Captain," Collins finally said, "I'm going to do you a favor and pretend you didn't come here today. You will return to your troops and take whatever assignment I give you, just like every other regiment. I took a chance on you, and I stand by my decision, but if you start trying to undermine my authority and question my orders, then there will be no place for you in this army. Am I understood?"

Anna's face fell. She opened her mouth to try and respond, but the General held up a hand.

"I'm going to assume you agree with me and will thank me for being so nice," he said. "Now, if you'll excuse me, I have a lot of work to do."

Anna nodded and walked back to the barracks with a heavy heart. Perhaps challenging the General wasn't the smartest thing she could have done. But she couldn't just sit back and watch her troops get sidelined when they could do so much more. At least she'd made her point. Maybe if she kept a respectful distance for the next few days, he'd think about what she'd said.

"Anything exciting for us?" Rebecca called, interrupting Anna's thoughts.

"Just barrier patrol," Anna replied. Her troops groaned, and she continued, "Sorry, everyone, but barrier patrol is an important job too. I know the afternoons are dull. Just try to make the best of it and get through it."

Their patrol that afternoon was without incident. After the breach, refugees had been reminded about the Sanctuary's rules for civilians and given strict orders to stay away from the barrier. Aside from her own troops, Anna didn't see anyone all afternoon. Even the other regiments used the inner training areas.

As she walked along the barrier, she thought about how her interaction with the General would affect her troops. They all wanted a real assignment, and she'd likely just ruined their chance. Guilt settled heavily in her stomach and she could barely look at Alex and Liam. Collins was in command, and she'd insulted his orders and his leadership. She made up her mind to apologize to the General at the next Assembly.

~ 19 ~

As darkness fell over the Sanctuary, the lone soldier stood at the edge of the barrier. He carefully surveyed the area before leaving the grounds and heading into the forest. He walked for a few minutes, shivering as a cold wind swept through the trees. He tightened his jacket against the breeze and scanned the shadows for movement.

"You'd better have some information for us," a voice said from beside him. "His Majesty does not like to be kept waiting." Two wraiths materialized from the shadows. They brushed past him, their darkness caressing the soldier, before stopping across from him in the clearing.

"Your wraiths got through the barrier, didn't they?" the soldier responded.

The wraiths glared. "Only to be killed as soon as they set foot on the grounds," one said.

The soldier threw his hands up in defense. "It's not my fault they couldn't handle a few soldiers. But now you know it works. You could keep trying."

"Perhaps. Do you have anything else useful for us?"

"I'm trying," the soldier grumbled. "The Council is very protective of the mission logs and assignments."

"Try harder," the wraith replied, red eyes flashing. "If the King doesn't think you're doing your best, he may have to rescind his offer."

"He can't—" the soldier protested.

"You dare question our King!" The other wraith's eyes narrowed and a low growl started in the back of his throat.

"No," the soldier said, his chin trembling in fear. "Please. I'll get the information. Besides, it's not like you have anyone else in the Sanctuary. You need me."

The shadows shook with anger. "For now. You may have a deal with Roland, but you weren't the only coward who sought us out."

The soldier winced. "Like I said, I'll get the information. I just need a little more time."

The red eyes focused on him, hard and skeptical. "There's a small shack a mile north of here with a few dakas. Send us what you can. If you're smart, you'll hurry."

"I do know something."

"Well?"

"Collins is supposed to be heading out tomorrow. I'm not sure where they're going, but I know they'll be coming back through Anazize next week."

"You'd better be right," the wraith said with a snarl. He motioned to his partner and the two faded back into the trees. Moments later, they were gone.

The soldier collapsed to his knees, breathing heavily from the encounter, as soft hoots began echoing from the trees once again.

⚡ 20 ⚡

The next week at Assembly, Anna didn't see General Collins anywhere. She wanted to apologize to him for what she'd said. She spotted Major Ravenall and approached her.

"Major, where's General Collins?"

"He's out on assignment. I'll be running today's Assembly. Actually, I'm glad you're here early. The General wanted me to give you your assignment as soon as possible. You'll be going to Unalique to salvage supplies. The village should be empty, but the villagers didn't have time to grab more than the bare minimum as they fled. You'll need to leave immediately so you can return to the Sanctuary before dark. Here's a map along with some other details about the village and surrounding area."

She took the scroll from the Major's outstretched hand before saying, "Thank you, Major. We'll leave at once."

Anna saluted and left the room. The General was giving her a chance and there was no way she was going to waste it. She rushed through the Sanctuary halls back to her barracks, where she had left her troops under Alex's command. As the barracks came into view, she could see her troops out front running hand-to-hand combat drills.

"Gear up!" she called. "We've got an assignment!"

"Really? Outside the barrier?"

Anna nodded, a big grin on her face. "I want everyone ready to leave in ten minutes."

That was all her troops needed. They picked up their weapons and rushed to gather what they needed for their trip outside the barrier. Anna went to her trunk and grabbed the old bag she'd taken from the safe house, putting her hunting jacket in along with a small bag of nuts and jerky she kept tucked away for such an occasion. She also grabbed a few bandages in case an emergency should arise.

Anna then returned to the entryway and went over to the racks where she kept her weapons, though there weren't many to speak of. Some regiments had returned with a few gold weapons, but the armory was still stretched too thin for anyone to have extras. She examined the pair of steel swords she had gotten from the armory. They had nicks and dings all along the blades and the grips were wearing thin, but they had held up through training so far. She also had her mother's dagger, and the gold dagger she'd saved General Collins from at the barrier. Anna buckled the worn leather sword sheaths around her waist and tucked a dagger into each boot.

Shouldering her bag, she went outside to wait for her soldiers. She didn't have to wait long, though. It seemed everyone was eager to begin their first real assignment. When they were all assembled in front of the barracks, Anna led them to the southwestern tree line, a path most regiments took to leave the barrier in case any wraiths were watching the main southern entrance. Before they left the safety of the barrier, Anna turned back to debrief her troops.

"Alright, now, I know everyone's excited, but I need you all to keep your heads. We're going on a simple reconnaissance mission. There's a small village about half a day's walk west of here, from which some refugees arrived yesterday evening. They said there'd been a wraith raid, and the Council wants a report of the village's status. We're to survey the village and salvage what supplies may be left, if any. In the unlikely case of survivors, we will escort them safely back to the Sanctuary. Any questions?"

"Do you think we'll run into any wraiths?"

"I hope not. It's unlikely the Council would have sent us out on our first mission if it were especially dangerous. They actually switched our assignment with another regiment because there were reports of a wraith squadron heading toward our original target. I expect that at most we'll see a few animals. But we'll still be ready for anything, including wraiths—no letting our guard down until we're back at the Sanctuary. Any other questions?"

"Come on," Liam said, "let's go already!"

Anna smiled wryly and nodded. She led her regiment past the barrier and out into the unknown forest. Without the golden tint of the barrier, the trees looked greener and the sky bluer. She and her troops walked through the trees in silence for a few miles, admiring their surroundings. Anna inhaled the fresh scent of new leaves and dirt, loving the aroma. It reminded her of climbing trees just outside the Fort. She longed to spend the day relaxing in the forest, to stop and search for the small animals she could hear calling to one another, but she had a job to do. This was her first real mission, and she couldn't afford to be distracted. She called for her troops to stop.

"Take a few minutes to drink some water and rest. Then we'll get going again." Anna pulled out the map the Major had given her. "We should be near Anazize now, which means we've still got about eight more miles until we reach Unalique."

A few minutes later, everyone was rested and ready to march on. Anna told them to stay as quiet as they could, but conversation bubbled up among the troops. They were all excited to be outside the Sanctuary, combined with the lingering fear, despite Anna's reassurance, that they could run into wraiths.

Anna had the most experience facing wraiths, followed by Alex and Liam. The others had likely never encountered one, save for a few in the initial attacks on their villages. If they messed up on their first real mission, they might not get another chance. She doubted the General would tolerate her yelling at him again. Lost in her thoughts, she barely noticed they had reached what remained of the small village of Unalique.

"Alright, everyone," Anna said, "we need to make this quick. We want to be back at the Sanctuary by nightfall. Oliver, Ele, Rebecca, and Liam, you'll be lookouts. We don't have enough people to surround the entire village, so spread out around the perimeter and watch for anything suspicious. The rest of you, pair up and search the buildings. One person inside, one person covering them from the door. Collect anything that might be useful: food, medicine, clothes, and any other supplies you might find lying around."

Anna's troops rushed to follow her orders. Oliver and Liam helped Rebecca up to one of the roofs so she might have a better vantage point. Anna positioned herself at the town center to watch their progress and keep a lookout for any movement in the shadows of the homes. She turned her gaze toward the southern end of the village. The birds had suddenly gone quiet.

Her breath caught, fear slowly creeping through her. She scanned the dark shadows of the trees for any sign of movement. Taking a few steps forward, she narrowed her eyes, trying to focus on the shadows flickering and wavering among the trees. Slowly, a wraith emerged from the shadows, followed by fifteen to twenty others.

"Wraiths!" Anna cried, not taking her eyes off the threat.

The first one Anna saw smiled widely, showing off sharpened fangs. Anna had never seen a female wraith before—they were every bit as beautiful and terrifying as the stories had said. Her eyes glowed more brightly than any other wraith's that she'd seen, save for Roland. Her skin was pearlescent, yet shadows moved just beneath the surface of her face. Her dark hair was almost one with the trees behind her, and tendrils of darkness followed her out of the shadows. Anna could feel her pull and yearned to lay down her weapons and surrender, but a voice in the back of her mind snapped her attention back to the present danger. The female gave a signal and the wraiths advanced into the village.

Anna drew her swords and charged the oncoming wraiths, with her troops following closely behind. The humans formed a tight circle, protecting their backs. Anna attacked the first wraith she saw, swinging her sword with as much strength as she could muster. Anna could see surprise flood his face, just before she turned him to dust. She looked for the next opponent to fight. As she slashed at her opponents, cleanly taking the head off one of the nearest wraiths, one of her swords shattered, the weak steel unable to withstand the constant hammering of the battle. She turned again as the leader stepped forward

"You're more trouble than you're worth," the red-eyed horror snarled, drawing her swords, and Anna almost pulled back as she saw the golden blades coming toward her, glinting dangerously in the sunlight. Anna summoned her courage and gripped her remaining sword tightly, bracing herself for the coming duel. She knelt and grabbed her mother's dagger from her boot with her free hand just before the wraith reached her.

Raising her sword, she pushed up to a standing position. She met the wraith woman's blades, blow for blow, moving in close so she might use her dagger in place of her second sword. The wraith lunged at her right side, and Anna felt a sharp sting across her ribs. She shook off the pain and focused on keeping the golden blades as far away from her as she could. Twisting her dagger, Anna hooked it under the guard of one of the wraith's swords and sent it flying away.

The wraith looked at Anna in surprise, and Anna took advantage of her hesitation to knock away her other weapon. Before the wraith had the chance to do anything, Anna thrust her sword through her neck, killing her. Dust slowly fluttered to the ground, almost hovering as it slowly descended. Anna had the urge to wave a hand through the strange darkness, but refrained, not knowing what the effect might be.

She turned from the small pile of dust and saw that her regiment had the rest of the wraiths well in hand, defeating them soundly. She ran a hand over her ribs, fearing what she might find, but there was no blood. She glanced down at her side, but there wasn't even a scratch.

But what about the stinging? she wondered. *Maybe the wraith woman just grazed me with her blade.*

Anna disregarded the thought and scanned her troops, surveying each one closely. Mariana and Jonathan were helping Rebecca down from the roof, and all three of them looked okay. Some of the leather armor Ian and Liam wore now bore deep gashes, but there was no blood. Kyree had a large cut across her forearm, but it didn't look too deep.

"Is everyone okay?" Anna asked, worried that someone might not be able to walk back to the Sanctuary.

"Anna, Ele!" Rebecca called. "Come quick!"

＊

Across Istamba, a shadow floated down a darkened hallway, gliding over the worn stone. The form flickered slightly as it came to a stop in front of a door, the gold face slightly open to reveal a lavish study inside. A broad desk stood in the middle of the room, the wood a deep brown so dark it was almost black. Gold trimmed the edges of the desk and reflected the bits of light around the room. The walls were draped in black fabric that appeared to absorb whatever light hit it.

"I do not appreciate your hesitation," came a voice from within. "It suggests failure."

The page pushed open the door and stepped inside. Sun streamed in from a single window, filling the small room with golden light, and deepening the shadows clinging to the walls. King Roland stood facing the window. His eyes were closed to the brilliant palette of orange and red filling the sky. Breathing deeply, he could almost taste his victory. He had sent his mate out to kill the Sanctuary's General. Without their leader, the humans would surely crumble.

He turned slowly from the window and opened his eyes.

"Good news, I trust," Roland said, his words dripping from his mouth like venom.

"The information from our informant in the Sanctuary was correct. The scouts, though difficult to catch, are easily defeated," the page responded.

"Hmmm. Perhaps associating with that human wasn't a mistake." Roland strode over to his desk and examined the map spread out there. A sharp pain sliced through his chest and he doubled over, grasping the sides of the desk for support. The wood splintered under his grip and the gold edging broke away.

The page took a hesitant step forward. "Do you need a healer, my King?"

Roland hissed, baring his fangs. "I am not sóme weakling human."

A wave of nausea hit him.

"Send a daka to Unalique immediately," he gasped out. "One of my personal servants should be there with Vivian. I want to know what happened."

"Of course, my Lord. Right away."

The page scampered away, eager to be free from the King's presence.

≈ 21 ≈

Anna rushed over to where Rebecca was kneeling over Oliver, who lay on the ground, clutching his left arm in pain. Tears pooled in his eyes and his face was red.

"What happened? Is he turning to shadow?" Anna asked, glancing nervously at Oliver.

"No, I don't think so, but his shoulder doesn't look like it should. Did anyone see what happened?" Rebecca asked.

Anna shook her head. "I was fighting a wraith."

Ele hurried over and examined Oliver's shoulder.

"Ele?" Anna asked. "You've taken a few healing lessons. Is it broken?"

"It doesn't look like it," Ele said. "I think it's just dislocated. I can put it back in, but I'll need someone's help to hold him down."

"I'll help you," Anna said. "There are bandages in my bag."

Ele nodded and grabbed Anna's bag from where she'd dropped it. Walking back over to Oliver, she knelt down by his side.

"Someone get him something to bite on," Ele said as she pulled out the spare bandages. "This is going to hurt, and we don't want anything out there to hear him."

Anna held Oliver's upper body down while Ele pulled his shoulder back into place. He grunted in pain, his cry muffled by the jacket arm he had clenched in his teeth. They made a makeshift sling with the bandages to keep his arm in place. Once they were sure it was immobilized, they pulled him to a sitting position.

"How do you feel?"

Oliver groaned. "It hurts, but not as much as before. I just want to get back to the Sanctuary." He dabbed at his eyes, his teeth still tightly clenched.

"We'll get you back," Anna said, "but we need to finish this mission first. I want three groups. Rebecca, Liam, Michael, you'll continue as lookouts. Alex and Ian, you start going through the weapons and armor left behind by the wraiths. Try to give it to whoever killed the wraith, if you can. Mariana, Jonathan, Kyree, and I will pair off and look inside the houses. Ele, look after Oliver. Make sure he doesn't fall asleep or go into shock. I want this done quickly. The sun's already starting to set and we need to get back to the Sanctuary as soon as we can."

Anna and Jonathan went over to the nearest building, and Jonathan went inside to see if there was anything to salvage while Anna covered the door. The other groups got to work as well. Soon, Anna's group had finished searching through the ruined buildings and rejoined Oliver and Ele in the center of the village.

"Anna," Alex called, "everything left behind by the wraiths has been collected and put in piles. This one's yours, and these are Jonathan's, Kyree's, and Mariana's."

"Great."

Anna walked over to the pile Alex had gestured to. The last wraith she'd killed had been well-armed and had left behind a good number of things. There were two matching swords that fit Anna's preferred fighting style perfectly, with fine leather sheaths. A twin pair of daggers in a matching dual sheath fit snugly at the base of her spine so she could grab them easily from her lower back. The wraith had also left behind a solid gold breastplate and matching bracers for her forearms, as well as cuisses for her thighs.

"I'll say one thing for this wraith," Anna remarked, "she certainly had good taste in weapons."

Anna bent down and picked up the final thing the wraith had left behind—a small leather bag. She unbuckled the top and sifted through the items inside. There were a few worn pages with writing she couldn't make out, a small, leather-bound book that looked like a journal, a folded map of Istamba, and a small picture preserved in a spotless gold frame.

"Oh my goodness," Anna said, holding out the picture, "this is a portrait of King Roland."

"Ew," Kyree said, making a face.

"Does that seem odd to anyone else?" Liam asked.

There was a murmur of agreement, and Anna turned back toward the small pile. The first few wraiths she'd killed had also left behind some nice weapons as well, and any that weren't wanted by her own troops would be put to good use by other regiments. Picking through the remainder of the pile, Anna got the feeling that the group of wraiths had been more important than she'd originally thought. Anna picked up the breastplate and held it out in front of her.

"Do you really think that armor's going to fit you?" Rebecca asked.

"Any gold armor should. I assume it's made the same way as their weapons. Haven't you ever noticed that when you use one, the grip will shrink to fit your hand better? I have a feeling the armor will do the same thing."

Anna slid the breastplate over her head and let it rest on her shoulders. It was much too large at first, but after a few seconds, it shuddered and shrank to fit Anna's form perfectly. Anna repeated the process with the other pieces of armor. Satisfied, she buckled the swords around her waist and fixed the daggers to her back.

"Everyone, put on whatever armor you can, but be sure to wear a jacket or something over it for now. The gold will reflect light and give away our position. Don't leave any weapons behind, gold or steel. Ele, Liam, help Oliver along. I don't want to stop until we're safe behind the barrier again."

As they walked back through the forest, Anna began flipping through the journal she found in the wraith's bag. Most of the scribbling was incomprehensible, and Anna guessed it was some kind of code or shorthand. Various sketches of the Sanctuary from different angles were tucked into the pages. These wraiths had been able to get all the way to the barrier without anyone knowing it, which was a little unnerving. The few readable journal entries would be of good use to the General, and perhaps the code for the rest could be broken. She turned the book to the back cover and found a name embossed across it. *Vivian Sandoval.*

"Has anyone heard of Vivian Sandoval?"

Jonathan furrowed his brow. "I haven't, but I have a feeling that regiment was rather important."

"What makes you say that?" Ian asked.

"Most wraith troops I've come across don't have full armor and they all have one or two weapons, but that group had two or three weapons each and every one of them had nearly a full set of gold armor. Only higher-ranking wraiths travel that heavily armed. Besides, there was something very familiar about their leader. I swear I've seen her before."

The conversation died, as Anna lost herself in thought. Though the group had many miles still left to cover, they were silent for the most part. While they'd talked and laughed on the way, the thought of another attack now kept them silent and fearful, especially considering Oliver's injury. Eventually, the sun disappeared behind the trees and night began to cover the forest.

"How much farther, Anna?" asked Alex. "It's getting awfully dark, and I don't want to be caught outside the barrier before the sun completely sets."

Anna pulled out a map and located their approximate position.

"Only another couple of miles. We'll get there before full dark."

Sure enough, the shimmering gold of the barrier came into view not long after Anna had spoken. They picked up their pace a little, and none of them relaxed until they were all safely inside.

"Ele, help Oliver to the infirmary," Anna said. "Ian, Mariana, Alex, get the extra weapons and supplies to the storage rooms. The rest of you, get some sleep. The officers may want to question you tomorrow about the raid today."

"What are you going to do?"

"I have to file a report. I'll be back soon."

Anna left her regiment and headed toward the Council chambers. Though it was past sunset, they were still meeting, and, Anna suspected, waiting for her regiment to return, since the 77th had arrived back at the Sanctuary later than they were supposed to. She walked up to one of the guards posted at the door and asked to be let in.

"I've just returned from a reconnaissance mission, and I need to report."

The guard nodded. "Name?"

"Captain Lieay."

"Wait here."

He knocked, and a page opened the door. The guard whispered something Anna couldn't hear before closing the door again. A few minutes later, the page opened the door and motioned for Anna to step inside.

"Captain Lieay," said Althea, "I'm glad to see you've returned. How did your regiment fare?"

"The mission was a success, but we were attacked. We killed the attacking wraiths, but there was something odd about them. They—"

Anna didn't get to finish as General Collins burst into the Council chambers.

"We have a problem," he announced, clearly agitated. "The mission we just got back from wasn't the attack we thought it was going to be."

"What do you mean, General?" Althea asked.

"Our scouts had reported that a high-profile wraith troop was going to be at Parnally, so we switched assignments between regiments to put my regiment in place. When we got there, there were only seven low-level wraith scouts. The wraiths must have learned that we were coming and changed their plans. Who was assigned to the reconnaissance mission at Unalique?"

Anna's head snapped up. "We were."

The General stared at Anna in surprise. "Your regiment? What happened? I need to know everything."

"We handled it. They attacked, we fought back. It really wasn't—"

"Who were they?"

"I don't know exactly. We all noticed something was different about them, and Jonathan Greggory said their leader looked familiar. They were heavily armed and most of them had full armor. Even the wraiths that attacked my home didn't have that much armor. The leader was a female. She had these in her bag," Anna said, holding out the journal and maps. "I think her name is on the inside cover. Have you heard of Vivian Sandoval?"

Gaping, the General took the journal and maps. "What happened to her?"

"She's dead."

"Are you sure? How can you be positive?"

"Well, considering I stuck my sword through her neck and she turned to dust, I'd say she's gone. Why? Who was she?"

"She was Roland's mate."

Anna gasped. "She carried a portrait of Roland!"

"Anna, we need a full report. Start from when you arrived in the village."

"Okay." Anna described everything she could remember. As she talked, the room seemed to get quieter and quieter. The General began pacing, and Althea's eyes never left her face. When she finished, Anna folded her hands in front of her and waited for someone to break the deafening silence.

"And what of your troops? How many injured or dead?" Althea demanded.

"One of my troops dislocated his shoulder and I sent him to the infirmary, but aside from a few small cuts and bruises, everyone else is fine."

Althea gaped at Anna. Anna wondered if she should say more, or just let Althea think things through.

"Thank you for your report, Captain," the General finally said. "After a mission, a regiment normally has the next day off, so take tomorrow to rest and recuperate. You may return to your troops."

Anna nodded. "Thank you, General."

She saluted and left the chambers, contemplating the odd meeting.

King Roland paced in his library, anxiously awaiting the news from Unalique. Surely, the humans wouldn't have been able to defeat his mate and her men. They were some of the best fighters he had.

"Mm . . . my . . . my Lord . . ." stammered a page.

The Wraith King slowly turned to the page, jaw clenched.

"I hope you have good news to deliver." Roland spoke slowly, drawing each word to a point.

"Well, um . . ."

"Spit it out, will you!" he snarled.

"We sent a daka to Unalique as you instructed, but there was no answer. We sent our nearest scouts, but all they found were piles of dust."

"What?" Roland grabbed the edge of his desk and threw it to the side. Vials of ink crashed to the ground, staining the rolls of parchment and maps that had slid to the floor. A dagger bounced and clattered into a corner. The desk itself slammed into the wall with a loud *thunk* that reverberated through the room. The King crossed the floor in two wide steps and seized the page by his throat.

"I'm so sorry, my Lord," the page choked out. "Your servant managed to survive the attack; he met with the scouts. He said the whole troop was taken out by a small human regiment."

Roland stumbled back, hand clutching his chest. "My Vivian," he mumbled. "My Queen, my Vivian." His eyes snapped back to the page, and he grabbed his arm.

"Which Regiment? Was it General Collins?"

"No, my Lord. It was a group of children."

"Children? And who killed Vivian?"

"It was a Captain. Captain Lieay."

Roland screamed and hurled the page against the nearest wall. The page slid to the ground from the force of the impact, but he scrambled to his feet as quickly as he could.

"Lieay?! When I gave the order to attack their Fort, I thought I made it very clear that I wanted every Lieay *dead*. And now I hear that one has escaped and killed my mate?"

Roland screamed in rage and destroyed what remained of his study. As he stood amid the debris, he glared at the small sliver of moon adorning the night sky.

"Find out where Captain Lieay is now," he commanded. "I have a debt to settle with her."

❧ 22 ❧

"Captain, wait!"

Anna turned back to see General Collins rushing after her. "General?"

"I was very impressed with how you and your troops handled yourselves in Unalique. Many regiments wouldn't have come back from a fight like that in one piece. In addition, you have dealt a large blow to Roland and his forces. They will be seriously disheartened by the loss of their Queen. Each of your troops will receive Stars of Valor and you are being promoted to Major. Please promote your Lieutenant to Captain."

"General, I—I don't know what to say."

"No need to say anything. Just keep up the good work."

"I . . . Thank you, Sir," Anna said, staring as he pinned her new Major's pin to the exposed fabric on her shoulder above her armor.

"I'll see you at Assembly in a few days, Major."

The General paused as if unsure. He placed one hand on her shoulder, then removed it. With a small wink, he walked away, leaving her standing in the hallway, open-mouthed. She touched her right shoulder, feeling the cold metal of the new pin. It felt right there, visible to wraiths. Visible to anyone else who would try to kill her friends.

She made a mental note to move her first Star to her shoulder as well, and returned to her barracks where her regiment was waiting. She took off her armor and hung it up, along with her new weapons, before going into the main sleeping area. When she entered, her troops were still up, unwilling to go to sleep until they'd heard what had happened with the Council.

"Is Oliver alright?" she asked.

"He'll be fine," Jonathan said. "Ele is with him in the infirmary. What did the Council have to say? Did they give a reason as to why they didn't warn us of the danger? Or didn't they know?"

"There was a mistake regarding the assignments. Regiment 21 was originally supposed to go to Unalique, but they heard of a high-profile wraith group that was supposed to be at Parnally. Unfortunately, the wraiths scouts discovered our plan to attack them there, and they diverted to Unalique, where they found us. But the Council is very pleased with our performance. They'll be sending over Stars of Valor for each of us, and they promoted me to Major."

She reached over and unpinned Alex's Lieutenant pin, replacing it with the Captain's insignia.

She twirled the Lieutenant's pin in her fingers, and she remembered how she'd felt on first seeing it. Though it had been a few weeks since she'd last been promoted, it all still felt so new. "I know you're all tired, but with Alex promoted to Captain, I'm free to select a Lieutenant. I'm open to your input."

Anna looked at the group expectantly. No one wanted to speak first.

"I suggest Liam," Michael finally said.

"Oh, I don't think . . ." Liam began, then paused and collected his thoughts. Clearing his throat, he said, "I'm flattered, but I don't think I would make a good leader. Thank you, but I respectfully decline."

Anna nodded. She thought Liam underestimated himself, but she couldn't select a leader who wasn't committed to the job. "You don't give yourself enough credit, but I won't force you into anything. Any other thoughts?"

"Well," Rebecca said, "I think Jonathan deserves a chance. He's lived here the longest, and he would make a great leader."

Rebecca's recommendation was met with nods of approval.

Jonathan had been a calming voice of reason since the regiment was created, and he was well-liked. Anna agreed, and now that she and her second were both younger, having Jonathan as a formal officer brought her comfort.

"Jonathan, do you accept this promotion?"

"I do. Thank you all."

Anna stepped forward and pinned the metal insignia on his right shoulder, mimicking her own pins' new placement.

"So, what now?" Liam asked.

"It's pretty late, so we should probably get some sleep. The General said we have all day tomorrow to rest, but I'd like to do a little group training. I think we need some practice fighting together as a large group."

Her troops groaned, and Anna waved them down. "It won't be that bad. We'll take it easy."

A few weeks later, Anna left Alex in charge of training while she went to the weekly Assembly. They'd been given a few more assignments for barrier patrol, but because of their success in their first mission, she continued to remain optimistic about their potential assignment this time. She was one of the first to arrive at the meeting room and was immediately pulled aside by Major Ravenall.

"Wait a moment, Major Lieay," the older officer said.

"Major Ravenall, what can I do for you?" The words caught in her throat; she hadn't considered that this woman who she admired was now her equal, at least by rank.

"General Collins is away on another mission and he left me to run today's session. He wanted to send you to Corosia. We've heard reports of a few humans stuck there, and we'd like you to retrieve them."

"Corosia?" Anna repeated. "That's an overnight mission. I didn't think the Council would allow us to have such an assignment."

"The General believes you're ready," replied the Major, "as do I. You and your regiment have done well so far. This is a great opportunity to prove you're capable of more."

"Thank you, Major. We'll leave at once."

The Major nodded. "The supply rooms should have your rations and supplies ready. Good luck. And come home safe, Major."

Anna saluted and walked briskly back to her barracks. She wanted to leave as soon as possible so they could travel as far as they could while it was still light out.

"Gather what you need to be out in the forest for a few days," Anna shouted as she reached the barracks.

"We're going on an overnight mission?" Kyree asked.

"Yes. There are a few humans in Corosia who need help returning to the Sanctuary."

"Are we really ready for this?" asked Michael.

"The General seems to think so," Anna replied, "and I do too. Ele, go to the infirmary and request mission first aid supplies. Kyree, Michael, Liam, go to the supply rooms and request rations for the 77th. They've been given our assignment information and should have everything ready."

Kyree nodded. "We'll be back soon."

Anna looked around at her remaining troops. "Jonathan, go to the command rooms and see if they have extra amulets we can take. I have my own, but I don't think anyone else does. Everyone else, pack up. I'd like to get as far as we can before it gets dark."

Ian caught Anna's eye just before he started packing up. She'd been wondering if she should address what he'd said to Colonel Wells a few weeks ago, but she didn't think he'd take kindly to eavesdropping.

"Ian," she said softly, "can I talk to you for a moment?"

Ian glanced around the barracks. "I guess."

Anna waved him over to the back of the room so they wouldn't be overheard. "I've been thinking about something a lot the past few weeks, and I couldn't decide whether to bring it up with you or not."

"If this is about me giving you a hard time when we first started—"

"No," Anna said, holding up a hand. "Do you remember when you went to exchange your sword? I know Colonel Wells spoke to you."

Ian opened his mouth to respond, but shut it immediately. He looked down at the ground. "Major, I . . ." he fell silent.

"I just wanted to say thank you," Anna said, and Ian's eyes snapped to her face. "You didn't have to defend me to the Colonel, but I really appreciate that you did. The way you questioned my choices helped make me a better leader, and what you said to Wells . . . it meant a lot to me."

Ian looked away, uncomfortable. "I just spoke the truth, Major. I didn't do anything special."

"Nevertheless, thank you." She briefly placed a hand on his shoulder before walking back to her trunk. "And my friends call me Anna," she said over her shoulder. As she turned back around, she thought she saw a smile cross his face.

Jonathan entered the barracks, catching Anna's attention. "They only gave me five," he called as he rejoined the group, "but I have my own." He pulled a pendant free from his armor. "It was a gift from your parents before I left the Fort."

Anna stared at the object, immeasurably moved to know that her parents had trusted Jonathan enough to give him such a precious item. She'd been pushing thoughts of them away but couldn't avoid the memories now, and so it took her a minute to regain a voice steady enough to reply. "I just hope we won't need them. Will you distribute them? I don't think it matters who carries them, but . . . maybe choose the ones you consider most responsible?"

The rest of her troops returned not long after, excited to venture into the forest once again. Anna led them out on the western side and kept them at a steady march as they made their way to Corosia. This journey started out much more smoothly than their first mission. After their success at Unalique, everyone was more confident in their abilities, and the thought of meeting a wraith wasn't nearly as intimidating.

Anna's eyes constantly shifted to watch the shadows, but she felt like she didn't have to be as worried about her troops in a fight, now that they knew what to expect. They still kept their voices low and listened for the unseen animals, but they were all relatively comfortable walking through the trees.

Shadows began to grow around them as they walked, and the sun sank lower and lower. A few of them began to fiddle with the amulets, the translucent pieces catching the light from the sunset. Anna pulled out a map and saw they were close to an old village. The crooked homes appeared in the gaps between the trees, and Anna called for them to stop.

"We can stay here for the night," she said, studying the map. "It should only take us a few hours to get to Corosia in the morning."

"Where are we?" Michael asked.

Anna scanned the map again. "I think we're in Habelit."

Ian looked around at the empty houses. "There's not much here."

"After people started moving north trying to escape the wraiths, most of the other villages evacuated as well, even if the wraiths never came near them. Aside from the mountain villages in the far north, I think the only people still in their villages are those too scared to make the trip to the Sanctuary on their own. That's where we come in."

"I can't believe everyone just had to leave," Ele said, peering into one of the homes.

Oliver came to stand next to her. "That's why we joined the army, right? To stop this from happening."

Ele nodded and took a deep breath.

"Do we have to sleep in the houses tonight?" Liam asked. "They seem kind of spooky."

"We can make camp in the town center," Anna answered. "Jonathan, please work out watch shifts. I'd like three people on guard throughout the night. Also, I know we didn't see any wraiths on our way here, but I don't want to start a fire tonight."

Her troops nodded and went about setting up camp. Kyree, Ian, and Mariana took first watch, and the rest of them settled in for the night.

Anna was woken early in the morning along with Alex and Rebecca for the final watch. As the sun rose over the top of the trees, she roused the rest of her troops to continue on to Corosia. She slowed their pace as they reached the village. They carefully walked past the first few houses, but saw no one as they wove through the lopsided homes.

"Hello," Anna tentatively called out. "We're soldiers from the Sanctuary. We're here to escort you back there safely."

A door of one of the houses slowly opened and a face peered out from behind it. A few people emerged, and a family came out from another home. A young boy clutched his mother's skirts and a little girl hid behind her brother

"You're from the Sanctuary?" a man asked. "But you're children."

Anna swallowed her annoyance. "We may be younger than the average soldier, but I promise you we're capable. If you'll grab your necessities and whatever personal possessions you can carry, we'll start the journey back."

The man nodded and disappeared into the house again. Moments later, he came back out with a few other people. Each had a small bag slung across their back. The family came back out from their home carrying what supplies they could.

Anna turned to her troops. "Help them carry whatever's left. The Sanctuary is in no position to turn down supplies."

After some shuffling of packs, the refugees were grouped together in the town center with Anna's troops standing off to the side.

"Everyone ready?" Jonathan asked.

The refugees nodded.

"Great. Anna, are you ready?"

"Shh," Anna said. She was staring intently at the southern edge of the village.

"Anna," Alex whispered.

"Jonathan, Ian, Mariana, with me. The rest of you, protect them."

Anna drew her swords and crept toward the edge of the village, with Jonathan, Ian, and Mariana close behind. As she got closer to the tree line, she could see red eyes peering out at her. Five wraiths jumped out of the trees at them. Anna took the head off the first one before he could attack, and engaged a second while her companions took on the others. They were only scouts, weak compared to the wraiths they'd fought before. Mariana spun around Anna's back and jabbed her blade at a wraith's midsection. Metal hit metal, the sound reverberating through the trees. Ian thrust his spear through one of the last wraiths, and dust trickled to the ground.

After the last wraith had disintegrated, Anna turned back to her troops. "Let's get moving. There may be more of them, and I'd like to get as close to the Sanctuary as we can before nightfall." She motioned to the refugees. "You stay toward the middle of our group just in case."

One of the men stepped forward. "Why should we listen to you?"

"As a Major, I am the ranking officer here. You will listen to what I say," Anna said with a cold look. "So stay toward the middle of my troops, and we won't have a problem. Let's move out."

Anna stalked off into the forest and Jonathan hurried to catch up to her.

"That may have been a little harsh," he said.

Anna scoffed. "Would it have been harsh if Colonel Wells said it? Or General Collins? I'm tired of not getting the respect the other officers are given. It shouldn't matter that I'm fourteen. It shouldn't matter that I'm a girl. What matters is that I've proven my skills as a warrior and a leader."

"Okay, okay," Jonathan said, laughing. "I understand where you're coming from. But if it makes you feel better, Collins had to fight to earn his respect as well."

"Not as hard, I'd imagine," she paused and glanced at Jonathan, "but thanks."

The rest of the day passed without incident. The refugees were silent for the most part, only asking for water or a break. The regiment had to slow their pace so the refugees could keep up, but the civilians still complained about how fast they were going. When they stopped for the night, they were only ten miles from the Sanctuary. Anna considered continuing, but the refugees' complaints had become louder and louder the more tired they got. She didn't like the idea of spending the night in the forest, since the additional untrained people would be difficult to guard.

She scanned the refugees' faces once more. The little boy was rubbing his eyes and the girl had fallen asleep in her father's arms. The others looked almost as exhausted as the children. Her mind made up, she signaled to her troops to set up camp and distribute the extra rations.

"We're just outside of Telarta," Anna announced. "That leaves us only ten miles to get to the Sanctuary tomorrow. I know wraiths don't generally come this far north, but with the extra people, I want four-person watches tonight. I'll take a double shift."

Ian woke Anna in the middle of the night for her watch. She rubbed the sleep from her eyes and sat up against the trunk of a tree. A few hours into her watch, one of the refugees woke up and came to sit next to her.

"I'm never going to get any sleep," he grumbled. "How do you and your troops do it?"

Anna smiled in the darkness. "We were all nervous on our first mission. I just had to keep telling myself not to give up. We joined the army to try to make a difference, and if a few nights in the forest is what it takes, that's what we'll do."

"I don't think I'll ever get used to it. I'm Kaiden, by the way. Kaiden Wooley."

"Anna Lieay."

"Lieay? You wouldn't be related to—"

"Yes," Anna interrupted. "They were my parents."

"Ah. Your determination to fight makes more sense now."

"We all wanted the chance to avenge our friends and family. You're lucky you still have yours." Anna frowned and gazed off into the darkness. She didn't want the memory of her parents to fade, but it was becoming a little frustrating to only be known for their accomplishments.

"I just hope this war will be over soon. I don't want my children to be raised in fear."

"We'll stop the wraiths," Anna said firmly. "If you'd like to try and sleep a little more, you'll be perfectly safe. I promise."

Kaiden nodded. "I suppose I can try." He rose from the ground and went back to lay next to his children. A few moments later, Anna could hear soft snoring coming from his direction.

"I will stop Roland," Anna whispered to the night. "He won't tear any more families apart."

Anna remained leaning against the tree for the rest of the night. She woke everyone early, and they broke down their camp quickly. They were all eager to return to the Sanctuary.

Anna smiled when she saw the familiar gold shimmer of the barrier. Major Ravenall met them on the southern quad.

"Major Lieay, I assume everything went alright."

"There were a few wraiths at the village, but it wasn't anything we couldn't handle."

"Good." Major Ravenall turned to the refugees. "There's hot food in the dining hall, and a soldier will show you where you can stay."

"Thank you," one of the men said, and they all left with food on their minds.

The Major turned back to Anna. "You and your troops have the rest of the day and tomorrow to rest, as usual, but be ready to attend the General Assembly in two days."

"Thank you, Major."

Anna led her troops back to the barracks to unload their weapons. She followed them back into the sleeping quarters where they all looked at her expectantly.

"Did I miss something?" she asked, confused.

"Well," Oliver began, "we thought that we needed something to energize us and set us apart from the other regiments, and we came up with a cheer."

"A cheer?"

"For the record," Jonathan interrupted, "I was against this."

Oliver rolled his eyes. "The rest of us think it's awesome."

"When did you have time to do this?" Anna asked.

"We've been working on it every time you were at Assembly," Kyree said.

"You mean the times I left you to do conditioning drills?"

Her troops glanced at each other, but no one seemed very sorry. "Well, we found a better use for our time."

Anna chuckled. "Okay, let's hear it."

Oliver smiled and looked at the rest of the troops, "Seven-Seven!" he yelled.

"Hoo-hoo-hoorah! Hoo-hoo-hoorah! Hoo-hoo-hoorah!" everyone yelled back.

"How long did that take you?" Anna smirked.

"Hey! We thought it was good. Besides, I think it gives us some character. What's wrong with it?"

"Nothing. I like it."

Jonathan let out an exasperated sigh while Oliver and the rest of the group grinned.

"I believe we've started a tradition," Liam said.

even-seven!" Anna called when she glimpsed the Sanctuary towers through the trees.

"Hoo-hoo-hoorah! Hoo-hoo-hoorah! Hoo-hoo-hoorah!" everyone echoed.

A few weeks ago, Collins had sent her and her troops to restock and repair the safe houses between the Sanctuary and Fort Lieay. They were in terrible shape, and the Council had been neglecting their upkeep for far too long. It had been a longer mission than most, and Anna had almost said no when the General first asked her, but it had been a great bonding experience for her and her troops.

As they broke through the barrier, she saw General Collins coming out to meet them on the southern quad.

"Major, I take it the mission went well," Collins said.

"That it did, General. The safe houses are stocked, and Roland is down about fifty more soldiers."

He nodded. "Well done, Major. Since the mission took so long, the next two days are yours to recuperate."

"Of course. Thank you."

Anna led her regiment back to the barracks and took off her weapons and armor with a grateful sigh. She rolled her shoulders to alleviate some of the soreness from carrying so much weight the past few weeks.

"The General said we have the next two days to rest," Anna said, "so you all can do what you'd like."

"What are you going to do?" Liam asked.

"I'm headed to the library," Anna said. "I know we restocked the main safe houses between here and Fort Lieay, but I thought there were more safe houses throughout Istamba. I just can't remember where."

Liam shrugged and rolled over on his bed. Within a few moments, soft snoring could be heard coming from his direction.

"I think he's got the right idea," Mariana said as she too lay down on her bed and closed her eyes.

"I'll come with you to the library," Alex said.

Anna smiled, and the two left for the main building. She and Alex took opposite sides of the library, looking for something that might tell them about the other safe houses in Istamba.

"What about this?" Alex asked. "The spine says, 'The Watchtowers and other Ancient Buildings.'"

"Maybe," Anna said.

Alex pulled the book from the shelf, but it only came out halfway. There was a small click and the bookcase swung backward with a cloud of dust.

Alex's eyes went wide. "Oops."

"Oops? That's amazing!"

Anna grabbed a torch from the wall and entered the darkened room. She saw two torches flanking the door and lit them to reveal another, smaller room with books and scrolls. A small table littered with more scrolls sat in the center of the room.

"It doesn't look like anyone's been in here in years," Alex said. He lifted up one of the books to try and read it, stirring up a cloud of dust in the process. He coughed, and the book fell loudly to the ground.

"Hey," Anna called from near one of the shelves, "these journals look like a complete set." She grabbed an armful and set the journals down on the table.

"Ransley Elwin." Alex read off one of the covers.

"You read some and I'll read through the others?" Anna asked.

Alex nodded, and they each picked up a journal, squinting to read the cramped handwriting.

The first journal Anna picked up contained detailed accounts of supplies stored in the Sanctuary, as well as the comings and goings of people, no matter if they stayed a night or a few weeks. There were notes from every Council meeting, though Ransley Elwin wasn't actually a Council member. Very rarely were there any passages about wraiths, as though the man didn't care about them at all. Mostly, he described how and why everyone he met annoyed him and how he should be in charge of the Sanctuary.

After about an hour, Alex threw down the journal he was holding in disgust.

"I don't know how you're still reading this stuff," he said. "All he does is complain."

"Well, this is interesting," Anna said.

"Let's hear it."

"'The whole of the Sanctuary has been halted in shock. Alistair Lieay has given a demonstration of his power that will surely allow me to expel him from Istamba indefinitely. He destroyed an entire regiment of wraiths in a single blast of golden light. When he turned around to face the surprised onlookers, his eyes were glowing with the same strange power and his body was shaking with dangerous rage. He let loose a yell, and a second wave of power was released upon the Sanctuary. Two of the watchtowers were turned to rubble, and a shimmering veil has descended around the perimeter. He then collapsed from the effort and still lies on the southern quad, as all are too scared to go near him.

"'This display of magic is surely all I will need to turn the Council against him permanently, for none of our magicians have a strength anywhere near what he has shown. I only hope this strange barrier surrounding our Sanctuary will not harm our people.'"

"So your ancestor created the barrier?" Alex asked.

Anna nodded. "I guess so, but there's more. 'Despite his anger and the obvious threat that Lieay poses to the Sanctuary, the Council has rejected my request that he be expelled from our company. They say that his power could be of great use and that we must take the risk. To add further insult, he has been asked to head the magicians' task force. I have heard they plan to enact Straga Impreva upon our best warriors. I have argued against this course of action at every opportunity. The spell has never been attempted, and the repercussions of attempting it are a mystery. I fear it may kill our greatest fighters and leave us far worse off in this war, but the Council has dismissed my worries and advice. They have a sickening faith in Lieay that I cannot understand, especially since they discovered that the shimmering barrier he has placed around the grounds repels wraiths.'"

"This guy really hates your ancestor."

"So it would seem." She continued to read aloud, "'I shall never forgive Lieay for what he's done. He led the magicians through Straga Impreva. Every magician lost their power and half of them perished. Twenty soldiers volunteered for the spell; my own brother volunteered without my knowledge. Eight of the soldiers perished, my brother among them. Lieay has gone too far this time. Surely now the Council will see him for the villain he is.'"

Anna paused and skimmed through the next few pages, "It doesn't look like there's much more of importance. He just continues to complain about everyone in the Sanctuary."

Anna thumbed through to the end before setting aside the journal and continuing on to the next in the series. Alex wandered over to see what else was on the shelves. A few minutes later, Anna gasped and nearly dropped the journal she was holding in surprise.

"Everything okay?" Alex asked.

"Depends on your definition of okay."

"What does that journal say?"

"'I have reached my fiftieth name day and had to watch everyone celebrate Lieay's latest achievement. He had just returned from a campaign to enact barriers around various places across Istamba. I have been contemplating my future for some time now and have finally reached my decision. I will leave this Sanctuary and Istamba. I have heard of a land across the southern sea, and I will seek a better life there.'

"It then picks up a few months later. 'Even across the sea, I cannot escape from Lieay's supposed greatness. They tell stories of his strength in all the villages I've been to. I cannot understand their fascination with him. Therefore, I have left civilization in search of an ancient cave that is rumored to contain the first blood of humanity. Supposedly, the first blood will grant whoever drinks of it immeasurable strength and power. Everyone I've spoken to claims it's a myth, but in my experience, all myths stem from truth. I am deep in the mountains and haven't seen anyone in months. My food supply is dwindling and I fear death is coming quickly.'"

"He just dies?" Alex asked.

"Will you stop interrupting?"

"Sorry," Alex said sheepishly, "go on."

Anna shook her head before continuing, "'I have found the cave. The walls are filled with the stories of creation. Though they are scratched into the wall, they are filled in with gold. However, the true treasure lies deep within. At the back of the cave flows a spring of blood. I could not resist my thirst and tasted of the spring. The blood burned through my body, erasing all sense of humanity, leaving behind strength and power like I've never known.

"'Using my newfound strength, I have destroyed the cave's entrance so that none may take advantage of this gift that I have been granted. I have been reborn, and with this comes certain responsibility. I will cast off my human past and become Ezra Roland, King of the Wraiths. I will return to Istamba and wipe out the family that has done so much wrong to my own. Lieay and his descendants will cower at my might, powerless as I conquer their land.'"

~ 24 ~

So Roland—the Roland we're fighting—used to be human and a resident of the Sanctuary?" Alex asked.

"It looks that way."

"Is there anything else in the journal?"

"No," Anna said. "It just ends."

"That's too bad," Alex muttered. "I would have liked to know how he got back to Istamba."

"Maybe there's another journal on the shelves somewhere and I just missed it."

The two began searching through the remaining books to try and find another matching journal, as thoughts swirled through Anna's mind.

"Anna," Alex called, "I think you should look at this."

Anna walked over to look at the box Alex was staring at. Engraved on the front was *Alistair Lieay.*

Anna gasped. "Amazing."

"I know, but it won't open."

"Let me see," she replied. As soon as she touched the lid, it opened with a soft click. "Maybe he used some kind of magic so that only he or one of his family could open it." Anna stared at the box for a few moments, wondering what to do. "Why don't we take it back to the barracks? I bet the rest of the regiment will want to know about this."

"Really?" Alex asked. "You don't think we should keep this to ourselves?"

Anna raised one brow. "They're our friends, Alex. And this is probably really important. I want them to know."

"I guess just as long as no wraiths find out," Alex said quickly.

Anna nodded and cradled the box. Aside from her mother's dagger, this was the only thing she had from her family. Everything else had been left at Fort Lieay and was likely destroyed by the wraiths in the raid.

When they got back to the barracks, Anna set the box on her bed and sat down. Alex woke everyone, and the two quickly explained what they had found. Though most had just woken up, they were all eager to know what secrets her ancestor had left behind. She opened the box, and gingerly pulled out a book nestled inside. The edges were lined with gold and the cover had a carving of the Sanctuary, also made of solid gold. The book was obviously old, but it was still in pristine condition. She flipped it open and leafed through the gold-lined pages.

"Whoa," she said, "this is a spellbook."

Jonathan's head snapped up. "Impossible. I thought all magical artifacts were destroyed centuries ago."

"So did I," Anna muttered. She flipped through a few more pages before a title caught her eye. "Straga Impreva."

"What?" Alex asked.

"Straga Impreva," she repeated, "it means Warrior Enhancement. Must be that spell Ransley mentioned."

"Are you sure? If we could recreate it, we could defeat the wraiths once and for all. How does it work?"

Anna skimmed the page and turned to the next one. It read 'Frata' or healing. She could barely make out a few frayed edges in between the two pages, as if some had been ripped out.

"Bad news. It looks like there's a few pages ripped out. All it says here is what happens to the subjects of the spell."

"What else was in the box?" Rebecca asked.

Anna glanced down in her lap and pulled out one of a pair of journals. Her brow furrowed upon reading the text.

"Is everything okay?" Jonathan asked.

Anna nodded slowly. "Yes, it just looks like he wrote these in Ancient Stambian."

Ele groaned. "So we'll never know what they say? I don't think there's anyone alive that knows how to read Ancient Stambian."

"Actually, I can," Anna said, her face turning red from embarrassment.

"Really?"

"Yes. My father found some old books in a crypt underneath our keep and taught himself. I found the books one day and begged him to teach me. I can't really speak it, but I can read enough to translate."

"Seeing as you're the only one who can understand them, will you read aloud?" Oliver asked.

"Sure, but it'll be slow going. It's not easy to read and translate at the same time," she paused so she could put herself in the right mindset to read the old language. "'War has broken out across Istamba, and it's high time the northern and southern territories unite to vanquish the wraiths once and for all. I have led my troops north to the Sanctuary as a sign of good faith, and they in turn have welcomed us as friends and allies. I have sent my magicians to join their task force, but I have resolved to keep my own magic hidden. I know not the strength of the northern magicians, but if they are similar to my own men, my greater power may not be well-received. One man remains suspicious of my men and me. Ransley Elwin seems intent on blocking my progress for peace at every turn. My only consolation is that everyone dislikes him. The Council is deaf to his words. I don't know if they are keeping us close because they truly want to be allies or if they are just using our resources to win this war. I hope for the former, and I will strive for friendly relations for as long as I can.'"

Anna paused for a moment, skimming over some pages. "Sorry.

A lot of this middle section just describes technical details about the war. Here's something interesting. 'My magic has been revealed. I forgot how volatile my emotions make my power, and lost control. Ransley was yelling at me for losing some men in our latest campaign. All the while, a wraith regiment was advancing on the Sanctuary. My anger got the better of me and I let my power loose. I managed to aim it at the wraiths and ended up destroying the entire regiment. I could still feel my power surging. I let it escape into the air, creating a shimmering barrier around the Sanctuary, but destroying two watchtowers in the process.

"'I believe this barrier is made out of my magic and will keep the wraiths out, but that remains to be seen. I know Ransley will be requesting that I be expelled from the Sanctuary, but I hope the Council will see the value in our continued alliance.'"

"Wait," Liam interrupted, "your ancestor created the barrier?"

"That's what I said," Anna responded. She skimmed over a few words before she found her place again. "'Barely a day has passed since my outburst of power, and already people are praising me. The magicians' task force is requesting I lead them. I wish people would stop idolizing what I've done. My magic may be powerful, but it is based on emotion. Therefore, I cannot always control it. I have noticed that, because of my power, I'm a fair bit stronger and faster than my peers and am more easily able to fight our enemy. The Council has ordered me to lead the task force through Straga Impreva to enhance the abilities of some of our stronger fighters. I am worried, though. This spell has never been attempted, and for good reason. The price of failure is death. I will warn the Council once more, but if this is the price for an alliance, I will respect their wishes.'"

"Ha! He didn't like the Council either," Oliver said, laughing.

"Shh," Rebecca scolded, "I'm listening."

Anna raised her voice to be heard over the conversation. "'In an effort to dissuade the Council from performing the Straga Impreva, I've created hundreds of protective amulets. I've imbued small pieces of steel with my own magic. My magic transformed the steel, making the metal translucent and almost opalescent. After being left in the sun, the amulets can store a single blast of light energy for the night. Should a wraith attack the wearer, the light would solidify them for a moment, allowing the human to run. Hopefully, this will be enough to discourage the Council from forcing us to enact a dangerous spell.

"'I do not understand the Council. They are calling the Straga Impreva a success. Of the twenty soldiers who volunteered, only twelve survived the process. Over half the magicians involved perished from the magical strain. The other magicians survived, but lost their abilities. Aside from myself, the only magicians left are healers, and they are very weak in skill. I fear we may be the last in Istamba. How twelve enhanced warriors are better than a team of magicians is a mystery to me, and yet the Council is pleased. I am leaving the Sanctuary soon. I have told the Council I will try to create more barriers around some houses throughout Istamba, but I really just need some distance to clear my head. I hope these houses may help lost humans stay safe from wraiths. Perhaps in the forest, I may find answers.'"

Anna stopped. "That's the end of this journal."

Alex handed her the other one. "This is the only other thing in here of use. The scrolls are blank."

She opened it and read the first few pages silently. "There's a lot missing. This picks up nearly thirty years later."

"What does it say?"

"'Just when I thought we were done fighting, another supposed Wraith King comes to claim Istamba. This one is worse than the last. He is intent on ruling everything and killing all but a few humans to keep as slaves. He calls himself King Roland, but I see him for who he truly is: Ransley Elwin, intent on righting supposed slights against himself while he was a resident of the Sanctuary. I have tried to propose a diplomatic solution to this feud. Ransley was once a trusted ally, and I thought he might be open to negotiating peace; however, each messenger I send never returns. I cannot justify this hope for peace any longer. Whatever reason Ransley has to hate us so much, he refuses to share. Sometimes I wonder if he even knows why he's fighting anymore.'"

"Wow," Michael said. "At least your ancestor tried for peace."

"A lot of good it did him. He basically killed all his messengers by sending them to Roland," Kyree argued.

"Wait," Mariana said, holding her hands up, "if there wasn't a peace treaty, why did Roland stay in the city for so long? I mean, he didn't leave for hundreds of years."

Anna rolled her eyes. "Maybe if you let me finish the journal, we'll find out."

A few troops mumbled apologies and Michael turned bright red. Anna gave a soft smile so they would know she wasn't really angry and kept reading. "'I believe I have a solution that will allow humanity to continue living here in relative peace. For some reason, Roland hates me above all other humans and has demanded my surrender a number of times. I know that if I were to agree to his demands, he would never keep his word; however, I believe I have succeeded in creating a magical pact, that, once enacted, cannot be broken. If this works, only I will need to surrender, and Roland will be confined to the wraith city for a thousand years. If this is my last act alive, it will be worth it to save my people.'"

Anna flipped through a few more pages. "The rest is just records of his people and supplies. It looks like there are also a few spells in the back."

"This is a lot of information to process," Jonathan said, "but I don't know how any of it will be of use to us."

"If there were still magicians in Istamba, the spellbook might be of some use, but I think you're right," Anna said. Even though there were no longer magicians in Istamba, she would still keep everything she'd found. Just having something from a family member, even if he'd lived almost a thousand years ago, made her feel closer to home.

Anna sifted through her ancestor's box again. She picked up one of the scrolls and stared at it. It didn't make sense for him to lock up a blank scroll. She unrolled it and looked at the blank page. It shimmered gold for a moment and something began to appear on its surface.

Anna sucked in a breath as words formed. She skimmed the scroll before reading aloud, "'I have placed a powerful spell upon this scroll, as well as the chest which houses it. Only those I most trust, myself and my family, may gain access to this knowledge. Upon this page, I leave my final secrets, for tomorrow, I shall surrender to King Roland to ensure the safety of my people.

"'Firstly, I have taken the spell of Straga Impreva from the master book and destroyed the instructions, for the risk is too great to ever use it again. However, in the second scroll, I have copied the knowledge so that my descendants may perhaps improve upon it. My hope is that they will have read my account of the spell and will take caution before performing it. In addition to the instructions, I have listed those twelve warriors who survived this dark magic.

"The Council does not know the intricacies of magical inheritance and does not understand that magic can only be passed to direct descendants. The death of the magicians during the Straga Impreva has diminished the availability of magical lines in the land. I believe, though, that the descendants of the warriors who survived the spell may also show signs of enhanced ability, should extreme stress cause the gift to reawaken.

"'Secondly, I have recounted the method of my creation of the barriers and the amulets. Members of the Sanctuary have no doubt been trying to recreate it, but only my abilities can fully allow the magic to work. Though magic is quickly dying out from this land, perhaps my own descendants will retain my power.

"'Finally, a word of caution to those who do retain my ability. You may believe it a gift, but only through extreme emotion may the full range of it be reached. As such, once awakened, it is unpredictable, and the likelihood of controlling it is quite low. Even dormant, it will enhance your natural abilities, and I would suggest not trying to awaken it further, for though it may seem a gift, it is, in reality, a curse. May the strength of humanity govern this land now and forever.'"

Anna reached the end of the scroll and fell silent.

"So that's how magicians came about?" Rebecca asked. "Through family lines?"

"I guess," Jonathan said, "and that makes sense with what little lore we still have about magicians as well."

"Hmm," Anna said. She grabbed the other scroll and unrolled it. Sure enough, the blank page shimmered and revealed the lost spells. She skimmed the page and her mouth dropped.

"Ele, let me see your right arm."

Confusion crossed Ele's face, but she extended her arm. "Is my arm important or something?"

Anna crossed over to Ele's bed and looked just below her elbow on her right forearm. Three dots, no larger than freckles, marked the skin in a perfect triangle.

"Anna?" Oliver asked. "What is it?"

Anna sat back on her bed. "I always wondered why we were better in training than everyone else," she mumbled, before speaking up. "Everyone, look at your right arm, just below your elbow."

"Three dots? What does that have to do with anything?" Ian asked.

"My ancestor said that marking appeared on the warriors who survived the spell. It's written here," Anna said, motioning to the scroll.

"Hmm," Jonathan said, "I don't have that."

"So we're all descended from the enhanced warriors of the Sanctuary? That's amazing," Liam exclaimed. He eyed Jonathan. "Well, almost all of us."

"And you still can't beat me in a duel," Jonathan said, laughing. "Besides, I like my family just the way it is." He leaned back against the wall.

"This actually makes a lot of sense," Alex interjected. "Surely you've all noticed how much better we are at fighting. If we're descended from these warriors, perhaps the spell they survived is still in our blood. Maybe this war with the wraiths has triggered some residual magic and activated the spell in us."

Anna pulled up her sleeve and stared at her own arm. "I don't have the mark either."

"Yes, but that scroll said his descendants would have magic that enhanced their abilities. Meaning you."

"That's all well and good, but I don't have any magic."

Jonathan jumped in. "Perhaps you don't have his power, but your abilities are still enhanced. I remember your parents seemed stronger than was natural. Even if you don't have actual magic, its effects still remain within your family."

"I suppose." Anna paused, uncomfortable with where the conversation was going. "Isn't dinner supposed to be ready soon?"

Not a minute after she spoke, the bell rang and they all leapt up, racing each other. It had become customary for whoever got to the dining hall first to start their cheer.

A few days later, Anna left her troops to run some group drills while she went to the General Assembly. She took her usual place in the back of the room, trying to ignore the looks from the other officers. Oliver had been talking with his parents about being descended from ancient warriors, and the story had spread through the Sanctuary like wildfire. Granted, she hadn't told her troops to keep it quiet, but she hadn't expected people to latch onto the story so quickly.

The only good thing that had come of the rumor was that the officers seemed to have more respect for her and her troops now, especially considering her success with each of her missions. Every now and then, her thoughts would return to the conversation she'd had with General Collins at the beginning of the war. Everything she'd done to prove herself to the officers was bringing her closer to her dream of reclaiming her parents' land. Now that she had the respect of the soldiers, she just had to work on maintaining the respect of the refugees.

"Major Lieay," said the General, and she turned her attention to him. "There's a group of wraiths holding the village of Oracha. We think they're trying to push into our territory. I'm sending you and your regiment to take care of them and reclaim the village."

"We will leave at once, General," she said.

"Good, dismissed."

General Collins began speaking to one of the Captains who

hadn't received a mission yet, as Anna left the Assembly. She hurried back to the barracks.

"Troops," she said, "we're headed to Oracha. We'll be in the forest overnight, so grab what you need for the next few days. This one's dangerous, so Ian, Mariana, Ele, go to the supply rooms and grab rations and emergency supplies. They should have our assignment already. Alex, could you grab some amulets?" Anna said.

Her soldiers nodded and went about performing the various tasks Anna had assigned. A few minutes later, Ian, Mariana, and Ele had returned and started distributing rations among the troops. Anna shouldered her pack and glanced around.

"Where's Alex?" she asked.

"Not sure," Jonathan responded. "Grabbing a few amulets shouldn't take long at all."

Finally, Alex returned to the barracks, and Anna gave him a questioning look.

"What?" he asked.

"Where were you? Getting amulets doesn't take that long."

Alex sighed. "Sorry. Someone from my village was in charge of the amulets today. I hadn't seen anyone from home in so long, I just couldn't help talking with her."

Anna's face softened. She wished someone else from Fort Lieay had survived. "I know how you feel. Let's get going."

They departed from the southwest side of the barrier, Anna leading the group.

"I'd like to go at least twenty-five miles today before we make camp," Anna said as they marched. "That way we should reach Oracha by midday tomorrow."

◆━━◆

When they approached Oracha the next day, Anna stopped her troops under the cover of the trees to discuss their plan.

"Our scouts didn't say exactly how many wraiths were going to be here, but I'd guess around thirty. Any less and they'd have a hard time covering the whole village. We should be able to take them if we surprise them. We can use the trees around the village as a cover; one group will circle around and we can attack from two sides. Split into two groups and try to make them even in terms of weapons. Alex, you take one group around to the far side of the village."

Alex nodded and led his group away through the trees. Anna directed her group closer to the destroyed homes. The roofs were sagging on most of the homes and walls had been burned on others. A few sagged against one another as they fought to stay upright.

Anna peeked around the side of a jagged wall, being careful not to touch the splintered edges. A group of wraiths were talking in the town center, and a few others patrolled the perimeter. Figuring Alex had made it around to the other side, she signaled to her group and they rushed into the village. As she ran at the wraiths, she caught sight of Alex and his group charging out.

Distracted by the two groups, the wraiths didn't know which way to focus. In their confusion, they hesitated. Anna swung her sword in a wide arc, taking the head off the nearest wraith while her troops killed some of the others before they could mobilize. She and Kylie darted through the middle of their ranks, dividing the wraiths even further. Anna occasionally caught glimpses of Rebecca and Michael firing arrows into the battle. She blocked a sword coming at her head and made eye contact with the startled wraith. Recognition momentarily flashed in his eyes before she stabbed him with her sword and turned him to dust. She turned to engage with the next wraith she saw, hoping the battle wouldn't last much longer.

After pulling her sword free from the disintegrating form of the last wraith, Anna said, "Check inside the houses for anything useful, but make it quick."

Her troops cleaned the dust off their weapons before starting to hunt through what the wraiths had left behind.

"It's almost too easy," Liam said, as he examined a pair of daggers one of the wraiths had dropped.

"I'd rather have easy battles we all come home from," Jonathan responded.

Liam looked away, his face reddening, and continued to look through the wraiths' weapons.

Anna cleared her throat to get their attention. "Let's focus and then get moving. I'd like to make it to Habanic before nightfall."

Meanwhile, across Istamba, King Roland was glaring at a map of the land, trying to anticipate the movements of the human troops. "Well?" he demanded angrily.

One of his advisors shifted one of the gold towers on the map. "What if we moved these troops north? Then—"

"No," barked the King. "That leaves this village too far from any of our troops."

A soft knock sounded at the door, and a page stepped inside.

King Roland looked up from the map. "This had better be important," he snarled.

"Yes, my Lord," the page said with a deep bow. "We just received a daka from our contact in the Sanctuary. The 77th Regiment has been assigned to reclaim Oracha. They are unlikely to return to the Sanctuary by nightfall and will have to spend the night in the forest."

Roland smiled and glanced at the map once more. "Marius and Lucian's regiments should be relatively close. Send them. I don't want those humans returning to the Sanctuary."

"Do you want them all killed?"

"I want to kill the Lieay girl. She killed my dear Vivian, and I will make her pay, myself."

"And the rest?" asked the page.

"Bring a few back alive. They can serve as a warning of what the future holds for those humans still hiding in their Sanctuary."

"What of our scouts holding the village?"

"They are already lost," Roland said with a wave of his hand.

"Of course, my Lord. I'll send a daka with your orders."

Roland dismissed the page and turned back to the map. The humans had become more daring, and he'd had to pull many of his troops back, tightening the perimeter around his city. With the 77th out of the way and the Lieay bloodline finally crushed, the humans would crumble.

~ 26 ~

Anna shouldered her pack and waited for her troops to join her at the edge of the village.

"I think we're ready," Alex said, after glancing around at the empty houses once more.

"Good." Anna motioned to her troops, and they began the march back to the Sanctuary.

After walking for a few miles, she noticed the birds had gone quiet. Only wraiths could make the animals run and hide, but she hadn't seen any. A few of her troops noticed the sudden silence, and Anna saw worry cross their faces. She picked up their pace and pulled out her map to trace a new course.

After a few more miles, she noticed quiet in the trees once again. Fear gnawed at her stomach as she continued to change their course. She and her troops moved more and more quickly, while still trying to make the least amount of noise as they could and scanning for any potential attackers. They'd long since ceased any conversation.

The afternoon slowly turned to evening, and it wasn't long before Anna began to have difficulty seeing the path ahead. She squinted at her map, trying to discern their location using the last bits of sunlight left in the day, and motioned for Jonathan to come closer.

"I think we have to make camp," she whispered, still worried about the possibility of something lurking in the trees.

Jonathan glanced around the small clearing they had stopped in. "I don't like it. We're too exposed."

"I don't either, but I'm not sure what else to do. We'll make too much noise if we try to continue on to the Sanctuary tonight. It's too cloudy for us to use the moonlight."

"True," Jonathan conceded. "I don't relish the thought of stumbling through the trees without any idea where we're going. But I still don't think we should camp here."

Anna weighed the options.

"Let's get the opinion of the others." She motioned to the rest of her troops to group up. "Alright, I think we have to make camp here for the night. We'll make too much noise trying to stumble through the forest in the dark. I know we don't usually camp like this, so I'll leave it to you. If you think we can continue, say so now."

Her troops glanced at one another.

"I don't like it," Rebecca said, "but at least if we camp, we minimize the chance of being found. Stomping through the trees makes too much noise."

"Surely we aren't that far from the Sanctuary," Liam countered. "I think we could make it."

"We could make it if we could see," Ian said, scowling.

Alex shook his head. "We need to camp. It's too dangerous to continue, and we'll end up drawing a lot of attention if we try."

"I want to know what you each recommend," Anna said. "Hand up if you want to camp."

Eight hands raised.

Anna sighed. She was leaning toward camping, but it was nice to know her troops agreed with her decision.

"Alright," Anna said, "we'll stop here for the night. But only set up the bare minimum, just in case we need to leave quickly. We're very exposed as it is, so I want four people on watch all night. Get as much rest as you can. We move at dawn."

Her troops formed their normal watch groups and spread out in the clearing. They arranged themselves in pairs, trying to make it look like the clearing was empty. Anna could tell they were nervous, though they tried to hide it. Usually, when they were outside the Sanctuary at night, she'd time their days and plot their course so that they would end at a village to camp. Wraiths generally avoided the villages, and the old houses provided some shelter and safety, even though many were falling apart from neglect.

The trek back to the Sanctuary worried her. It felt as though wraith scouting groups were everywhere, but with her course changes, she never did see one. At times, she almost felt as if they were being herded by the patrols. She didn't really want to make camp, but she didn't trust the forest enough to continue.

Anna settled into an uneasy sleep, only to be woken a few hours later for her watch. She rubbed the sleep from her eyes as she stood and surveyed the camp. Her troops had done a good job of concealing their presence. All weapons and traces of gold armor had been hidden. Had she not known they were there, her eyes would have slid past, seeing nothing out of the ordinary.

As she scanned the small clearing once more, darkness seemed to shift in the corner of her eye and her head snapped around to examine the bushes. She was trying to make sense of the shapes when the clouds shifted, allowing moonlight to filter through the trees. Red eyes peered out through the bushes. Anna went cold and her chest tightened.

"Wraiths!" she cried, drawing her swords.

Her troops were up in a flash, circling together so they couldn't be attacked from behind. Wraiths emerged from behind the trees in all directions, and the shadows around them thickened. Anna felt the familiar warm tingle fill her limbs as she prepared to fight, but they were at a disadvantage in the middle of the night. Their swords would only pass through the wraiths' shadowy forms, doing no damage. The humans' only hope was to escape by catching the wraiths off guard.

The wraiths were expecting a fight, but Anna had another idea. Though they'd only used the strategy in their training games, each of her troops knew the signal. She held her amulet up as high as she could and it released the blinding light of the sun it had trapped inside.

"Scatter!" she yelled as loudly as she could.

Her troops, surprised at first, turned northeast and fanned out through the trees, running toward the Sanctuary. Her call had the desired effect. The wraiths, blinded and weakened by the light trapped in the amulet, offered no resistance as Anna and her troops shoved past them.

Between the darkness and the trees, Anna quickly lost sight of her friends, but she wasn't worried. They couldn't have been more than fifteen miles from the Sanctuary. Now that they didn't have to worry about being silent, passing through the trees became a much easier task. She focused on one step at a time, intent on putting as much distance as she could between herself and the wraiths.

After about an hour, she could finally make out the shimmer of the barrier, glinting in the moonlight. Pushing past her exhaustion, she sprinted the final yards and came to a halt just inside the barrier. She turned to go back for her troops, but stopped. She wouldn't be able to see anyone in the dark and they were all far too spread out. She'd just have to hope that they'd all make it safely in.

Alex came crashing through the trees a little way to her left, with Liam close behind. One by one, her soldiers came running through the barrier out of the darkness, stopping in front of her and trying to catch their breath. Anna counted everyone, including herself. Her heart sank and her breath quickened.

"Ten," she whispered.

Jonathan stared at her, eyes wide. "What?"

"Ten." She frantically scanned everyone's face. "Michael. Where's Michael?"

There was a scream from the forest where they had just come from, but it was abruptly cut off. Anna felt her heart leap into her throat and her breath came out in strangled gasps. She squeezed her hands into tight fists and took a step back toward the forest, but Jonathan caught her before she could leave.

"I have to go back." Anna struggled against his grip.

"Anna, you can't." He said. "You can't take them all on at once. Not at night."

"I can't just leave him," she pleaded.

Jonathan turned her around to look in her eyes. "Getting yourself killed won't help anyone." He straightened and addressed the group, his voice thin and faltering, but with authority that dared anyone to argue. "Return to the barracks and sleep. Now. We'll regroup in the morning." He placed a hand on Anna's shoulder, as if offering permission for her to stay.

"Promise me you won't leave," he whispered.

Though it tore her soul to do so, she was weary and decided to trust her officer. "I promise," she whispered.

Heads low, and with a few muffled sobs, her troops followed Jonathan, trudging off to the barracks. Anna sank to the ground, her shoulders drooping and her fingers curling into the rocky dirt. She stared longingly out past the barrier, willing Michael to come back. Alex sat down beside her, pulling her shaking form close. She looked over in surprise; she thought he'd left with the others.

"It's alright," he said, "we were bound to lose someone eventually."

She recoiled at his casual statement. "I don't care," Anna whispered, "I should've done something. I should have—"

Alex glanced behind them before speaking. "You still could. You could go after him."

Anna shook her head. "Jonathan was right. There's nothing I can do in the dark. I don't even know if he's still alive."

She scooted closer to Alex, seeking comfort. Pressing her head into the side of his jacket, she allowed sleep to take her.

◆━━▶

As sunlight rose over the trees, the warmth of the new day woke her. Birds gently called to one another, their cheer deepening Anna's sorrow. She took a hesitant step toward the barrier. The sun was out. She'd have an advantage of any wraith out in the trees. She took another step before closing her eyes and turning away from the barrier. Jonathan was right. She couldn't go after Michael. She didn't know where the wraiths had taken him; she didn't know if he was even alive. And she wouldn't break her promise.

She clenched her hands into tight fists as the previous night's events replayed over and over again in her mind, the blinding light from her amulet flashing and illuminating the small clearing. The wraiths' faces contorted in pain as they blinked against the sudden light. Her troops' eyes narrowed in determination despite their fear. And more than everything else, she could still see Michael's face. She could see his mouth set in a tight line as he notched an arrow and held the bow out in front of him, half drawn. She could see a smile tugging at his lips when she yelled 'scatter' and he turned to run for the Sanctuary.

She clenched her fists tighter, until they hurt, hoping the pain would chase away some of the numbness in her heart. Her fingertips felt wet, and she opened her hands to look at them. Small cuts had been gouged in her palms from her nails, crisscrossing the old scars on her skin. Small drops of blood beaded from the new wounds. She didn't mind the pain. She'd take more if it meant having Michael back. She'd even take his place. As commander, it was her responsibility to protect her troops, and for the first time, she felt as if she had truly failed them.

A warmth radiated from her palms, and her eyes snapped back to her hands. The heat increased until it felt like her hands were on fire. Her breathing sped up as she fought the new pain. Gold light shimmered around the small cuts and they slowly closed as she watched, until there was nothing but unmarked skin left behind. The heat faded, leaving Anna staring at her hands in shock.

I must be seeing things, she thought, *I haven't slept, and with Michael* . . . She stopped her train of thought and dropped her hands to the side. She couldn't forget about Michael.

"Did you sleep at all?" Alex asked, coming up beside her and taking her hand in his.

"A little," Anna muttered. She tried to walk away, but Alex kept hold of her hand.

"Anna . . ."

She collapsed against Alex, silent sobs shaking her whole body. "It's my fault. Michael would still be here if it weren't for me."

"You got the rest of us back safely," Alex reminded her, squeezing her shoulders comfortingly.

"I chose to alter our course; I stranded us in the middle of the forest at night."

"We had to avoid the wraiths, right? What else could you have done?"

"I don't know. Something. Anything." Anna let out a shaky breath and pulled herself away. "I know we have today off, but if anyone wants to train, will you take over? I'm going back to the barracks to try to get some more sleep."

Alex agreed, and Anna wearily left the quad.

27

Anna woke just as the sun was beginning to set. Though she'd tried to sleep, she'd tossed and turned all day, shadows and darkness consuming her dreams. She didn't feel rested at all. She didn't really feel anything. Alex walked into the sleeping area just as she was getting up.

"Feel better?" he asked.

Anna scoffed. Her friend was dead, or worse, and she was supposed to feel better after a few hours of unsatisfactory sleep?

"Not even a little," she finally said. "Where is everyone?"

Alex shrugged. "Jonathan reported to Collins while you were asleep. Everyone else is scattered about the Sanctuary. They're all still trying to get over Michael."

Get over him? Of course they were; it seemed an insensitive way to say it, but in her training she'd learned that losing a soldier often brought tension to a team. Knowing this, Anna didn't say anything. The silence stretched between them.

Finally, Alex said, "Let's head to the quarry. You need some distance."

Reluctantly, she let Alex lead her to the northern part of the barrier. They wove through a few trees before leaving the grounds. The pair reached the quarry and sat against one of the boulders. Anna tilted her head back to watch the stars. Sadness welled up within her and she couldn't stop the tears from pooling in her eyes. She knew she hadn't been sleeping as much as she should the past few weeks, and with Michael's loss—

She took a deep breath and sat up again.

"I hate this war," she said.

A funny look crossed Alex's face. "It'd be strange if you didn't."

"I know. It's just . . . when I started fighting and training, my only thought was to avenge my people and my parents, and hopefully to reclaim my family's land." She paused and sighed. "But it didn't feel real until now. Every time we went on a mission or fought a battle, it felt like we were playing a game. Now Michael's gone and it's my fault." She pulled her knees to her chest and buried her face in her arms.

"I know what you mean," Alex said. "Sometimes I wonder what would happen if we just surrendered."

Anna's head snapped up and she stared at Alex. "Surrendered? Are you serious?"

"We wouldn't have to fight anymore. We wouldn't have to see our friends die."

"But we would be slaves, and the wraiths would still kill whoever they wanted to anyway."

"How can you be sure? Maybe the only reason they're so cruel is because we keep challenging them. Maybe if we tried for peace—"

"We don't want their kind of peace, trust me."

"But how do you know what their kind of peace is?" Alex asked.

Anna's eyes narrowed as she continued to stare at him. How could he not know what the wraiths would do? "You've heard about the holding camps. That's all they want from us—slaves to make their lives easier. How could that possibly be better than fighting for our freedom?"

Alex shrugged. "It was just a thought."

"Mmm." She sat in silence for a few moments, thinking about what Alex had said. It was borderline treasonous. She wouldn't say anything to the General, but he needed to be more careful about what he said and where. She'd talk to him tomorrow. Now, she was far too tired to care.

"Come on," she finally said, "we should get back before we're missed."

She stood, not waiting for his answer, and the pair made the trek back to their barracks.

The next morning, Anna led her troops in a few training exercises and some conditioning workouts before leaving to attend the General Assembly. She had to keep from scowling when she entered the Assembly. Instead of awe and respect, the other officers gave her looks of pity. Of course losing Michael had been hard on her and her troops, but it wasn't as though she were the only commander to lose a soldier. The other officers had lost three each at least, and they never got those kinds of looks.

What hurt the most was the look the General gave her, like she was a child who had just woken from a nightmare. When he finally got to her assignment for the week, she was grateful to leave.

"Major Lieay I'm sending you to check on Telarta," Collins said as he handed her a small scroll detailing the assignment. "Dismissed."

She saluted and left the room. Since the army had managed to push the wraiths back quite a way, some of the civilians residing in the Sanctuary had moved back to their homes. Most of the people who left had only come to the Sanctuary after regiments had been sent to bring them in, and they'd been eager to return to their homes. Their villages were very close to the Sanctuary, so most of them had never even seen a wraith. Though the nights were tense, the residents were able to return to something close to a normal life. The Council made sure to send regular missions to these nearby villages to make sure they were safe.

She returned to her troops and announced their assignment. "Gear up. We're headed to Telarta. We just need to make sure the settlement there is doing alright."

Her troops packed up their weapons and headed out. Since

Telarta was only ten miles from the Sanctuary, they were back by dinner.

For the next few weeks, they received similar assignments, rotating through different villages. General Collins claimed it was good for the people to see the 77th. He said that their presence gave everyone a morale boost, but Anna knew he was keeping them close on purpose. They had lost Michael, yes, but that didn't mean her whole regiment was so distraught that they couldn't function. She made up her mind to talk to the General after the day's General Assembly, hoping she could prove to him that they were still a strong unit.

"We do have one final piece of business," said the General as he stood in front of the Assembly. "There is a mission that needs to be assigned; however, it is extremely dangerous. I will be asking for volunteers, mainly because the soldiers assigned may not come back." He paused once more. The officers in the Assembly said nothing, waiting for him to reveal the mission.

"Our scouts say that there are a large number of slaves being held just outside the walls of the wraith city. I am taking my troops to the north side, but we need a regiment to go to the east side as well. The rescue of the slaves is our first priority, but—"

"I volunteer," Anna called. She stood up so the General could see who had spoken.

"Major Lieay. You volunteer your regiment so readily? You haven't even heard all the details."

Anna's mind raced. Really, she wanted to know if Michael had been taken to the holding camps, but the General would never accept that as a reason to go on the mission. She had to make him see that she and her troops had the best chance of succeeding.

Gathering her thoughts, she chose her words with care. "I fully understand the dangers and what could happen if we fail. I may not know every detail, but my troops and I joined this army to help humans free themselves from the wraiths, and I intend to pursue that goal, no matter what."

"That's all well and good, Major, but you must know the risks."

Anna swallowed. She didn't like the idea of putting her friends in danger, but they wanted Michael back just as much as she did. If it was possible to save him, she knew they'd take the risk.

"With all due respect, General, you can't keep my regiment here forever. Yes, we lost a brave soldier, but one failure has not made us incapable. My regiment and I can handle this. I understand the risks; we all do, but wars cannot be won without sacrifice. You are committed to this mission, and so am I."

Collins' face drew into a grimace, and Anna wondered if she'd gone too far. She straightened her shoulders and kept her gaze fixed on the General. She knew that she and her troops had proven themselves time and time again, and she wanted the respect that came with those feats. After a long pause, she still hadn't broken eye contact, and the General finally looked away.

"Very well, Major. Have your regiment prepare for the journey. We'll leave tomorrow morning. If you'll come by my office after dinner, we can discuss the mission further."

"If you would, General, I'd like my troops to hear what you have to say."

Collins stared at her for a few moments, and she wondered if he still disapproved of her leadership style. Officers normally only told their seconds such information.

Finally, Collins gave a curt nod. "I'll be by your barracks after dinner to discuss the mission further with your entire regiment."

Anna's shoulders relaxed, and she allowed herself to blink. "Thank you, General."

He nodded and addressed the entire Assembly. "You all have your assignments. Dismissed."

28

General Collins gathered his papers and left the Assembly before any of the officers could bother him with questions. He tried to make it look like he was far too busy to be disturbed. Aside from a few salutes, he passed through the Sanctuary without any interaction.

After reaching his office, he shut the door and collapsed in his chair, contemplating the mission he was about to set out on. It was extremely dangerous to venture so close to the wraith city, and he had purposefully kept all prior assignments well away from it. However, the war had come to a relative stalemate in the past few months. He kept sending out small reconnaissance missions. His troops might kill a few wraiths, but they'd lose a few of their own to the enemy, and neither side gained any ground. And then there was the loss of the boy. He refused to sit back and watch his troops die, one by one, without an end in sight.

The Council was breathing down his neck, always asking when the war would be over or when Istamba might be safe again. With each day that passed, he was losing their faith. He knew he had to do something to reinvigorate his troops and strike a hard blow to the wraiths. Rescuing a large group of slaves and returning them to their families would accomplish both goals. Unfortunately, to do so meant putting some of his best soldiers closer to death than they'd ever been. It was a risk he had to take, despite how it tore at him to even consider it.

His thoughts turned to Major Lieay and her regiment. Of all the soldiers he'd seen go through training, he was especially impressed with that group. They were exceptional soldiers, and their success had inspired the people of the Sanctuary. He'd heard the rumor that they were descended from the great warriors of legend, but he wasn't sure how much truth there was in it. They did seem to be stronger and faster than his older, more experienced soldiers, but they also trained a lot harder than most regiments did. And after what they'd seen, who knew what stories kids that age would invent to keep their sanity.

Major Lieay had changed so much from the little girl who had saved him on the quad nearly two years ago. With everything that had happened and through all her successes, he could see more and more of her parents within her. He had met them a few times before Roland had attacked Fort Lieay, and, despite his being a respected General when they met last, he remembered being in complete awe of their presence. They stood tall and proud, as any leader should. They were logical rulers, and their kindness and fairness shone through in every action they took. But even after everything they'd done, there was still a dangerous edge to them that had always made him uneasy.

Perhaps Anna had a dangerous edge too, and he just hadn't seen it yet.

If only they'd made the decision to depose the Council and unite the north and south into a single kingdom, perhaps things would be different now, but Anna was right in her assessment. They wouldn't have wanted to put their people through a war. Though, if they had taken control, perhaps the war would have been won by now. Both were formidable warriors, which was probably why Roland chose to target them with the majority of his forces.

"You alright, General?" a voice said.

Collins looked up to see Colonel Grimshaw peeking into his office.

"Just thinking."

She came in and sat down in one of the chairs across from Collins.

"Major Lieay giving you problems?"

Collins stared at his second. Iyla Grimshaw was more perceptive than he gave her credit for.

"Maybe."

"She's strong," Iyla said.

Collins barked out a laugh. The way Anna had stood before the Assembly, confidently offering herself and troops to protect her people, showed how strong she truly was. And the way she had stared him down—not even the 2nd General had the nerve to challenge him like that. Yet, even in her brazen immaturity, she was able to stand her ground and offer a constructive defense that left him no choice but to give her the mission.

"She's just like her parents," Collins said.

Iyla smiled. "You know those kids'll be in an awful lot of danger, right? I've seen the mission reports. Roland's forces are targeting them."

Collins nodded. "Anna killed Roland's mate. It only makes sense he'd want revenge."

"I think it's more than that. Their successes empower our forces like nothing I've ever seen. They can't be taken."

Collins didn't respond. He didn't like the idea of putting any regiment into this kind of extreme danger, but the possibility of losing the 77th almost made him want to back out of his plan. He couldn't bear to think of what Roland might do if he managed to capture Anna or any of her troops. They would doubtless be made into an example to scare any humans who might continue to resist the Wraith King's rule. The more he thought about it, the less he wanted to send Anna on this assignment, but after going through his options, he didn't know what else to do.

"You're not backing out, are you?" Iyla said after a few moments.

"No," Collins said, "I'll just have to find a way to explain to them how much danger they'll be in, and hopefully they'll still make the trip."

"Good," Iyla said, smirking, "because you know they're likely the only ones who have a chance of succeeding in this mission. And I include us in that assessment."

"Don't tell the rest of our troops," Collins said. He shuffled through a few of his papers before standing and saying, "Get to the supply rooms tonight and gather what we need. I want to leave as early as possible in the morning."

"Yes, General," Iyla said. She saluted before leaving his office.

⚞ 29 ⚟

After the General dismissed the Assembly, Anna hurried back to the training ground where she'd left her troops. When she got there, they were all circled around Liam and Ian, who were wrestling on the ground. She placed her hands on her hips and *tsked*. This was not what she'd meant when she said to run one-on-one combat drills.

Clearing her throat, she said, "Interesting strategy, though not one I would use."

Everyone turned toward her sheepishly. Liam and Ian stood and attempted to brush the dirt and grass from their clothes and straighten their appearance.

"We were just, um—"

"Right," Anna said, letting a small smile escape. She was confident in her troops' abilities, and some fun was probably good for them. "Everyone, prepare for a long trip. We have a new assignment. Ian, Mariana, Kyree, get to the supply rooms and request rations. Ele, get to the infirmary for emergency supplies. Jonathan, request a few additional amulets; see what they'll give you. Hurry back. There are some things about the mission that I need to tell you before the General comes by after dinner. The rest of you, pack up."

Anna walked back into the barracks to pack her things. Alex fell into step beside her.

"Why does the General want to talk to us?" he asked.

"It's about the mission. I don't mean to keep information from you, but I want everyone together before I explain."

Alex didn't push. Less than an hour later, Ian, Mariana, and Kyree returned with their supplies, followed closely by Ele and Jonathan. When she saw that they'd returned, Anna called everyone to the roof to explain their latest mission.

"At the end of Assembly today, General Collins asked for volunteers for a rather dangerous mission. I know we don't revel in the thought of risking our lives, but given the mission, I believe we are the regiment best suited for it."

"We wouldn't have joined the army if we weren't prepared to handle a little danger," Jonathan said.

"Some scouts have reported that the majority of the wraiths' slaves are now being held just outside their city walls. The General is planning a rescue with a simultaneous attack on the north and east flanks of the city. He'll be taking the north side, and we will attack the other."

"Anna, you don't think—never mind."

"What is it, Kyree?"

"Well, Michael wasn't taken all that long ago, maybe he—"

"The thought did cross my mind," Anna interrupted, "and that's part of the reason I volunteered us, but I don't want anyone saying that to the General. We can't let our guard down, and if the General thinks we aren't completely focused, there's no way he'll let us go. Venturing this close to the wraiths' city is dangerous, but we'll be careful, and we'll all return. However, I need you to understand something very important. If the recent attacks on our missions show anything, it's that the wraiths are targeting our regiment—they want *us* for some reason. We must not be taken alive."

Anna emphasized her final sentence and waited for her meaning to reach them. Her troops glanced at one another as realization sunk in. A few swallowed nervously, but most just nodded in understanding.

"We can handle ourselves," Ian finally said, "and I believe I speak for everyone when I say we know you wouldn't ask something of us that you wouldn't do yourself. We will follow you anywhere."

Anna relaxed a little. "Thank you. I don't want to frighten you all, but I want to make sure everyone understands the consequences. Enough of this for now; dinner should be ready soon."

As if to emphasize her point, the bell rang, sounding the next meal. Her troops cheered and raced each other to the dining hall as usual. Anna gave them a slight head start before rushing after them, catching up easily. As they reached the halls of the main building, they began their chant, as had become customary at every evening meal. Some of the officers still opposed their cheering, but Collins continued to allow it. Anna figured that it gave people hope. If they remained happy, despair couldn't live within the Sanctuary.

After dinner, Anna led her troops back to the barracks to await General Collins. They didn't have to wait long. Just as most had settled on their beds, a knock came at the main entrance. Anna rose and admitted the General, inviting him into the sleeping area. At his entrance, her troops rose and gave a quick salute before returning to their relaxed positions.

Anna worried at the breach in protocol. It was customary to salute a superior officer and remain in salute until told to be at ease. Anna had long since disposed of the practice within her regiment, and that relaxed attitude tended to carry over to other officers. Collins didn't say anything, though, and Anna went to her own bed and sat.

"General," she said, "thank you for briefing us personally."

"Yes, of course. I wanted to solidify our plan before reaching the city, in case any unfriendly ears are listening. I'd also like to reiterate the risks involved in this mission."

"I've already briefed my troops on that matter."

"Are you sure, Major?"

"General," began Ian, "we all understand what we'll be walking into. At the risk of sounding conceited, we know of our importance to the Sanctuary, and we know the wraiths would be extremely pleased to have any and all of us as prisoners. We've been following Anna for some time, and we're confident that she'll lead us through this mission safely. While we intend to come back from it, I can assure you that we're all prepared for what needs to be done in case of failure."

Anna saw Collins stiffen at Ian's words, and she couldn't help but feel proud. Ian had proven that they were as strong and brave as any adult regiment, and it showed how loyal they all were to the cause. Anna wondered if the General's men showed the same confidence in him, but quickly dismissed the thought; she didn't want to think ill of the General.

The General raised his chin. "You continue to surprise me, Major, as does this regiment. It's an unfortunate topic, but it must be discussed. I've constructed a plan with my second, and you need to be made aware of the situation we're walking into. The wraiths have no idea we're coming, and I've let them hear of a few false assignments to distract them.

"We'll travel as a large group for a few days, but eventually, we'll have to split up. Our shared journey will take about six days before we reach that point. My goal is to attack both flanks of the city at the same time. We don't know exactly how many slaves are being held there or what condition they're in, but we want to bring as many back as we can. We won't be able to carry enough food and supplies there and back, but hopefully, we'll run into some game on the way. Did you have any questions about the specifics?"

"Not at the moment," Anna replied.

"Good. We'll leave tomorrow at dawn."

As Collins turned around, Anna stood and called to her troops, "Seven-Seven, salute!"

For a moment, she feared their hesitation, but Ele shot to her feet, Ian following closely behind. As one, she and her troops offered a unified salute. The General surveyed the room, and a smile played at his lips.

"As you were," he said, and the soldiers sank back to their seats. Anna tried to catch the General's gaze, but he was already gone. Anna turned back to her troops.

"One more thing before we leave tomorrow morning," Anna said, "I don't want anyone bringing armor, aside from leather padding. I know this will leave us more vulnerable, but the gold is reflective, and it could give away our positions. Try to leave as much gold here as you can. That extends to weapons as well. I'm not asking you to go unarmed, but I do ask that you take only the bare minimum.

"If possible, choose weapons that will be easiest to conceal. Ian, I know your expertise with your axe, but I'd rather you take a sword. Rebecca, take your bow. We may need the long-range help." Anna paused to take in her troops' expressions. She knew they didn't like the idea of leaving their armor behind, but she didn't want to take any chances. "Get some sleep. We're leaving early tomorrow, and we'll be out in the forest for a while. This may be the last good night's sleep you'll have for some time."

Anna fell into a light sleep, but was awoken a few hours later by the sound of someone shuffling nearby. She sat up slightly and looked over to Alex's bed, only to find it empty. She glanced toward the door and saw the back of him disappearing out of the barracks. She rose quietly and followed him out.

"Alex?" she called softly, once they were both outside. "Is everything okay?"

Alex turned around, obviously startled at her appearance. "I couldn't sleep and thought a walk might do me some good."

"I'm nervous too," she said. "I'll walk a lap with you. Maybe it'll help us both sleep a little sounder."

Alex gave her a small smile, and the two started along the edge of the barrier. They kept up a brisk walk, in silence, making sure to stick to the shadows; they didn't need anyone seeing them out after curfew. Finally, they came back around to their barracks and slipped inside, lying down quietly in the dark.

"Good night," Anna whispered.

"Good night," Alex responded.

Anna lay awake for a while longer, listening to Alex's breathing become deeper and slower as he slipped into sleep. Relieved that he'd been able to calm his mind, Anna fell asleep too, visions of shadows consuming her dreams.

‮30‬ 30 ‮ى‬

Anna stared at the shadow of a tree, examining it for movement.

"Is everything alright, Major?" General Collins called from the middle of a small clearing.

Anna stared at the shadow for a second longer before turning to the General. "Yes. I'm just jittery, I guess."

Collins nodded. "Of course. We're close to the enemy's city, after all." He turned to the troops scattered about in the clearing. "Set up camp and watches, but no fire." He didn't need to explain why; they were deep in wraith territory.

Anna nodded in agreement and sat down with her back against one of the trees. For the last five days, her regiment had been traveling south with the General's regiment. Though they hadn't run into any wraiths, she couldn't shake the feeling that they were being followed. She wouldn't have been able to sleep at all, but the added security of the General's men helped a little. She pulled out her maps and motioned for the General to sit beside her.

"This looks like our last night together," she said. "If these are correct, we'll need to split up around midday tomorrow."

"I noticed that as well," he responded. "Try to keep the same pace we've had the past few days. We need to make sure we attack at the same time, so they aren't able to send warning."

Anna pointed at two spots on the map. "If we reach here and you reach here by sundown tomorrow, that should get us close enough to make camp without being noticed. Then we can attack at dawn the next day and still have plenty of time to retreat."

"Looks good to me."

Anna stared at the map and bit her lip. "I do have one concern."

"What is it, Major?"

"How will we get everyone away without being recaptured? I know my troops and I could hit the target and retreat easily, but the humans we're rescuing will slow us down. They're bound to be weak, and there aren't enough of us to defend them."

"I've been thinking about that as well. According to our scouts, these towns filled with slaves are holding areas rather than actual villages. The wraiths only keep the slaves they're currently using in their city; the rest are held in these makeshift camps until they're needed. They're returned to the holding camps when they've become too weak to work, if they haven't died.

"There will be some wraiths keeping guard, of course, but we should be able to handle them. They don't guard the holding camps heavily because they see their human slaves as weak, and the wraiths would never expect our army to attack so close to their city. As long as we don't let any guards escape to raise an alarm, we should be a few days away before they're due to be relieved."

"I hope you're right. Those people will only get one chance."

"I am confident in our plan, Major. It will work." He paused. "It has to. Now, get some sleep. You may not have much of a chance tomorrow night, and I need you at full strength."

"If you say so. Good night, General."

Anna got up and went to find a sleeping spot for the night. She found Alex and Jonathan and settled herself next to them, but couldn't sleep. She turned over on her side and tried to calm her racing mind. Traveling with Collins and his regiment over the past few days had been comforting. Her regiment was the smallest in the Sanctuary, and dividing up the watches when they spent the night in the forest was always difficult when they were on their own. Though they were now in wraith territory, traveling with more people had given her a feeling of safety, and the duty of night watches was shared. She couldn't help but think about what would happen when they split up.

She shifted on the hard ground and tried to find comfort as the night grew colder. Thoughts of the mission clouded her mind, and she tossed and turned all night. Every time she closed her eyes, she relived the moment when Michael was captured. She heard his scream over and over again while shadows closed in and consumed her and her troops. Finally, she gave up trying to sleep and just stared into the darkness around her.

As the first rays of sunlight filtered through the trees, both regiments were up and ready to get moving. They swept away all evidence of their stay before marching on. Very few words were exchanged between the soldiers. Even Oliver was too nervous to make any jokes this far into enemy territory. As they had predicted, they reached their splitting point just before midday. They stopped for a brief rest before they said their goodbyes.

"You know the plan, Major?" asked the General one last time.

Anna pulled him away from their troops so they wouldn't be overheard. "It's not the plan I'm worried about."

"They aren't expecting us, Major. Everything should work out in our favor."

Anna glanced around at the trees before answering. "I know we've planned everything, but—" she trailed off.

"But what?"

She sighed, searching for the right words. "General, since this war started, I've fought when and where the missions have taken me, and I've never questioned it. I know in every war there are bound to be losses, and I've made my peace with that. But I can't ever remember being as scared as I am now. What if I've just led my regiment, my friends, to a fate worse than death?"

Anna looked away from the General, and tears threatened to spill. Losing Michael was one of the hardest things she'd had to deal with in the war, and now she might lose more of her friends. She'd always played the strong, confident leader—if she hadn't, he and the Council wouldn't have let her fight—but standing here, so close to the city, she couldn't help but feel like a frightened child searching for a safe place. Collins placed his hands on her shoulders and forced her to look at him.

"Anna," he said softly, "I know you're scared, and honestly, I am too. I'm terrified. What we're about to do goes against years of instinct and training, but those slaves are counting on us. I need you to be strong, but if your resolve is faltering, I can't send you into battle. I don't want to send you back, but neither will I force you to continue."

"General—"

"I don't mean to negate your feelings," he said, "but right now I need you to be the strong warrior I know you are. I need you to be the leader I know resides within you. Can I count on you to finish this mission?"

Anna let out a shaky breath. She never knew how the General saw her, and his words chased some of her fears away.

"You can count on me. We'll see this mission through."

Collins nodded. "I'll see you back at the Sanctuary, then."

He extended a hand, and she grasped his forearm briefly before they each went to rejoin their troops and set out.

"General," Anna called, and he turned back. "Thank you." She smiled before disappearing into the trees after her regiment.

Despite her fear, Anna put on a brave face. The General's words had helped a lot. She was still scared, but her fear was more manageable, now that she knew the General had confidence in her. Besides, she needed to be strong for her troops. The less nervous they were, the better chance they'd have to rescue those being held by the wraiths.

Finally, she saw the tower she and the General had decided her group needed to reach. It was an old Sanctuary outpost, hundreds of years old. Unfortunately, since it was just an outpost, there was no protective barrier. She called for a halt and turned to her troops.

"We're about a half day from our target," she said in a low voice. "At dawn tomorrow, we'll move forward, as the General and his men move as well. If we've planned everything correctly, we should hit each side of the city at the same time, catching the wraiths by surprise. Is everyone clear on the plan?"

Her troops mumbled their agreement.

"Good, then we won't speak of it any more tonight. I know it's not ideal, but I want everyone to sleep in the trees. We no longer have the added safety of the General's regiment, and since we're so close to the city, the trees may provide us with some extra protection. Go in groups of three or four and have someone on watch throughout the night. Get as much rest as you can. We want to be at our best tomorrow."

Anna ended up in a tree next to Alex and Liam.

"I'll take first watch," Alex said. "Liam, will you take second?"

"Sure." Liam adjusted his position slightly on his branch and tightened the rope around his waist before promptly falling asleep.

"How does he do that?" Alex asked.

"I have no idea," Anna whispered. "It takes ages for me to fall asleep."

"Hmm. How do you think it will go tomorrow?"

Anna sighed. "Honestly, I have no idea. The General and I have tried to plan for everything we could think of, but I can't help wondering if we've missed something."

"I guess there's nothing we can do about it now."

"Alex—"

"Hmm?"

"I need you to stay strong. I've seen you hesitate before, but we can't afford that now. Those people in there need us. I've just been noticing you've been a little . . . reserved lately, whenever we fight the wraiths."

"I didn't realize I was hesitating," Alex said, drawing back. Anna felt bad; she didn't want to offend him.

"I just want to make sure everything is okay. I can't have you pausing in a fight when it could cost you or someone else their life. I need you to go all in, strong and determined. I know you can do it."

Alex hid his face. "I'm fine, really. I guess I just expected this war to be over a long time ago."

"I know what you mean. I can't believe it's been two years."

"Yeah, and Anna, don't worry about me tomorrow. I'm sure everything will go according to plan."

"I suppose."

"Anna?"

"Yes?" She altered her position to see his face better. She couldn't quite make out his expression, but sadness hung in his eyes.

"No matter what happens, just know that I care about you. Okay?"

"I care about you too," she said. She shifted a bit on the branch, trying to get comfortable.

Anna dozed off, only to be awakened in the early morning by Liam so that she could take her turn on watch. She adjusted her position in the tree, rubbing her eyes. She'd barely slept a handful of hours over the past few days, and it was starting to affect her thoughts. She was struggling to think clearly, and the burning of her eyes was a constant reminder of her weariness. She pulled out her waterskin and splashed a bit of water on her face, the cool liquid sharpening her vision slightly.

If she listened closely, she could faintly hear her troops breathing. The silence chilled her. They had long since left the sounds of animals behind. Even the smallest birds, save for the dakas, knew better than to go so close to the wraith city. The minutes felt like hours, until finally, the dark of the night gave way to a cool, grey morning. Once Anna could see bits of golden light peeking through the trees, she signaled the others on watch to wake everyone.

Once they were assembled on the ground, she faced her troops. "We'll most likely encounter wraiths from here on out. Any we see will need to be taken care of before they see us and raise the alarm. If we are discovered, all will be lost. Move as quickly and quietly as you can while remaining hidden. The sooner we reach the target and accomplish our goal, the more daylight we'll have in which to put distance between ourselves and the wraith city. Let's move."

Luck was on their side. They only encountered five wraiths throughout the morning, and Rebecca and Kyree easily took them out before they saw any sign of the 77th regiment. Anna eyed the sky nervously as the sun crept higher. Since they'd had to move slower through the trees, they hadn't been able to attack at dawn like she'd planned. Just before midday, Anna was relieved to see a break in the trees. She motioned for her troops to hide in the bushes surrounding the clearing in which the first holding camp was situated.

The clearing was relatively small, but Anna could see the huge wall surrounding the city in the distance. An artificial cloud hung over the city, blocking most of the sun. The cloud was a deep black near its center, but weakened to a light grey as it thinned over the outskirts of the city. The sun burned through the cloud as it reached the city walls and beyond, so the holding area wasn't covered at all. Though the cloud couldn't reach them where they hid, Anna felt suffocated by it all the same. It looked heavy, as if it might drop from the sky at any moment, crushing anything it touched.

Anna turned her face to the sun, soaking in its rays and allowing it to push the darkness from her mind before she turned her attention to the holding area. Ten makeshift huts formed a circle, blocking most of their view. A single tower was visible just above them, and Anna could see a large bell at its top. If she wanted to win the battle, and live, she had to keep the wraiths from ringing that bell. If they did, escape would be nearly impossible. She didn't see any wraiths patrolling the outside of the circle, nor could she see any slaves. Anna motioned for her troops to gather together so she could talk to them.

In hushed tones, she explained her plan. "Did everyone see the bell tower? I'd bet that's the only way they can alert the city. Our first priority is to surround that tower to ensure that no one can get in there to raise a warning. Once that's blocked off, the only way for them to warn the city is to run. The sun is high, and the sky is relatively clear, so we shouldn't have to worry about them turning to shadow. Rebecca, I want you on a roof somewhere. Any wraith that tries to run, you stop."

Rebecca nodded. "None of them will get away."

"Good. I didn't see any patrols on the outside of the huts, so we should be able to get all the way there before being spotted. I don't want anyone trying to free the humans until we're sure every wraith is dead. If civilians start running around, they may get hurt. They'll be safer locked up until we're ready to leave. I'd guess there could be twenty to thirty wraiths here, maybe more, so be prepared for the worst."

"We're ready when you are," Jonathan whispered.

"Let's get to it, then."

Anna led them back to the edge of the clearing. Checking once more for wraiths on the perimeter, she signaled for her troops to approach the huts. As she got closer, her frantic heartbeat calmed. After so many battles and missions, she felt like her feet were moving on their own. Her vision focused and her senses heightened, ready for the fight to come.

Once they reached the ring of huts, they broke in half, Alex leading one group right and Anna leading the other group left. They both stayed in the shadows of the huts, trying to conceal their presence for as long as she could. Anna peeked out from behind one of the structures to assess their situation.

"How many wraiths do you see?" Jonathan whispered from behind her.

"About twenty, but I can't see the entire quad. I'd guess there's at least ten out of sight, maybe more."

As she was trying to come up with a plan, a wraith walked right by their hiding place. Seeing them, he started and reached for his sword. Before he could sound an alarm, Anna grabbed him as Jonathan reached around to kill him. A few other wraiths noticed the disturbance and turned their way.

"There goes our surprise," Anna groaned. "Rebecca, get on that roof. The rest of you, to the bell tower!"

～ 31 ～

Anna and her group sprinted toward the bell tower; seeing them, Alex's group did the same. Anna reached the tower first and started climbing after the single wraith who had managed to beat them there. He was fast, but Anna had spent her whole life climbing trees and towers. She fell into a rhythm, closing the distance between them. Grabbing his leg, she yanked, causing him to lose his grip and fall to the ground. Anna made her way back down the tower and jumped into the battle. Her assumptions had been correct. Just over forty wraiths were guarding the small area, but in direct sunlight, they were no match for her and her troops.

Swords clashed and muffled cries rang out. Anna focused on the wraiths in front of her, ignoring the various flashes of her troops darting through the wraiths. Her swords moved on their own, blocking and jabbing, as she anticipated every move in her mind. Dust filled the air, and she cut her way through the haze, intent on ending the battle as soon as possible.

As Anna thrust her sword through one of the last wraiths, she heard someone call her name. She looked up to see Rebecca waving her arms and pointing at a wraith running out of the area. Another look at Rebecca, and Anna saw the archer was out of arrows, having used all of them to stop wraiths that fled.

Drawing a dagger, Anna aimed as best she could and hurled the small blade at the escaping wraith. The dagger caught him in the lower back and sent him sprawling onto the ground as she ran toward him. He was distracted long enough for Anna to catch up and take off his head.

Anna stood and brushed the dust from her knees, heaving huge breaths in and out. The wraiths here were dead, and now she could turn her attention to rescuing the slaves and leading everyone back safely. Anna turned to her troops, who were still surrounding the tower waiting for orders.

"Ian, Mariana, Liam, help Rebecca down, and you four are on lookout duty for any approaching wraiths. Oliver, Ele, see what they left behind. I'd like to take any weapons that we can. The rest of you, start letting everyone out of the huts. We need to get them back to the Sanctuary as soon as possible."

Her troops immediately went to work. None of them were eager to stay this close to the wraith city any longer than they had to. Anna climbed a little way up the tower to observe their progress and keep an eye out for anything suspicious.

Her gaze settled on one of the huts. It looked similar to the barracks she and her troops resided in, save for the bars and locks on the doors and windows. She assumed the huts were nothing more than long rooms meant to imprison the slaves. Faces crowded each of the barred windows, curious about the disturbance outside. When they realized humans had come to rescue them, everyone that Anna could see started waving or calling out.

As her troops opened up each of the huts, people came streaming out. Many were confused to see young soldiers, but they hobbled to them, nevertheless. Some even began to cry, overwhelmed that they'd finally been rescued. After being locked up for so long, most were gaunt and weak, and marked with wounds and bruises, but Anna didn't see anyone who couldn't walk on their own. Once everyone had been let out, Anna did a quick count. She estimated that there were just over a hundred and fifty rescued humans here. Her heart swelled and felt heavy at the same time. On one hand, all these people were free; on the other, she wasn't sure how she was going to get them all back safely.

"Attention, everyone," she called, "I am Major Lieay. I know you're all anxious to be free of this place, and we will get you back to the Sanctuary as quickly as possible. However, we will need your help and cooperation to do so. If my troops give an order, it is to be followed without hesitation. If any of you know how to wield a sword, please tell me or one of my troops. We'll be in wraith territory for a few days, and we may encounter more on our journey north. We'll be moving quickly for the next couple of days to put some good distance between this place and us, so those of you who are able, help those who are struggling."

Anna jumped down from the tower and walked through the crowd. They all parted as she passed. She heard numerous calls of thanks, and pride swelled within her. She had helped these people regain their lives, and she wasn't about to let them return to slavery. These people deserved so much more. Her hands clenched around her sword hilts, and she marched back to the others.

When she reached Alex and Jonathan, she said, "I'd say there's about a hundred and fifty people here, and that's just a guess. We don't have nearly enough food for them, so hopefully we'll come across some game on the way back. I think we should divide them into small groups and put one of our soldiers in charge of each group. Any who can fight should be armed and evenly distributed. It's going to be hard getting everyone back, but I think if they cooperate with us, we can do it. Jonathan, would you begin organizing them into groups? Alex, follow me."

Jonathan nodded and went to give Anna's orders to the rest of the troops. Alex followed Anna, confusion marring his face. She motioned to Kyree as well, and led the pair of them to the edge of one of the huts, away from everyone else.

"This is going to sound ridiculous," Anna began, "but I think the three of us should stay behind."

"Are you kidding? Why would we willingly stay here?" Kyree asked.

"I think we can do some good. I was looking at what the wraiths left behind, and they all had matching uniforms. I think we may be able to sneak into the wraith city itself and get some valuable information. I'm sending the rest of the regiment back under Jonathan's command, but I'd like you two to stay with me. You both are good at fighting in close quarters and can easily conceal your weapons. I know this sounds a little reckless, but will you do it?"

Alex and Kyree exchanged a look.

"It's not like I have anything else to do," Alex said.

Kyree rolled her eyes. "Oh, very enthusiastic. I don't think I'll ever know how you come up with your ideas, Anna, but I'll stay. Maybe we can finish this war off."

Anna smiled and reached out to grasp Kyree's hand. She held it a long moment. "Thank you. If you see a weapon you want, grab it before they leave, and meet me back here. I'm going to tell Jonathan."

Anna walked back over to Jonathan. More murmurs of thanks followed as she passed. She gave the grateful people a few small waves, but didn't turn her head.

"Anna, good," Jonathan said, "they've all been put into groups and we're ready to leave."

"Great job. You'll be in charge of leading everyone back safely. Alex, Kyree, and I are staying to see what else we can learn. Tell the General we'll be back as soon as we can."

"You're staying? Anna, don't you know how dangerous this is? I can't allow this."

"You don't have a choice." She stood taller. "I order you to lead these refugees back to the Sanctuary without us," Anna said with a hard edge to her voice.

Jonathan blinked. Anna felt slightly guilty, but she squashed the feeling immediately. Though she'd never actually used her rank so directly, it was within her rights to give commands. She knew this was something she had to do. If it was a mistake, it would be on her shoulders. Forever.

"Very well, Major," Jonathan said stiffly.

"I'm sorry, Jonathan, but this is something we have to do. We may not get a chance like this again. We'll be safe, I promise, and if everything goes well, we should only be a day or two behind you."

"You can't promise that," he muttered. "You always were too stubborn for your own good."

"Well I *am* a human."

Jonathan grinned, and the brief iciness between them melted. He placed a hand on her shoulder and squeezed it tightly.

"Stay safe," he said softly.

"I will, and I'll see you in a few days."

"Yes, Ma'am," he said, with a salute. Anna turned and walked over to Alex and Kyree, leaving Jonathan staring after her.

"Alright," he called loudly, "let's move out!"

The people they'd rescued from the slave camps followed without hesitation. The soldiers glanced back at Anna, Alex, and Kyree in confusion, but followed Jonathan as ordered. Once the large group had left, Anna, Alex, and Kyree picked through the uniforms the wraiths had left behind to find something that would fit. They secured their weapons and pulled the helmets on.

"Hopefully, these will hide that we aren't shadow. We shouldn't have to conceal our weapons anymore either. They are from wraiths, after all."

"These helmets are absurd," Alex complained. "None of the wraiths in the field wear them."

"I bet it's to intimidate the slaves. If they're too scared to revolt, they're easier to control," Anna replied. "The city entrance shouldn't be too far. You two ready?"

"No," Kyree said, "but let's go."

Anna gave a wry smile and led the pair out of the deserted town. After walking for a little way, they saw a large set of gates and could just make out buildings beyond. The large doors of the gates were open wide, and Anna shuddered. It looked like an open mouth, ready to swallow them whole.

"I don't see any guards," she whispered, "but once we're in, look for hiding places and escape routes. Keep a sharp eye out. We may have to run for it at any moment."

The two nodded their understanding and followed Anna through the gate. Anna had heard stories of the wraith city, but she still had to stop herself from staring in awe. Most of the buildings were as tall as the Sanctuary's tallest tower, and every building had some sort of gold ornamentation. Anna saw a small alcove out of the way and led Alex and Kyree there. The streets were empty, which made sense as it was near the middle of the day. Not seeing any wraiths, Anna turned to her companions.

"That building over there looks like a guard house. Maybe there's some information there that we can use. Kyree, you're the smallest—do you think you can get in while Alex and I stand guard? Kyree?"

Kyree was staring at something down the street and didn't appear to have heard anything Anna said. Alex grabbed her shoulders and shook her out of her daze.

"Kyree," he said, "now is not the time to become distracted."

Kyree's eyes found Alex's. "Michael," she gasped, "he's down there."

Anna snapped her head around to look where Kyree had been staring. There was a cage on a raised platform in the middle of the street. Inside, she could barely make out Michael's face.

⚘ 32 ⚘

Anna gasped upon recognizing her friend. When he had been taken near Oracha, she never thought she'd see him again. Horror and joy fought to overtake her, glad to see him alive, but not knowing what they'd done to him.

"Do you think he's dead?" Alex asked.

"Of course not!" she snapped. "His eyes are open. Kyree, I want to rescue him as much as you do, but we need to get into that guardhouse to see if there is any useful information. Then we can go after Michael. Alright?"

"Shouldn't we go after Michael first?" Alex asked.

Anna shook her head. "He's in the middle of the street. I know we haven't seen any wraiths, but we can't risk it just yet. We need to go after that guardhouse first."

Kyree nodded. "I understand. What do you need me to do?"

"You're the smallest, so you've got the best chance to sneak inside while Alex and I stand watch. Grab anything that looks like it could be important. Journals, maps, notes, whatever you can find. Then we'll work on getting Michael out."

"I've got it," Kyree said. With a sharp breath, she turned toward the tower. "I'll see you soon."

She slipped across the street and snuck in the door. Anna and Alex eyed their surroundings nervously, but no one came their way. A flash of light from the guardhouse drew their attention, and Anna felt panic well within her. She took a step toward the guardhouse, ready to help Kyree, but Alex pulled her back.

"Give her a chance," Alex whispered.

Anna clenched her jaw, unwilling to leave Kyree alone, but nodded. She'd draw too much attention if she tried to help.

Kyree emerged a few minutes later with a small bag. Anna brushed some dust from the bag, her brow raised in question.

"Are you okay?"

"There were a few wraiths, but I took care of it. My amulet's depleted, though."

"That's alright," Anna said. "I still have mine. Now, about Michael . . . Alex, can you still pick a lock?"

"Shouldn't be a problem."

"Good. It looks like there are some steps leading up to the cage, so if we act like we're just soldiers checking in on him, no one should give us a second glance. Kyree and I will conceal you while you pick the lock. We'll probably have to run for it, but hopefully it will look like we're just moving him somewhere else. My only concern is his condition. If he's unable to walk, trying to get him out of here might mean none of us make it."

"We'll cross that bridge when we come to it," Kyree said. "Let's get going before the sun sinks any lower."

Anna nodded and motioned for Alex to go first. "Act confident, like you belong here. Kyree and I will flank you."

They marched up the street in a triangle formation. Anna scanned the street, looking around as much as she dared, but didn't see any wraiths in the streets. When they reached the platform, Alex went up first, and Anna and Kyree followed, positioning themselves to hide what he was doing with the lock. Anna assessed Michael's condition as she ascended the platform. One leg was extended and the other was tucked awkwardly underneath him. He looked far too thin, and his hair hung limply from his head, partially covering a bruise on his temple. Various cuts crisscrossed his arms, and his clothes were torn and bloodied. A large gash ran along one of his shoulders; fresh blood dripped down his arm, pooling next to where he sat. One of his boots had been lost at some point and his foot was covered in dirt and grime. The other boot had been mangled near his shin, as though something had chewed on it.

Michael flinched and looked away when he saw them coming, but Anna caught a glimpse of the fear shining in his eyes, though his face remained passive.

"Michael," Alex whispered, "stay calm and look defeated."

Recognition dawned and he turned his head toward them. "I can't believe . . ."

"Can you walk?" Kyree said quietly.

"My ankle hurts a lot, but I don't think it's broken. I won't slow you down."

"Hurry up, Alex," Anna hissed. "The longer we're here, the greater the risk."

"It's open."

Michael stepped out of the cage, and Anna and Alex made a show of grabbing him by the arms like they would a prisoner. Michael winced, and Anna felt a pang of remorse. He had to be in pain, but if she and Alex weren't rough, they might give themselves away. They marched him down the platform with Kyree close behind. Anna felt a raindrop hit her hand, and glanced up toward the sky.

"Uh oh," she whispered.

"Clouds are moving in quickly," Kyree whispered back. "We have to pick up the pace."

Anna nodded, and she and Alex helped Michael walk faster. Anna glanced nervously at their surroundings, the day growing darker and darker as clouds moved in to obscure the sun. The rain began to come down hard. The humans made it halfway down the street before they were stopped by a wraith in full armor. Anna's eyes flicked downward to see his legs shifting between shadow and flesh.

"Where do you think you're going?" asked the wraith. "That prisoner is supposed to stay in his cage."

Anna's heart leapt to her throat and her mind went blank. "We, uh, received orders to transfer him to one of the camps outside the city," Anna said nervously.

"I wasn't made aware, and take off those helmets. They aren't to be worn outside the holding camps. Who are you?"

The wraith bent to peer into the visor of Anna's helmet. Seeing blue eyes instead of red, he drew his sword, but Anna was quicker. She drew one of her daggers and sliced him across the neck.

"Help Michael to the gate and head east," she said. "I'll cover our retreat."

Alex and Kyree each took one of Michael's arms and half ran, half dragged him to the gate. Anna was close behind, facing the wraiths that had come out of the buildings to stop them. She glanced down the street and saw her friends had almost reached the gate. She finished off one last wraith before sprinting after them. As they passed through the heavy black doors, Anna led them eastward.

"We need to keep running for as long as we can," Anna said between breaths. She pulled her amulet free of her armor and located the small dot. "There should be a safe house directly ahead of us. If we can make it there, we may have a chance."

"How far?" panted Alex.

"Not sure. We'll just have to keep going until we see it."

"We'll never make it," gasped Kyree.

"We have to. It will take a while for the wraiths to mobilize. We'll get there."

The day got darker and the rain continued to pelt the small group. Anna looked at Michael repeatedly. His face was contorted in pain and he winced with each step. Alex and Kyree were being as gentle as they could, but speed was more important than comfort.

Finally, the sun disappeared below the horizon, and Anna began to worry even more. The trees all looked the same and she couldn't tell how far they'd run. She breathed as deeply as she could, but her muscles burned with each step.

"Are we almost there?" Alex asked nervously.

"I think so, but it's hard to tell."

They pushed on through the trees a little while longer, until Anna breathed a sigh of relief. "I think I can see it."

A few minutes later, the group stumbled inside a small safe house. Michael tumbled to the ground and breathed out a weak thanks, before rolling to his side. Anna managed to latch the door before she collapsed next to her friends. She reached over to offer Michael some water, only to see that he and the others had fallen asleep almost instantly. Exhausted herself, Anna took a small sip of water and joined them. The night passed in a blink, and Anna had to force her eyes open as the sun streamed in. She shook her companions awake.

"I know we didn't get much sleep last night, but we have to get moving as soon as we can," she said.

Alex tried to rub the sleep from his eyes and stumbled toward the door.

"Wait," Anna said, "we're still pretty close to the city. There may be wraiths out there." She went to the back of the hut and peeked out of the window. She couldn't see any wraiths, but knew they could be hiding in the trees.

"I'll slip outside and look around. Find something to bind Michael's ankle. If they're out there, we may have to run for it."

"How far is the next safe house?" Kyree asked.

Anna shook her head. "Too far. But I figure as long as we keep moving, we should be able to stay ahead of the wraiths."

Kyree nodded and began searching through the crates to see if she could find anything useful. Anna snuck out the window and climbed a tree within the safe house barrier. She could barely make out a few birds calling to each other. She carefully dropped down from the tree and circled around to the front of the safe house. Knocking on the door, she softly called for them to come out.

"I can hear some birds nearby, so we should be alright to leave, but we may run into scouting groups. Michael, are you okay?"

"My ankle hurts, but I should be able to walk with a little help. I don't think I can run anymore. I'm sorry."

Anna shook her head. "Don't be sorry; you've been through a lot."

Michael's face reddened and he looked away. As he turned, Anna thought she saw tears pooling in his eyes.

"How are we supposed to reach the next safe house?" Alex asked. "You said yourself, wraiths are bound to be out on patrols throughout this area, and none of us are ready for a fight."

"I can distract them," Anna said, trying to think of a plan. "Michael, we'll help you along as best we can. Once we get to the first safe house, more are lined up all the way back to the Sanctuary."

"Anna," Kyree said, "you've only slept for a handful of hours in the past few days. Even at your best, it would be difficult to outrun all those wraiths. We have to find another way."

"The only other way gets us all captured. This way, at least you can make it back."

"I have an idea," Michael said softly.

"What?"

"The old houses around here aren't very sturdy. We could take a few apart and set up a fire with some leaves. The wraiths would see the smoke and come here while we slip away to the next safe house."

"You want to start a fire in the middle of the forest?" Alex asked. "We're trying to get away from the wraiths, not torch ourselves!"

"Not if we set it in a large clearing. The fire doesn't have to be big, just smoky."

Anna thought for a moment, running through the possibilities in her head. Michael's plan was risky, but it was better than anything she could think of.

"Okay," she finally said, "I can't believe we're doing this, but let's get started. Kyree, Michael, you stand guard. Alex and I will take apart one of the old homes and gather some greenery."

Her companions nodded and set to their tasks. After a while, Kyree left Michael on his own so she could help the others dig a shallow trench around where the fire would be. They hoped the trench would prevent the fire from spreading. When that was finished, Kyree dug another trench leading away from the pit to the edge of the clearing.

"What's this for?" Anna asked, motioning toward the trench.

"If we line it with tinder and kindling, we can light it here and let it spread to the main kindling. It will give us more time to leave before the fire really gets started and draws attention."

"Hmm. That might actually work. Alex, bring some of those smaller pieces here."

Alex finished laying the wood and leaves in the main fire pit before beginning to line the trench with small sticks and leaves. The whole process took the group a little less than an hour. Once finished, they stepped back to look at what they had done.

"It's not perfect," Alex said, "but hopefully it will do."

"It will," said Michael. "It has to."

They picked up what few supplies they'd managed to salvage. Alex and Kyree helped Michael up and supported him as they walked to the edge of the trees. Anna made sure the stolen maps and notes were secure before drawing out her flint.

"Are you ready?" she asked.

Alex nodded. "Now or never."

Anna struck the flint, lighting the dry leaves at the end of the trench. The flames moved along the trench more quickly than she'd expected.

"Go, go!" Anna said, ushering the others away from the clearing and further into the shelter of the trees. They moved slowly to begin with, making sure to stay in the brush as best they could. Their whole plan relied on the wraiths thinking they were dumb enough to light a fire. Anna looked back the way they'd come and saw smoke rising above the trees.

"They should be able to see it. We need to hide. I think I hear someone coming our way."

Kyree and Alex helped Michael under a bush and rearranged the leaves so he couldn't be seen, then climbed a tree to hide in the branches with Anna. They secured themselves just in time to see two wraith scouts stop right where they'd been standing.

"Did you hear something?" the first one asked.

"Could be a bird," replied the second. "We don't normally come this far east, so we're bound to scare off a few animals."

"I don't know. What if it's the humans?"

"Don't you see the smoke? Only a human would be stupid enough to start a fire like that, especially in our territory."

"But . . ."

"Come on. Whoever catches the humans gets first blood."

The pair continued on, excited about the prospect of a fight. Once she was sure they were gone, Anna dropped down from the trees, with Kyree and Alex close behind.

Anna helped Alex pull Michael from the bush. "That was close."

"I agree," he said. "Let's get to the safe house."

The four moved through the forest as fast as they could, but even at their accelerated pace, they didn't reach the safe house until well after nightfall. Once through the barrier, they all began to breathe a little easier. Anna opened the door to the hut and waited for everyone to get inside before shutting it tightly so their presence wouldn't be discovered. They all collapsed on the floor of the house, desperate for a rest. The past few days had been exhausting, and it wasn't long before Anna could hear the steady breathing of sleep. She took a few deep breaths to calm herself before falling asleep as well.

King Roland twirled a dagger in his hand while circling the messenger kneeling before him.

"How many slaves did we lose?"

"Um, nearly three hundred, my Lord."

"Three hundred," the King said. "The last estimate was half that. Are you so incompetent that you cannot count mere humans?"

"There was another attack, my Lord, on the eastern holding area."

Roland cracked his neck and came to stand in front of the messenger.

"So," he began slowly, his voice low but deadly, "not one, but two human regiments ventured to my city, stole my slaves, and returned to their Sanctuary unharmed, while none of the scouts in the forest had any idea of their movement. Did I miss anything?".

"Well—"

Roland grabbed the messenger by the throat, hoisting him off the ground. "Well?!"

"A few humans entered the city. They stole our weapons inventory lists and troop movement reports from the guardhouse near the entrance. They, um—"

"They what?"

"They also took the human soldier from the cage near the entrance. The soldier from the 77th Regiment."

The King hurled the messenger against the wall with a scream that was heard throughout the city. He stormed from the room and stalked down to the chambers where his advisors were planning attacks. Upon his entrance, they all ceased their activities and bowed deeply.

"My Lord, though we haven't heard from our contact within the Sanctuary for a few weeks now, we have just finished a plan that should cripple the humans for good."

"Should? Or will?"

"Will, my Lord. Tanaba Ridge only has one entrance. If we trap the human army there, even their best regiment would have no hope of escaping. One hundred of your finest soldiers are on their way now."

"Double it."

"Double? That will take more time . . ."

"I said double it! And I want the Lieay girl dead *now*! Send a message to our contact in the Sanctuary. I want this war ended once and for all."

⚘ 33 ⚘

General Collins led his group north, his troops spread out through the large groups of rescued citizens. Their attack had gone exactly as planned. There were very few wraiths guarding the northern holding area, and his regiment had freed the humans easily. The trip back, however, was more stressful than he had anticipated. He wanted to return to the Sanctuary as quickly as possible, but the refugees couldn't keep up with a soldier's march, especially in their weakened state. Grudgingly, he slowed their pace, but that was only the first of his troubles.

He and his troops were able to carry supplies for themselves, but feeding everyone on those rations was impossible. Even if he'd had enough food, the refugees would still need to be carefully monitored. The wraiths had barely given them enough nourishment to survive. If they ate too much too fast, they could become ill. He hated having to deny them anything, but he kept telling himself it was for their own good.

As they came to a stop for the night, he directed his troops to set up camp and distribute water and a small ration of food to everyone. A few of his troops took some of the stronger refugees out into the woods to hunt. He settled against a tree and watched the activities of the camp.

"General Collins?" one of the refugees asked.

He glanced over at the man who had spoken. He was leaning heavily on a makeshift crutch, and his foot was bent at an awkward angle. He needed to get back to the Sanctuary as soon as possible, or else his leg would never heal.

"I just wanted to thank you," the man continued. "You don't know what it was like in the city. They forced us to work until we dropped, and then they'd beat us until we got up again. Some of us were beginning to think we'd been forgotten, but you never did forget about us, did you? We knew you'd come back for us."

Collins swallowed hard, feeling tears starting to form. He held them back, though. He couldn't allow himself to be distracted; not while so many were counting on him to get them all back to the Sanctuary. There wasn't a whole lot of room for emotion in his position, and for good reason. He was used to his soldiers leaving him alone, save for logistical questions.

"Excuse me, General," Colonel Grimshaw said, "could we speak for a moment? Privately."

The refugee looked between the two of them before saying, "I'll take my leave. Thank you again, General. For everything."

Collins watched the man leave and motioned for his second to sit. "What did you need, Iyla?"

She smirked. "Nothing. I just figured you could use a little assistance."

Collins sighed deeply. "I don't understand why they insist on sharing their experiences. I know they're grateful and I'm glad we were able to get them out, but we still have a long way to go to get back to the Sanctuary, and listening to stories isn't going to help anyone."

"It helps them."

Collins gave her a funny look. "How?"

"They don't know how else to express their gratitude except to tell you what you saved them from," Iyla said.

"It's not that I don't care," Collins told her. "I just have a lot more to worry about right now."

Iyla gave him a soft smile and laid a hand on his shoulder. "I know you're not used to all this mushy feely stuff. We'll do what we can to keep them away. You just focus on getting us back safely."

She stood and walked away, leaving him alone. He took a deep breath and examined his map. If they angled their route east, they could cut some time off the journey. He wanted to get out of wraith territory as fast as possible. His men were barely managing to stay awake, and the refugees were too weak to fight anyone. By going directly north, he hoped to avoid most, if not all, wraith scouting missions.

So far, his hunch had been correct. They had encountered a few wraiths in the beginning, but they were taken care of easily. He only hoped that the lack of wraiths in their path didn't mean that there were more in the way of the 77th.

Eight days after the attack, General Collins finally saw the towers of the Sanctuary behind the shimmer of the barrier. He heard the horn announce their presence and called for everyone to stop just inside the safety of the barrier.

He turned to address the gathered citizens, trying to imagine their ordeal within the slave camps. "I know you all are anxious to find your family and friends, but we need to address your wounds and injuries first. This is Captain Price. She will help you transition to your lives here." The General turned away and murmured to his second, "I need to report to the Council. Take care of things here and make sure the lookouts are watching for Major Lieay. I want to be informed as soon as they return."

"Yes, Sir."

The General walked purposefully to the Council chambers. They needed to be notified of his victory immediately.

"I need to speak to the Council," he said to the guards outside.

The soldiers' eyes shifted back and forth. "They're in a private session, General. I'm sorry, but we can't let you in," one of them said.

Collins sighed. While most of the soldiers respected him as their leader, there was still a small faction of soldiers who thought the

Council should be in complete control of Istamba. Apparently, in his absence, the Council had chosen soldiers from the latter group to guard their chambers.

"Tell them I've returned from my mission," he said.

"General—"

"That's an order."

The guard nodded and slipped inside. He returned a few moments later and motioned for the General to enter..

"General Collins," Althea began, once he was standing before them, "I'm glad to see you've returned. How fared your mission?"

"For my part, exceptionally well. We managed to save over one hundred slaves."

"And what of the other regiment?"

"We haven't heard from them yet, but we did have to take different routes back. If everything ran smoothly, they should be here within the next day or so."

"Good," Althea said. "We shall await Major Lieay's report, then."

The next day, General Collins was pacing on the southern quad. The 77th probably wouldn't return for a few hours, but he still worried. What if something had gone wrong? He knew they could handle themselves in a fight, but they could have kept running into scouts, or worse, full regiments.

A horn sounded, and he peered out beyond the barrier. He could just make out a group of people approaching the barrier. It took all his restraint to wait for them to reach the Sanctuary instead of rushing out to meet them. After what seemed like an eternity, a huge mass of rescued citizens had assembled before him, with the soldiers of the 77th at the back.

He gave this group of newcomers the same orders he'd given to the group he brought in and sent them off, eager to speak to Major Lieay. However, as he surveyed the soldiers before him, he realized that the Major wasn't with them. A man stepped forward and spoke.

"General Collins, I'm Lieutenant Jonathan Greggory."

Collins nodded, recognizing the officer. "Where is your Captain and Major Lieay?"

Jonathan looked at his feet and sighed. Shaking his head, he looked back at the General, "They, along with one other soldier, stayed behind to infiltrate the wraith city."

"What?! That wasn't in her orders!"

Jonathan's mouth tightened to a line. "She was adamant that I lead the refugees back safely. She said she should only be a few days behind us."

Collins ran a hand through his hair. That girl annoyed him to no end. If she wasn't Anna Lieay, he'd have expelled her long ago. But he still believed in Anna, and her schemes tended to work out. He only hoped this wasn't the time when her luck ran out.

"Thank you, Lieutenant. Take your troops back to your barracks and rest up. Until the Major gets back, you'll be free from responsibilities."

"That's not necessary, General. We don't mind helping out."

"You've earned it. Of course you can train, but take it easy. The past few weeks must have taken a lot out of your soldiers. When the Major returns, I want to be notified immediately."

"Yes, General; thank you." Jonathan saluted and led the regiment back to their barracks for some much-needed rest.

⚞ 34 ⚟

Six days later, Anna caught a glimpse of the Sanctuary's towers through the trees and gave a grateful sigh. Trekking through the forest and dodging wraiths had made the last six days miserable. Michael spotted the towers as well and insisted they pick up their pace. He waved away his companions' protests about his injuries, and Anna finally obliged. Now, as they approached the Sanctuary at a light jog, Anna understood his hurry.

They were so close; it would be awful to fail at the last moment. They'd dodged wraith scouts for the past six days and didn't know how many more they could handle. She checked every other minute that the stolen journals and notes were still secured at her side. She was paranoid that they'd be lost, after all the risk and effort it had taken to acquire them.

As the three of them stepped through the barrier, they all exhaled in chorus. Anna handed Michael over to Alex and Kyree, the weariness evident on their faces. She wanted to collapse on the quad herself, but she knew she still had responsibilities to take care of.

"Get him to the infirmary. I need to find General Collins. Get some rest, but don't go far. I expect Collins will want to speak with each of you."

Alex pointed behind Anna. "Isn't that Collins heading toward us?"

Anna turned around. Sure enough, the General was advancing quickly in their direction. Anna couldn't quite decipher his expression. She thought she could detect relief in his eyes, but his mouth was set in a scowl.

"What were you thinking, Major?" Collins barked. "Willingly staying in wraith territory? Do you understand how important you are? I'm considering discharging you from the army."

Anna scowled. She'd spent the past few days running from wraiths, trying to get her comrades back safely. Though they'd managed to find a safe house each night, they'd hardly slept, and the exhaustion was starting to get to her. Arguing with the General was the last thing she wanted to do.

"You know, you threaten to discharge me an awful lot," Anna snapped. "It's starting to lose its effect."

The General gritted his teeth, and she wondered if she'd gone too far this time.

"General," she said, trying to smooth things over, "I'll explain everything, but my troops are exhausted and our latest rescuee has wounds that need attending."

The General's eyes narrowed slightly, but he turned his attention to her companions. He scanned the trio, seeing how Alex and Kyree had to hold Michael up, though they were nearly collapsing themselves.

"Get to the infirmary, all three of you. I have a feeling Reyla will want to keep you overnight just in case."

Kyree breathed out a 'thank you' before they trudged off to the infirmary.

"Major, come with me. The Council will want to hear your report. And might I suggest being a bit more respectful to them? They aren't as forgiving as I am."

Anna nodded, and the two began walking to the Council chambers.

"I'm sorry, General," she said as they walked, "but we had to take the chance while we could. Staying in the city was a difficult decision; I did my best to make sure the risk was worth it."

"I understand better than anyone, Major, but the Council won't."

When they reached the door, Collins stopped Anna before entering.

"Anna," he said softly, "be careful what you say in there."

She was caught off guard by his tone. "What do you mean?"

"From what I've heard, since we left two weeks ago, Colonel Wells has taken advantage of your absence to denigrate your name and skills as a leader. I've heard rumors that a few of the Council members are on his side, but I'm not sure how much truth there is to the rumors. I was angry with you on the quad, but I know you wouldn't have stayed without good cause. I know you want this war ended as much as I do."

Anna frowned. "What am I supposed to say, then? If the Council's already against me, there isn't much I can do."

"Just tread carefully and make sure you don't say anything that could be used against you."

"I'll do my best," Anna responded. "I like to think I'm doing some good for Istamba, and I don't intend to stop."

"Please," he repeated. "Be *careful*."

Anna squared her shoulders and entered the Council chambers, determined to appear strong despite her exhaustion. The Council was assembled in their usual places, and Colonel Wells was seated at the end of their table, a smug look on his face. Collins entered behind Anna and took his usual place off to the side of the large room.

"Major Lieay," Althea began, "I trust you have a good explanation for endangering not only yourself, but two other soldiers by recklessly remaining in wraith territory."

"I don't believe what I did was reckless, Ma'am. I saw an opportunity to gain some valuable information, and I took it. In addition, we rescued a soldier being held within the city, one of the men from my regiment. I believe it sent a message to King Roland. Not only were we able to travel to his city and rescue our people, we infiltrated the city itself."

"As admirable as it is to save a fellow soldier, that doesn't excuse your actions," Colonel Wells said.

"Please, Colonel," Althea interrupted, "let the Council handle this. Did you say something about information?"

"When we snuck into the city, we found a guardhouse close to the gates. Inside, we found some journals and notes that hold critical information. I have them here." Anna pulled the journals and notes from the satchel and set them before Althea. "I had a chance to look through them on our way home. There are weapons inventory lists and troop counts, as well as tentative plans to move against us. I know what I did was risky and dangerous, but this is war. I understand what I did wasn't within my orders, but I made the decision to stay behind and gather information that I believe can help us win the war."

Anna folded her hands in front of her and waited for the Council to speak. Colonel Wells smiled broadly.

"Major, would you give us a moment? Colonel Wells, would you step out as well?"

Anna nodded and stepped into the side room with Colonel Wells following closely behind. He sat near the back of the room, fiddling with his officer's pin. She ignored him and positioned herself near the door. So long as she remained quiet, she could just barely hear the Council talking within. She only hoped Colonel Wells couldn't hear anything.

"Well," Anna heard Althea say, "what do you make of the situation, General?"

"What Major Lieay did was dangerous, but I think it would be a mistake to dismiss her from the fighting force—when we should be rewarding her for her bravery. Because of the risk she took, we have important information that we can use to our advantage. The message she sent to Roland was clear as well; even his city itself is not safe from us. Additionally, she succeeded in her original mission to rescue the slaves. I would recommend Stars of Valor for each of her troops, and an additional Star for the three that stayed behind with her."

A faint smile played at Anna's lips. Even after everything she'd done, the General was still fighting for her. She only hoped the Council would be able to see things from her point of view.

"Thank you for your input, General," Althea said. "This Council has made a decision. Despite what you may have heard from other officers, I can assure you this Council makes its own decisions. Now that you have returned, we are more prepared to deal with Colonel Wells. His actions have been proven not to suit our best interests, as I'm sure you'd agree."

Anna glanced over at the Colonel. What *had* he been doing? She flicked her eyes away before he caught her staring, but she missed the rest of Althea's words.

"Good," she heard someone say. "Call the Major and the Colonel back in."

Anna leapt back from the door and turned away so it wouldn't look like she was listening, though she was dying to know what she'd missed. The door opened, and Colonel Wells sauntered back into the main Council chambers. Anna rolled her eyes at his back and followed.

"Major Lieay," Althea said, once she was standing before the Council again, "while you did not directly disobey orders, you deliberately risked your life and the lives of two other soldiers by choosing to enter the dark city without first conferring with your leadership. In such cases, the offending officer is stripped of their titles and honors and discharged from the fighting force permanently, pending further disciplinary action."

Anna winced. When they laid it out like that, what she'd done sounded a lot worse.

"However," Althea continued, "you demonstrated an ability to act under pressure and with bravery. And you not only succeeded in rescuing over one hundred slaves and recovering one of your own soldiers, you also succeeded in bringing back valuable information that may help us end this war once and for all. Therefore, this Council has decided to promote you to Colonel, and you and your troops will each receive Stars of Valor."

Anna swelled with pride and her chin rose a fraction of an inch.

"You must be joking!" Colonel Wells shouted.

"Colonel Wells, hold your tongue!" Althea commanded. "This

Council has made one other decision. You have been accused of undermining another officer behind her back and attempting to have her deposed by bribing other soldiers. You are also suspected of attempting to bribe Council members. You will be suspended, pending a formal hearing. Dismissed."

"You can't just—"

"Colonel Wells, you are on dangerous ground as it is. Don't make things worse for yourself. You have been dismissed."

Wells glared at the Council for a moment before throwing a scathing look at Anna and storming from the Council chambers.

Collins sighed and shook his head. "Althea, will you send a few of your soldiers to detain the Colonel?"

Althea gave a curt nod and signaled to a page before turning back to Anna.

"Apologies, Colonel Lieay. Here is your new command pin. Who was it that you saved from within the city?" Althea asked.

"Michael Telin," Anna answered, still slightly in shock from her promotion.

"When he is well enough, we would like to speak with him. For now, go to the infirmary to have any injuries tended and get some rest."

"Yes, Ma'am," she said.

"Dismissed."

Anna saluted, grateful for the Council's decisions. She didn't like having to stay the night in the infirmary, but she wasn't about to push her luck any further. She entered the infirmary and saw Alex and Kyree speaking with one of the Sanctuary's counselors while a healer checked their minor wounds. Michael was lying in a bed next to them, sound asleep. She sat on a bed near her friends and held out the Major's pin to Alex.

He took it before saying, "You're joking. They promoted you again?"

"Yes, and they suspended Colonel Wells. Apparently, he tried to bribe Council members while we were gone."

"I wish I had your luck," Kyree said. She rolled over and quickly fell asleep. Anna stared at Kyree's back. She didn't see herself as lucky. If she were, she'd still have her parents.

"Night," mumbled Alex as he rolled over too.

Anna banished her memories before pulling off her boots and weapons and placing them under the cot. For the first time in days, she felt safe. The barriers around the safe houses were nice, but with the wraiths chasing them, every sound made her jump, expecting a potential attack in the dark. It didn't help to know that on rare occasions the barriers *could* falter and let a wraith through. Here, others were on patrol and she could let go. Her lids closed on their own and her exhaustion finally took over, sending her into a deep sleep.

Golden light filtered through the high windows in the infirmary, shining on Anna's bed. She stretched lazily, feeling more rested than she had in the last few weeks, when she heard cheering and yelling coming from the hallway. She sat up in time to see her troops burst through the doors, making a beeline for their small group of cots. She smiled. Trust her troops to make an entrance. She stood and was quickly caught in Jonathan's embrace.

"Don't you ever do that again," he scolded. "We were worried sick."

"No promises," she said wryly.

Each of her troops embraced her, Kyree, and Alex in turn. Even Ian managed a one-arm hug, though Anna knew he'd never admit it. Finally, the commotion woke Michael, who struggled into a sitting position.

"Hey guys," he said.

They all gaped at him before barraging him with questions, well wishes, and hugs, when a healer interrupted.

"I know you all are excited, but Soldier Telin still needs some care, and you are disrupting my patients. All of you, out." She turned to Alex, Kyree, and Anna. "You three are free to go with them; just take it easy for the next few days. Now, shoo!"

Her regiment said their goodbyes to Michael before rushing to the barracks, eager to hear the whole story. Anna and Alex brought up the rear, glad they didn't have to run for their lives anymore. When they reached the barracks, her troops immediately bombarded her with questions about why they stayed behind, what the city was like, and how they managed to get away. Anna waved down their questions and had them settle in for their story.

"If you'll all be quiet, we can tell you what happened."

Her regiment settled down, eagerly awaiting the tale. Once they were silent, Anna began recounting their story. She told them how they'd used the wraiths' uniforms to sneak in, how they stole the journals and found Michael, and finally how they'd survived the long trek north, running and hiding from the wraiths. Alex and Kyree would occasionally fill in a few details, but they left Anna to speak for the most part.

"It was a good thing we restocked the safe houses a few months ago," Anna finished. "I don't think we would have made it otherwise."

"Is Michael alright?"

"Michael should be fine, but I don't want everyone bothering him at once. He's been through a lot, and it's highly unlikely he'll be out on missions with us anytime soon. He's having a hard time getting what happened out of his mind. He'll have to recount his experience to the Council, but he mentioned that he has no desire to speak of it, so please don't ask. If he talks, fine, but respect his silence." Anna paused to make sure her troops had got the message. "One last thing: the Council promoted me to Colonel, and thus Alex to Major and Jonathan to Captain. And I'm authorized to commission a new Lieutenant."

"I'd like to put Oliver's name out there," Ele said shyly.

"Oh, awkward," Oliver said. "I was going to suggest Rebecca. While it would be interesting to be an officer, I'm not really a leader. I think Rebecca would be much better than me."

Rebecca blushed. "I'm flattered, and I'd love to. But that's up to our Colonel." She beamed back at Anna.

Anna made her decision. Jonathan handed over his Lieutenant pin and Anna fixed it on Rebecca's right shoulder next to her stars.

A few days later, Michael returned to the barracks, much to everyone's delight. As Anna had requested, they avoided the topic of his capture and imprisonment as best they could. Anna could tell they were all burning with curiosity, but it was evident he wasn't over it. Every now and then, Michael would drift off in conversation and then rapidly change the subject. He did participate in some of their training exercises, but mostly sat off to the side.

The rescue of the slaves had the desired effect. The people of the Sanctuary were filled with new hope for the future, and the atmosphere in the Sanctuary was happy and full of life. The wraiths tightened the perimeter around their city, leaving most of the forest alone. With the lack of wraith troop movements and attacks, there wasn't much for the regiments to do. Anna and her troops, with the exception of Michael, were often assigned to check up on various human settlements around the Sanctuary.

While the refugees went about their daily lives, Anna noticed she saw General Collins around less and less. When she did see him, he was darting in and out of the Council chambers at all hours, likely planning some sort of attack. All she had to do now was wait for the next big mission—and hopefully, the end of the war.

⚜ 35 ⚜

Adaka flitted from branch to branch, catching the attention of the soldier watching the sunset. He scanned the quad to ensure that he wasn't observed before sneaking past the old buildings and venturing through the barrier and into the woods.

He walked for a few minutes before the forest around him went silent and a shadow emerged from behind one of the trees.

"It's been a while," the soldier said. "I thought you were satisfied with my information sent by daka."

The wraith stepped closer to the soldier. "His Majesty wants this war ended."

The soldier scoffed. "Don't we all."

"We intend to cripple the humans, but his Majesty has an important task for you."

The soldier paced back and forth between the trees. "I'm already sending you information. I don't think there's much more I can do."

"You can kill the Lieay girl."

The soldier stared at the wraith. "You want me to kill Colonel Lieay? Are you insane? Not only is she a great soldier, but she—"

"She what?" the wraith snarled.

"It's just not possible," the soldier said, shaking his head. "She's too well protected; especially while she's in the Sanctuary." Unwilling to argue the point, he pivoted on his heel and headed out of the clearing.

"You will be turned immediately following her death."

The soldier turned back toward the wraith, stunned by his words. "Even if the war is still going?"

The wraith nodded. "Yes, but as I said, we will be crushing the humans sooner than you might think. As soon as Lieay is dead, you will be granted a place in our city. King Roland himself has decreed that you will have a position of honor among our ranks.

The soldier took a deep breath. "Very well. I should have an opportunity to kill her the next time she goes out on a mission."

"Do not fail us," the wraith whispered as it blended back into the trees, leaving the soldier alone in the night.

The soldier glanced back at the Sanctuary. Could he really kill Anna after everything they'd been through?

He stared up at the moon, then back at the shadows around him. The humans deserved to crumble. The Sanctuary deserved to burn. He deserved vengeance after they'd abandoned his people and left him to fend for himself against the bandits that had murdered his family.

Could he kill Anna to finally gain some peace for himself? Yes, he could.

The soldier turned and walked back toward the Sanctuary, carefully re-entering the barrier unnoticed. He was just walking back around one of the old buildings when he heard a voice call his name.

"Alex? What are you doing out here?" Anna asked.

Alex looked at Anna's loyal, kind face. "I thought I saw something in the trees," he lied smoothly. "Turns out it was just a bird."

Anna smiled. "Well, it's past curfew. We should probably head inside the barracks.

Alex nodded. "I'm right behind you."

A few days later, Anna was watching Mariana and Ian spar with Liam and Rebecca in front of their barracks when a page came running up to her.

"Colonel Lieay, the Council needs you immediately. It's urgent."

Anna nodded. "Right. Alex, take over here. Continue partnered combat drills."

Anna nodded to the page and followed him back to the Council chambers, where she was admitted immediately.

"Colonel Lieay, we have a problem," Althea said.

"What is it?"

"We intercepted a daka carrying information about a small group of wraiths at Tanaba Ridge. General Collins and his regiment left two days ago, and today, one of the soldiers returned, badly injured. The soldier said they were ambushed and trapped in a small safe house. It's clear now that the wraiths intended for us to intercept the information. We are sending your regiment to rescue the General and his men."

"Of course. We'll leave at once."

Anna took the mission scroll from Althea's outstretched hand, saluted, and left the Council chambers. As soon as she was out the door, she sprinted back to the barracks. Her troops looked up when they saw her coming.

"Everything okay, Anna?" Ele asked.

"No," she said. "Two days ago, General Collins went out on a mission. There was supposed to be a small group of wraiths camped out at Tanaba Ridge. Unfortunately, there were too many wraiths for them to handle, and they became trapped in the safe house with many soldiers injured. They did manage to get a single soldier out to report back to us and ask for help. The Council is sending us to retrieve the General and his men—and, hopefully, get rid of the wraiths while we're there."

"So, what are we waiting for? Let's go." Liam said.

Anna looked at her troops.

"I'm not going to lie you. This mission—" Anna trailed off, not quite sure how to explain her feeling of certainty about the situation. "It's a trap. I know it is, and General Collins is the bait. I can guarantee that we'll be walking into an ambush; it's one that we may not come back from. This mission is far more dangerous than going to the city, because they know we're coming. I won't ask you to throw your lives away for this mission. So if anyone wants to stay behind, they can, with no judgment or repercussions. I'm going after Collins, but I don't expect anyone else to come with me."

Ian glanced around before speaking up. "I could do with an adventure. I'm in."

"Right," Mariana echoed, "and we aren't about to leave Collins to fend for himself."

There was a murmur of agreement among the rest of the troops.

Jonathan stepped forward. "You're our leader, Anna. We'll follow you."

Anna's heartbeat echoed in her ears. She almost wanted to order them to stay at the Sanctuary, but they'd never let her go alone, and she couldn't leave the General. He'd become like a father to her, and there was no way she'd leave him to the wraiths.

"Michael, I know you're getting better, but I want you to stay behind. You're still a liability in battle." Anna looked at Michael and saw relief etched on his face. They both knew he was in no way ready for a fight. "The rest of you, gear up. We need to leave as soon as possible."

Her troops jumped up at once, and a few left for the supply

rooms, returning as quickly as they could. Anna followed the others into the barracks and grabbed the bag she kept prepared for situations like this. She threw in a few extra daggers, and strapped her spare short sword to her back before going outside to wait for the rest of her soldiers.

"Good luck," Michael said.

Anna briefly rested a hand on his shoulder in what she knew could be a permanent farewell. "Let's move out."

Her troops shouldered their packs and followed Anna to the western exit route.

They traveled all day, trying to make light conversation, but it felt forced. They couldn't help but think of how Michael had been taken by the wraiths, and how damaged he still was from what they'd done to him; it was impossible not to fear for what was to come. They managed to make it to Ephesia, which only left about half a day's travel to Tanaba Ridge. They broke into their normal watch groups, but very few of them actually slept; they were all too anxious.

Anna had intended to let them sleep a little longer, but they were all up at dawn anyway, so they proceeded. As they walked, Anna couldn't avoid the fear that she was about to lead her friends to certain death. She shook away her negative thoughts and checked her map one last time before calling for a halt.

"Alright, we should be just a few miles out from the Ridge. As I said before we left, we are most definitely walking into a trap, but since we're aware and prepared for it, they won't be able to surprise us. The General and his men are our top priority. Their messenger said most of the soldiers were injured, so we won't be able to count on them for much help. Now, the safe house is small enough that we should be able to surround it. When we reach the clearing, I want everyone to get to the house and put it at your back. I don't care what you see or hear; if our backs are covered, that's one less way for us to be attacked. It's going to be a hard fight, but I believe in each and every one of you. Are you ready?"

"Lead on, Anna," Mariana said. "We know the plan."

Anna nodded and led her troops through the forest. Once she

could make out the clearing, it was easy to see what a perfect trap it made. Red sandstone cliffs arched behind the safe house, cutting off any escape route to the north. The only entrance was through the forest from the southwest side, which could easily hide enemies. Tanaba Ridge was beautiful, but deadly.

Anna began to hear rustling in the trees, though she couldn't actually see any wraiths. She and her troops broke into a steady jog. The closer they came to the clearing, the more noises they heard, and the faster they went. As soon as they emerged into the clearing, they sprinted to the safe house, trying to get there before the wraiths closed in. Once she had her back to the house, Anna could see her surroundings more clearly. Wraiths emerged from the trees and shadows on every side. Their sheer number was enough to finish off both regiments easily, but Anna refused to go down without a fight, and she knew her troops wouldn't either.

"You okay in there, General?" she shouted at the house.

The door opened a crack and she saw the General staring out at her. His face was drawn, and he had a long cut running from his right temple down to his chin. Dried blood was caked around his face and covered his hands. His troops must have been in worse shape than the Council's words had suggested.

"You shouldn't have come," he rasped. "They've set a trap, and now they'll kill us all."

Anna gave him a small smile. "I know. But we had to try."

Anna turned back around just in time to see a dagger coming for her chest. She raised a sword and batted away the oncoming blade with a grunt. The dagger landed harmlessly to her left, and Anna surveyed the wraiths stepping out from the trees. She was able to see about a hundred wraiths, and she knew there were more on the other side of the safe house.

She adjusted her grip on her swords. To her right, she saw Rebecca notch an arrow, her eyes narrowed as she surveyed the clearing. Glancing back to her left, she saw Alex heft his sword and shift from foot to foot in anticipation of the fight to come. Anna nodded to him and tried to smile reassuringly, but she knew it didn't reach her eyes.

"You ready for this?" she asked Alex.

"Not at all," he replied. His eyes were hard and his mouth was set in a tight line.

Anna stared at the circle of wraiths, dread settling in her stomach.

"Seven-Seven!" she yelled.

Her troops were silent for a moment before their cry echoed off the stone walls of the Ridge, "Hoo-hoo-hoorah! Hoo-hoo-hoorah! Hoo-hoo-hoorah!"

The wraiths charged, and Anna lunged forward to meet them, letting loose a raw-throated yell. Alex was right beside her. She swung her swords faster than she ever knew she could, but the wraiths just kept coming. The seconds turned to minutes, the minutes melted away, and yet the fight wore on. Anna wanted nothing more than to drop her swords and end it, but she continued to push herself. *Humanity is Strength* pulsed through her mind, urging her to keep going.

She thrust her sword into wraith after wraith, visualizing each of her next moves in sequence. Even with all the conditioning, her limbs burned and her lungs ached. Her swords grew heavier and harder to hold as sweat covered her palms.

As she spun to the side, she saw Rebecca being drawn away from the safe house and she dashed over to her side. She managed to push Rebecca back to the safety of the wall, but in doing so, she was forced out into the army of wraiths alone. Wraith attacks came from all sides. Though she wore armor, it didn't protect against the numerous bruises each blow gave her. She swung her swords furiously, deflecting attack after attack, but she could feel herself wearing down.

Her attacks became weaker and weaker. Instead of delivering killing blows, she barely managed to scratch her opponents. Her legs began to wobble, and she gave in to the pain and exhaustion, dropping to one knee. Her breath came in short bursts and she saw black spots in her vision, blocking out the faces of her enemies.

Anna saw a sword coming straight for her head, and fear filled her entire being. Her body froze and she couldn't force her arm up to block the blow. Suddenly, the sword clattered to the ground, and the wraith holding it fell to dust as another blade was forced through his chest. Anna blinked to try and clear the haze of exhaustion and panic from her mind, when a hand entered her field of vision. She took it, and a strong arm pulled her to her feet.

"You didn't think we'd leave you out here alone, did you?"

Anna felt a smile pull at her lips. "General," she gasped out, "thank—"

"You can thank me later." He swung his sword to block a wraith's attack and turned back to her. "Catch your breath. But there are still many more to fight."

General Collins launched himself back into the fray. Anna saw him pull a wraith away from Rebecca while a few of his soldiers emerged from the safe house and joined the fight. Though he and his soldiers were obviously exhausted, the extra people helped to embolden her own troops, and Anna felt hope fill her once again. She took a firm grip on her sword and charged back into the battle, slashing at the wraiths surrounding her friends. Even though only a few of the General's soldiers were able to join the fight, it was enough to finish off the remaining wraiths.

After dispatching the final wraith, Anna stood tall, rolling her shoulders to alleviate some of the soreness. Looking around, she could see that nearly everyone had received some minor wounds. If it hadn't been for the armor they'd won from previous missions, they would all be in much worse condition. She felt numerous bruises beginning to form all over. She gingerly touched her jaw and felt the warm wetness of blood. Aside from a few more small cuts, she would be fine to continue, and she turned her attention to the rest of her troops.

She saw Alex struggle out of his armor. As he dropped it to the ground, Anna noticed the breastplate was heavily dented in the center, but he seemed to be unharmed. Ian looked the worst of everyone; the wraiths must have targeted him because of his size. Anna could see a large gash running from his forehead to his ear.

His legs were trembling and covered in blood from a dagger firmly lodged in his right thigh.

"Everyone, patch up your wounds as best you can," she said, feeling infinitely weary. "Ask for help if you need it. I don't want any injuries getting worse through lack of care."

Ele pulled out the emergency supplies she'd brought and tended to herself first, ripping a length of bandage off to wrap around a gash in her arm, so that she could help everyone else. She started with Oliver; after reprimanding him for re-spraining his arm, she set it again for him. Carefully, she worked her way through the soldiers, ensuring that they could at least make the walk back to the Sanctuary.

Anna looked up as General Collins walked over to her.

"General, I—"

Anna's words were cut off as he pulled her into a tight embrace.

"Thank you, Anna," he whispered.

She pulled back and stared at his face. Blood was dripping from a new gash on his cheek and tears glistened in his eyes.

Anna smiled softly. "I think I should be thanking you."

Collins gave a dark chuckle. "Let's head home."

Anna nodded and turned to face her troops. "Back to the Sanctuary," she called out.

Her troops started their cheer, bringing a smile to the General and his men. They all walked back toward the forest where they had entered the clearing. Alex, however, hung back. Anna turned to see what kept him, and she was surprised to find him glaring at her in fury, his jaw clenched, his whole body shaking with rage. Letting loose a yell, he swung his sword in a wide arc at her head.

⚘— 37 —⚘

Anna barely had enough time to raise her sword to block the attack. The blow jarred her whole arm as she pushed Alex away from her.

"Why can't you just die?" Alex screamed.

He charged Anna again, and they exchanged a few more blows. Her troops tried to help, but Anna waved them away.

"Everyone, stay back," Anna called. "That's an order." Anna knew Alex's fighting style better than anyone else did. She wouldn't allow her troops to get hurt from this.

"You think you can face me by yourself?" Alex taunted.

"What are you doing, Alex?"

"What I should've done a long time ago. Just think how the King will reward me."

Anna shoved him back once more. Hatred gleamed in his eyes, like nothing Anna had ever seen. Suddenly, everything made sense: his hesitations in battle, his odd remarks concerning the war, his sneaking off all the time.

"You're my oldest friend here, Alex; don't make me do this."

"As if you could," he spat out. "You've always been weak. All humans are."

"You're human!"

"Not for long."

"So that's what he promised you. You really think Roland will keep his word? After everything?"

"It wasn't the wraiths who killed my parents, Anna, and now I'm going to help bring down the people who did."

Anna pushed off from Alex once more, and tears threatened to spill from her eyes, but she held them back. His movements became wilder as he thrashed at her with his sword. All hope of bringing him back to the Sanctuary alive left her head as pure survival instinct overtook her. Her muscles burned from the recent battle, but it was plain that Alex wouldn't hesitate to kill her. She lunged at Alex with all her strength and ripped his sword away. Before he could react, she plunged her blade into his chest, right to the hilt.

"I'm sorry," she whispered as he sank to the ground, unmoving.

Anna let out a sharp huff and dropped her eyes to his body, blood still dripping from the sword in her hand. She sucked in a short breath, the air cutting its way through her lungs. Looking back at her comrades, she locked her jaw and marched over to the group.

"Let's go," she said.

"What about his body?" Rebecca asked, her voice barely more than a whisper.

"Roland can have his spy. We need to get as close to the Sanctuary as we can before nightfall."

Without waiting for a response, she marched into the trees.

The journey back to the Sanctuary was tense and difficult. Most of the General's men needed assistance walking, and everyone was exhausted and in shock from Alex's betrayal. Aside from a few terse orders, Anna didn't speak to anyone. Jonathan and Ele tried to comfort her, but she didn't want sympathy; she didn't deserve it. Every time she moved, her chest tightened even more. She knew there were risks involved in war, but to have a threat come from a trusted friend—

Collins waved everyone else back so he could walk next to Anna. "Anna," he said.

She couldn't look at him. "I'll hand in my resignation as soon as we get back."

"Resignation?"

"He's likely the reason the war has gone on for so long. He's my responsibility, which makes this my fault."

"Anna," Collins said, "do you have any idea how many times I've failed? How many times I've made a mistake? Even this last mission—I should have realized it was a trap, but I went anyway. It's my fault so many of my soldiers are injured right now. I'm the reason your troops are injured right now. But that's no reason to resign. Mistakes are a part of life. It's how we learn, it's how we grow. Mistakes are what makes us who we are. I know things seem dark right now, but the Sanctuary needs you, your troops need you, and I need you." Collins paused and gave Anna a searching look. "Can I count on you, Colonel?"

Anna took a deep breath. "I won't resign." She increased her pace to leave the General's side. While his words had helped a bit, guilt still gnawed at her stomach. She needed time to think.

When they finally reached the Sanctuary, the General sent both his men and Anna's to the infirmary and led Anna to report to the Council. When they reached the chambers, the Council's guards let them in immediately.

"General Collins, I'm glad to see you're alright," Althea said. "If you will give your report, and then we would like yours as well, Colonel."

The General nodded and began his story. "As you know, we intercepted a daka with information about a wraith troop near Tanaba Ridge. We left that afternoon and stayed in Ephesia that night before making it to the Ridge the next afternoon. We didn't see any wraiths at first, but then they began to appear out of the forest from all over. It was as if they were herding us, and we had no choice but to fall into their trap. We managed to get to the safe house, but many of us were badly wounded in the process. The safe house provided us with a small respite from fighting, but we couldn't stay there indefinitely. We created a distraction and one of my soldiers managed to get away.

"In retrospect, he got out too easily. I believe the wraiths were setting a trap for the 77th and using us as bait. Eventually, Colonel

Lieay and her soldiers showed up and fought their way to us. When the fighting started, a few of my troops who were still able to fight went outside with me to help. Together, we managed to defeat the wraiths." The General stopped his report there. Anna supposed he was waiting for her to address what had happened with Alex.

"Thank you for your report, General. Colonel, if you would give us your report of what happened."

"We left almost immediately after you last called me here. We made it to Ephesia the first day and stayed there for the night. Before we reached the Ridge, I stopped my troops and told them my plan. I knew we'd be walking into a trap, but I hoped that anticipating it would help. I knew the general layout of the safe house and the ridge, but until I saw it, I never realized how perfect it was for an ambush.

"When we reached the clearing, my troops and I sprinted to the house and surrounded it. My hope was that our backs would be covered and we might have a better chance. My troops and I fought for what seemed like forever, but we finally managed to defeat the wraiths. I doubt we would have succeeded without the General's help, though. All of my troops were exhausted, but we weren't too badly wounded. We salvaged some of the wraiths' weapons and prepared to leave.

"Then . . . my second-in-command attacked me. From what he said, I'd guess he'd been conversing with the wraiths since the beginning of the war. He claimed that Roland would turn him if he killed me." Anna fell silent, unsure of what else she could say.

"And what happened to your second?"

"He's dead. I killed him."

Althea didn't speak for a few moments. Anna saw numerous emotions cross her face, from shock to anger, before she fixed her face into a mask.

Althea nodded. "It is truly unfortunate that one of our own thought allying with the wraiths was better than helping his own kind. We will start forming strategies to root out any other possible spies. General, how many of your troops will be out of commission?"

"Everyone needs some sort of medical attention, but only seven of them will be unable to fight for some time."

"Colonel, what of your troops?"

"One is still recovering from his stay in the dark city, and one is dead. Otherwise, everyone should be able to fight again after some rest."

"Thank you for your reports. Colonel, you are dismissed. Get your wounds attended to and rest for the next few days. You've earned it. General, if you'll stay, there are a few things we need to discuss."

Anna nodded and saluted before leaving. She walked slowly away from the Council chambers, heading to her barracks. A few soldiers saluted her on the way and a few others congratulated her on the most recent victory. Word had spread quickly of what had happened at Tanaba Ridge. She herself had killed over fifty wraiths and was being called a hero by all, but Anna didn't respond to anyone. She couldn't. She was afraid of what might happen if she opened her mouth. The shock was beginning to wear off, giving way to numbness.

"Anna," a voice called.

She turned to see Jonathan striding toward her.

"I know it's a little soon, but someone needs to clean out Alex's bunk, and being his commander, the job falls to you. If it's too much, I can take care of it."

Anna shook her head. "No," she replied, her voice cracking, "I'll take care of it. I need to face it eventually. Might as well be now."

"I could come with you, if you like."

"No. I'd really rather be alone."

Anna tried to make her lips curve into a smile, but her heart wasn't in it. Instead, she briefly rested a hand on Jonathan's arm, and continued on to the barracks. She walked in tentatively, hoping no one would notice her, but the barracks were empty. Anna guessed her regiment was giving her time.

She walked over to Alex's trunk and opened it. It was only half full. Like her, he'd come here with nothing. She took out the two shirts and the jacket and stared at them. He'd retrieved these from the safe houses they'd stayed in just after they'd met. She wondered if he'd been plotting against his own kind even then.

She forced herself to set the clothing aside. It would need to be reused, given to other soldiers. The Sanctuary wasn't in the habit of wasting anything. His armor was next. Most of it would be divided between the members of the 77th, but some of the more common pieces could go to the Sanctuary's armory. They would be happy to have some of the gold weapons.

Aside from a few more pieces of clothing and some maps and strategy plans, the trunk didn't have much else in it. Anna moved the weapons and armor into the entry area of the barracks for her soldiers to pick through, and went back to retrieve the clothes. He'd always seemed so normal. Sure, he didn't talk about his past very much, but not many people did here. Somehow, Roland had managed to ensnare Alex with false promises.

She stared at Alex's empty bed, fury filling her every limb. The numbness and sadness evaporated, replaced by fire and anger. She hated the wraiths and the war, but most of all, she hated Roland. He had been the first to strike, to rekindle the old war between wraiths and humans. He'd attacked her people, had her parents murdered, and now, he'd forced her to kill Alex.

Anna left the barracks to see the sun setting over the trees.

I will kill Roland, she thought, *along with every last wraith in the land.*

38

King Roland stared at the one-page mission report that had just been placed on his desk. Though he'd read the report already, he couldn't help but read it over and over again.

Tanaba Ridge attack: Defeat. No surviving wraiths. All humans returned to the Sanctuary.

That was it. The entire report. Granted, there wasn't anyone left alive to give a full report, but he suspected that wasn't the only reason behind the bare-bones information. He was furious. His advisors had assured him that the ambush would crush the humans, and thus, he had left it to them to plan the full attack.

That was obviously his mistake.

His advisors and officers had been utterly useless, and yet he continued to rely on their help. It was time to take this war into his own hands.

Roland stormed into the throne room where his officers and advisors were already assembled. At his entrance, they all fell silent and bowed their faces to the floor. Terror and hatred permeated the air. Though he very rarely used his persuasive influence on his own wraiths, he wanted them all to cower at his disappointment. He paced back and forth in front of them, glaring.

"Two years," he snarled. "Two years, and the humans have yet to crumble at my feet. Two years, and I am no closer to ruling Istamba. Two years, and all I have to show for it is an army of worthless imbeciles!"

"We did manage to wound the General's men."

"Wounds can be healed! You didn't manage to kill any of the humans. Two hundred wraiths, and not a single dead human."

"There was a body, my Lord."

"Of the useless spy!"

His troops began to shake, and one of his advisors spoke up. "My Lord, we could launch a counterattack. Lucian and his troops can be near the Sanctuary within a day."

"No," Roland barked, "not Lucian and his troops. I have sent attack after attack and all you bring back is failure. Ready all available troops. This time, I myself will lead my army to crush the Sanctuary once and for all."

39

A few days later, Anna gathered her troops in front of the barracks.

"Is there a reason we're up so early?" Liam grumbled.

Rebecca elbowed him, and he scowled at her before moving to the other side of the group.

Anna rolled her eyes before saying, "I know we're tired, but now is not the time to slack off. So, in light of our most recent mission, I'd like us to run some multi-person drills. I want one person fighting at least two others, then add a third opponent if you can manage it."

Her troops nodded and wearily split up into groups. Ian squared up against Mariana and Kyree, while Anna faced Oliver, Liam, and Ele. Anna ducked under Oliver's sword and turned her own to block Liam's. Standing up again, she raised her foot and kicked Ele back from her open side. Twisting, she disarmed Liam with a quick move. Elbowing him hard on his shoulder and kicking the back of his knee, she sent him to the ground, and turned to face her remaining opponents.

They made the mistake of standing next to each other, so she could attack both at once. Now evenly matched with her two swords, she easily gained the upper hand. Ele squinted as one of Anna's swords reflected the sun—Anna took advantage to disarm her as well. Oliver, distracted by one sword, didn't have time to block the other as it easily disarmed him.

"Dead," she proclaimed, holding a sword to each of their throats. Liam, watching from where he'd fallen, rolled over with a groan and got up, dust covering his right side.

"Every time," he said. "Do you have to hit so hard?"

"A wraith wouldn't soften their blows, and neither will I," Anna said.

"Anna!" Jonathan called, jogging up to their sparring area.

"Yes?"

"The General wants to speak with you. He's near the east barracks."

"Thanks. Take over here. Multi-person sword drills. One against at least two. Three if they can manage it."

Jonathan nodded, and Anna trekked across the Sanctuary grounds to the east barracks where she found General Collins observing some training exercises. She walked up to him and saluted.

"Ah, Colonel."

"You wanted to see me, General?"

"Yes. I wanted to speak to you about something of great importance, but I do have a question first."

"Oh?"

"Are you alright?"

"What do you mean?"

"Ever since the raid at Tanaba Ridge, you've been different. I've heard you've barely rested and have hardly stopped training long enough to get a meal. And you haven't given your troops much of a rest either. I know Alex was a good friend of yours, but life still goes on."

"I'm fine, and I don't see the problem with training. Tanaba Ridge was a deep blow to Roland, and now's the time to strike. You said you had something important to speak to me about, and if that was it, I'd like to return to my troops."

"I'm sorry, Anna. I'm just concerned about you, and I'm not the only one."

"General, please. I've told you I'm fine, and I am. So, if that's all . . ."

"Actually, it isn't. General Rike returned from a mission just before we returned from Tanaba Ridge and was wounded quite severely. He has now handed in his resignation, which means we're looking for a new 3rd General. I've spoken with General Horne, and he and I agree that you're the strongest candidate."

"Me? A General?" Anna asked, while apprehension grew in her chest. She'd allowed a traitor to go unnoticed. How could she be a General?

"Of course. Only ranking officers are eligible candidates, and out of the active officers, you are the best choice. You've proven yourself to be a strong leader and an amazing warrior. Not only that, your success has inspired the people of the Sanctuary in a way that many of the other officers cannot. I understand if this is too sudden, but I'd like to announce your promotion at the celebration tomorrow afternoon. If you accept, that is."

Anna took a deep breath. Perhaps she could use this promotion to make up for her mistakes. Maybe she could do even more good for her people.

"I'm honored, General. I would be happy to accept."

"Fantastic. I'd like to keep this quiet for the moment, if you don't mind. I don't want rumors of General Rike's retirement spreading to the wraiths."

"Of course, General. If that's all, I'd like to return to my troops."

"Until tomorrow, Colonel." General Collins surprised Anna by saluting her first, a sign of great respect. She saluted back.

◆━◆

The next day, Anna left her troops getting ready for the celebration, and went ahead to the main hall. General Collins had told her to arrive early so they could discuss how her promotion ceremony would go. Anna approached the platform where she saw the other senior officers already sitting. General Horne and General Collins were also there.

"Ah, Colonel Lieay. We've been waiting for you."

"Sorry, Sir. I was caught up."

"General Horne has a few announcements to make, and then I'll proceed to give a run-down of our latest victories. After that, I'd like to announce your promotion. When that's been announced, I'd like you to say a few words, if you don't mind. It doesn't have to be much, just something to preserve moral. Many of the soldiers already look up to you, and with General Rike's retirement, it will be good to show solidarity between the ranking officers."

"I don't mind saying something, though I wish you would have told me sooner."

The General laughed. "You'll do fine. The rest of the soldiers should be arriving soon. You can take a seat."

Anna took the open seat that General Collins pointed to. While she was sitting there, Anna took the time to survey the hall, set up as it was for this gathering instead of meals. They didn't normally have large meetings with all troops attending except for the barest minimum needed on patrol duty, but the Council was beginning to see a loss of spirit among the refugees and soldiers alike, and had asked General Collins to do something about it.

Anna and the other Colonels were up on the platform, sitting in an arc on one side. The Council arrived and took their seats on the other side of the platform. The two Generals sat directly in the middle, and an extra chair was placed next to them where General Rike would normally sit. He, however, was still unable to leave the infirmary.

The rest of the hall had rows of chairs that were slowly filling with soldiers trickling in after finishing their various assignments. Once everyone was assembled, General Collins called for silence. Althea then stepped up to address the crowd.

Anna tuned out most of the ceremony. She personally thought it was a waste of time, but what the Council wanted, the Council got. She contemplated what she was going to say to everyone after the General formally promoted her. She'd never been one for big speeches, and she'd never spoken in front of so many people before.

Just before General Collins stepped up to speak, she figured she had some idea of what she could say. Collins' voice brought her back to the present.

"Soldiers, one last thing before I let you return to your training. As some of you may have heard, General Rike has returned from his latest mission gravely injured. He is still recovering as we speak, but he has decided to withdraw from the fighting force. Which means we need to appoint a new 3rd General. I've spoken with the Council, and we have unanimously agreed that Colonel Lieay will take his place."

The General's last few words were drowned out by cheering and applause from the crowd.

"Please," the General shouted over the noise, silencing the crowd, "calm down. Colonel, if you'll rise."

Anna stood from her seat and moved to stand in front of the General.

"Colonel Anna Lieay," he began, "the governing body of this Sanctuary, acting in accordance with ancient laws set down by our ancestors, has placed special trust in your ability to command your fellow soldiers. In view of your achievements on the battlefield and your demonstrated potential to serve in higher standing, you are hereby promoted to the rank of 3rd General. Do you swear to uphold the laws and traditions of this Sanctuary to the best of your abilities?"

"I do."

"Do you swear to protect the people of Istamba against the might and terror of wraith rule?"

"I do."

"Do you swear to embody the ideals of our creed, *Humanity is Strength*, to the best of your abilities?"

"I do."

Collins fixed the General's pin on Anna's right shoulder, just above her Stars of Valor. "Congratulations, General."

He finished by saluting Anna, and the rest of the Assembly stood and saluted her as well. Anna turned to face the room and motioned for everyone to sit down.

"Soldiers of the Sanctuary," she said, "these past few years have been difficult for all of us. We've lost friends and family, but through everything, we are still here. We are still fighting, and we have endured. Now we are closer than ever to defeating the wraiths and reclaiming Istamba for humanity. Thank you."

Anna bowed her head and sat back down. When the applause died down, General Collins stood up once more.

"Soldiers, thank you for your attendance. Please return to your regular assignments."

Anna walked off the platform and headed straight back to her barracks. Under normal circumstances, she would be ecstatic. Not only had she taken on and defeated more wraiths at once than anyone else, at fifteen, she was the youngest General in human history. She should be celebrating with her friends, but all she could think about was Alex. She'd been able to push his betrayal from her mind so far. She'd thrown herself into training and pushed herself harder than ever. She quickly wiped her tears with a sleeve as she heard elated yells coming her way. Oliver and Ele were leading the rest of her troops to find her.

"Why didn't you tell us you were going to be promoted?" Oliver asked.

"Because you can't keep your mouth shut," Anna said with a smile. "Collins wanted it to be a secret until it was official, but we do have a few things to take care of. Everyone in."

Anna held the barrack door open as everyone funneled in.

"Alright," Anna began, "with my promotion and Alex's loss, Jonathan, you are now a Colonel, which makes Rebecca a Major. That means I'm free to appoint a Captain and a Lieutenant. Now—"

Three sharp blasts interrupted Anna. She looked at Jonathan, eyes wide.

"Barrier alert, south side! Go!"

She and her troops grabbed their weapons and tore out of the barracks, heading for the southern side of the Sanctuary. They were the first soldiers to arrive, as most were still socializing in the main hall.

Anna looked out past the barrier. She couldn't see any wraiths, but that didn't mean they weren't out there. The sentries had a much better view of the forest in their high towers that stood at each of the four corners of the Sanctuary. To have sounded such an alarm meant there was something big coming toward them. Anna saw movement about a hundred yards out and slightly to her right. It was a wraith. She was smiling broadly, showing her fangs.

Anna's eyes narrowed. She sheathed both her swords and took off running after the wraith. She didn't think twice about leaving the safety of the barrier, nor did she hear Jonathan shouting at her to return. Only one thought consumed her as she ran toward the wraith. *Revenge.*

"Anna! No!" Jonathan yelled at Anna's back.

Blood pounded in Anna's ears, blocking out Jonathan's call. Her vision narrowed, and she quickly closed in on the wraith. She threw one of her daggers. It struck the wraith's calf and caused her to stumble. Anna pulled out her swords and beheaded her with a swift cut.

"Quite impressive."

Anna turned to face the voice coming from her right. As she looked around, she realized she was completely surrounded. In her haste and blind rage, she hadn't noticed she was running straight into a trap, with no reinforcements and no escape. The wraith that had spoken stepped forward.

"King Roland," Anna said, surprised at the strength in her voice.

"General. Congratulations on your promotion. Too bad it will be short-lived."

He leapt at her in a move so quick, she barely had time to react. She brought her swords up just in time to meet his as they engaged in a deadly match. Anna was a fantastic dueler, but even she was outmatched by Roland's speed and strength. She was easily able to combat his soldiers, but he was a Wraith King, fueled by all that he had turned. Their strength was his strength, and he easily wore Anna down. He struck her right shoulder hard, causing her to drop the sword from that hand, but Anna raised the sword in her left hand and caught the guard of one of his swords, yanking it from him.

Evenly matched again, they pushed off one another only to surge back again. Overconfident, Roland left a small opening, and Anna managed to give him a shallow wound on his side. Taking advantage of his surprise, Anna knelt and grabbed her mother's dagger from her right boot. Roland, furious that Anna had drawn first blood, attacked with more ferocity and Anna couldn't hang on. Her left arm, already weak from so much fighting, began to spasm, and Roland sent her sword to the ground with a loud clang.

"Bravely fought, General," Roland mocked as he leveled his sword at her stomach, "but it's time for you to die."

Anna stared down the length of the sword. Fury and rage swelled within her. Adjusting her grip on her dagger, she angled the point forward. She grabbed Roland's sword arm and pulled herself forward, twisting to the side as best she could but still feeling the blade slice into her abdomen.

"Funny, I was thinking the same thing," she said.

She seized his shoulder and thrust the dagger through his neck. The shock had just barely registered in his eyes before he disintegrated to a pile of dust at her feet.

Anna stared at the pile of dust, eyes wide. She hadn't expected that to work, and she still didn't fully believe he was dead. Her head snapped up as snarling and hissing filled the air around her. The wraiths surrounding the small clearing were advancing toward her, their red eyes flashing in anger. Anna grimaced as she spun in circles, trying to distract herself from the pain in her stomach while trying to figure out a way to escape. The wraiths came closer and closer and Anna's breaths came out in ragged bursts. Fear settled in her stomach before ice rushed through her veins and heat flooded her face.

Gold weapons flashed in the sun all around her, and she couldn't see past the crowd of red and shadow.

I am going to die, she thought.

She squeezed her eyes shut as the wraiths advanced, preparing for the final blow, but it never came. She felt as if time around her had stopped; she could no longer hear the threatening noises coming from the wraiths. A heavy silence surrounded her, and all she could hear were her own deep breaths, ringing in her ears.

When she opened her eyes, her whole field of vision was tinted gold. She glanced down at herself and saw a golden halo of light surrounded her like a cloak. She felt powerful, strong. As she flicked her eyes back up, she saw a sword coming straight for her chest. A piercing scream escaped her lips, and a surge of energy bust from her hands, striking each of the wraiths, snaking through their ranks and turning them all to dust.

Her breathing slowed, and the gold faded from her vision as the light faded from her person. She stared at the ring of dust, her mind unable to comprehend what had just happened.

Rustling came from one end of the clearing and Anna wearily turned her head to see Jonathan and the rest of her regiment appearing from the trees.

"Anna?" he said.

Jonathan's eyes slowly took in the thick ring of dust around her before moving down to her midsection. Following his line of sight, she saw that she was wet with blood; Roland's sword had cut deep. The adrenaline from her fight began to fade, and pain started to spread from the wound. Anna's legs, already tired from fighting, gave out as she collapsed in a limp pile on the forest floor.

"Anna!"

Jonathan rushed forward and tried to keep her awake. "Don't go to sleep. Stay with me," he implored.

Anna's eyes fluttered and her vision blurred. The shapes around her became nothing more than huge blobs, slowly losing their color.

"Jonathan . . ." she whispered before her eyes shut and everything went black.

40

General Collins surveyed the massive crowd that had gathered to hear his speech. In the week and a half since Roland had been killed, many refugees had left the Sanctuary, yearning to return to the life they'd had before the war. Still, there was a large enough crowd left to make him slightly nervous. He took a deep breath to calm his nerves before mounting the stage and facing the crowd.

"Soldiers and citizens of Istamba," Collins began, "we are here today to celebrate a momentous occasion. Our war with the wraiths has finally ended!" The General paused as the crowd cheered. "Today, we recognize the great deeds of our heroes and the sacrifices of our fallen. Any who have fought these past few years, please stand. Citizens, look around you. Let us have a round of applause for our brave warriors!" The General paused again as everyone applauded their heroes.

"Now, I'd like to take a moment of silence for those who have fallen in battle, for those loved ones we have lost. Remember, those who are no longer with us did not die in vain. They gave us the chance to live a happy life, free from the wraiths' oppression.

"There is one last person we have to thank for our victory: the great General Lieay! It was her bravery and strength that led to our victory. She herself was the one to wield the blade that ended King Roland's life, but in doing so, she withstood a grave injury. The Council and I have decided to present her with an award for special services to humanity."

The crowd applauded once more.

"As many of you may have heard, we have begun relocating people back to their homes and villages. Some soldiers are returning to their homes as well and have volunteered to escort groups of civilians. I can assure you that the forest is safe once again, but the soldiers are there for your peace of mind. Thank you, everyone, for your support and service over these past few years. Now, we can look toward a bright future!"

The General stepped down from the stage and walked back to his office, the sounds of applause and celebration fading with each step. Reaching his office, he shut the door and collapsed in his chair. After all these years, there was finally peace, and he didn't know what to do with himself. After the civilians returned to their homes, he was going to leave for a small western village. The Council had asked him to stay on and manage the Sanctuary, but he wanted a quiet life. Besides, the Sanctuary was keeping track of every soldier that was returning home in case the need for them arose again.

His thoughts went back to Anna and the day she'd killed Roland. He'd heard the horns sounding an attack and rushed to the southern barrier, only to see Anna running into the trees after a wraith. Her second had turned to him for orders, and the two of them had decided to take the regiment and follow Anna out into the forest. When they reached her, there was nothing left of the wraiths but dust. Judging by the thick ring of dust that surrounded Anna, he guessed there had been a great number of wraiths in the clearing, but in her wounded state, there was no way she would have been able to defeat them all.

He couldn't figure out how Anna had possibly defeated so many on her own, especially when he had to save her at Tanaba Ridge. Unfortunately, with her grievous wound, she had passed out almost instantly. They'd rushed Anna's inert body back to the Sanctuary, but based on the healers' looks, no one had thought she was going to make it.

She'd always been such a strong warrior, but seeing her in the infirmary, pale and weak, he was struck by how small she was.

He'd never really considered how much she had sacrificed for the Sanctuary and her people, but she'd set aside her whole childhood to fight the wraiths. She'd changed her entire life to help them.

That girl. Sure she'd followed orders, but loosely, always having her own interpretation. She'd ignored common sense time and time again, and nearly killed herself in the process. Despite all this, he owed her his life. They all did.

He rifled through some of the papers on his desk. Though the war was over, he still had mountains of work to do. The people living in the Sanctuary had begun to return to their villages almost immediately. No one really wanted to stay at the Sanctuary longer than necessary, and he was having a hard time assigning enough escorts for the massive amount of people vacating their temporary homes within the old stone walls.

Then there were the soldiers. Roland and his wraiths were gone, but the Council still wanted a record of everyone who had fought and where they were all heading after they left the Sanctuary. They said it was in case of an emergency, but he suspected it was a power move. They wanted to keep a watch on anyone who might threaten their rule in the future.

A knock on his door startled him.

"Come in," he called.

A page entered. "The Council requests your presence."

The General sighed, getting up from his desk. "Very well. I'll be right there." He closed his office door behind him and walked toward the Council chambers. Now that he was playing politics with the Council, he almost missed the war. At least *that* he understood.

⚜ 41 ⚜

Pain. Darkness. More pain. Anna knew nothing else. Then she felt a warm hand embrace her cold one. It gave her a comforting squeeze. Anna's eyes felt heavy as she tried to pry them open.

"Anna?" called a soft voice.

Anna tried to make her mouth move, but all she could manage was a soft groan. Finally, she was able to open her lids a small crack. Light flooded her eyes, causing her to scrunch up her face in pain. Groaning again, she forced her eyes open and stared past the headache, trying to make sense of the bright blur in front of her.

"Take it easy."

Anna recognized Jonathan's voice coming from one side of her. She felt a glass being pressed against her lips, and drank the offered water, relief filling her as it washed the scratchiness from her throat and the dryness from her mouth. Blinking to clear her sight, she slowly shifted her head to bring Jonathan into view.

"Jonathan? What happened? Where am I?"

"You're back at the Sanctuary, in the infirmary."

"Infirmary?"

"You very nearly died. We managed to get you back here in time."

"How long have I been here?"

"About ten days. You've healed surprisingly quickly, but I still had the healers keep you asleep for most of it. I knew you'd try to leave if they didn't."

Anna rolled her eyes, but gave him a small smile. He was right. She'd always hated infirmaries and never stayed long, no matter what her injury was. She thought back to the last thing she could remember, trying to shake the sleep from her mind.

"Roland!" she exclaimed. "The wraiths!"

She tried to sit up, but Jonathan pushed her back down.

"I said take it easy, and don't worry about the wraiths. They're all dead."

"What happened?"

"You don't remember?"

"Vaguely. It all happened in such a rush. But Roland—I killed him."

"Yeah." Jonathan's brow furrowed. "About that, Collins and the rest of the regiment and I, we didn't get there in time to see the fight, but it looked like you killed a few hundred wraiths all on your own. How?"

Anna gingerly shook her head. "I don't know. I nearly skewered myself to kill Roland, and after that, everything else is pretty much a blur."

"Hmm," Jonathan said. "If I were you, I'd think up a better story for when Collins comes to ask you about it. I know you're still not fully healed, but considering what happened, I doubt he'll accept 'I don't know' as an answer."

Anna looked away, and silence stretched between the two as Anna thought about Jonathan's words. Even if Collins asked, how could he expect her to give more of an explanation than she had? It wasn't like he could do anything to her if she couldn't explain.

"What's happened over the past few days?" Anna finally asked.

"We brought you back here as fast as we could. It didn't take long for the news of your victory to spread throughout the Sanctuary. The Council sent scouts to search the forest, and they couldn't find signs of wraiths anywhere, so it's been decreed that the wraiths are gone. Collins thinks they all fled across the southern sea once their king was killed.

"A few groups of refugees have already left for their homes, but most of the soldiers are still here. They also had a big awards ceremony. Collins wanted to wait for you, but I told him you'd rather not be the center of attention anyway. Anyone who fought was recognized, and those who made the most difference received special thanks. They gave you a medal. Here."

Jonathan set a gold medal in her hand. It was shaped like a shield about the size of her palm. On the front was the seal of the Sanctuary: two swords crossing in front of a hand clenched in a fist. Their motto, *Humanity is Strength*, was etched along the bottom with decorative scrollwork around it. Anna turned the medal over to see a second inscription.

"Special Services to Humanity," Anna read off the back.

"Yeah. It's a little dramatic, but you deserve it. You ended the war. You're the reason everyone can return home and start their lives again."

"Not everyone."

"Don't do that, Anna. You saved so many people."

"I suppose. When can I get out of here?"

"That didn't take long. You were lucky. It was a clean cut and didn't hit any vital organs. You healed remarkably quickly, but you'll still feel weak for a while. Just take it easy over the next few days. I know you want to leave, but I really think you should stay here. At least for another day."

"I guess I can manage another day. I am pretty tired still. Do you mind if I get some sleep? I don't think whatever the healers gave me has completely worn off yet."

"Of course. I have to take care of a few things, but I'll be back when you wake up, and probably with the rest of the regiment. They're all anxious to see you."

Anna smiled and closed her eyes. She heard Jonathan rise and leave the infirmary. His footsteps grew more and more faint until she could no longer hear them at all. Sitting back up, she looked around the hall and saw no one. Pulling back her blankets she stood, nearly collapsing from the effort. She wore an infirmary robe, but she saw that someone had brought her clothes and placed them at the foot of the bed.

Her armor had been returned to the barracks, for which she was grateful. She didn't think she could lift too much in her condition. She pulled on the brown leggings and her hunting boots before easing the simple cotton shirt over her head. It was light enough not to rest too heavily on her wound, and loose enough that the bulkiness of the bandages wasn't noticeable. Whoever had brought the clothes had also brought her the old hunting jacket she always wore when she wasn't in armor. She was glad for its warmth as well as the comfort of something familiar.

Next to where Jonathan had put the medal, she saw both her General's pin and her mother's dagger. She assumed Jonathan had brought them both. She was glad, though. She always carried the dagger with her. It was small enough to conceal but big enough to do good damage in a fight. It always gave her comfort to have it close, which Jonathan knew. She tucked the dagger in her boot and slipped the medal and the command pin into her jacket pocket.

Quietly and carefully, she made her way out the back of the infirmary. She didn't want to attract any attention. The people might see her as a hero, but all she wanted was to leave and start a new life like so many of the refugees. She used back hallways and shadowy corners to her advantage as she made her way over to the supply rooms. When she got there, she found it, thankfully, unguarded now that the war was over. Though the walk over hadn't been difficult, she was in no condition to face anyone. She grabbed a small shoulder bag from one of the rooms and filled it with food and some extra clothes from two of the other rooms. She also found a few extra bandages and threw them into the bag as well.

As night fell over the Sanctuary, Anna made the trek up to the northern end of the Sanctuary to the forest practice area, figuring that no one would come looking for her there. Pulling out the spare jacket she found, she curled up and slept under the roots of one of the larger trees. She woke up a few times during the night from the pain in her stomach, but it wasn't anything she couldn't handle.

When she woke the next morning, she checked the bandages. The wound was fairly small, and it went all the way through the right side of her midsection, but it was clean and had closed tightly. Jonathan was right; she'd healed very quickly. She figured the wound would be nothing more than a small scar in a few more weeks. She wrapped the bandages back around her stomach and stood, gingerly stretching so as not to break open the wound. She then made her way around the edge of the barrier back to the southernmost side. Anna didn't want to stay here longer than necessary, and she was eager to get going.

She snuck out with one of the massive waves of refugees attempting to return to their shattered homes and broken villages. She left everything in her barracks, only carrying the things she'd taken from the supply room, her mother's dagger, her command pin, and her medal of honor. Though she wanted to leave the war behind and forget everything that had happened, she couldn't leave without those few items. The dagger hadn't left her side in two years and the pins—they served as a reminder of all she had lost. As she reached the southern tree line beyond the barrier, she looked back. She could just barely make out Jonathan talking to Oliver and Ele. She felt bad for not saying goodbye, but she figured it'd be easier that way. She'd see them again, one day.

She couldn't talk to Collins; she didn't know how. She honestly didn't know what had happened after she'd killed Roland. She remembered a golden light surrounding her and killing all the wraiths, but she couldn't explain it, and she didn't want to. She was tired of being in the spotlight, always being watched by the Council, the General, and the other soldiers. And with everything that had happened, thinking about the past had become too painful. Now, she had a life to live.

Anna turned her back on the Sanctuary, forcing herself to only look forward.

◆━━◆

She traveled south for a few days, following the trails of other refugees, but staying far enough away so as not to have to make conversation or travel with them. Just before nightfall, she would break off and find a safe house to sleep in. The wraiths may have been killed or just vanished, but she was still nervous. After defeating Roland, the Council had supposedly sent out scouts to confirm that every wraith that Roland had ever created had died with him. However, she couldn't stop the nagging feeling that they'd missed something.

Seven days after leaving the Sanctuary, Anna reached the marker for the path that would lead back to her old home, Fort Lieay. She started down the path, only to freeze after a few steps. Could she really go back to the place where her people had been killed? Could she walk into the banquet hall and live where her parents had been murdered?

"Miss?"

Anna turned to see a middle-aged man staring at her with a questioning look. He was obviously a refugee, but she'd never seen him in the Sanctuary.

"Are you headed to Fort Lieay?" he asked.

"Oh, I, um . . ."

"I've heard there isn't much left. I'm heading west. There's a settlement there that has been rebuilt. You can come if you like. We're always happy to have more people."

"Did you fight in the war?" she asked.

The man gave a small smile. "No. I helped maintain the gardens and the water system. I don't think any soldiers are living in the village, but I'm sure it's perfectly safe, if that's what you're worried about."

Anna took a deep breath. At least she wouldn't have to worry about any questions.

"I'd love to join you," Anna replied. "I don't really have anywhere else to go."

"I'm James, by the way, James Grigg. My wife should already be at the village. She left the Sanctuary to get settled as soon as the war ended."

"I'm Anna."

James looked at her, expecting more, but Anna wasn't ready to give out her past. James swallowed his questions and led the way to his home. Anna glanced back at the forest one last time. If she were to leave the war truly behind, General Lieay would have to disappear, to become nothing more than a distant memory.

Taking a few quick steps, Anna caught up to James, who gave her a reassuring smile. More relaxed than she'd been in a long time, Anna missed the red eyes glaring at the passing refugees from the shadows.

⚡— About the Author —⚡

Ryanne Glenn is a member of the Northern Colorado Writers in Fort Collins, CO, where she attends Colorado State University. She is pursuing a degree in Chemical and Biological Engineering with a minor in Biomedical Engineering. She loves to golf, though after playing for twelve years, her handicap should be much lower than it is. Between writing and classes, she often visits her hometown of Fruita, Colorado, to spend time with her family and two dogs, Coco and Pebbles.

Ryanne started writing short stories when she was ten and was first published in Fruita's local newspaper. She took her first creative writing class in high school, and was inspired to expand her writing into poetry and longer stories. After struggling with depression in her first year at college, she turned back to writing as a healthy outlet for her emotions. She wants to write strong female role models and is excited to share her stories with the world.

⟡— Acknowledgments —⟡

So much time and love went into this book, but it absolutely wouldn't have gotten finished without help.

To my family, for supporting me always, but especially to my mom. No matter what my problem was, whether it be grammar, odd scenes, or entire rewrites of the story, she was always there to help. Her insight and ideas added a lot to the story, and it wouldn't have been the same without her. Whatever happened with the book, she was supportive and excited to help with every part of the process.

To my friends, Jazz and Katie, I don't know where I'd be without you. No matter how wild things got, you always stuck with me, and made everything seem a little less dark. And you never refused to read whatever I put in front of you, whether it be a small paragraph or whole chapters.

To my amazingly wonderful critique partner, Linnea, I can't even begin to describe what you've done for me. You helped me push my writing to a new level, and provided a ton of inspiration through your own writing journey. Keep being awesome!

To my publisher/editor/supporter/everything else, Emily, thank you for taking a chance on me. Through all the rounds of edits and the craziness of getting this book going, you were always there to lend a hand. Your support was invaluable through this process. Thank you times a million for believing in me.

To the entire NCW Community, I can really only say thank you about a million times. Even if we've never met, being part of a group of writers means so much. It didn't matter if I was at the conference, a class, or just a writers' meet up, I always felt like I was welcome and valued.

To my proofreaders, Brian and Deborah, thank you so much! The little details can make or break a book, and catching those errors was so helpful.

To my beta readers Bella, Gemma, Delaney, George, Walter, and Emily, I hope you enjoyed the story as much as I enjoyed writing it! I think it's so important to read, no matter your age group, and you were the first ones to see this story as more than a draft. Thank you so much for your time, and hopefully you'll be just as excited about book 2!

And finally, to everyone who helped polish up the final product, Keith, Camille, Jenny, and Chris, you are all amazing. You helped turn a draft into a product that I couldn't be more proud of.

— Ryanne

Continue Anna's story in

DESCENT OF SHADOWS
BOOK TWO

atthisarts.com